The Cash-Strapped Cutie

"This place is a gold mine."

Cal smiled with bemused skepticism. "A gold mine?"

"Well, it will be when I'm through with it," Natalie conceded, lifting her chin imperiously.

He rolled his eyes in disbelief. "I'd bet a hundred dollars that you'll be out of here in six weeks."

Six weeks! She could barely stomach the thought of staying in that house six minutes, but she couldn't allow his challenge to go unanswered. "Your wager is accepted, Mr. Tucker."

She would fix up the house and make a big success of her inn and show all these mountain folk that they couldn't best a Winthrop!

He sighed. "All right. But I hope it's not just some foolish prickly pride making you stay here."

"You needn't worry about my motives, Mr. Tucker."

"Well, maybe I'll have some extra cash soon." He extended his hand with a grin.

She took it and shook it firmly. "No, you won't," she said sweetly. "*I* will."

For more, turn to page 9

Jake was not the lover Laramie had expected.

He was much more. A wonderful surprise.

"Are you always like this?" she asked.

"Like this?" Idly his forefinger caressed her leg.

"You're being sweet," she said. "Cute. But I won't tell anyone."

Looking disgruntled, he said, "I'll give you cute," and pressed her back on the bed.

"Jake," she said, laughing, then repeated it— "*Jake*"—not laughing. Not breathing. Her eyes closed. Her hips began a slow, languorous movement.

After a moment, she protested, "This isn't fair." She squirmed out from beneath him. "Very nice, but not fair. I'm an equal opportunity gal." She pushed him down on the bed. "Get naked, bucko."

She grabbed the black Stetson from the bedpost and put it on. "This," she said, straddling him, "is what we in the club call the *ride 'em cowgirl* position..." She threw up one hand like a bronc rider. "Yee-haw!"

For more, turn to page 197

HARLEQUIN DUETS

ISBN 0-373-44104-5

THE CASH-STRAPPED CUTIE
Copyright © 2000 by Elizabeth Bass

KEEPSAKE COWBOY
Copyright © 2000 by Carrie Antilla

This edition published by arrangement with Harlequin Books S.A.

® and TM are trademarks of the publisher. Trademarks indicated with
® are registered in the United States Patent and Trademark Office, the
Canadian Trade Marks Office and in other countries.

Visit us at www.eHarlequin.com

Printed in U.S.A.

The Cash-Strapped Cutie

LIZ IRELAND

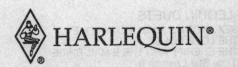

HARLEQUIN®

TORONTO • NEW YORK • LONDON
AMSTERDAM • PARIS • SYDNEY • HAMBURG
STOCKHOLM • ATHENS • TOKYO • MILAN • MADRID
PRAGUE • WARSAW • BUDAPEST • AUCKLAND

Dear Reader,

In the final installment of my LONE STAR LAWMEN trilogy, love takes on its toughest adversary—Cal Tucker, the once-burned, romance-shy ex-deputy of Heartbreak Ridge. Or, as newcomer Natalie Winthrop refers to him, "the poster child for heartbreak."

Cal might be avoiding romance like the plague, but he has a hard time dodging Natalie, his troublesome and beautiful new neighbor up on Heartbreak Ridge. When danger threatens Natalie, Cal drifts back into his old lawman world…but are his efforts out of duty, or love?

I hope you've enjoyed all three books in the LONE STAR LAWMEN miniseries. I have to confess, I'll miss hanging out with Merlie, Jerry, Jim and the rest of the gang at the Feed Bag diner!

Best wishes,

Liz Ireland

Books by Liz Ireland

HARLEQUIN DUETS
14—SEX AND THE SINGLE COWPOKE
22—THE LOVE POLICE
33—THE SHERIFF AND THE E-MAIL BRIDE
    (Lone Star Lawmen I)
35—THE DEPUTY'S BRIDE (Lone Star Lawmen II)

1

"OH MY GOD. Oh my God. Oh...my... Gaaaawwwwwwwwwd."

As Natalie Winthrop gaped at the architectural monstrosity before her, the words repeatedly tumbled out of her mouth in a horrified whisper. The desperate mantra did her no good of course. Nothing could help her now. But reciting the words, using her East Texas accent to drawl them out as long as possible, somehow seemed all that was standing between her and complete, utter despair.

What had happened? How had she tumbled so far, so fast?

Two days ago she'd been sitting on top of the world. She was the grand prize winner of a raffle for a charming hilltop mansion in West Texas—a beautiful house she was going to transform into a wildly successful country inn. Winning the house had opened up possibilities, made her take decisive actions. She'd cashed in all her chips—traded in her Lexus for a Volkswagen Beetle, consigned the last valuable pieces of her wardrobe, rented out her condo with a six-month lease and loaded all her worldly possessions and furry friends into her new car and left her old life for good.

More agonizing still, she'd abandoned a perfectly good groom-to-be practically at the altar because she'd thought she'd found something better than marriage.

Now she was staring at that something—the quaint hilltop mansion that was actually a borderline ruin—and she felt like the world's biggest sucker.

She was hard-pressed to mentally conjure the drawing of the stately mansion that had appeared in the advertisement asking entrants for one hundred dollars and an essay explaining why such a turn-of-the-century charmer should be theirs. Art certainly hadn't imitated life in this case. Instead of a graceful house there was a rambling, slouching edifice that looked as if a sneeze would knock it over. No cheery shrubs like those that had been promised stood sentinel under the windows—just piles of leaves forming impromptu compost piles. Shutters, on those windows that still had them at all, hung askew or flapped precariously in the breeze on rusted hinges. The porch sagged like an old mattress. Windows on all three floors were broken, and the shingle roof could only be considered half there.

Good heavens. She had abandoned her life, everything she knew, dear old friends and a fiancé, even, and for what?

A ruin!

Finally giving into that dire despair, she sagged against her Volkswagen's hood, buried her face in her sheepdog Mopsy's fur and let out a wail they could probably hear back in Houston. She wasn't certain whether crying made her feel better or worse. Her mother, Helena Foster Winthrop of the Fosters of River Oaks, had admonished her that a woman's tears should always be a means to an end. But as far as Natalie could see, this *was* the end.

The end of her hopes!

The end of her money!

The end of everything!

With all her heart she wanted to take a flying leap off the side of the mountain that so precariously propped up her house. Or better yet, douse the "mansion" in lighter fluid, ignite it and then hurl herself onto what was left of the roof as if it were a gigantic funeral pyre.

This might as well be her funeral because as far as she could tell, her life was over. Over!

In this moment of self-indulgent woe, she saw that she had been limping toward this sad conclusion for a year now. Because it was nearly a year ago to this very day that Malcolm Braswell, her late parents' trusted advisor, accountant and estate executor, disappeared into thin air with all her money.

Well. He didn't get everything. That slippery rascal hadn't been able to touch her family's River Oaks mansion with its antiques, wardrobes full of furs, minor masterpieces of painting and sculpture, tapestries and other objets d'art. When she had sat down and estimated her net worth even after Malcolm Braswell had done his worst, she was pleased to see that she was still a relatively wealthy young woman.

But that had been a year ago.

After all, she was a Winthrop, and she wasn't exactly accustomed to living like a pauper...or even an everyday rich person. She had appearances to uphold, charitable obligations, and tastes that had always been considerably beyond even her prereduced means. But what could she do? If she had suddenly up and announced that she was broke, she would have been a laughingstock. She would have lost all her friends, who at the first whiff of money troubles, wonderful caring people though they were, would drop her like a hot brick. No one would invite her anywhere. Her social life would have gone the way of the dinosaur, the dodo and Neil Sedaka.

So for a year she'd kept mum and quietly tried to find Malcolm Braswell through a private detective, which had cost more than she expected, with no results. Meanwhile, she slowly sold off a painting here, a sculpture there, and did a passable job of keeping up appearances. She prayed that by the time her house was picked clean of all its treasures, the dastardly accountant would be found or she would have discovered some other way of getting by, some pot of gold at the end of the rainbow.

But money, even when she was keeping an eye on it, seemed to slip through her fingers as fast as ever. Faster, in fact. She was shocked to discover a Winslow Homer drawing barely paid her bills for a month. The fur vault covered a Christmas so less festive than what she was used to that she practically felt like a little soot-covered waif in a Charles Dickens story. Though she was feeling the pinch, she kept spending as liberally as she could. Her friends weren't fools; they could sniff downward mobility a mile away. If she was going to trick them into believing she still had tens of millions at her disposal, she had to keep up with the Joneses, which in her rarefied neck of the woods required throwing parties, buying clothes and the usual whirlwind jaunts to Sun Valley, St. Kitts and Vail.

In other words, she blew it. Completely. Like those dizzy dames in *How to Marry a Millionaire*…only there didn't appear to be a Mr. Moneybags at the end of her rainbow.

By summer, she'd been forced to sell the River Oaks house and buy a condo in a less fashionable neighborhood—claiming to one and all that she simply couldn't bear the memories of her old home. She resorted to things like budgeting for groceries, bathing her dogs herself instead of getting them groomed at Pampered Pooches and consigning her clothes. Then, just when she thought she'd reached the lowest ebb, just when she thought she was going to have to pack it in, move to a city where no one knew she used to be rich, and maybe even resort to getting a job, a miracle happened.

More specifically, Jared Huddleton happened. And not only that, he proposed marriage.

Deliverance!

Jared had moved to Houston earlier in the year, and she'd latched her matrimonial hopes onto him, since not only was he someone independently wealthy and physically appealing in that slick *GQ* way, but he barely knew her and wasn't liable to notice the bare spaces on her walls where masterworks used to hang, or the fact that her summer wardrobe was the same as last summer's. She couldn't have been happier.

For a while.

As their wedding date drew near, niggling doubts crept up on her, and for the first time in her life, Natalie actually wrestled with an ethical qualm. The awful truth was, though she was overwhelmingly relieved and grateful that Jared was actually going to marry her, rescuing her, no doubt, from a lifetime of drudge work and a certain future as a strictly bargain shopper, she didn't really love the man. In her desperate straits, that should have been a laughable obstacle. After all, she was a Winthrop, descended from a long, proud line of women who had married for not just convenience, but for luxury. Her own mother, who had loved her husband dearly, wasn't so impractical that she wouldn't have pooh-poohed any hesitation from a woman in Natalie's position. "Don't be a nitwit, darling," she would have said, and given her a Tom Collins and a bolstering pat on the shoulder.

But her mother wasn't there anymore to spout her socialite's wisdom. Natalie was all alone, and suddenly she was filled with trepidation at the idea of marrying Jared. Marriage was forever, and she still had hopes that someday her private detective would hunt down Malcolm Braswell. She'd never stopped keeping an eye out for get-rich-quick schemes. She'd nearly forgotten the ad she'd found in *Texas Monthly* for a house on Heartbreak Ridge in the mountains in West Texas. When she'd seen the drawing of the picturesque manor house, she'd immediately envisioned herself making money by actually utilizing her talents at gracious living. She could open an inn that all her rich friends would pay top dollar to visit!

She'd sent in a hundred dollars—this had been before she'd started consigning clothes, or she never would have choked up that much cash and then had forgotten the drawing. It wasn't until she was having her final fitting for her wedding dress that she received the big news. She'd won! Right there, in her cheap copy of a designer dress, she'd whooped and skipped around her bare-walled condo for joy. With the house, she thought she'd been given the key to her future survival.

Now all that joy was gone. Her whoops were wails.

The key she'd been handed was a key to disaster. Not that the house she was staring at even needed a key. Aside from the several broken windows, there was that crater-size hole in the roof that was a welcome mat for vermin and which, she supposed, any person could also crawl through.

How could she have been such a fool? What was she going to do?

She was sniffling in shameless self-pity and reaching for a tissue when, as if she needed more trouble, all hell broke loose. Mopsy let out a yodeling howl and began springing angrily around the car. Bootsy and Fritz launched themselves out of the back seat and ran circles around the car, barking and yapping like dogs possessed. Her British shorthair cat, Winston, hissed his annoyance from the safety of a cage, but Armand, the cockatoo, was nowhere near so restrained. He burst into a guttural parrot rendition of *The Flight of the Valkyries*—his favorite opera melody.

What was happening? Natalie's heart was beating as quickly as a hamster's. As a pounding sound came near, the dogs tore off down the road to meet a man on horseback who appeared suddenly, careening toward them down the hill.

A shriek rose in Natalie's throat. She wasn't afraid of horses, but the man atop this horse scared her silly. With long blond hair flowing in an unruly mane behind him and a months' worth of ragged whiskers and clothes so beat-up she couldn't tell if or when they had ever been washed, he was easily the wildest looking man she'd ever seen—if he was really a man at all! He had a profile like a Greek god's, a body she could discern, though covered with a Clint Eastwoodstyle poncho, was better than her personal trainer's, and blue eyes that glittered like fire and ice. He was half Adonis, half Sasquatch.

She realized that she was holding her fist to her mouth as the man thundered close, and she forced herself to assume something like a casual stance. Then she caught sight of something else that had the dogs so riled—a dead rabbit thrown over the back of the man's saddle—and she lifted her hand back up to her mouth to keep from being sick.

The dogs couldn't have been more thrilled, however. Aside from the rare T-bone steaks she always prepared for their birthdays, this was probably the closest any of them had come to raw meat. She called their names, afraid they'd be trampled.

The man reined in the painted horse and the beast wheeled, his hooves spewing dirt and grass in all directions. "What are you doing here!" He had to yell over three barking dogs and Armand's Placido Domingo imitation. Not to mention, Fritz, the Chihuahua, was leaping straight up at the man's heels in an attempt to reach that poor bunny.

"Fritz, down!" Natalie stared at the intruder in annoyance. What kind of greeting was this? "I might ask you the same question!"

"Lady, I live here."

Fresh tears spilled onto her cheeks. "Oh, great!" Not only had she been swindled into buying a rattletrap, but it was an already inhabited rattletrap! "On second thought, you're welcome to it. Just don't sue me when the place collapses on you!"

He frowned, flicking an annoyed glance between the still hysterical Fritz and the house. Then he gaped at Natalie. "Are *you* the sucker who Jim Loftus horn-swoggled into taking that thing off his hands?"

She reached forward and snatched Fritz away. When the Chihuahua bared his teeth at the man, she couldn't have been happier. "Yes, I am the sucker," she said with as much pride as she could muster. "And as such, I demand that you move your things off my property."

He barked out a laugh. "Oh, I get it! You thought I meant I lived *here.* But I really meant that I live in that house up the hill...see?"

He poked his head in the direction of a little cabin about a quarter mile away. It was a simple two-room hunting cabin, rustic in design, probably without any amenities at all other than running water and a wood-burning fireplace.

But from her distressed vantage point, it looked like Cinderella's castle at Disneyland. She squirmed with envy. What she wouldn't do to swap houses with Daniel Boone here!

"I'm so used to being alone up here," he explained, "that when I heard your car I figured somebody must be lost, or in trouble."

She grunted. "Right on the last count."

His icy blue eyes narrowed curiously, then he frowned as he listened to the wordless opera coming from her Volkswagen. "What's that racket?"

"Armand."

"What?"

"My cockatoo," she explained in a louder voice. "Once he starts on Wagner, there's no shutting him up."

"Good God. Dogs *and* birds."

"And a cat," she added. "Winston's in the back seat."

His eyes looked her up and down lazily for a moment, but his gaze was hardly flattering. "Where are you from?"

Thoughts of the city she left behind only made her more miserable. "Houston."

He shuddered visibly. "*That* explains it."

She tilted her head. "Explains what?"

"City slicker!" He practically spat the words.

City slicker? That was a phrase she'd never heard outside of the movies! Was he for real? "And what would you know of Houston. You've probably never even seen it!" He looked as if he'd never been off this mountain.

"My parents retired there."

Someone in his family had sense, then.

"City folks like you have no call to be here," he said.

"I guess I've as much right as you do," she retorted indignantly.

"I've lived here all my life."

No kidding...the man was so rustic he might have been half mountain goat. His brown jeans sticking out of that poncho fit like a second skin, and those boots of his had a layer of dirt and mud an inch thick.

She drew up proudly, straightening her lemon-yellow silk blazer—the one she'd thought would be so appropriate for a stylish hotel proprietress. The thought of her newly punctured self-image only made her madder. "That still doesn't alter the fact that I now own this property."

He grunted. "Lady, you wouldn't be out here if that old swindler Jim Loftus hadn't shorn you cleaner than a spring lamb. Even at that I reckon you won't last out here a month."

The challenge in his voice rankled; partly because there was so much truth in what he said. "I'm still weighing my options."

He hooted. "Oh, that's right. I heard in town that you were the one who was going to turn Jim's place into a swanky hotel. Everybody got a big kick out of that."

Her face burned as she remembered the optimistic, effusive essay she'd written about all the things she would do to transform the abandoned house into a luxurious inn. And that it would bring no end of commerce to the little town of Heartbreak Ridge, which was a twisty mile drive down the mountain from the house. That her writing had attracted top prize simply for its comic value was humiliating past all endurance. Especially when she imagined a whole town jeering at her like this filthy ruffian!

"I'll have you know that I don't intend to be the butt of some pathetic town joke. I have means at my disposal, and influence. Why, my father played golf with the famous attorney F. Lee Bailey! Believe you me, I'm going to use every connection and every penny I have to sue the pants off Mr. Jim Loftus! By the time I get through with him, he won't even have a toothbrush to his name. He'll be making license plates!"

The wooly one rubbed his beard and waited for her harangue to end. "Well, now, actually, I checked out this raffle business."

"You did?"

"Sure. For one thing, it sounded fishy. For another, I didn't exactly relish the idea of having a neighbor."

Naturally! "And?"

He shrugged. "Turns out it's all perfectly legit."

She tried not to visibly sag.

Darn! Not that she could have actually sued Jim Loftus. Her father hadn't really golfed with F. Lee Bailey; they'd just belonged to the same country club. And she couldn't have afforded his services in any case. But she'd at least hoped to scare Loftus with a few threats…if he ever returned from Honolulu, the destination he'd fled to the very day she'd been notified of her big win. No doubt he'd dropped the key in the mail as he was hotfooting it to the airport.

The fact that there was yet another man in the tropics enjoying her money was depressing in the extreme. "Well, I'm certainly going to report him to the Better Business Bureau—you can depend on that!"

"From F. Lee Bailey to the BBB," the man mused, taking a moment to stare at her till she wanted to squirm. "Think of it this way. You only paid a hundred dollars. Heck, even if you bulldoze the house, the land it's sitting on is worth more than that."

"If I bulldozed the house, where would I live?"

He nodded. "You have a point."

But his statement captured her interest. "This land…does it have anything on it?"

"Wildlife."

Hmm. "Could you grow anything on it?" She couldn't see herself living off the land, but someone else, some nut, might like it for that reason….

He shook his head. "Nope."

"Are there any mineral deposits?"

He laughed. "No gold in these here hills, ma'am."

She huffed in frustration. "Well is there any reason

imaginable that someone would want to buy this land?''

''I can't think off the top of my head, no.''

She felt like screaming. ''Then it's not worth a hundred dollars. It's not worth fifty dollars or fifty cents or even a plug nickel!''

''Well…maybe it would be once you got the house fixed up again.''

So they were back where they started. ''But where would I begin? I wouldn't be surprised if the electricity doesn't even work.''

He frowned. ''Course not.'' When she looked up at him, startled, he added quickly, ''Oh, but it did. Once.''

''*Once?*''

''About ten years ago…before the mouse and fire ant infestations.''

She groaned.

''Oh, don't worry, the fire ants are under control.''

''And the mice?''

He grinned. ''Think of it this way. Your cat's gonna love it here.''

Natalie was horrified, but she couldn't help hanging onto the man's every word. He might look like something out of the cast of *Deliverance,* but he seemed to know what he was talking about. ''Are there any other problems I should know about?''

He hesitated. ''Well the roof, naturally. That's probably the biggest single repair, if you don't count the plumbing.''

''What's wrong with the plumbing?''

''There isn't any.''

For a moment, she simply stood there, blinking. She couldn't have heard him right. Every house had plumbing nowadays. Plumbing was a necessity. It was practically the bedrock of civilization....

She gaped at the house, then at her definitely *un*-civilized neighbor, and felt herself quaking in the marrow of her bones.

"*No plumbing?* No way!" She stomped her foot, raging at no one in particular. "This is the limit! The end!" A few other choice words—mostly epithets for a certain Jim Loftus—flew out of her mouth. She kicked a rock with the toe of her lemon-yellow Amalfi pump and railed at the unfairness of it all. She was so consumed with anger for a few moments that she didn't realize what the man on the horse was doing.

He was laughing at her. He wasn't just chuckling, either, but letting loose a full-throated, knee-slapping, finger-pointing gut buster.

Natalie froze. This was it. At last she'd hit rock bottom. She was finally hearing the sounds of taunting that had led her to the extreme measures she'd adopted over the past year to ensure that *no one* would ever know that she was poor and thus jeer at her.

She'd dreaded it because deep down she knew she deserved to be laughed at. Because she was a fool and lost almost all of her money to a crooked accountant, and then gave more money to a sleazy detective to track down the accountant. Because she was so desperate she tried everything she could think of to keep the world from discovering her reduced circumstances. Because she'd almost married a man she didn't love, rather than gather the gumption to go out and find a job just like everybody else.

Now, in spite of everything, this creature had spied

her desperation and was laughing at her, and yet instead of crumbling or flying to pieces, something completely unexpected occurred. From somewhere within, some wellspring of pride she'd never guessed she had, she reached down and gathered courage.

How dare this rustic reprobate laugh at her—how dare anyone! Was she at fault for having been robbed and cheated?

Well, maybe she was—there was no denying she'd been gullible and foolish—but what good did he think his laughing would do her?

She squared her shoulders and leveled a withering glare on him. "I don't see what's so funny about another person's misfortune. But if you think I'm going to turn tail and run back to Houston, Mr. Whatever-Your-Name-Is—"

He cut off his laughter with a tight snort. "Tucker. Cal Tucker."

"Mr. Cal Tucker, if you think that I'm going to turn tail and run, think again! I have a plan for this house, and I'm going to carry it through. Discovering that my new home has a few deficiencies..." *No plumbing—oh Lord!* She lifted her chin to hide her panic. "Well, that's just a minor setback, that's all."

Her brave words, emotional as they were, stopped his laughing but failed to wipe a smug grin off his face. "Lady, you won't last six weeks."

"You said that before!"

"I know your type."

She scoffed at his arrogance. "Do you have any idea who I am?" She'd only just now remembered herself. "*I* am the great-granddaughter of George Nathan Winthrop."

"Never heard of him."

"He was a great cattle baron, and one of the first men in this great state to strike oil!"

He looked woefully unimpressed. "I've still never heard of him."

She lifted her chin imperiously. "Be that as it may, you can bet your bottom dollar that George Nathan Winthrop didn't look at the ugly black gunk spurting **ou**t of the ground and throw up his hands in despair. He knew nothing of oil, but he learned, and he profited. He knew a gold mine when he saw it, and so do I."

The man smiled with bemused skepticism. "Are you calling this house a gold mine?"

"It will be when I'm through with it."

He cackled. "I don't know about my bottom dollar, but I'd sure bet a hundred dollars that you'll be out of here in six weeks."

Six weeks! She could barely stomach the thought of staying in that house six minutes, but she couldn't allow her odious neighbor's challenge to go unanswered. "Your wager is accepted, Mr. Tucker."

She would fix up the house and make a big success of her inn and show all these mountain folk that they couldn't best a Winthrop!

He sighed. "All right...but it's gonna be like taking candy from a baby."

His smug tone set her teeth on edge. "Is it just me you have a low opinion of, or is it all women?"

He shook his head. "I've never met a woman yet from a city like Houston who was worth a damn when it came to surviving in this country. I doubt you'll be an exception."

"And what makes you think that?"

"Lady, even your dogs look like they won't survive without plumbing."

Insulting her dogs. Now that was low.

"My canine companions are no reflection on my fitness for the task ahead, I assure you."

He sighed. "All right. But before we seal the deal, I hope it's not just some foolish prickly pride making you stay here. Because sometimes it's better just to cut your losses."

And do what? There wasn't an option available to her now that seemed any less foolish than accepting this man's challenge and staying here to try to renovate the rattletrap she'd been suckered into owning.

"You needn't worry about my motives, Mr. Tucker."

He grinned. "Well, maybe I'll have some extra cash soon." He extended his hand with a grin.

She took it and shook it firmly. "No, you won't," she said sweetly. "*I* will."

His other hand came around and patted hers—a touch she hadn't expected. Nor did she expect the jolt of sensation at having this furry creature's paw over hers. She looked into his icy blue eyes and saw a spark in them that she hadn't seen in any man's since first meeting up with Jared.

Her lips parted. In shock.

Surely whatever weird, perverse attraction she felt to this person had to be just a result of nerves! After all, it had been a long, disappointing and exhausting day. She was dragging. Her resistance was low.

Very low, apparently.

He let go of her hand and leaned forward. "Well good luck to you anyway, Miss..."

She lifted her chin. "Natalie Winthrop."

"Oh right." He laughed. "How could I forget the illustrious Winthrop name?"

"Thank you for your best wishes," she retorted sarcastically.

He nodded. "If you ever need help or just some neighborly advice, just remember that I'm right up the hill." He nodded again toward the rustic little cabin.

Neighborly advice—yeah, right! The only kind of aid she could imagine him giving her would be a shove off the mountain.

He took in her crossed arms and stubborn stance and grinned. "See ya later, Natalie." He quickly wheeled his horse so that she had to jump back out of the way.

And with that, her new neighbor left as abruptly as he had appeared, the unfortunate bunny flopping behind him.

2

AS HAD BECOME HIS CUSTOM in the past three days, Cal arose early, washed, worked around the house, then, at around ten o'clock, took his morning coffee out on the porch, settled comfortably in his favorite rocking chair and leaned back to enjoy the show.

For sheer entertainment value, Natalie Winthrop was the best thing to come along since Monday Night Football. Not to mention, her efforts to fix up her house were a hundred times more amusing than anything he'd ever seen on Bob Villa's program. He didn't even own a TV these days, but he just bet if she'd had an eye toward television production, Natalie could have put on a humdinger of a home improvement show. *This Old Shack,* perhaps, or *Natalie's Home Fiasco.*

Today his neighbor was working on her roof. Or, more specifically, in lieu of actually fixing the roof she was going to attempt to tape thick plastic sheeting over the elephant-size hole that left the roof gaping open to the elements.

Good luck, lady, he thought, smiling as he always did as he watched her tackling one of her projects with Martha Stewart pluck. Unfortunately Natalie rarely ended up with perfect Martha Stewart results. Yesterday it had taken her hours and hours to board up a few windows, having first mismeasured and then bought the wrong size boards. Then, during an attempt to attach several boards together and thus save herself a second trip to the hardware store to get bigger ones, she'd slammed a hammer against her hand, resulting in something Cal hadn't seen since the days when Michael Jackson topped the charts. Break dancing. She'd finally decided to join the boards together with her brand-new hot glue gun, but then, when she'd nailed them against the windows, the glue hadn't held, and the boards were going every which-a-way over her windows. So she'd used duct tape to finish off the job, ending up with a crooked patchwork of gluey boards and shiny silver tape that was the finest example of inept home repair he'd ever seen.

Today's would be a more straightforward, albeit much more difficult, job.

He watched her scramble up the ladder she'd brought back from town yesterday strapped atop her red Volkswagen Beetle. The vehicle looked as if it were new, which was hard to believe, if she bought it when she knew she was moving to the mountains. Hardly a practical purchase. But Natalie Winthrop, granddaughter of the oil baron, which he supposed made her something like a baroness twice removed, didn't look as if she had the sense God gave an earth-worm.

Of course, considering where she came from—no doubt some neighborhood in Houston with big fancy yards owned by women who had never in their lives pushed a lawnmower—he doubted a woman had to rely on her intelligence, and a woman as good-looking as Natalie Winthrop had probably been even less dependent on her brains than most socialites. Even Cal, who considered himself pretty much immune to the superficial beauty of women, had to admit that his new neighbor was an eyeful.

Not that her beauty had anything to do with why he was watching her so closely, he told himself. The reason he was snooping on Natalie's home improvement work was to gauge just how soon he'd have his mountain back to himself.

Pretty soon, it looked like. The woman didn't have a prayer of making her little scheme work. Not going about it the way she was so far, at least.

He was watching Natalie, who was crouching uneasily on her roof, but in his mind's eye he was suddenly seeing Connie, his ex-wife. She, too, had been a pretty debutante type, spoiled and impractical, who had thought it would be "fun" to live in the sticks. He'd met her in San Antonio and after a whirlwind courtship, he'd brought his dazzling bride back to Heartbreak Ridge.

Naturally he'd warned Connie of the dangers of living in a small town—had enumerated them many times in fact. The boredom. For entertainment, most folks were slaves to the satellite dish. There was one place to eat in town, the Feed Bag, and Jerry Lufkin, the owner and cook there, had never even laid eyes on a sun-dried tomato or cooked *nouveau* anything. Cal had warned Connie of the gossip mill, and the fact that everyone in town seemed to take pride in knowing everyone else's business, and telling them so. He'd chewed her ear off about the yawning distances that must be traversed to get absolutely anything done. He'd cautioned her about all these things, but when she suddenly found herself experiencing them, Connie professed shock.

After a month, she'd professed exasperation.

After three months, she hadn't bothered professing anything, she'd just started letting fly with the insults. She called him a two-bit deputy, sleepwalking through life in a Mayberry throwback town. She'd said she was bored—with Heartbreak Ridge, with satellite TV, with *him.* She told him he'd never amount to anything, never do anything important, because his world was so isolated, so provincial, so small. Moreover, she told him that if he wanted to spend the rest of his life handing out speeding tickets, that was fine and dandy with her, but she didn't intend to spend one more minute smothering in small-town America.

And then she'd slammed the door behind her, leaving a mostly empty bottle of Chanel Number Five as the only evidence she'd been there at all.

Cal had to admit to himself that he'd seen it coming. But what he hadn't foreseen was Connie's parting insults making a direct hit on his ego. *Sleepwalking?* Practically every man in his family as far back as he could remember had chosen law enforcement as a career, so he had automatically slipped into the job of deputy sheriff under his uncle, Sam Weston. He hadn't given the matter two thoughts. He'd just thought that for the rest of his life he'd coast along, get married, have kids.

But when her walking out sent his life kerblooey, he'd begun to second-guess his old assumptions. He didn't want to do anything anymore because everyone, including himself, had just assumed he would. He wanted to take some time off and make up his own mind about what kind of life he wanted to live.

People in town had been shocked when he'd resigned his job at the sheriff's office and moved up to his family's hunting cabin on Heartbreak Ridge, with nothing but a set of encyclopedias for company. His little brother, Cody, had stayed on in their house and taken over Cal's deputy duties. And, ironically, during Cal's year-long sabbatical, *Cody* had gone through major life changes. He'd discovered his true calling as a rancher, and had even married. Whereas Cal, so far, had only come to one clear conclusion about his life: He didn't want to share his mountain with a harebrained female with three loud dogs, a cat, and a parrot who thought he was Pavarotti. He didn't want to be around any woman who reminded him of Connie.

End of story.

He took a slug of coffee and grunted. Connie! It had been weeks since he'd thought of her…his recovery had been imminent…and now look! A woman showed up on his mountain, and suddenly he couldn't get his ex-wife out of his mind.

That's just what women did to men. Distracted them.

Or maybe it was love that did that.

Cal wasn't a big fan of love anymore, either. At the very least, it was wildly overrated.

Of course, love had worked out okay for his uncle, Sam. The sheriff had fallen in love with some woman he'd met over the Internet, and improbably, their marriage seemed to have worked out. So far. Even his own little brother, Cody, had fallen into something— love or maybe insanity—with the unlikeliest person, a local girl named Ruby Treadwell, and now they were married and seemed to be happy out on their new ranch, raising sheep and llamas and bees and who knows what all else. Nothing so practical as a cow, Cal was certain. But both those relationships were young, and though Cal wished Sam and Cody well, Connie had topped off his tank with skepticism.

The fact of the matter was, after his marriage to Connie, he had come to a few distinct conclusions about love. One was that it made people liars. Something about being attracted to a person of the opposite sex not only set off hormones, but he was pretty certain sparked glands that compelled people to tell little falsehoods. Such as Connie telling him that she wouldn't mind living in the country a bit. Or that she could live without mochaccinos from Starbucks and didn't need Lord and Taylor nearby to make her happy. She claimed she would be perfectly happy just quietly reading a book on weekends as long as she could be with him.

And love had made him believe her words when every other instinct was telling him that she didn't know what she was talking about. She'd always lived in the city. And during their courtship he'd never seen her read anything more substantial than the latest copy of *Vogue*.

In the middle of his musing on his love theory, Natalie disappeared.

One minute, he'd been looking right at her as she'd hovered on her roof. The next minute, she was gone. It was as if she'd fallen into a black hole—literally! The only remnant of her was a sheet of plastic flapping in the wind on her roof.

He bolted up to standing, sloshing his coffee cup down abruptly on the porch railing. Good heavens. *Had the woman actually gone through the roof?*

He cringed almost guiltily, as if her calamity were some sort of cosmic wish fulfillment. God knows he wanted the woman off his mountain, but he didn't want her dead.

Fast as a whip, he jumped off the porch and sped down the hill to see what was left of his neighbor.

As THE DUST SETTLED around the fallen debris—and Natalie supposed she had to consider herself the main part of that debris—she marveled again at the incredible swan dive from success to complete, utter failure her life had taken. In the space of one short year, she'd gone from living the American dream to its worst nightmare. From divine wealth to Dogpatch in one catastrophic misstep.

A year ago she would have never worried about a roof. A roof? The last roof problem she'd endured was when she'd had *pâte de foie gras* on an overly crunchy baguette that had scraped the sensitive upper palate of her mouth. In fact, she'd never quite understood roofing at all, come to find out. She'd assumed that there was a lot of material between a roof and the floor below. A ceiling, for one thing. But apparently in some cases—in this house, for instance—ceilings weren't something you could count on to be there to break your fall!

Her breath was still coming in shallow gasps when she heard a commotion below. First there was a pounding—distinct from the pounding of her head—and then the dogs went nuts, barking like mad and hurling themselves against the front door. Armand let fly with his doorbell imitation. There followed louder, more insistent pounding, more cacophonous barking, and a louder cockatoo doorbell.

Just what she needed. A social call!

Natalie tried to move, but she was afraid she was

paralyzed. Sooner or later whoever it was would either leave or figure out that the door wasn't locked. Naturally the locks on the house didn't work. That was another thing she would have to fix before all her rich friends would pay her two hundred and fifty dollars a night to stay at her exquisite country manor....

She felt a tear drip out of the corner of her eye and didn't bother to try to wipe it away. She was too tired to move. In fact, after three days of laboring to make the house minimally inhabitable—three days of eating packaged food and one makeshift shower that consisted of dumping a bottle of Evian over the top of her head—she finally felt defeated. Utterly defeated.

Heavy footsteps sounded in the hallway below, rattling the rafters and sending a mouse scurrying into one of the many rodent bunkers lining the walls of her new attic.

"Natalie?! Natalie, are you all right?"

Her eyes rounded and her spirits roused at the now nearly unfamiliar sound. A human voice!

Someone was calling her name!

She hadn't spoken to anyone besides hardware salesclerks for days. She wasn't entirely certain she was still capable of making conversation, or that even if she did, the natives would be capable of talking back at her. So far, they'd mostly just gawked at her. But for novelty's sake, and the sake of her sanity, she was willing to give communication a whirl.

"I'm in the attic!"

Bootsteps clambered up the two flights of stairs with what sounded like amazing agility. Behind those, she could hear the frantic scrambling of three sets of paws as Mopsy, Bootsy and Fritz tagged close on her visitor's heels. In the next instant there was a clomp, a canine shriek and a muttered curse. Her visitor had tripped over Bootsy.

She was just trying to push herself up to her elbows when suddenly her dreaded neighbor Cal Tucker skidded through the attic entrance.

"What happened to you?" He was practically shouting at her.

In the next moment she was in a sea of fur and tongues that no amount of pleading or pushing away could get rid of.

"Are you all right?" Cal asked.

Five seconds ago she would have answered that question with a definite no. Of course she wasn't all right. She had spent three days living on Vienna sausages and Pop-Tarts. She had labored nonstop to laughably little effect. Her clothes were filthy, her hair was grungy and her body was stiff and achy from sleeping on the floor. She'd spent more money trying to patch holes in the house than she'd even paid for the honor of purchasing this, her own personal death-trap.

Not to mention, she'd just fallen through the roof.

So no, she definitely did not consider herself *all right*.

But was she going to tell that to Cal Tucker, the neighbor who had been sitting on his porch for three days watching her like a hawk, no doubt praying for a calamity just like this one to befall her? You bet your bippy she wasn't!

She bolted up to sitting—and felt as if she'd just scrambled her brains. Placing her hands on either side of her to keep her balance, she declared, "I'm just f-fine."

"You don't look fine," he said.

"Mopsy, down!" True to her name, Mopsy was licking Natalie's face, which wasn't helping her compose herself any. She turned back to Cal. "Then why did you ask me if I was three seconds ago?"

"Because three seconds ago you didn't have a complexion like green cheese."

Reflexively she lifted her hands to her face, then nearly collapsed. Before she could fall, however, Cal swooped down on her and swept her into his arms.

Finding herself suddenly airborne, she squeaked out a protest. "Put me down!"

Instead of heeding her instruction, he headed out of the attic and down the stairs with the dogs scrambling back down in a chaotic jumble of fur.

"Did you hear me?" Natalie repeated, her arms crossed. She certainly wasn't going to wrap her arms around him, Scarlett O'Hara style!

He nodded curtly. "And in case you haven't noticed, I'm ignoring you."

She clucked her tongue in outrage. Did the man think he could just barge into her house and pluck her off the floor like some Neanderthal brute? Was this how neighbors behaved in this neck of the woods?

He let her stew down two flights then carried her into the kitchen, where he hefted her onto a counter, since there were no chairs anywhere in the house. She silently thanked heaven that she had managed to get the kitchen clean before this humiliating event... though it had taken an entire morning and an economy-size can of scouring powder to scrub all the grime away.

He stood in front of her, arms crossed, while

Bootsy did a figure eight between his legs. "These mutts of yours are real nuisances."

Mutts? That was the limit!

"How dare you come in here and haul me around like a sack of potatoes and then insult my dogs, who, for your information, are *not* mutts. Bootsy is a pug, Fritz is a purebred Chihuahua of excellent pedigree and Mopsy is an English sheepdog!"

"And you know what they all have in common?" He grinned. "They're all nuisances!"

She wrinkled her nose. "I would think a mountain man like yourself would at least have an affection for creatures from the natural world."

"I do have a fondness for animals, if they serve some kind of purpose. But lady, these silly pooches of yours don't look much more familiar with the natural world than you are."

She lifted her head. She wouldn't dignify a slur on herself with an answer, but where her dogs were concerned, she could allow no insult. "They're all excellent watchdogs."

"Is that why they jumped up and licked me when I busted down your door?"

She opened her mouth to really let him have it, but he lifted a hand and looked around him, stopping her. "Got any water?"

"There's just the tail end of a bottle of Evian," she admitted. She didn't add that most of it had been used for bathing.

"What about the pump?"

"It's not working."

He frowned. "How can it not be working? It's manual."

"I'm telling you, it doesn't work."

"Are you sure you did it right?"

"Of course!" Did he think she was a complete idiot? "I pumped the handle and nothing came out."

With a long-suffering sigh, Cro-Magnon Man pivoted on his heel and marched out the back door toward the big pump outside the kitchen.

She had to see this! Eager to witness her insufferable neighbor with egg on his face, she hopped down from the counter, wincing as her sore muscles protested when she hit the ground. She and the dogs traipsed after him out the door.

At the well, Cal was already giving it his best shot, pumping the handle fiercely. To her immense satisfaction, nothing was happening.

"Told you so."

And as she stood, arms crossed, grinning at his foolish insistence on trying to show her up, she allowed herself to appreciate for the first time—objectively, as a scientist might appreciate a perfect germ under a test tube—just what an ideal specimen of the male physique Cal Tucker was. His arm muscles bulged impressively, as did several sets of muscles beneath his T-shirt. His faded jeans hugged his legs loosely, tightening around his hips and taut buns in the most eye-catching way. What a shame that such a sexy body had to be wasted on such a loathsome, arrogant character.

As she stood staring at him with all her scientific objectivity, a miracle occurred. Her pump spurted water. Muddy brown water—but water all the same! Wounded pride collapsed in the face of unspeakable joy.

She'd be able to have a bath. A real bath!

She gasped and ran forward. "How did this happen? What did you do?"

She couldn't even work up any outrage. True, Cro-Magnon Man had triumphed...but at least she had water!

"It's called priming the pump," he explained. "You have to get water into the line before it will start pouring for you. Didn't you know that?"

She put her hands on her hips. "Who do I look like, Mother Jones? Besides, if I had known, I would have done it myself."

"The trouble is you're trying to do too much yourself. Too much that you don't understand."

She drew up to every centimeter of her five-foot, five-inch height. "It's not that I don't *understand*, it's just that I've never done a lot of these things before. But of course I can learn. I'm very good at learning. I made excellent grades in school."

He released an exasperated breath. "You don't know a soul out here, do you?"

She shook her head, just barely able to keep her lip from trembling. It bothered her to have her isolation and loneliness spoken of aloud. She'd been acutely aware of being here by herself these past days. She'd missed picking up a phone and calling her friends. But even if she had a phone, would Missy Pendleton understand, much less care, about how outrageously expensive lumber was? And how long would Clarice Biddles, her sorority house roommate from college days, listen to her whine about something that had to do with neither men nor the country club?

"How are you going to learn to fix up your house

if you have no one here to show you?'' Cal asked her.

She had him there. "I have a book."

He gaped at her, and she turned and led the way back into the house, where she presented him with her valued copy of *The Southern Estates Complete Home and Garden Book.* She'd bought it in Houston, knowing it was bound to come in handy.

Cal took the book from her and began flipping through its thick glossy pages. "This isn't going to be any use," he said in a disgustingly know-it-all tone. "This is all about decorating."

"Well, isn't that what I'm doing?"

"Sure…after you put in the roof and plumbing and fix the electricity and get the foundation leveled off."

He did make it sound daunting. "You don't have to tell me there's work to be done. I'm doing my best."

He sighed. "Look, I don't know why we're arguing."

"Because you came over here to pick a fight."

"No, I didn't," he assured her. "I just happened to notice that you…well, that you were having a little trouble. I think you need to get some professional help. I can give you some names, especially of people who could fix your roof and basement."

She thought quickly. She'd already gone through more money in three days than she'd budgeted for several weeks. "I'm not sure…I'll have to think about it. You might not be able to tell, but I'm actually making quite a bit of headway on my own."

"Uh-huh." He didn't look convinced by her perky tone.

"But I certainly might come to you for a few names if I happen to hit a roadblock."

He stared up the mountain toward his house. She wished he'd make up his mind to go there.

"Listen, I don't mean to butt into your business," he began, hesitating just a little, "but since we're neighbors and it's sort of in my interest to make sure you're safe over here so that I won't worry every time I hear your dogs barking or your bird starts squawking his head off, and since I just happen to be going into town today, why don't you do me a favor and let me buy and install some dead bolts for you?"

She cocked her head. *Let him?* It was the first kindness anyone in Heartbreak Ridge had paid her. In fact, she'd begun to wonder if the people around here just intended to stare at her for the rest of her stay here. Cal's offer gave her hope.

"You would do that for me?"

The grudging shrug he sent her let her know he was acting outside his better judgment. "Call it a housewarming gift. Between neighbors."

She almost felt guilty for thinking of him as Cro-Magnon Man. "Well, thank you. The truth is, I haven't gotten around to worrying about the locks yet..."

Actually she'd worried about them plenty. Unfortunately she could no more install a dead bolt than she could walk on the moon. She wondered if Cal could, either, but he did seem pretty sure of himself.

He grinned. Strangely his smile seemed almost friendly.

Handsome, even.

She smiled back, yet gritted her teeth against the way her pulse danced at the sight of her neighbor's smile. Those toaster pastries must have been frosted with loony dust to make her start lusting after Alley-Oop.

"I'll see you later," he said. "Try not to kill yourself in the meantime."

She crossed her arms. "Don't waste your worry on me. I'll be here."

That was just the problem. She would be here, she feared, living right alongside good-looking, infuriating Cal Tucker, till doomsday.

In town, Cal bought the locks at the hardware store then strolled over to his old stomping grounds, the sheriff's office. As he walked in the door, his uncle's secretary, Merlie Shivers, looked down the bridge of her nose, on top of which perched a pair of cat glasses with rhinestones in the corners.

Her wide eyes feigned shock. "Well, if it isn't the old man come down from the mountain to spread his wisdom!" She bent from the waist in mock reverence. "What have you come to tell us, oh wise one?"

Cal smiled. He'd worked as his uncle's deputy for four years, so he was used to being the butt of Merlie's jokes. "The end is near. Do you really want to spend eternity in overalls?"

Merlie cackled. She wore the same blue overalls to bed, Cal was certain. "I certainly wouldn't want to spend it with a scraggly old beard like yours," she sassed back. "Why don't you get a haircut and shave? Who knows, it might make you feel like joining the human race again."

"That's what I'm afraid of."

His uncle, the sheriff, came out of the back office

and clapped him on the back. "What brings you to town, stranger? Ready to come back to work?"

Sam was always after him to come back to work. Really, Cal sort of missed the job. He hadn't while his little brother was serving as deputy, but Cody had gone off his head two months earlier, marrying some crazy woman and deciding to become a rancher. A sheep rancher! Cal still had a hard time wrapping his mind around the idea.

But now seeing his old desk empty, and his uncle working solo, he sort of felt nostalgic for the old days of hanging around town and occasionally doing some good for people. Not nostalgic enough to actually commit to the job, however. He didn't believe in doing things by halves, and if his heart wasn't in it, he didn't want to be a policeman. "I'll give it some thought, Sam."

Sam smiled, a little disappointment showing in his eyes.

"How's Shelby?" Cal asked, changing the subject.

At the mention of his wife, his uncle's face lit up like a million-watt bulb. "Great! You should come over to the house sometime, Cal, and see her and Lily. Lily's so big now you won't even recognize her. She's crawling." He laughed. "You could see some of the home movies I've made, too."

Merlie laughed. "Oh, Cal wouldn't want to miss those. Last time I was at *chez* Weston I was treated to a fascinating feature-length documentary of Lily gumming a banana."

Cal laughed. It would never cease to amaze him how crazy Sam was about his wife's kid, who Sam treated as if she were his very own. But maybe having been there at the baby's delivery gave him some special bond. Lily's every coo and burp was greeted with oohs and ahhhs of appreciation. Cal half suspected the real reason his uncle wanted him back as deputy was so Sam could spend more time at home documenting Lily's phenomenal accomplishments.

"As long as you're here, Cal," Merlie said, "I might as well see if you're willing to adopt."

He blinked in confusion. "Adopt what?"

Merlie reached inside her desk's file drawer and pulled out a fat, furry orange ball. "Tubb-Tubb junior."

Instinctively Cal backed away. One thing he didn't want to do was start collecting responsibilities, such as turning himself into some pathetic creature like that Natalie woman. "How did that happen? I thought your cat was...you know..."

Merlie laughed. "Emasculated? He is. Only you have to admit, this fuzzball bears a striking resemblance. Maybe they're cousins or something. Anyway, I found him on my doorstep." She looked genuinely surprised. "Some joker around here obviously has me mistaken for a soft touch."

Sam winked at Cal. "Can't imagine why."

Everybody knew that Merlie's Tubb-Tubb was the fattest, most pampered animal in the state of Texas. This kitty would probably suffer a similar fate.

"I hate to disappoint you, Merlie, but I'm not in the market for kitty-cats. I was just wondering if either of you knew of somebody handy in need of work."

Merlie frowned. "What kind of work?"

Cal stuck his hands into his pockets. "Oh, fixin' up a house." If it got out that he was helping his new neighbor, he'd never hear the end of it.

Unfortunately Merlie had the nose of a bloodhound when it came to sniffing out gossip. "Don't tell me you've already made friends with the innkeeper!"

Sam translated for Cal. "That's what folks at the Feed Bag are calling our new resident. 'Cause the essay she wrote about the house talked about turning it into a fancy inn."

Merlie laughed. "Everybody's speculatin' whether she can stick to the fancy part, or whether she'll wimp out and go for the Heartbreak-Hotel-Elvis-Cheezoid stuff. You know, renaming that asphalt road of yours Lonely Street and doing the place in white sequins?"

Cal winced a little at that unwelcome prospect, but at the same time, he shifted uncomfortably, feeling torn. He'd greeted Natalie Winthrop's harebrained plan with as much scorn as anybody in town, but he'd also been witness to the hell she was going through. In fact, he was amazed the poor woman hadn't inadvertently killed herself. But if she was alive, it was probably just barely by her standards. Though he'd only seen her once close up in the three days since he'd first come upon her crying against her Volkswagen, he could tell the woman was a shadow of her former self—more scraggly, more desperate, and even slightly more humble.

"What's she like, Cal?"

He laughed. "What's that expression about if you can't say anything nice about someone...?"

Merlie nodded. "She's been to town several times and hasn't spoken a word to anybody except the clerk at the Western Auto and Leila Birch at the Stop-N-Shop, who put some Pop-Tarts in a bag for her. And then the only thing she said was thank you."

"That sounds polite at least. Maybe she's just shy," Sam said.

"She said plenty to me," Cal told them. "You folks should be grateful she kept her silence."

"What are you helping her out for if she's been so rude to you?"

Sam grinned. "You saw the woman, Merlie. She's pretty."

Cal sputtered indignantly. "You call that pretty? They're isn't a hair on her head that hasn't been dyed that society dame blond."

"Good figure, though," Sam pointed out.

"City women buy those, too. She probably has a personal trainer. Unfortunately nobody's trained her to have common sense."

Merlie laughed. "Of course, you wouldn't be prejudiced against city women, would you, Cal?"

At the not-so-subtle reference to Connie, he felt his face pale. "This woman's a worse case than even Connie was. She keeps babbling on about some grandfather of hers who was a millionaire, plus she's got these pets that are so spoiled they probably have their own bank accounts."

Merlie, doting parent of a twenty-pound feline, frowned judgmentally. "That's city people for you!"

There was still one thing about Natalie that seemed especially puzzling to Cal. If the woman was so rich, why didn't she do the sensible thing and use all her wealth to hire some hotshot contractor to fix up her house?

Then again, what business was it of his?

He folded his arms, wondering for the umpteenth time why he was bothering to get involved at all. He had a hundred dollars riding on her not making it through six weeks, and without his help, she probably wouldn't. Heck, he doubted she would last very long even with his help.

Trouble was, he couldn't just sit idly by anymore while she flailed around that old rattletrap, dying of thirst and falling through cracks. That's where she had the advantage over him. Winning a bet was one thing; watching her slow demise by home maintenance incompetence was something else.

"Sounds like you've got more company up there than you bargained for," Sam observed. "If you left her alone, maybe she'd go away faster."

He shook his head. "It would be like leaving a wounded squirrel on the side of the road. To be humane, you should either shoot it or give it some help." He sighed. "Guess I can't shoot her."

"Now *that* wouldn't be neighborly." Merlie laughed. "Or lawful."

The trouble was, ever since he'd held her lithe, supple body in his arms that afternoon, and looked into those brown eyes snapping with fire, his thoughts had turned more toward kissing her than killing her. For *that* he needed to be locked up!

Sam gave the matter some thought. "Well, I suppose you could ask Howard if he needs some work."

"Howard Tomlin? That old recluse?" Merlie professed shock. "I'd be surprised if he could even lift a hammer anymore!"

"I saw him just the other day," Sam answered. "He's pretty spry for a man in his late seventies."

Cal nodded. Better yet, he bet Howard would work for cheap.

Natalie Winthrop might make out like she was a big wheel, but he had the sneaking suspicion that there was a dire reason the baroness was being tight with her pennies.

"Thanks, Sam. I'll look up Howard this afternoon."

But that, he promised himself, would be absolutely the last time he put himself out on behalf of his new neighbor. Presenting her with the handyman and some new locks would be his first and last present to haughty Natalie Winthrop. From there on out, the baroness was on her own.

3

CAL HAD LIFTED NATALIE'S spirits when he told her that he'd found her a handyman, but one look at Howard Tomlin and Natalie's heart sank like the *Titanic*. She wasn't getting professional help, she was getting Mr. Magoo! It took the man five minutes to climb out of his antique pickup; she couldn't imagine asking him to actually climb a roof. The guy shuffled instead of walked, and his glasses looked as though he was peering at her through the bottoms of Coke bottles. When he spoke he hollered at her as if he were speaking through a megaphone, piercing her eardrums, but Cal swore that was just because Howard was accustomed to being alone all day and therefore had forgotten to put in his hearing aid. It seemed without his hearing aid he couldn't hear *or* gauge how loudly he was speaking.

Natalie didn't know what she was going to do. She didn't want to hurt the man's feelings, but wasn't she herself liability enough for one work crew? She just had to tell the man she couldn't use him. But when she looked at him peering at her through those thick glasses...

"I, uh, I'm afraid the wages I can offer you might fall short of what you hoped..." she said, praying the subject of money would bring a quick end to Howard's reentry into the workaday world.

"WHAT?"

She took a deep breath to gather both lung power and courage. She just didn't have the heart to tell him that he looked like calamity in work boots. "I CAN'T PAY YOU MUCH!"

He blinked at her through his Coke bottles. "CAL DONE TOLD ME YOU WERE THE HIGH AND MIGHTY SNIPPETY TYPE," he squawked at her. "BUT DON'T THINK YOU CAN EXPLOIT ME ON ACCOUNT OF MY AGE. I'M A MEMBER OF THE AARP AND I KNOW MY RIGHTS AND I WON'T WORK FOR A DIME LESS THAN SIX DOLLARS AN HOUR."

Six dollars an hour! The man could probably make that busing tables! His statement so astonished her that she blurted out the very words she'd been determined not to say.

"YOU'RE HIRED!" Never mind that Howard Tomlin was legally blind and couldn't climb a ladder. She thrust her hand out at him with more enthusiasm than if she'd picked him from among one hundred strapping young candidates. "WHEN CAN YOU START?"

Howard looked annoyed. "GUESS I MIGHT AS WELL START NOW, SINCE I DROVE UP ALL THIS WAY. I RECKON I COULD PUT IN THOSE LOCKS."

And without more ado, he shuffled back out to his truck to get his tools. Remembering something, she ran after him. "Mr. Tomlin? Mr. Tomlin?" Receiving no response, she stopped, put her hands on her hips and yelled at the top of her lungs. "HOWARD!"

He turned.

"THE HOUSE DOESN'T HAVE ANY ELEC-

TRICITY. IT MIGHT MAKE THINGS DIFFICULT FOR YOU.''

''ELECTRICITY?'' He wrinkled his nose. ''NEVER LIKED THE STUFF.'' He turned and stumped away.

He would love it here, then, she thought ruefully. She was walking back to the porch where Cal was standing when she heard a tuneless bellow behind her.

''IN THE VALLEY, WE SHALL MEET ON A BEAUTIFUL MORN!''

She frowned. Oh, no—he *sang* at the top of his lungs, too!

Inside, prompted by the sound of something approaching music, Armand started warming up his Verdi with a favorite snatch of *Rigoletto*. Between the two of them, Armand had the better voice.

Cal was waiting for her, arms crossed. That smug look was back. ''The baroness and Howard Tomlin. A match made in heaven.''

She scowled at him. ''DO YOU—'' She cleared her throat and started over at normal volume. ''Do you spend your entire life smirking at people?''

''Hey, I just helped you! Even though it was against my best interests, I might add.''

As she tossed a glance back at Howard, who was still unknowingly singing a duet with her parrot, leaning so far over into his truck bed that she feared he might tip over, she wasn't so sure. ''I half suspect Howard is your secret weapon.''

He laughed. ''That man can fix anything.''

She pursed her lips thoughtfully. So much in her life needed fixing, it seemed. Maybe she should have sent Howard after Malcolm Braswell.

But at any rate, Cal had already given her more aid

than she'd expected, especially considering he had a hundred dollars riding on her failure. "Thanks," she said belatedly. "I didn't mean to sound like an ingrate."

He answered with a mock bow. "You're welcome."

She shifted, uncertain what came next. Maybe his volunteering to leave...

That, unfortunately, wasn't forthcoming. He just stood there smiling at her in that knowing way he had about him, as if he were aware of her absolute most embarrassing secret.

"So what brings you here, Natalie Winthrop?"

She stiffened in surprise at the question. "I should think that would be obvious." She gestured at her house in one sweep, like Vanna White revealing the bonus round puzzle on *Wheel of Fortune*. "My mansion."

He shook his head. "Nope. Sorry. Not buying it."

She laughed nervously. "There's nothing to buy, Sherlock. No mystery to solve. I was cheated. End of story."

"But why would a hoity-toity dame like yourself go looking for houses in Heartbreak Ridge in the first place? *That's* what I wonder about."

She shrugged, her discomfort level increasing exponentially. "Who isn't interested in get-rich-quick schemes?"

"Rich people. Which you claimed you were but obviously now aren't."

Good Lord—he *did* know! Or if he didn't, he was on the verge of guessing. The possibility of that filled her with dread somehow. She lifted her chin a notch. "What on earth makes you think that?"

"Because you wouldn't be living out here if you had a dime to spare on a hotel. I know your type."

His sneering tone made her want to scream in frustration. "How do you know?" she asked. "Are you an anthropologist? Have you done a study?"

He snorted. "Lady, I've practically earned my Ph.D. in your kind."

Her kind. Her type. For heaven's sake, what was he talking about? She couldn't begin to grasp the category he was placing her in. Blondes? Inept housekeepers? Chumps? She wagged a finger at him. "I don't claim to understand *your* type, you mouthy mountain man. All I know is that you've bet I will turn tail and run, but I won't. So standing here and insulting me won't get you any closer to your hundred dollars."

He took in her words with a complacent smile. "It was a man, wasn't it?"

She rolled her eyes. "I don't have the foggiest idea what you're talking about."

"A boyfriend," he clarified. "A failed love affair that sent you off searching for some pie-in-the-sky dream life. Or maybe he dumped you, and you decided to resign from the world for a while."

After he'd stated his latest hypothesis, she had a flash of insight. "Why? Is that what *you* did?"

His arrogant mouth snapped shut, and for a split second she felt like jumping up and down and whooping in triumph the way sailors in old World War Two movies did when their torpedoes blew up an enemy ship. *That* would teach him to engage in wild speculation about her private life!

Slowly his face turned from its customary sneer to an unhappy mask, and after a moment of staring into those blue eyes clouded with some unknown sorrow, Natalie felt a shiver go through her. To her astonishment, his expression tugged at her pity. Something terrible must have happened to Cal Tucker to create that impenetrable shell of his.

But then, she knew a little bit about that. Oh, her history hadn't made her a cranky recluse—far from it. But for the past year, she felt as if she'd just been putting on a mask every day out of desperation, trying to hide the fear roiling inside her—fear that people would discover Malcolm Braswell had cheated her.

Was that what Cal felt? Fear?

Remorse filled her for having triggered unpleasant feelings; after all, he *had* helped her. She didn't want to revel in another's pain. "I'm sorry if I was rude."

His face registered no acknowledgment of her apology. "Well, I'd better be going." He stepped down from the porch, brushing right past her.

He was just going to walk away? "I said I was sorry," she bit out.

"I heard you."

She crossed her arms, growing furious at the man. Not accepting an honest apology—how childish, how arrogant! She regretted even extending the apology, if he was going to be this way about it. She had half a mind to take it back.

Though that *would* be childish....

Instead she glared at him as he went over to his blue truck, which was parked next to Howard's and looked like its grandchild. When he looked up at Natalie, she could see there was no love lost on his side, either.

She shifted testily, uncomfortable with the disappointment tweaking at her. She didn't like people not to like her. But Cal Tucker's opinion didn't matter one way or the other.

Did it?

Cal drove off without another word. Without a wave, even. Natalie just stood on her porch, stunned by the fierce emotions she and her good-looking new neighbor seemed to set off in each other.

"SHAME WHAT HAPPENED TO THAT BOY," Howard said as he came up the steps, lugging a green toolbox with rusted hinges.

"WHAT HAPPENED?" she asked, trying not to sound too eager for gossip about the neighbor she couldn't care less about.

"THE LOCAL SPECIALTY." Howard shook his head mournfully. "HEARTBREAK!"

THUNDER CLAPPED AS A STORM charged over the mountain, but it just seemed to echo the clamorous storm that had been brewing inside Cal ever since he got back from his neighbor's house. His snippy, unpleasant neighbor, he might have added.

There he'd been, trying to help her, and she'd up and insulted him! Not only that, but her barb was so on target it made him wonder if she hadn't heard talk in town about what had happened between him and Connie. Even after a year and a divorce, that wound still felt fresh—and leave it to the baroness to rub a little salt on it for him!

He felt like railing at fate—or whatever had brought that woman here. Of all the people in all the world, Jim Loftus *would* have to choose some incompetent society tootsie to move into that damn house! There had been over five hundred entrants in the house raffle to choose from—couldn't he have picked a nice retired couple? Or a quiet old guy who minded his own business and liked to fish? Or just someone *sane?*

He frowned as the rain that had been threatening for over an hour finally began to do a war dance on the roof. The trouble was, he was partly glad Natalie was in that house. That old deathtrap was just what a woman like her deserved. Watching her make a big flop of the renovation was going to be a pleasure. Even with Howard's help she wouldn't be able to make that place livable, and with having to pay him maybe she'd run out of whatever money she had left just a little bit faster.

The prospect of her giving up made him rub his hands together with glee, like the Grinch contemplating spoiling the Who's Christmas.

Why, besting Natalie was going to be nearly as wonderful as triumphing over Connie would have been!

Not that he understood quite what "triumph" would be in that instance—having Connie crawl back to him? He didn't want that!

Lightning struck nearby, followed by a deafening clap of thunder, and he ran over to the window and looked down the hill.

The big house was dark except for a faint glow emanating from one room. A smirk touched at his lips as he imagined the sad little scene being played out below…. Natalie would be huddled in the one corner of the house that didn't leak water through the ceiling—if there was such a place—hovering over a candle. No doubt a woman like her was afraid of lightning, and since this storm was a doozy, she was probably petrified. He pictured her honey-blond hair falling in her face like it sometimes did, her pretty brown eyes wide with fear. She'd be clutching one of those pathetic, overfluffed dogs of hers…

His smirk slowly morphed into a thoughtful frown.

In his imagination, the big fuzzy dog jiggled with fright. It was whimpering, even…

He stood stock-still in the middle of the room that doubled as a living room and kitchen. Who knows how long he stood there, his face going slack with sympathy, the ice around his heart slowly melting as the picture became more and more real to him. Natalie's house had no heat, no light, no place to keep dry. The fierce wind whipping at those rattling old windows, some of them poorly patched with duct tape, would be enough to scare even the most seasoned Heartbreak Ridge folk.

Damn!

He pivoted and stomped to the front door, cursing himself for being a million kinds of a fool even as he threw on his raincoat and smashed his hat on his head. That infernal woman had no business being here…no business making him feel sorry for her! But the simple fact was that he did, and he wasn't going to get any sleep until he checked up on her.

He sprinted out to the truck and tore down the hill as fast as the blinding rain would allow. The storm was so heavy that the road between his and Natalie's looked as if it might be washed out before the night was over.

He jumped out at the bottom of the hill, ran to the door and knocked. Inside, the parrot did his doorbell imitation. The dogs as usual went nuts; he could hear them jumping up and down and running their paws over the door. He turned the doorknob to go inside, but when the thing wouldn't open, he remembered that Howard had installed locks.

"Who is it?" Natalie called from inches away.

He rolled his eyes. "It's me, Natalie. For God's sake, open up!" Naturally the porch leaked. Actually it more than leaked. He was getting as drenched standing at her doorstep as he would have standing out in the middle of a field.

The parrot chimed again and she turned the key in the lock. When she swung the old heavy door open, he sucked in a breath of surprise. She was standing in an old flannel nightshirt and some sweats, and she looked every bit as forlorn as he'd imagined. Rain poured into the front room, and in one little corner where the cockatoo's cage stood, a small candle flickered restlessly. The damp room smelled of wet dog and parrot and some other pungent, familiar scent.

His nose wrinkled as he zeroed in on Natalie as the source of the smell that bothered him. "What's that you're wearing?"

She blinked. "Chanel."

He might have known—she even *smelled* like Connie! The very idea made him want to whirl on his boot heel and run right back to his truck. Yet he remained glued to where he was.

The dogs whimpered and jumped at his legs, and Natalie just continued staring at him with those big eyes of hers. Shadows from the candle flickered across her high cheekbones, making her complexion seem a little more perfect. But her hair hung in limp tired strands, and thin collarbones jutted out of the neckline of her floppy nightshirt. She looked like a waif.

"Come on," he said, clamping down on one of

those thin arms. Perfume or no perfume, he couldn't just leave her here.

She dug in her heels before he could drag her out the door. "Come on where?"

"I'm taking you to my house." Now that he thought about it, they needed to blow out the candle. He strode across the room. "Get whatever you need for the night, and let's go."

To his surprise, Natalie didn't argue. This was a first!

"Okay," she said, "you grab the parrot cage and I'll try to find Winston. He hates storms." She was about to wander off in search of the cat when he grabbed hold of her again, stopping her.

"Pardon me?"

Big brown eyes blinked up at him, alarmed. "I can't leave them here!"

"It's just overnight," he said.

"But look at them," she pleaded, pointing to her trembling pups. Back in his own house when he'd been imagining the scene here, he'd been wrong about one detail. It was the silly Chihuahua with his bug eyes that appeared the most terrified. Not to mention, the fat little pug dog was shaking so that his loose skin jiggled and quivered as though he had Jell-O under his fur. "They're scared to death!"

"My house has two rooms," he informed her. "And a bathroom."

She put her hands on her hips. "Well *this* house has about two square feet that's usable, so you're doing pretty good from my vantage point. Besides, Armand really shouldn't be here in the cold and damp—it's bad for him."

"He's a bird!"

"He's a *tropical* bird. His native habitat is a rain forest."

"See—rain!"

She thinned her lips impatiently. "Just grab the cage, would you? And put it in the back seat of my Volkswagen. I'll get Winston, and the dogs can ride with you." She turned on her heel as if the matter was all settled.

He grumbled as he heard her run up the stairs calling for Winston. Good grief—he'd come over to help and now she was turning him into her zookeeper! As he tried to figure out how to detach the bird's cage from the stand it rested on, dogs bustled around them, their nails clicking around his ankles, tripping him up.

A pathetic shriek went up and he realized he'd stepped on the fat one. He looked down apologetically. Chubbo had buggy eyes, too. Sad buggy eyes. Pathetic!

He grabbed hold of the handles on the side of the cage and lifted it. An *oooof!* of surprise came out of him. The thing felt as if it were made of cast iron!

He sighed. "Okay, guys, let's go."

The dogs danced toward the door, and he stepped on the pug again. It let out another piercing yelp, which apparently cued the bird to burst into song— some wordless but familiar tune that reminded him of something one of those three annoying tenors on public television might sing.

"God help me," he muttered to himself as he banged out the door into the pouring rain. "I try to rescue a woman and I end up getting force-fed culture from a bird!"

"In case I didn't say so before, thank you for bringing us here," Natalie told Cal as she settled onto his couch with a cup of hot tea. Having spent the past days living off processed foods, hot anything to her now seemed like a luxury. Bootsy and Fritz joined her on the couch, while Mopsy curled on an old braided rug at her feet.

"Does this house belong to you?" she asked.

Cal moved toward his rocking chair, nearly tripping over Winston, who wove between his legs. They'd draped a dark towel over Armand's cage, so the room was silent except for a crackling fire. "It's my family's hunting cabin."

She wrinkled her nose at the deer head mounted on the wall just above her. Poor Bambi! She hated the thought of it meeting such a scary end, then being stuffed and nailed up as interior decoration.

"Wait—don't tell me," Cal said with a snort. "You don't approve of hunting."

She smiled, trying to remember that she was a guest. If she were in Japan, she would accept raw fish from a host without any lectures about bacteria. The same manners were needed, she supposed, when dealing with a barbarian. "I'm sure killing things is a very absorbing hobby."

He laughed. "Just as I suspected—a bleeding heart! You probably wouldn't hesitate to order venison from a five-star restaurant."

She was afraid her blush told the awful truth. Like a foot stepping on the proverbial banana peel, the moral high ground slipped out from under her. "I wouldn't *order* it." Though she'd had a delicious venison steak at a dinner party just last month...and since it was all there was, what choice did she have but to eat it? And the caterer for her wedding reception had talked her into veal cutlets on the buffet. From a bleeding heart point of view, eating veal put you on a moral level with Attila the Hun.

She wondered what had happened to all those little veals after she canceled the wedding. She hoped the caterer had done as she asked and donated the lavish feast to the local food bank. She smiled, thinking of her black-tie banquet, complete with the cupid ice sculpture, being transplanted from the Hilton to a soup kitchen.

"Something wrong?" he asked.

She shook her head, a little troubled. "Just thinking."

He held his steaming mug in his hands and nodded knowingly. "It's that guy, isn't it?"

"What guy?"

"The fellow who dumped you. You can't stop thinking about him."

Apparently *he* couldn't stop thinking about him, though she'd assumed after she'd put him in his place this afternoon that he would have learned to avoid this subject. "For your information, I didn't get dumped. I did the dumping myself."

He looked as if he'd just swallowed a frog. "I should have known."

She lifted her chin a notch. "Besides which, that was *not* who I was thinking about. Jared rarely crosses my mind."

"Jared!" he said in disgust.

"That was my fiancé's name. Jared Huddleton."

"Why did you dump him?"

"That's none of your business!" She couldn't bring herself to admit that she'd dumped him for her house—the house she couldn't sleep in during a rainstorm. Cal already thought she was an idiot! She wasn't even sure she could explain to anyone the exact circumstances that made her flight to Heartbreak Ridge, to the unknown, preferable to the sure thing of marrying Jared. "Anyway, it's a long story."

He grinned. "The night is young. How close were you to marrying this Jared character?"

"About sixteen hours." His jaw dropped, and she added quickly, "But it was for the best. Ours would have been a disastrous marriage."

"Apparently!"

"I realized I didn't love him."

"Then why did you get engaged to him?"

She cast her eyes down to the rug and patted Mopsy absently. "I...I thought it would be a beneficial arrangement."

Cal snorted. "I get it. He was loaded, but in the end you couldn't go through with it."

She didn't answer. Her red face probably spoke volumes, anyway.

"A real heartbreaker," he said, his voice almost a sneer. "I guess you've come to the right place."

She chuckled anxiously. "That heartbreak business is just a gag, right? Howard was telling me a little about it today."

She didn't add that they'd been discussing Cal at the time.

His expression turned dead earnest. "It's no joke to the people living here. There's not a family around that hasn't been hit pretty hard by heartache."

It was on the tip of her tongue to say there was barely anyone in the world who hadn't, but she could see from his expression that he was in no mood to debate the town's love curse. For whatever reason,

Cal obviously saw himself as a poster child for his hometown affliction, the crown prince of heartbreak—nothing she could say would change that.

"You know," he said suddenly, "women never cease to amaze me. They'll leave a guy flat and then feel sorry for themselves."

She squared her shoulders. "I didn't realize I was supposed to be representing my entire sex. Have you always been this hostile to all women?"

"It's a more recent development," he grumbled, taking a swig of tea.

"I see," she said. "Ever since your wife ran out on you..."

His blue gaze narrowed. "Who told you about that?"

"Howard. It seems even the town recluse—the *other* one—knows you've been holed up here moping. No doubt you've also been waiting for some unsuspecting female to come along so you could vent your rage on her. How gleeful you must have been when I drove up!"

He barked out a laugh. "Gleeful!" His voice was about three octaves higher than usual. "Lady, do you think I'm enjoying having my solitude shattered?"

She twisted her lips. "You were the one who invited me to stay the night."

"And look what happened!" He gestured around him in a sweeping motion. "I end up with a roomful of fur and a mouthy woman who wants to pry into my psyche!"

She practically quavered with indignation. "Who was the one who started asking prying questions about my would-be marriage?"

He ducked his head—the closest he would come to confessing being in the wrong.

She sighed, reminding herself he'd been trying to be nice, in his own way. At any rate, she should at least be grateful for having a dry place for her and the animals to sleep. Not every neighbor would have taken her in as Cal had. She feigned a yawn. "I'm sort of tired...maybe we'd better go to sleep?"

It would be better than staying awake longer and arguing.

He nodded, and when he got up and stretched, she couldn't help but feel a grudging admiration for the way his chest muscles pushed against his T-shirt. He was one of those rare men who filled out their clothes like fashion models without appearing to have spent a million hours in an expensive, mirror-lined gym. Cal was just naturally well built and graceful—and he looked completely comfortable in his skin.

But it was what was going on in that head of his that gave her the willies. Serious ex-wife fallout there!

Of course, there was no telling what kind of shape the ex-wife was in. Maybe she was a basket case, too.

She forced a smile. "Where do I sleep?"

He nodded toward the couch. "You're sitting on it."

A couch! It would be a hundred times better than the floor she'd been sleeping on...and yet she'd caught a glimpse of Cal's king-size bed with its mattresses piled waist high and she'd practically lusted. Not after Cal, but a decent night's sleep.

She realized now, as her shoulders sagged a little in disappointment, that she'd been hoping he'd do the gentlemanly thing and offer to sleep on the couch himself.

Cal Tucker. Gentlemanly. Fat chance!

Five minutes later Cal had her set up with sheets, blankets and a pillow. "Okay, baroness," he said. "Sweet dreams."

She bristled at the sobriquet, but tried not to let her annoyance show too much. "Good night," she said sweetly.

When she was alone and sank onto the soft cushions, she let out a sigh. This was the softest bed she'd had since leaving Houston. It felt close to heaven, actually. She might have some sweet dreams after all.

Except that when she closed her eyes, she couldn't stop picturing Cal's muscles rippling against his undershirt...and remembering that wonderful bod was alone in a king-size bed just twenty feet away...

4

RIGOLETTO BEGAN AT DAWN. And not the whole opera, either. That damn bird knew just about as many snatches of that work as Cal himself did, which was to say, not very many. Cal only opened his eyes enough to see that it was still mostly dark, then he flopped over with a groan.

With his next breath, he inhaled a pile of fur.

Cal coughed and propped himself up on his elbows, frowning at the hulking sheepdog eyeing him in startled innocence through his veil of fur. "Wait a minute!"

How the heck did Mopsy get into his bed?

In the next moment, two more sets of eyes were peering at him over Mopsy's back—the bug eyes of the Chihuahua and the sleepy eyes of Natalie.

"What's the matter?" she asked, yawning.

He rocketed off the bed as if he'd been launched by NASA and gaped at her, astounded. He was awakened by a Verdi-squawking bird to find himself sharing his king-size bed with two mutts and a very shapely woman, who, the last time he checked, were tucked into the sofa. And she had the audacity to ask _him_ what the matter was?

"What are you doing in here?"

She shrugged her stiff shoulders. "I needed somewhere to sleep."

"What was wrong with the couch?"

"It was fine until Bootsy climbed in with us. You wouldn't believe how loudly that dog snores! It's a characteristic of pugs, I'm afraid. Snoring and shedding."

"Delightful."

"Plus, Bootsy might be small, but what a bed hog! She always wants to be smack-dab in the middle."

"Is that so?" He tried not to look too pointedly at the gorgeous body sprawled across the middle of *his* bed.

She nodded. "She can take up more space than you would imagine. So I decided to go where it was less crowded. It's not as if you were hurting for room, Cal."

"Now I am!"

She looked over at Mopsy and laughed. "How did she get in here?"

"You left the door open, obviously!"

She glanced up at him with raised brows. "Are you always this cranky in the morning?"

"When I find my bed invaded by two furballs, yes!" He didn't mention what seeing Natalie there, all rumpled and adorable with her nightshirt falling off one thin shoulder, was doing to him. From the next room the parrot launched into another fractured chorus, nearly sending him over the edge. "Is there any way to shut that bird up?"

Natalie jutted her chin up in her haughty Winthrop way. "I don't think I like the tone you're taking."

He practically quaked. "Lady, I don't like the liberties *you're* taking."

She grinned. "Not accustomed to sharing your bed, are you?"

"Not with canines, no."

"And women?"

He frowned as she gave his boxers and bare chest a quick once-over. "Listen, Natalie, I'm not a saint. And since you have a body that seems groomed for bedroom shenanigans, just the sort of thing to tempt the appetites of a barbarian like myself, if I were you I would take this opportunity to skedaddle back to the living room."

Even in the darkness he could see that her cheeks turned a few shades redder. "All right, if you're going to be that way about it. I wasn't throwing myself at you, you know."

He let out a sigh. Did she really think she had to remind him that she considered him unworthy? "I know."

She gathered up Fritz in the crook of her arm and ushered Mopsy off the bed, her proud carriage crackling with displeasure. "I didn't know you were going to be so huffy, or believe me I never would have come in here. Sorry we disturbed you!"

She pivoted on her bare heel and padded out of his bedroom, shutting the door firmly behind her. He had to stop himself from running after her. The apology on his lips was completely unwarranted. *He* was the one being put out here. *He* was the one who had extended hospitality and been taken advantage of. *He* was the one who was having to listen to some Metropolitan Opera reject at five in the morning!

Besides, maybe he could be nice to her later, at a decent hour. That was a less painful prospect than an apology.

He crawled back into bed and pulled the covers over his head, determined to muffle the off-key squawks of Armand, until he realized that there were no sounds coming from the living room at all. Natalie must have, as asked, shut him up.

That was one way she differed from his ex-wife. If he'd goaded Connie about the noise level, she would have simply made *more* noise. Of course, Connie wouldn't have been caught dead with a bird or a cat or a dog living in the house. She hated the idea of fur getting on her clothes, and Cal just couldn't picture her cleaning out a parrot cage. He was surprised Natalie would, either—probably she was used to having a houseful of faithful family retainers to take care of the unpleasant details of life.

Only she didn't have any servants now…

He frowned up at the ceiling, trying once again to figure out how such a rich, obviously spoiled woman ended up in a—well, he had to admit it—backwater like Heartbreak Ridge. She must have had some breakup with that fiancé of hers. *Jared!* he thought in disgust. What else would send her running out this far into the wilderness?

First he tried visualizing Jared—a slick, seedy, city guy, he decided. Glib and cheeky. Then he pictured the Natalie he'd seen yesterday morning, after she'd fallen through her roof, and tried to square it with a woman who would become engaged to Mr. Slick. Something about the equation wasn't adding up. He didn't want to give the baroness too much credit— she was a spoiled socialite, all right, but she wasn't a slick, glib, detestable one.

Or was she?

SHE'D NEVER SEEN SO MUCH frozen food in her life. Cal had enough stuff in his freezer to feed an army through the winter, and more beer in his fridge than Jared had ordered for his bachelor party.

That reminder of the life, the wedding and the man she'd left behind caused a little sigh to issue from her lips. She still felt foolish, throwing away a perfectly good fiancé...for what? To be the houseguest of a caveman with a well-stocked fridge and the manners of a troll?

Smart move, Natalie!

Jared had never snapped at her as Cal had this morning. Jared had always been the soul of patience with her, and had considered even her shortcomings charming. In fact, he'd never fought with her at all. Or even grumbled at her.

She frowned. There was something wrong with that, though she couldn't say just what. Jared always was a little short-tempered with others—the mechanic who couldn't fix his Mercedes, friends who left before paying their bar tabs, that kind of thing—but never once had he seemed irritated at her. He'd been the soul of kindness to her, in fact.

And she hadn't been able to fall in love with him! Was she a dope, or what?

She shouldn't be thinking of all this.

Food. She needed food. She rooted around the freezer for something that looked as though it might be transformed into breakfast, and pulled out a frozen pizza. She stuck it into the oven, then dug in the refrigerator for something besides beer. She grabbed a grapefruit, split it, then set about making coffee.

Luckily she was fairly adept at breakfast, she thought proudly. Cal obviously considered her spoiled and useless, but he would have to lose a little of that condescension when he stepped out of his bedroom and found a well-rounded meal awaiting him.

Of course, she didn't dwell too long on how eagerly she waited to see him step out of his bedroom. When she'd snuggled into his king-size bed, she hadn't had the vision of him in only those boxer shorts, or else she never would have been so bold. And he'd told her that *she* had a body made for sexual shenanigans! That man was the sexiest thing she'd ever clapped eyes on outside of a movie theater. In fact, she'd be willing to bet that his bod could give some of those Hollywood types a run for their money.

His temper reminded her of a few Hollywood types, too; unfortunately, mostly the ones who ended up on *Entertainment Tonight* for having shoved their fists into faces of cameramen.

She opened the oven and saw that the pizza beneath the broiler was bubbling nicely. The coffeemaker sputtered and puffed as it finished brewing. She opened the cabinets and managed to scrounge up two matching plates and arranged them on the table.

Within a few moments, sounds issued forth from inside Cal's bedroom, and she sat down restlessly, uneasy with the furious surge of her pulse as she waited for him to appear. Just because a man had a good body didn't erase the fact that he had the personality of a wild dog. The fresh mountain air must be going to her brain for her to start lusting after Cal Tucker!

"What's this?" Cal asked when he finally made his entrance in a loose plaid flannel shirt and his customary tight-fitting jeans.

"Breakfast." Her pulse skipped, but she was spared the pulmonary gymnastics she would have experienced seeing him nearly naked again. "Come 'n get it."

She poured him coffee and pulled the pizza out of the oven. He squinted at her choice of breakfast food, but to her shock, he didn't complain.

"I forgot to buy eggs last time I was in town," he said, almost apologetically.

Given the niceness of his tone, she assumed he must not be thoroughly awake yet. "This looked good to me anyway," she assured him, not adding that she was much better at defrosting frozen pizzas than scrambling eggs.

He said little as he scarfed down most of the pizza and his half a grapefruit and guzzled two cups of coffee. Finally, when he'd ended his meal, he looked her up and down and grinned. "Well, what shall we do today, baroness?"

She frowned, both at his derisive nickname and at the implication that they were going to spend the day together. "I don't know about you, but I'm going home."

His mouth twisted into a skeptical frown. "Have you looked outside? It's still raining."

"I have work to do."

He laughed. "Then I hope you're amphibian, because you'll probably have to tread water to get any work done in that house of yours today."

The thought of the house being even worse off today than it was last night made her shudder in dread. What could *worse* be? A Superfund cleanup site? Suddenly, her eagerness to be up-and-at-'em evaporated. "But what about Howard? He said he was coming in today."

"Howard's no fool. He won't show up till your

house has had time to dry out. Anyway the dirt road—now a mud road—up to your place is probably impassable by anything with wheels."

She sighed. "But I can't just stay here."

"Why not?" he asked dryly. "Don't we have fun together?"

Was he actually joking with her? And more amazing yet, did he really want her to stay?

She crossed her arms and leveled a skeptical glance on him. "Of course I *love* your company, but what about my animals? They need food."

He got up and opened a cabinet filled with canned goods, including a healthy supply of tuna. "Armand can eat fruit and crackers for a day, can't he?"

She nodded numbly. "Sure...but are you positive you want us all over here?"

He weighed the question. "Not really, but if you went back to that house, I'd probably just spend the rest of the day worrying about what kind of scrapes you were getting yourself into down there. Having you fall through the roof once wasted a lot of my time already." Before she could start yelling at him, he shrugged and added, "Besides, the rain's bound to clear out before long. I'll take you back down this afternoon."

What was the catch? There had to be one. He was being awfully considerate. Yet his blue eyes communicated that the offer had been extended in earnest.

"Okay...if I won't be in the way."

He practically hooted. "In a two-room cabin, how could you not be in the way?"

She popped out of her chair. "If you think I'm—"

He stood up and put his hand on her shoulders to calm her down, which actually had the opposite effect. True, she stopped speaking—in fact, her mouth felt so bone-dry she had a hard time even swallowing—but his touch on her was anything but soothing; her blood raced through her veins like a raging river after a typhoon.

"Will you stop being so touchy?" he asked.

"*I'm* not the one doing the touching here," she told him, casting a pointed glance down at his big hands over her shoulders.

He dropped them and stood in front of her awkwardly...during which time she wanted to kick herself for telling him to let her go. Now that they were down by his sides, she found that she missed the feel of those big paws of his.

"Well...what do you suggest we do?" she asked after a few uneasy moments of staring into his sexy blue eyes. "Have any movies?"

He shook his head. "Nope."

"Oh, well, maybe something's on TV."

"There is no TV."

She gaped around the combination living room-kitchen in amazement. This might have been the first time she'd been in a house without a television since...well, not counting her present accommodations, since forever! She blinked at him in amazement. "What do you do up here?"

He laughed and nodded to a set of books stacked in a corner. "I've been reading my way through the encyclopedia."

She put her hands on her hips. "No kidding? What for?"

"Maybe because I didn't go to college," he said. "I figure this is a cheap way to catch up on what I missed."

The response brought a chuckle to her lips. "I was wondering why you had so much beer in your fridge. Apparently you're trying to make up for all the keggers you missed in college, too."

He crossed his arms. "I just like to keep stocked up. I don't go to town much."

She tilted her head, interested. "But you just did. Was that for my benefit?" Surprisingly she was almost sure she caught a redness in his cheeks.

"Not entirely. I had some other business to attend to."

But she had the sneaking suspicion that he would have been happy to let his business wait if it weren't for her pressing need for a handyman. Natalie felt a sharp stab of appreciation for the aid he'd extended her, however grudgingly. "How far along are you in col—I mean, the encyclopedia?"

He grinned. *"J."*

"Hmm, a sophomore," she translated. "That's a very good year. The real world hasn't started closing in yet."

"I'd like to keep it at bay for as long as possible."

She tilted her head, hesitating. Maybe she shouldn't ask him the questions burning inside her, but she couldn't help it. "What were you in the real world?"

She'd never given any thought to the possibility that Cal had at one time had a profession. He seemed tailor-made for the role of recluse and annoying neighbor. Now she was prepared for any number of answers, from cowboy to construction worker to felon.

"Deputy sheriff of Heartbreak Ridge."

That was the one response she hadn't anticipated!

"No way!" His answer nearly floored her. "*You're* a cop?"

His lips twisted in that somber way he had. "Ex-cop. I resigned a year ago."

"When…" She didn't even have to finish her sentence with "…*your wife left you.*"

He nodded in understanding. "That's right."

A wave of sympathy moved through her. Strangely she understood that need to remake one's life after a romantic upset. Not that she had experienced heartbreak on the scale that Cal obviously had.

How strange! What could this wife of his have been like? And why had she left so abruptly? It had to have been abruptly to cause Cal to recoil from the world.

She knew better than to actually ask the questions, of course, but she filed them away for a later date.

"Sitting around reading *J* isn't very sociable," she said, knowing the man was praying for her to change the subject. "How about a game of gin rummy?"

Cal drew back as if she'd just suggested dancing on hot coals. "No, thanks!"

"What's the matter with cards? Given the fact that you consider yourself the king of heartache, you should be a fairly lucky man with a deck."

He frowned in distaste. "My little brother started playing cards with a woman to pass the time and within a few weeks they were married."

She tilted her head. "Did it end badly?"

"No, it hasn't ended yet."

"You mean they're happily married? From what I've heard, I didn't think happily ever after was possible in this town.

"Well, they're married," Cal conceded grudgingly,

but added, "If you call living in a fool's paradise happiness, then I suppose they rate as happily married."

She chortled at his assessment. "So even when people are married and happy, Cal the wise, old owl says they aren't really happy?"

The owl scowled. "They might be happy. But as far as I can tell, most marriages are just a matter of waiting for the other shoe to drop."

"You're a case!" She almost had to admire someone so relentlessly cynical. "So now, after your brother's brush with wedded bliss, you shy away from cards because you're afraid lightning will strike twice?"

"Something like that."

Amazing. A heartbroken ex-lawman with an aversion to cards. Filling the day was looking more and more difficult. She doubted he had any board games sitting around; besides she didn't particularly like those herself. There had only been one she was any good at, and somehow Cal didn't strike her as the *Candyland* type.

"Do you have any other suggestions for what we should do?"

"Sure," he said, a wry smile touching his lips. "How about teaching that bird of yours something worth listening to?"

ARMAND WOULDN'T SING Hank Williams, even after hours of tutoring. Cal would sing along to "Your Cheatin' Heart" on the phonograph, and the cockatoo would respond with perplexed silence, as if he'd never sung a note in his life and thought Cal was crazy to expect him to. It was very discouraging.

Leave it to Natalie to have a stubborn bird with no taste in music.

Natalie, who was working on an old jigsaw puzzle she'd found in a closet, looked up at around one o'clock and smiled in surprise at the window. "Sunshine!"

In the next instant, the two of them were both pressed up against the glass panes like housebound kids, staring in amazement at the rays shooting out of the sky as if they'd spent forty days and forty nights under a cloud, instead of one measly morning. Natalie whirled on her heel and began gathering up her things. "I should really be getting home now."

The thought of her leaving should have made Cal happier than it did. His house was way overcrowded, the pets had shed everywhere, and being locked up for this long with Natalie was revving up his libido in a dangerous way. He was too attracted to her for his own good. Every time he thought about her, he kept remembering Connie and how much they looked alike and how similar their backgrounds were. But every time he actually found himself gazing at Natalie in the flesh, Connie was the farthest thing from his mind. All he could think about was how good it would feel to run his hands through that long blond hair, or to press his mouth against her soft pink lips, or to feel her body up next to his...

Obviously he was losing his mind. As if singing old country western songs to a big white bird all day weren't evidence enough of that.

"I'll help you," he said quickly.

For the next half hour, they went through last night in reverse. The parrot cage was loaded into his truck, as was Winston. The dogs piled into the Volkswagen.

Then they all slid down the muddy road to Natalie's and unloaded everybody.

"That's strange..." Natalie stood frowning at her front door as Cal lugged Armand's cast-iron cage up the creaky porch steps.

"What's the matter?" he asked, about to step through the front door. Natalie stopped him with a touch of her hand to his arm. The contact went through him like a bolt of electricity.

But the look on her face told him that she'd only touched him because she was startled. She nodded at the front door's lock, which had been banged up pretty bad. There was also a big muddy footprint in the middle of the door. Someone had left a calling card—size twelve, if he wasn't mistaken.

Cal stiffened and reflexively pulled Natalie away from the door, away from any danger that might be inside. Though, on second thought, he doubted whoever had kicked the door in would still be around. It probably had happened last night, while they were sleeping; they would have heard a car today.

"It couldn't have been Howard," Natalie said quickly. "Howard has a key."

As if he would have suspected Howard of breaking and entering. "Believe me, when it comes to kicking in people's doors, I'd suspect Fritz before Howard."

"Then who could have done this?"

"Stay out here," he instructed.

"Alone? Are you nuts? I'm going with you!" she said, taking his arm as they stepped over the threshold.

Seeing the inside of her home was obviously a shock to Natalie. Not only was everything wet, but the intruder had thrown mud and broken more windows than had even been broken before. The house was, now more than ever, a disaster area, and by the time they had toured all the rooms, Natalie was practically quaking with rage or fear or a combination of both.

"Who would have done this?" she whispered again. "Who?"

"I have no idea," Cal said honestly. "Vandalism usually isn't a big problem in Heartbreak Ridge. Nobody from around here would do this."

She stiffened. "Are you insinuating that I brought an urban crime wave with me from Houston?"

"Oh sure," he quipped, "all you gangsta types from River Oaks, getting high on pedicure fumes and then driving ten hours to break into houses. That's immediately what popped into my head."

His stab at levity was met with a withering gaze. "Wiseacre." Her face pinched in thought. "Maybe a bunch of kids came through and decided to rough up the old place. Don't you think it could have been just kids?"

Cal couldn't pinpoint a single kid in the area mean enough to do something like this. Or stupid enough, frankly. Everyone in the area knew that he lived in the cabin right up the hill. What kid in his right mind would break into a house and risk being seen by the ex-deputy sheriff?

"After all," Natalie went on, "you insinuated that people in town have been making fun of me. What do they call me?"

"The innkeeper."

"Yes! That could be the problem—someone's probably just trying to undermine me. Someone who doesn't want me to start a business maybe."

Cal looked at her sympathetically. "There aren't any other hotels around here, Natalie. It's not as if you have a rival."

It wasn't even as if she actually had a hotel, either, or even much of a prayer of ever having one.

His disputing her theories only made her look depressed. "But if it isn't a kid, or a person angry about my coming here and opening a hotel, who could it be?"

Cal frowned. "That's what you're going to have to help me figure out. Let's go."

Her eyes rounded. "Go where?"

"Home," he said, then added, "I mean, to my place. You can't stay here tonight, with no locks on the doors."

She stared again at the big footprint in the middle of the door. "It doesn't look as if the lock was much of an impediment to my visitor last night."

He took her arm with one hand and hefted Armand's cage with the other. "We can get a new door."

"A sturdier one."

He grunted. "If sturdy's what you want, maybe we should look up whoever manufactured this damn bird cage. Alcatraz couldn't have heavier bars!"

He tugged her off the porch and loaded the cat, dogs and bird back into the vehicle and drove up the hill to his house again. Never in a million years would he have thought he'd be volunteering to have Natalie and her menagerie spend more time with him, but Natalie's house being busted into had thrown him for a loop. He felt angry, and protective and, frankly, baffled.

Sure, he'd been a deputy for several years before

quitting, but Heartbreak Ridge wasn't exactly a hot-bed of crime. He'd only investigated two break-ins before, and those had been of businesses, with money as the obvious motive. Did people think that Natalie had a lot of money socked away in her house some-where? That was a possibility.

Once they were seated in his living room with some hot cocoa mugs in their hands, he decided the grilling couldn't be put off any longer. "Did you no-tice anything that had been stolen?"

She shook her head.

Her face was still pale with fright, and he had to force himself to keep his hands around a mug of co-coa instead of reaching out to hold her. "No valua-bles?"

"No, not at all. I've left what jewelry I have in a lockbox in the trunk of my car."

Cal frowned. That didn't sound very secure either. "I suppose that's where you keep your money, too."

She laughed bitterly. "What money?"

"C'mon," he said. "You obviously have some-thing, or you wouldn't be trying to renovate that old shambles into an inn for rich folk."

Her face colored a deep shade of red.

"Would you?" he asked.

"Well...to be honest, I *do* have money. Fifteen thousand dollars."

"In cash?" His voice was a grunt of disapproval; if a woman was running around with that much moo-lah in the trunk of her car, she was dumber than he'd given her credit for!

But she shook her head, assuring him, "No, it's in the bank."

He nodded. Then, as the implication of what she

told him sank in, he felt the blood draining out of his face. "You mean *all* the money you have in the world is fifteen thousand dollars?"

Not that this was an amount to be sneezed at. Far from it. But for a baroness?

At his loud, skeptical tone, she looked more miserable than ever. "Yes, I'm afraid so."

"But what about your great-great-grandfather, the oil baron?"

"He left a bundle to my ancestors, who in turn passed it along to me."

"And what did you do to make the pile dwindle from millions to fifteen thousand?"

She exhaled a puff of air. "I blew it."

He frowned. "*All* of it?"

Natalie shook her head. "Look…this is a long story. Do you want the long version or would you rather just have it all in a nutshell?"

"I'd like to have it in full, from the beginning," he instructed, wincing a little at the *Dragnet* tone in his voice.

She smiled ruefully. "Okay," she said. "But you might want to heat up another pot of cocoa. This could take a while."

For the next hour he sat equally rapt and appalled by the story of Natalie and her crooked accountant and her attempt to hide the fact that she was quickly going broke. Had he said a woman like Natalie was his worst nightmare? She was worse than the worst! There wasn't a step she had taken in this whole mess that wasn't harebrained and wrong, from not informing the police of Malcolm Braswell's theft in the first place right down to entering Jim Loftus's seedy contest.

Still, oddly enough, he almost understood the misplaced pride that had driven her to sell family heirlooms and come within a hairsbreadth of marrying a man she didn't love.

Almost.

"For heaven's sake, why didn't you just get a job?"

"What could I have done?"

He barked out a laugh. "Good grief. Everybody can do something. And look at all the advantages you've had. You have a college degree."

"In art history." She ducked her head. "Not exactly a field crying out for employees."

He frowned. "Okay, so you couldn't have been a museum curator. But think of it. You could have been a salesclerk."

"I've never even worked a cash register."

He rolled his eyes. "They could have taught you that in a day, Natalie. It's not rocket science. And then you might have been able to hang onto some of your family's things."

"I couldn't have made enough money anyway. Who would pay me to do anything?"

In that moment, Cal looked into her soulful brown eyes and came to a startling realization. Natalie might be a baroness with a chip on her shoulder, but she also had a hell of an inferiority complex when it came to her worth as a human being. Her self-esteem had all been tied up in a bank balance.

"And what about all my friends? What would they have said? They would have deserted me!"

"Some friends!" he scoffed.

Somehow, even in the midst of telling him this sad story of hers, she still worked up enough pride to stick her chin out at him defiantly. "I didn't tell you all this so you could sneer at me."

"All right," he said, sighing. "At least now I know what the hell you're doing out here. And now at least I can figure out who's going to be staying in that crazy hotel you intend on opening...all these so-called 'friends' who wouldn't speak to you if they knew how little you have in the bank."

She crossed her arms. "That's why I've dreamed of opening the hotel. I'll finally have done something all on my own. And all these people, whom I was too afraid to tell that I needed to get a job, will be paying me to stay here and they'll be happy doing it."

He shook his head. "Natalie, I don't mean to be a doom-and-gloomer, but I just can't imagine Heartbreak Ridge ever becoming a Mecca for tourists."

"The town just doesn't have the right lure yet."

"But even if it did, and the tourists did come, it wouldn't be the same place. Frankly I wouldn't want to live here with a bunch of strangers crawling around. Would you?"

"Luckily *I* won't have to worry about that."

He frowned. "What do you mean?"

She laughed. "You don't think I intend on living in this place for the rest of my life, do you? Good heavens, all I want to do is set up the hotel, see that it's running nicely and hand it over to a manager. Maybe if this is a success, I'll go somewhere else and try there. Somewhere more stylish, though. Maybe Santa Fe, or the south of France."

Cal squinted at her. At first he couldn't tell if she was for real, but apparently, she was. For real. Realistic was something else altogether.

"I could never *live* here," she explained. "Not permanently. There's nothing to do, no people even—"

Oh, Lord. He let out an angry bray. "That would come as a big surprise to about sixty-two people who actually thought they existed in Heartbreak Ridge."

She clucked her tongue. "That's what I mean. Sixty-two! That's hardly anything at all. Of course the absence of people sort of adds to the rustic ambience, and that's all for the good from a business standpoint."

He wondered how Merlie, not to mention all the folks down at the Feed Bag, would take it if they learned that they'd been reduced to atmosphere. "Are you saying that you just look on all the folks here as just sort of props to add rustic local color to your hotel scheme? Sort of like a rural version of people dressed up in mouse suits at Disneyland?"

Natalie thought for a second. "Well, sort of, yes. That's a very good comparison."

It was all he could do not to boot her back down the hill, no matter what kind of psycho vandal was out there stalking her. *Like* Connie? She was a million times worse than Connie! At least his ex-wife had come here with the hope of finding that she liked it and fitted in. She'd failed, naturally, but maybe her intentions were good. The baroness, on the other hand, obviously saw everything around her—probably even him—as just so much scenery that she couldn't wait to get away from it all once her hotel was up and running. He felt nauseated.

She blinked at him. "Is something wrong?"

"Oh, no," he said in a clipped voice. "You've made everything very clear."

She tilted her head. "But are we any closer to explaining why someone would want to do me harm?"

He bit his lip. They weren't, but he, at least, was closer to understanding the initial urge he'd had to wring her neck. To think that he had felt sympathy for her, and was even attracted to her…and all the time she'd probably been picturing him swaggering around her inn as a sort of Wild West exhibit for her snotty friends. Another scatterbrained woman with unrealistic ideas!

Could he pick 'em, or could he pick 'em?

Of course, he hadn't actually *picked* this one. She'd just been inflicted on him.

He pushed away from the table and stood. He needed to get out of here, away from Natalie and her honey-brown eyes and that innocent look that hid the heart of a Leona Helmsley! It still wasn't dark yet; he could probably catch his uncle in town.

"Did I say something wrong?" she asked, looking a little flustered by his abrupt change in mood.

"Oh, no," he said, putting on his jacket and heading for the door.

"Where are you going?"

"To town." At her forlorn look, he gritted his teeth. Damn. How did she manage to tug at his heartstrings even when he knew she was his worst nightmare, a spoiled, wrongheaded city girl, the anti-Cal? "I'll be back before long," he assured her, in a tone that was gentler than he'd intended. "Keep the door locked while I'm gone."

"Cal?" She reached out and touched him, and he stiffened.

"What?" he bit out.

Her lips turned up in a sweet, grateful smile, and

her honey-brown eyes betrayed none of the razor-sharp hardness he knew was lurking in a brain that could think of people as *atmosphere*. "Thank you for all you're doing for me."

Her voice, soft and full of sincere emotion, tugged at him. A lesser man would be taken in by her. A weaker man might even find himself attracted to her. But not him.

Oh, God, please, not him.

Groaning, he spun on his boot heel and fled for town.

5

HE SHOULDN'T BE DOING THIS. Definitely not. Absolutely not. And yet here he was, as helpless as a cow in quicksand when it came to trying to stay out of Natalie Winthrop's problems.

Cal hazarded a glance over at his uncle, who was regarding him with such thinly veiled amusement that Cal wanted to scream. Of course, all during the drive to Heartbreak Ridge he'd been fighting the urge to come here. Natalie Winthrop represented everything he detested—if he had a lick of sense, he'd hotfoot it as far away from her as he could. Maybe join up with Jim Loftus in Honolulu and start the first chapter of *Avoiding Natalie Anonymous.*

Instead he found himself explaining in irritation, "I just can't stand back and watch while she's being victimized, Sam."

Merlie, who was sitting at her desk doing some of that eavesdropping she was famous for, let fly with one of her raucous cackles. "I seem to recall you sayin' something similar when you were hunting down a handyman. That you just couldn't stand back and watch."

"Well what do you expect me to do, sit in my cabin while *The Amityville Horror* is being relived just down the hill?"

Before Cal and Merlie could get into a serious fracas, Sam simmered them both down. "Now don't go popping your corks. Cal's right. This matter needs to be investigated. I'll go out and have a look."

Cal felt somewhat mollified. "I told her it wasn't kids."

"Nah, I can't think of a kid around here that vicious."

"Natalie thinks maybe the people here don't like the idea of her opening a hotel."

"That just goes to show how well she knows us!" Merlie exclaimed. "There hasn't been such entertaining speculation 'round the Feed Bag since the sheriff here decided to hustle himself up a wife on the Internet. Or at least since your brother hooked himself up with the town hell-raiser. For gossip value alone, the innkeeper's been worth her weight in gold."

Cal grinned. "I don't think the idea of being diner amusement would go over so well with her."

"Yeah, she looks like the high-strung type."

Merlie's comments made him chew on the idea of Natalie's attitudes. Maybe the locals hadn't been all that welcoming...which might be either the cause or the result of Natalie seeing them all as props in her life's little drama. Just rustic atmosphere. Who could say?

Or maybe—more likely—he was just making excuses for her.

Sam's lips twisted in thought. "Natalie couldn't think of anyone who might want to do her harm?"

Cal shrugged. "Nope. From what she told me, there are just people who have reason to avoid her like the plague. The man she dumped at the altar, some guy who stole all her money, some detective bilking her for what little she has left...why would these men come after her?''

"It's the dumped groom," Merlie said with certainty.

Cal and Sam turned on her. "What makes you say that?''

"Cause whenever there's a pretty girl involved, it's always the boyfriend."

Sam grinned. "Where did you cook up that theory? *Charlie's Angels* reruns?''

She folded her arms. "You know that old saying, 'the butler did it?' Well it's wrong. It should be 'the boyfriend did it.'''

"In Natalie's case, it would be 'the boyfriend did handsprings,''' Cal retorted. "That man's probably jumping for joy that he wasn't roped into a lifetime commitment as zookeeper."

Sam tapped his fingers against the top of the desk. "I wonder if this episode has anything to do with the raffle."

Cal straightened. "You mean that someone who didn't win the raffle might be trying to scare her away?''

"Exactly."

Damn. Why hadn't *he* thought of that. Except...

Merlie frowned. "I'd think whoever this jealous loser was would start countin' his lucky stars long before he kicked in the door of that rattrap!''

"Besides, there were over five hundred entries to that contest," Cal said. "How could we ever sort through them all? Especially when Jim's hiding out in Honolulu."

Sam shifted. "Well, it's worth a look-see. I'll try to track down old Jim."

"Why don't you tell him the coast is clear?" Merlie laughed. "I'd enjoy it if he came back and got to meet the Winthrop woman face-to-face. In hand-to-hand combat, Cal, who'd you think would have the edge, the swindler or the innkeeper?"

Cal grinned. "She's wilier than she looks."

"Hopefully it won't come to that," Sam said. "But I'll do my best to find out where Jim is tonight."

At the thought of having made more work for his uncle, a protest rose on Cal's lips.

Sam's brows arched. "Unless you want to stick around and do it yourself."

Cal shrugged, trying not to seem overly eager. It wasn't as if he were hankering after his old line of work. Yet it didn't seem right to drop this problem into Sam's lap.

Merlie eyed him knowingly. "You want that I should blow the dust off that desk of yours, Cal? Much as it pains me to say so, it would be a relief to have you squattin' there again."

Cal laughed. "I'm not coming back to work. I just don't want to cause Sam more trouble over that neighbor of mine."

Merlie's lips pursed. "Suit yourself." She pushed her glasses up the bridge of her nose and nodded to the ball of fur sleeping in her desk drawer. "I don't suppose you've changed your mind about adopting Junior, either?"

He grinned. "Nope."

She shot him her best sour look. "Fine. Then you can blow the dust off your own desk, Mr. Not-Ready-To-Come-Back-To-Work-Yet."

"Don't mind if I do."

"*I* wouldn't mind if you lopped that beard off,"

Merlie sassed back. "Has anyone ever mistaken you for a wooly mammoth?"

"They're extinct."

"One look at you and those fossil doctors might think they've got a live specimen on their hands."

Cal shook his head, but found his fingers brushing his beard self-consciously. Maybe he was due for a trim...though he hated for Merlie to think it was at her bidding. And he certainly didn't want anyone to believe a simple haircut had anything to do with Natalie!

When Cal returned to collect Natalie and meet his uncle at her place, Natalie couldn't help being impressed. Sam Weston was as tall and lean and handsome as a black-and-white movie version of a sheriff would have been. Gary Cooper in the flesh. In fact, she would have found herself mightily attracted to the man, if it weren't for Cal standing next to him. Cal, who sometime during the afternoon had treated himself to a haircut and a shave!

She could hardly peel her eyes away from him. She'd thought he was handsome before, albeit in that backwoodsman sort of way, but spiffed up he was a heart-stopper. His hair was still long, but so squeaky clean that her fingertips itched to touch it. And without the scruffy beard she could see now the chiseled outline of his jaw and the sensual curve of his lips. After he'd stepped out of his truck, Cal had shuffled his booted feet self-consciously for a moment while she had gaped at him. She just couldn't help herself, though. In what seemed like the blink of an eye, he'd transformed from Grizzly Adams into Brad Pitt!

Was this for her benefit?

She reprimanded herself for having such a dumb thought. For one thing, since arriving, Cal had studiously avoided meeting her gaze. Something she'd said seemed to have put a distance between them—as if there weren't a yawning gap to bridge already. She thought back over their conversations, and winced when she remembered the idiotic, flippant way she'd talked about the town. Of course she didn't *really* think the people were like men in mice suits at Disneyland. Only she didn't know any of them. To her, the individuals Cal knew so well were just people who had been gawking at her for a week, and whispering about her the moment her back was turned.

And they *did* look rustic…

Still, she was going to have to apologize. Her and her big mouth!

Cal led his uncle through the house, pointing out the damage that had been done by the nighttime marauder. Sam clucked his tongue, spent a long time dusting a few areas for fingerprints, but didn't seem to see anything that would give him a clue as to who might be a suspect. Since this was the first time, outside of a movie theater, she had ever seen policemen actually investigating anything, she'd expected a little more drama.

"So Cal tells me that you've had some financial difficulties."

She shot her neighbor a wry look. "You mean he told you I was robbed?"

Sam cleared his throat. "Well, yes. If you could tell me a little about this accountant of yours…"

Natalie did her best. But what was there really to tell? Malcolm Braswell had disappeared. Her money was gone. Why would the man come kick her door in when he was living high on all her money?

"And what about this detective you hired to find him. What was his name?"

"Lester Bybee."

The look Sam and Cal exchanged told her nothing more than she already knew. She should never have trusted a man named Lester.

"When was the last time you heard from Mr. Bybee?"

"He made his last report to me two months ago, during which he said that he might have a lead on Braswell in the Bahamas."

"Might?" Cal scoffed. "That's pretty vague."

"That's what I said. Then I informed him that I couldn't afford to pay him any more unless he produced something more substantial than mights and maybes. And that was the last I heard from him."

"I've got a friend on the Houston force who might be able to round up some information on Bybee and Braswell for us," Sam said.

"Joe Teller?" Cal remembered a detective who had called them on an auto theft case years ago.

"It's worth a shot. I can call him myself in the morning, if you want," Sam said.

Cal nodded.

When they were finished talking inside, Sam and Cal stood on her warped porch boards and stared out at the dark muddy driveway. "I saw those tire tracks earlier," Cal told his uncle.

He had? Natalie peered at the indentations in the mud in wonder. She hadn't noticed them, and he hadn't mentioned them to her.

"I assume they were made by a car. Not wide enough for a truck."

Sam pushed back his hat, looking pensively at the driveway. "Hard to say. Could be a small truck. Depends on how hard it was raining, too. We can't be certain even when the break-in took place."

"Night," Cal said. "We would have heard a vehicle during the morning, in spite of the rain."

Recalling something, Natalie couldn't help but pipe up. "Except remember, Cal? You were giving Armand singing lessons. Maybe that's why we didn't hear the intruder."

The sheriff's dark eyebrows shot up questioningly at his nephew. "Singing lessons?"

Cal ducked his head.

"Who's Armand?" Sam asked, looking around at Natalie.

"My cockatoo."

"I told you I took Natalie and her pets over to my house for the night," Cal reminded his uncle. He looked as though he'd rather drop the whole subject.

"Cal was trying to teach Armand some Hank Williams," Natalie explained to Sam.

Sam smirked. "That sounds like a worthy endeavor."

"It is, especially because Cal can't stand being awakened by opera. You should have seen his face last night when Armand started in on *Rigoletto*. He practically exploded off the bed."

Sam's face screwed up in confusion. "The cockatoo?"

"No, Cal."

The sheriff squinted at his nephew. "You were sleeping with the bird?"

Natalie shook her head. "No, Armand was in the living room. He can't sleep a wink outside his cage. Only Mopsy and Fritz and I were in bed with Cal at the time."

Cal cleared his throat. "Hadn't you better get home, Sam?" He tugged his gleeful, grinning uncle off the porch. "I'm sure Shelby's wondering what happened to you."

As he yanked his uncle down the stairs, he spared only a backward glare for Natalie.

Why was he so embarrassed? Surely his uncle knew that Cal's heart was impervious to a woman. Especially, as Cal put it, *her kind,* whatever that meant. She imagined him going into town and venting his rage about her to anyone who would listen in that café she'd seen in town, the Feed Bag. The place looked like one of those old-time diners that served everything swimming in grease.

Which, come to think of it, sounded pretty good to her right now. Her stomach growled, and she realized she hadn't eaten much since breakfast.

"You didn't happen to go into the store when you were in town, did you?" she asked Cal hopefully, once his uncle had said goodbye and was driving away.

His lips thinned as he looked down at her. Lord, he was handsome—even when he was annoyed with her. "Hungry?"

She nodded. *Hungry for him,* she could have added.

He sighed, shuffled his booted feet on her porch and stared longingly at his house. "I guess we could go out."

She practically leaped with joy. Out to eat! That almost sounded like what people did in civilization.

It seemed years, instead of mere days, since she'd stepped foot in a restaurant. "To the Feed Bag?"

From the look on his face, she might have suggested dinner at a rendering plant. "Good God, no!"

She frowned. She would have thought he'd be pleased that she wanted to patronize the local eatery; maybe the food there was even worse than she'd imagined.

"Where else could we go?" She hadn't seen another restaurant nearby. "I need to decide what to wear."

He looked at her clothing with distaste. A spiffy Norma Komali outfit was now just a mess. She had been working in it yesterday, and hadn't really worried about what she was wearing today. When Cal had come by last night, she'd just snatched up whatever was handy.

Even being ogled by his narrowed, disapproving gaze made her quiver a little inside. "Don't you have jeans?"

"I did—a very nice pair, too. Donna Karan."

The name didn't even seem to register on his face. "What happened to them?"

Heat crept into her cheeks. "I used them to plug a hole in the plaster."

Cal sighed. "Tell you what. Maybe we should do some shopping, starting with some stuff we need for your house. Lightbulbs, maybe a lamp or two, a heater…"

She shook her head. "What's the point, if the electricity doesn't work?"

"Then we need to get the electricity fixed."

"I didn't see the point of doing that before the roof was fixed."

Frowning, he looked up at her hole-ridden roof. "Maybe Howard can start on that tomorrow."

She looked aghast. "I can't put Howard on that roof—I'd sooner put him on a tightrope!"

He sighed. "Okay, *I'll* do it."

She looked at him in awe. "You? Do you know how?"

"I roofed my cabin."

She stared up at the cabin in amazement. A lawman *and* a roofer. This man never stopped pulling rabbits out of hats, it seemed. And how did people pick up so many practical skills? She couldn't even hammer a nail straight! "I couldn't pay you very much."

"Look, let's not worry about that now."

"But I have to." She tilted her head. "Unless you're so eager to get rid of me that you want to do it for free."

"It's not that—"

His words cut off abruptly, leading her to suspect that it *was* that.

She folded her arms. "Okay, I appreciate your offer."

"Good. Let's get a move on." He looked her outfit over again, and said, deadpan, "And don't worry about dressing for dinner. I promise not to spring any five-star restaurants on you."

"Wisenheimer." He was insufferable.

Unfortunately he also possessed a smile that could turn her heart into a brass band on the Fourth of July.

THE TROUBLE WITH WOMEN—*one* of the many troubles, Cal corrected himself—was that they were always so scatterbrained. Here he was trying to conduct important business at Heartbreak Ridge's hardware store, ordering materials for *her* roof, and Natalie was all over the place. Looking at fancy electric drills for Howard. Toys for the dogs. Toys for *him,* for heaven's sake.

Right now she was gazing at a dust-covered, cactus-shaped votive candleholder as if it were a jewel-encrusted wonder. "Isn't this neat?" she said excitedly. "They've got *everything* here."

He grabbed her arm. "I thought you were hungry," he growled at her. Not to mention, Lon Wallis, owner of this establishment, was eyeing them mighty peculiarly. He should have warned Natalie that their every move was being recorded for the town's very active gossip mill.

"I'm starving," she agreed.

"Well the sooner we finish our business here the sooner we can eat."

She reluctantly put back the candleholder. "Okay, but if you don't mind my saying so you could use some more decorative touches around that place of yours."

"And you could use a roof over your head, so let's go."

He tugged her along, but he supposed it was just too much to hope that they could make it to the front counter without stopping again. Lord, the way the woman was digging in her heels every five seconds you'd think they were in Bloomingdale's. "Oh, look!"

When Cal finally stopped halfway down the aisle from her, she was holding a basketball. He rolled his eyes. "Don't tell me you think I could use a basketball hoop, too."

"Why not?" She grinned and twirled the basketball on her finger almost expertly. "It'd give you something to do besides spy on your neighbor."

In truth, he was rather shocked by how much the idea appealed to him, though he'd rather die than show it. Mostly he just wanted to get her out of there before she broke something. "Basketball's not exactly a fun solo occupation."

"That's okay—I'd come play one-on-one with you."

"Yeah, right." He let out a sputtering laugh.

Her grin faded. *"Think fast!"*

Before Cal knew what was happening, the basketball was coming at him with cannonball speed. He reacted sluggishly, fumbling at the ball as it bombarded him in his chest. He let out a *ooph!* of surprise.

She laughed delightedly that her hidden talent could knock the wind out of him. "I was varsity all four years of prep school."

With the stinging brand the ball had left against his sternum, he didn't doubt it. He was annoyed, and he had to admit, a little bit impressed. "No kidding."

"I also excelled at field hockey," she said immodestly.

He put the ball back on the shelf carefully, as though it were a lethal weapon. "Let's see if you can excel at calculating roof area."

She let out a disappointed breath. "Spoilsport."

This time, he held onto her arm as he pulled her toward the counter where Lon was waiting, a chuckle on his lips. No doubt the basketball episode would be all over town before morning.

"Cal." Lon nodded. "What can I do you for?"

For the next half hour, Natalie obediently stood by Cal's side while he ordered roofing materials, growing paler as the purchases added up to thousands of dollars. "And this is just for the roof," he informed her as she meekly wrote out a whopper check.

"Now I know what you're doing." She eyed Cal suspiciously. "You're trying to win your six-week bet by making me a pauper."

He laughed. In all honesty, he hadn't thought about their bet much. "Just taking care of business."

She grumbled. "The business of getting rid of me."

The terrible thing was, staring at her now as she leaned against Lon's counter with that adorable pout on her face, he'd never felt *less* like getting rid of her. Even after this long day. Even after he'd decided that she was the most exasperating woman he'd ever run into. She worried her lower lip and his own lips itched to bend down and kiss her. In fact, he could almost feel his body swaying toward hers.

"Cal?" The lips he was staring at spoke his name, then said, more alarmed, *"Cal!"* He popped to, shocked at the direction his thoughts had swung. Oh, great. He was really cracking up now. He wiped a bead of sweat from his brow, trying to ignore the worried looks coming from both Natalie and Lon.

"Are you feeling okay?" Natalie asked him.

"Just hungry. Let's go."

He tugged her out of the hardware store and looked across the dimly lit street to the Feed Bag, whose lights were just winking off. He suddenly felt self-conscious about being a citizen of a town that closed down at eight.

Natalie let out a disappointed sigh. "Well, that's okay. I can't afford to eat now anyway."

He laughed. "I didn't really intend on taking you there."

"Then where?"

The nearest restaurant was a hike, but he'd promised Natalie. They drove out to the Tavern, where Cal hoped they could dine in relative privacy. No such luck, of course. It seemed he tipped his hat to someone at every table they passed on their way to a booth in the back.

Natalie was amazed. "You know everyone in the world out here, don't you?"

He shrugged. "After you've spent years handing out speeding tickets, there aren't too many people left to meet."

She laughed and set down to the business of ordering half the menu. Steak, potatoes, salad, two sides and two desserts. The woman could pack it away. Over the next hour he watched in amazement as she scarfed it all down, too. As she was finishing her second slice of carrot cake, he must have been staring, because she stopped self-consciously in midbite.

"What?" she asked, her cheeks bulging like a nut-laden squirrel's.

"I thought that basketball business was a joke," he said, "but you're still eating like you were on the varsity squad."

She swallowed with effort before breaking into chuckles. "I'm not usually this bad. Back when I had Gary looking after me—"

"Gary?" Cal was immediately suspicious. And, he hated to admit, jealous. "Who's he?"

She blinked. "My personal trainer."

He let out a breath of relief. For a moment he'd

thought they'd hit upon a new suspect to check into. "You two play hoops together?"

She shook her head. "Free weights. When it comes to basketball, I'm just a spectator now. And mostly I just enjoy the college stuff. In fact, during the March play-offs it's hard to get me away from the television."

He leaned back against his booth and felt almost loopy for a moment, remembering that time—before Connie, before this last horrible year and a half—when he'd spent the month of March staring at the small screen. He'd been alone then, or occasionally with Cody. And even though it was absurd, almost unmanly, sometimes he couldn't help thinking that it would be nicer to have female company, someone to cuddle with on the couch and join him in tossing popcorn at the screen when refs made bad foul calls.

A woman who enjoyed basketball play-offs.

He realized suddenly that he was looking into Natalie's beautiful face with something like yearning in his heart. For the second time tonight. *Oh, no,* he moaned silently in dread, *not again.* How could his feelings have turned from dislike into desire so quickly, so ill-advisedly? He hadn't kissed a woman, even wanted a woman, in a year, and that woman had been his wife.

Great. Traumatized by Connie, he'd waited an entire year since their breakup to think about kissing any woman, and then the only woman he'd found to want to kiss reminded him of…Connie.

Only she wasn't like Connie. Was she?

Her smile disappeared. "Cal, for heaven's sake, what is it? Are you sick?"

"No," he bit out. "Finish your coffee."

She stared at him anxiously. "Is it something I said about…basketball?"

"No."

"Maybe something I said earlier," she guessed erroneously. "I know! This afternoon. You were thinking about what I was saying about the town, weren't you?"

He couldn't even remember the conversation she was talking about for a moment, but she took his silence for an assent and slapped her hand against her forehead. "*Why* do I say such noodle-brained things? I just can't apologize enough, Cal. Talking about Heartbreak Ridge as if it were a movie set or something. *Rustic people.* I just don't know why these things come out of my mouth…maybe I'm a little jealous of the people around here."

That was weird. "Why?"

"Because it seems like such a close-knit community, and I've never had that. Oh, I guess my college sorority was tight-knit, but that was different. That was about money and being selective…this is about roots. I have the feeling that I would never belong here, that I would never fit in."

He wished that she hadn't apologized. He wanted to tell her it was true, that she would never fit in, that she should just go back to her selective little world and leave him to his rustic people. Instead he gritted his teeth and explained, "The natives are friendlier than you think, if you make half an effort."

Though could Natalie really fit in with the smart set at Althea's Nail Boutique? He couldn't exactly visualize her taking a seat at the Feed Bag's counter, either, or shooting the breeze with Jerry and his gang there.

"I'm not a snob, Cal."

He laughed skeptically, and her face reddened.

"You're always trying to peg me as some type, and don't think I haven't figured out why."

"Why?"

"Because if you reduce me to a kind or a type, you can explain to yourself that this is why you're attracted to me, and not because you actually might just plain like me." She crossed her arms and looked at him with smug assurance.

Now it was his turn to go red in the face. "That's pop psychology nonsense."

"You've never thought of kissing me?" she shot back.

"No!" Dustin Hoffman could have won another Academy Award for acting so brilliantly, yet she still levelled a disbelieving stare on him. He couldn't help asking, "Have *you*?"

"Sure. This morning when you woke me up, in fact. I thought you looked cute in your boxers."

Cute?

The tensed muscles in his body went slack.

"We'd better go," he said quickly. Suddenly the urge to get out of that restaurant was uncontrollable.

The whole drive home, he found himself mulling over that word. *Cute.* At first he didn't know why he was so bothered by it. Then, after about twenty miles, he figured it out. *Cute* was what women called babies. Puppy dog ears. Rooms decorated with chintz and ducks wearing bonnets. Cute didn't denote desire so much as the maidenly urge to pinch someone's chubby cheeks. Natalie had said she'd thought about kissing him. Maybe her idea of kissing and his idea of kissing weren't exactly meeting up at the same place.

When he had thought about kissing, there was nothing innocent about it. And as they sped over the winding roads in the darkness, he was hard-pressed to hold those thoughts at bay. The longer he drove, the closer he came to his house, the more hot and bothered he became, so that by the time he stopped in his yard, he was in a regular lather.

But still in control.

He took a breath and leaned over, intending on opening her door for her.

But something about reaching in front of her, being within touching distance of all that warmth, sent him haywire. Or maybe it was that Chanel perfume. He couldn't be sure. All he knew was that they hadn't said a word the whole way home, and they didn't now, either. He just heard a little gasp of surprise moments before his lips touched hers.

A split second later, she was in his arms. God, it felt good. *She* felt good. Natalie's lips were warm and inviting, pliant beneath his, and she wasn't the least bit maidenly. In fact, she sidled right into his embrace as if she'd been wanting this as much as he had. Her arms snaked up around his shoulders and she let out a satisfied moan as her lips parted for him and he deepened the kiss.

As he plundered her mouth, he found himself slipping, losing himself in the scent of her, the softness of her hair at his fingertips, the subtle shift of her body against his. The sensations roiling inside him were a relief after having his attraction for her pent up inside him.

Yet there was danger in her delicious response, too.

Because even though they were maneuvering in the cramped front seat, their bodies seemed to fit together perfectly. He pulled her closer, unable to help his hands from skimming her shoulders and her thin arms, which on closer investigation had hardy little muscles underneath that beautifully tanned skin. He couldn't help himself from pulling her round womanly hips closer to the fiery ache building inside him.

She moaned again, showing no sign of resistance to following where this was leading them. In fact, one of her hands reached down and touched his thigh, setting off a four-alarm siren inside his head.

He pulled away from her, practically panting with the effort it took him not to make love to her right there on the bench seat. It wasn't any easier when he looked at her honey-brown eyes darkened with desire blinking up at him in delight.

"Oh, Cal," she said quickly, "that was—"

"A mistake!" He rushed out the words.

She stiffened in his arms.

He could have spat out any number of other responses. *Incredible. Fantastic. Unbelievable. Earth-shattering.* But if he had voiced one of those words, he might have pulled her back into his arms and done something he'd later regret like crazy. Like make love to Natalie until dawn. Like get himself intractably involved with the last woman in the world he should be mixed up with.

Her lips parted. "What?"

"It was a mistake, Natalie. A slip."

Her gaze hardened. "Oh, I see."

"See what?" he asked.

"You were just testing the waters. Apparently they were a little too deep for you."

He rolled his eyes. "Why is it women always try to spin every moment with a man into an afternoon talk show thesis? We just shouldn't have done that."

She folded her arms and sank back as far into the seat as she could. "Fine. Enough said."

He sighed. "Look, I'm sorry. It's just that given who we are, and the fact that we seem to have very different ideas about things, it would be better if we hadn't done that."

She nodded. "In spite of the fact that you really have the hots for me."

"Right," he agreed quickly. She broke into a triumphant grin, and he felt his own face go red with embarrassment. "I mean no!"

"*This* should make the situation interesting," she said.

His brows lifted. "What situation?"

Her lips twisted into a wry grin. "Sleeping ten feet apart with only a flimsy door between us."

6

THAT DOOR, HOWEVER, remained firmly closed.

Which wasn't to say that the kiss was forgotten. Especially not by Natalie. Mistake, was it? A slip?

Natalie couldn't think of anything as wonderful as the kiss they'd shared in those negative terms. If anyone had slipped, it was Cal, allowing her to see a side of himself that he worked so hard to keep under wraps. His heart. She suspected that glimpse of him was what worried him more than anything else.

His thinking their kiss was a mistake, however, did not stop him from fixing her roof. He, Howard and Natalie worked nonstop every day for a week, and in the evenings Cal went down to Heartbreak Ridge to visit his uncle at the sheriff's office and sift through the essays of the other entrants of Jim Loftus's contest.

And all during this time, despite the fact that he thought kissing her was a mistake and swore that his earlier assessment that she was a pain-in-the-neck city woman hadn't changed, he allowed her to stay on as his houseguest. He even insisted that she sleep in the bedroom and he take the couch, since she could fit all the animals on the bed, and he could get some solitary peace in the living room. Despite his grumbling, she saw gallantry in his sacrifice.

In fact, there was something gallant in Cal, period.

He would have rather died than admit it, but lying just beneath all those Ralph Kramden ravings of his lurked the heart of a true Galahad. She carried that knowledge through the next week like the private thrill of a kid with a secret decoder ring.

Yet what really thrilled Natalie was that under the tutelage of Cal and Howard, she was in less and less need of rescuing. True, her Lexus money was dwindling rapidly and her house still lacked a few necessities like indoor plumbing, but she was beginning to figure out how to do things on her own. She was actually learning to patch Sheetrock and cut door molding. She helped them with the roof, and after a few mishaps like almost slipping off an eave and nearly hammering a shingle nail through her hand, she was on her way to becoming an able workman. Who'd have guessed? Not that she was about to put any of the local carpenters out of a job, but...

But there was something wonderful, almost exhilarating, in this new feeling she had. Why, it was almost as if, for the first time in her life, she was...*useful!*

The very notion still caused a ripple of astonishment to go through her. She'd never imagined herself, a Winthrop, ever being useful. Winthrops didn't *do,* they simply *were.* But here she was, half managing, half taking orders. And getting things done! It amazed her. She, who hadn't changed lightbulbs if a servant was handy to handle the task for her, was now able to scramble across a rooftop and nail a shingle in place. It was fantastic! She wished she had some pictures to show her friends back in Houston when this was all over.

If it ever was all over. Her notion of opening the

inn and then being able to escape was beginning to seem a little unfeasible to her now. For one thing, there was so much yet to do, she couldn't imagine the work ever being done. And then there was the matter of managing the place. How could she turn her hotel over to someone else to run? She couldn't imagine doing that any more than she could imagine handing a baby to a nanny to raise.

And then there was Cal. Strange as it seemed to her, she couldn't imagine going back to Houston and not seeing him anymore, either. Yet there was no question of her taking him with her, as if he'd even want to go. He would be a fish out of water amid her old stomping ground. Just to imagine him in a house in River Oaks or a rented villa on the Riviera or the Pierre in New York City brought a smile to her lips. Cal, trade in his faded jeans for Armani? His sweaty Stetson for a sporty beret? He was as much a part of Heartbreak Ridge as the Feed Bag or any other part of the town.

Of course, if she didn't make a success of her hotel, *she* might be a permanent part of Heartbreak Ridge herself. Not that the notion frightened her anymore. She was beginning to like it here. But the thought of never having money again still scared her. Her dwindling bank account held her in thrall every night. With an ever-quickening pulse she saw the balance on her checkbook sink like a bottomless elevator.

The question that had been plaguing her for a year now rang in her ears as strong as ever. But now on top of financial worries she had her Cal woes to add to the mix.

What was she going to do?

"I'M THINKING THAT WE might be barking up the wrong tree." Sam sipped his coffee and eyed Cal worriedly. "I can't help but think that the accountant is at the bottom of all this."

Cal was busy looking over papers Sam had just given him—the essays he and Sam had found after tracking down Jim Loftus and getting permission to get into his house and find the old raffle files. They might not hold clues to the identity of Natalie's mysterious intruder, but the essays were still giving him valuable information. In retrospect, Natalie's resort hotel idea didn't seem so odd when compared to people who'd wanted to turn Jim's house into a home for displaced ferrets or a mango plantation or headquarters for a group that called itself the Founders of the Kingdom of Texas.

Believe it or not, he might have ended up with worse nuts than Natalie living next door.

"Any news from our man in Houston?"

Sam shook his head. "No, Joe hasn't gotten back to me yet, although he did say they already had a complaint file on Malcolm Braswell—from other clients he ripped off when he left town. Apparently he isn't the most sterling character."

"Why does that not surprise me?"

He found himself hating Malcolm Braswell mightily, as well as any man who had ever cheated Natalie, including Jim Loftus. In fact, he'd felt very protective of Natalie this past week, though their kiss hadn't been repeated. His heart had been in his throat once when she'd nearly fallen off the roof. Every time she bumped her head or pounded a hammer on her hand, something in his chest caught. Which was strange. Because there wasn't anything the least bit lovey-dovey going on between them. In fact, though Natalie had paid close attention to him whenever he was instructing her how to perform some task or another, she'd otherwise kept very aloof from him. Distanced.

A little too distanced, to his way of thinking. He found he missed having her smile beamed his way. And the idle chatter she used to keep up when they were alone, telling him about parties she'd attended, silly things she'd done. He'd missed the camaraderie, even though they'd spent the lion's share of each day together.

Now how could anyone explain that?

The bell above the door clanged noisily, but not as noisily as Merlie's subsequent greeting as she approached his and Sam's booth. "Well if it ain't *Starsky and Hutch!*" she exclaimed before scooting in across from Cal.

Jerry Lufkin, the owner of the Feed Bag, was standing behind the counter manning the grill. "Don't razzle 'em, Merlie," he joked, "they looked like they were *talkin'* about work."

Amos Trilby, the pharmacist, who was sitting at the counter, grunted. "Or maybe Cal was tellin' Sam about the innkeeper lady he's keepin' company with."

"I'm not keeping company with her," Cal brayed back.

Ernest Stubbs, two booths back, sent him a big-toothed grin. "That's not what we've been hearin', Cal. Lon said you two was awful tight when you dropped by the hardware store one night."

"Said you all were frolickin' in the aisles," someone else put in.

Cal rolled his eyes then glared at Merlie for the rife

speculation she'd brought in with her. "We weren't frolicking. Natalie threw a basketball at me."

Jerry let out a gale of gleeful laughter. "Oh, so it's *Natalie* now, is it?"

"Of course it's Natalie," he retorted, "I can't very well call her innkeeper to her face."

Earnest grinned. "Especially not if ya'll are, you know, shacked up together."

At the expression "shacked up," Cal drew back in surprise. "We aren't shacked up."

"'Course not." Jerry winked at him. "Ya'll are just livin' in the same house."

Cal shot an accusing look Sam's way. Who else could have been telling them this stuff?

Sam shrugged innocently. "Howard had dinner here the other night. Said he was concerned about you soiling Natalie's virtue."

The other diners in the Feed Bag broke into delighted chortles.

"Oh, for heaven's sake!" Cal felt his face turning beet-red, which only agitated him more. "She's just stayin' with me 'cause that place Jim sold her is unlivable. It's just for convenience."

Jerry grinned. "Oh, it sounds convenient, all right. Not to mention cozy."

Cal glowered at them all. "Don't you folks have anything better to do than sit around all day talkin' about Natalie Winthrop? Jerry, you oughta rename this place the Chatter Box."

Jerry shrugged. "Okay, Cal. We won't mention her anymore."

Someone at the counter grumbled. "Then what the heck are we supposed to talk about?"

Merlie laughed and turned to Cal. "Okay, Romeo.

How about me askin' whether you changed your mind about adopting my little feline friend.''

Cal let out a groan. ''Don't tell me you're still trying to foist that little furball off on people.''

''Not people, knucklehead, just *you*. You're the only person I know without any pets.''

It certainly didn't feel that way. ''Besides having the innkeeper's menagerie on my hands, I own a horse.''

''A horse is different.'' She shrugged. ''Besides, if somebody doesn't take Junior soon, I'm gonna have to haul him down to the animal shelter.''

Cal's face fell. From his years as a deputy, during which he'd referred stray animal complaints to the county animal shelter, he knew that the facility was already full to bursting with unwanted pets. Several had to be put down each day, just because there weren't enough people willing to adopt. To think of that little kitty, that cute little hunk of fur sleeping in Merlie's drawer, being put to sleep just because he was too selfish...

He let out a sigh of resignation. ''Oh, hell.''

He should have let them all keep gossiping about Natalie.

NATALIE WAS GOING OVER her bank balance for the umpteenth time that night as she heard Cal's truck drive up from his nightly trip into town. Moments later he burst through the door, beaming at her.

At the sight of his smile, her worries momentarily slipped away and she jumped up from the table. It seemed ages since he'd sent her such an enthusiastic, unguarded grin. ''What is it? Did you find out who the intruder was?''

His smile disappeared for a moment. "No, in fact I need to talk to you about that later. But right now, I want to show you a surprise."

She nearly clapped her hands together like a kid on Christmas morning. "What is it?"

He made her turn around and close her eyes, which she did. Then, a few moments later, he tapped her on the shoulder. "Okay, you can open 'em now."

She followed his instructions, and when she opened her eyes, she nearly fell over laughing. In his out-stretched palms was the fattest kitten she'd ever seen in her life. Cradled in Cal's hands, the little orange tabby resembled a feline Buddha.

"Where did you get him?" she marveled.

"Oh, Merlie nagged at me and nagged at me till she finally wore me down." He added in a confusing rush, "It's a stray someone dumped on her because it looked like her cat. His name is Junior. Do you mind?"

Mind? She and the little tiger kitty took to each other like old friends, though Winston was a little jealous. What surprised her, though, was Cal's bring-ing home another animal when he'd done nothing but complain about his house turning into the National Zoo for almost two weeks now. Did this indicate a change in his attitude toward her? Maybe he was be-ginning to like the feeling of living in a menag-erie…maybe he'd just wanted to do something nice for Merlie.

Or for her.

She didn't dare pin her hopes too much on that last idea. She couldn't read too much into things—or, as Cal had expressed it so scathingly, make a talk-show thesis out of their every encounter.

After she and Junior were done with their initial bonding, Cal cleared his throat and reminded her, "I did want to talk to you about that other thing."

The break-in. Even though almost two weeks had passed with no further incidents, the memory of what had happened still had the ability to make her jump in her skin. She frowned. "Do you have any leads?"

He shook his head. "None to speak of. But Sam wanted me to bring a list of these people to you, to see if any of them might ring a bell. After all, your name was announced as the winner. Maybe one of the other entrants actually knew who you were..."

She pursed her lips doubtfully, but went along as he read off a series of names that meant zip to her. He might have been reading at random from the Albuquerque phone book. "None of these people is someone I know," she said, looking over the list herself. "What do we do now?"

He shrugged. "We're still trying to hunt down Braswell and the detective, Lester Bybee. No luck with either."

She harrumphed. "That doesn't surprise me. It wouldn't even surprise me if they're working together."

Cal shook his head and sighed. "You seem awfully complacent about this."

She shrugged. "This isn't new to me, Cal. I've spent a year with this problem, and anguished over it more hours than I care to admit. There comes a time when you have to let the strongest anger go."

He frowned, but said nothing.

She tried to jolly up the atmosphere a little. Of course, it was hard for her to be too gloomy when a kitten was playing with her shoelaces. "Let's have dinner. I thawed out some chicken."

They spent the next hour preparing and then devouring their meal. All her worries about money and break-ins fell away from her when she was with Cal. Maybe it was the fact that he was so strong, so competent—it didn't seem anything bad to her could happen when she was with him. Living with him was like having her own personal security device. Or perhaps the fact that he was so handsome merely distracted her from her problems. She spent far more time dwelling on how devastatingly sensual those lips had felt against her own than about a break-in at her house. She was ashamed of how much she wanted him, of the way her tummy did little somersaults every time she so much as thought of him. Why, it was almost as if she were falling in love!

Which of course was simply not in the realm of possibility. She'd never been in love, really, truly in love, in her entire life. That's why she'd fled her marriage—because she didn't think she was in love with Jared. But she'd just assumed when the moment did come when she realized she was madly, passionately in love with someone, she would be in somewhat more appropriate surroundings. Over a candlelight table in a five-star restaurant, perhaps, sipping wine and holding hands. Not in a two-room cabin with the remains of a meal consisting of chicken cooked in Campbell's Soup.

Was she in love? Could the impossible really have happened?

"Something wrong?" Cal squinted at her.

She blinked in astonishment. "No, not exactly."

"Well then what's the matter with you? You're all red-cheeked and glassy-eyed. Are you sick?"

She shook her head. "Oh, no! In fact..." If her cheeks were red before, they were probably scarlet now as she grappled with the problem of whether she should inform him of her discovery or not. What should she do? If he thought just kissing her was a mistake, the idea of falling in love with her was probably not high on his list of things to do before he died.

"It's just...I had a thought, Cal."

"About what?"

"About you and me, actually."

He shifted uncomfortably. Or maybe that was just her imagination.

Still, the wisest course might be to ease him into this by degrees. "Are you going to like having me for a neighbor?"

He grunted. "It's not you I'm worried about. It's that houseful of rich guests you swear you're going to have."

"That I will have," she corrected.

"Right. I'm not used to thinking of Heartbreak Ridge as a place where the elite meet."

"So if it was just me you had to deal with, that wouldn't be so bad?"

He looked at her as if she were crazy. "I guess not."

Her heart did a conservative but definite leap. It might not be love, but being able to stand her was a definite step in the right direction!

And maybe if he knew the changes she was going through, he would see that something developing between the two of them wasn't so unlikely as it had seemed to her, too, at first.

"That's good," she informed him, "because I can see myself becoming a permanent fixture here."

He frowned. "I thought you couldn't wait to leave."

"That was how I felt a long time ago."

He laughed. "That was how you felt last week!"

But so much had happened since then. *He* had happened since then. "Things are different now, Cal. You have to know that."

"Why? Because you have a roof now?"

"No, because I feel different. You saw me," she explained. "I worked like a dog this week. Wasn't I helpful?"

"Well, yes. After you stopped being a pain in the rear, you were almost useful."

She laughed happily. "You see! This is all new to me. Why, I don't think work is really as bad as I always feared it would be. There's something really satisfying about labor, isn't there?"

He looked at her as if she were speaking Chinese.

"Naturally you wouldn't understand how I feel because you've probably always been a handy person, but this is a whole new world to me. I think I could really make a go of it out here, especially if I had companionship."

He drew back, a distinctly unpleasant expression on his face. "You mean...?"

She leaned forward, hoping she could convey in simple language how important he was to her. "I mean you, Cal. I never in a million years expected to feel anything like this for you, but I do. I think we'd be good together."

She was impatient for him to kiss her again. For days, it was all she could think about. His firm, warm lips, those arms that rippled with muscles. She'd suspected it was just a matter of time before they couldn't help themselves and they were drawn irresistibly to explore each other again. She hadn't reckoned on it happening this soon, of course, but she hadn't expected her own feelings to blossom so quickly. Getting emotions involved in physical lust changed everything.

It made it all the sweeter.

Or, in this case, all the more confusing.

Because after her pronouncement, Cal wasn't exactly sweeping her into his arms and carrying her off to his bedroom to make wild passionate love. He wasn't even tugging her into his arms for a kiss. If anything, he leaned a little farther back in his chair, his expression frozen somewhere between disbelief and horror.

After a moment of him staring at her in this way, she shifted uncomfortably in her chair. "Did I say something wrong?"

He didn't move.

"Cal?"

Suddenly he shot out of his chair as though jet propelled. "Well, I'm bushed! Mind if we leave the dishes till morning?"

She blinked in astonishment.

Dishes? She looked around them, barely taking in the question. What about her confession...what about unbridled passion?

This was an area, it seemed, he didn't care to explore. She shrank in her chair and nodded numbly as he dashed away as quickly as he could make his escape into his bedroom. Apparently his days of gallantry were over, because he simply dropped some sheets and blankets on the couch for her before disappearing completely.

She drew up in shock. Here was yet another new experience for her. A rebuff!

NATALIE PEERED CAUTIOUSLY into Althea's Nail Boutique and Hair Salon. It was time, she'd decided, to do some investigating of her own. But not into her intruder, or Malcolm Braswell's disappearance. The object of her snooping was Cal.

She pushed through the door and found herself standing in a hair salon that looked like a movie set from the 1970s. The posters of pouting models on the walls were impossibly outdated; she could swear that one of them was sporting a Dorothy Hamill haircut. Olivia Newton John was blaring out from a boom box, and the pink vinyl booth where she was instructed to take a seat was certainly not of the twenty-first century. The most modern thing going in the place was the late-model Mr. Coffee emitting the aroma of freshly brewed Viennese cinnamon.

Flavored coffee...now even something that simple seemed an incredible luxury.

"I'll be with you in just a sec," a woman in a turquoise smock who could only have been Althea informed her. "Just let me stick Shelby over here to soak in her conditioner. You weren't lookin' to get a perm, were you?"

"Just a trim," Natalie said, following the proprietress's instructions to help herself to a cup of joe.

Heaven knows she needed a haircut. She would have suspected her appearance had something to do with Cal's rebuff the night before; only Cal didn't really strike her as the type of man who would be turned off by a few split ends. No, there was something else at work here. Some wall they kept bumping up against every time she thought they were actually making progress.

After a few moments, Althea motioned her over to take the place the woman named Shelby had vacated, although Shelby didn't stay put for long. As soon as Althea had reclined Natalie into that horrible neck contraption at the sink, the other woman's beautiful green eyes suddenly peered down at her, too.

"You're Natalie Winthrop, aren't you?"

Althea shot Shelby a look and whispered scoldingly, "'Course she is!" She turned on the water and began shampooing Natalie's head.

Natalie blinked in surprise. She hadn't introduced herself to Althea, or anyone else in town. But then, she supposed there weren't many newcomers in this place.

"I'm so glad to meet you!" Shelby said, and the welcoming grin on her face made Natalie believe her words. "Finally someone in town greener than I am!"

"Shelby here's the sheriff's wife," Althea explained. "They just married a little while ago."

"It's been over five months!" Shelby corrected.

Natalie smiled. "I've met your husband."

"Yes, he told me about you." Shelby crossed her arms and grinned. "And I must say, the way he described you made me mighty jealous! But now I can see he was only reporting the facts."

Natalie felt herself blush. A shame Cal couldn't find her at least as attractive as this stranger in the beauty parlor did! "I'm sure you have no worries as far as your husband's concerned. He was full of talk about you and your baby."

"Sam dotes on that little girl!" Althea said, scrubbing Natalie's scalp within an inch of its life.

Shelby continued to study her during her condition and rinse. When Althea pulled Natalie upright again, Natalie caught the two women exchanging glances that made her very nervous as she was hustled back over to the cutting chair.

"She looks like Connie, doesn't she?" Shelby whispered to Althea.

Althea nodded. "Pretty close." She ran a comb through Natalie's hair and made a professional pronouncement into the mirror. "Thicker hair, though."

"I saw the wedding pictures," Shelby said, then caught Natalie's eye in the mirror. "When I first saw you walk in, I was confused. I thought for a moment that you were her."

"Who?" Natalie asked, about to bust with curiosity.

"Connie."

"Cal's ex-wife," Althea explained.

Natalie drew back in surprise. No wonder she sometimes caught him looking at her funny! But on another level, she was shocked. All these weeks, she'd thought his comparisons of her to his ex-wife were just because their backgrounds happened to be similar. To think that they actually looked alike gave her a funny feeling. As if she'd stepped into a Hitchcock movie.

"You mean you've been living up on that mountain with Cal all this time and he hasn't told you about her?" Althea asked.

"Well, no…not in any detail. He seems to want to avoid talking about anything to do with his divorce."

"Naturally!" Shelby said. "Sam says ever since Connie left town, Cal's been just like a turtle with his head stuck in, emotions-wise. But I just assumed that you and Cal…"

"That we what?"

Althea laughed. "Well, you know how gossip is. Two young attractive people, away up there on that mountain…"

She shook her head adamantly. "Oh, no. We're not intimate, if that's what you think."

Althea and Shelby exchanged not-so-subtle glances in the mirror.

Natalie knew she should cool it and let the subject drop, but she couldn't help asking, "Aside from looks, what was Connie like?"

"A piece of work!" Althea gesticulated with her scissors. "The most spoiled woman you could imagine. Rich and pampered. Didn't do housework—she'd always had a maid. Somebody at the Feed Bag reported that she couldn't even locate the on-off switch on a vacuum cleaner."

"So she *was* rich."

"Oh, my, yes. I thought women that pampered only lived in harems, or royal palaces. But she was a regular princess herself. And she just couldn't stand it here. Didn't like the isolation, missed the city life, missed her wealthy friends, I think. She didn't last four months before she went running back to San Antonio. Poor Cal's been a wreck ever since."

That's what Howard had told her. That's what Shelby had said, too. But now Natalie was beginning to piece together a disturbing picture. Blond. Rich. Pampered.

It was her all over!

No wonder Cal had been so horrified when Natalie had appeared on his mountain. Poor guy. She probably reminded him exactly of the woman he'd lost!

At the same time, however, the thought of him confusing her with his fickle ex-wife infuriated her. How dare he think she was just like that other woman! Why, he knew that she wasn't rich anymore. And she'd proven, hadn't she, that she wasn't afraid of hard work? For heaven's sake, she hadn't toiled as much in her whole life as she had under Cal's direction. It was one thing for him to think of her as a shallow, unrealistic city girl when they'd first met, but didn't their time together mean anything? So many big changes were happening to her, she'd thought they'd be obvious to everyone…especially Cal.

But Cal was apparently so prejudiced against her he couldn't even see what was going on right under his nose, that she was a changed woman. A more mature woman.

By the time Althea had finished clipping an inch off her hair, and she and Shelby had finished gossiping about the dear departed Connie, Natalie was boiling mad.

She couldn't wait to confront Cal. How dare he conflate her with his ex-wife. How dare he prejudge her just on appearances!

She paid Althea and took Shelby's phone number with promises to meet for lunch at the Feed Bag someday soon, then jumped into her Volkswagen and roared up the mountain. Halfway home, however, her thoughts were interrupted by an explosion—and the car lurching almost out of her control.

She let out a scream of surprise, thinking that the sound was gunfire at first before she realized she'd had a blowout. Her frantic mind tried to figure out what to do, but bad instinct took care of that for her. In her panic, she'd let up on the clutch and suddenly the car jounced to a stop on the shoulder of the road.

For a moment she just sat draped over the steering wheel, gazing in disbelief over the steep drop off the mountain a mere yard or so away. She could have been killed!

She was lucky to be alive, but how could this have happened? Her car and its tires were brand-new. Naturally it didn't help that she'd spent the past few weeks bouncing around on these uneven rural roads, including her own unpaved and rock infested driveway.

She got out to inspect the tire, but all that she could tell, in her limited knowledge of the automobile, was that yes indeedy the tire was flat. What was she going to do now? The only time she'd had this problem before, she'd simply pulled her cell phone out of her purse and called the auto club.

She didn't have her cell phone with her anymore, though. To make matters worse, it was getting dark. And cold. She jumped back into the car and turned on the engine so she could sit in the warmth of the heater for a while. She felt miserable, and took a moment to dwell unhappily on all of the things that had gone wrong in her life lately. Her money disappearing, her horrible house, Cal rebuffing her…and now this! It was as if all of life's problems were assaulting her at once, overwhelming her when she was beyond her usual means for dealing with them. She was even out of range of AAA.

Life wasn't fair.

She must have been crazy to come here!

What was she going to do? As far as she knew, she and Cal were the only ones who lived off this road. Cal wouldn't be coming down. Maybe Howard would, but she couldn't say for certain that he hadn't already gone home for the day. She'd probably missed him.

What a mess! God, what she wouldn't do to be home again. If only she were back in Houston, or at least somewhere with a public transportation system. Houston had all those buses. Granted, she'd never stepped foot on one…but she would have if she'd been in a jam like this one. Now her whole life seemed like it was in a jam. Her house wasn't live-able, her car wasn't drivable, and she was falling in love with a man who, for all practical purposes, wasn't lovable.

At least, he didn't want to be loved.

Or at any rate, not by a woman like her.

A woman like her! She grumbled to herself and tapped her nails angrily against the steering wheel. Now she understood all his references when she'd first arrived to "her kind" and "her type." As if she'd been molded in the cookie cutter shape of his ex-wife! It just made her blood boil every time she thought about how he considered her just a…

Suddenly, her whole body froze as a horrible truth dawned on her. *Just a pampered…fickle…helpless city girl.*

Good heavens! He was *right!*

Oh, she'd thought she'd changed, but the minute

she was faced with adversity in the form of a flat tire, she'd failed the test. She'd buckled in self-pity. Her only thought had been of going back to Houston. Her only action had been to hover in her car, wasting battery juice on the heater, hoping for rescue.

Rescue that wasn't coming.

When would she ever learn? Taking a deep breath, she did something she couldn't remember doing in her entire life. She leaned over to the glove compartment, got out her car's instruction manual and started reading to figure out how to get herself out of this fix. Come hell or high water she was going to change that damn tire!

Naturally the authors of the owner's manual tried to make certain that her efforts were prodigious by phrasing directions as confusingly as possible, but she took the problem step by step. Actually, the hardest part by far was just figuring out the jack, and where exactly to put it, and how to get the car lifted. Especially when she had to decipher sentences such as, "Underneath the vehicle near each wheel, there are bosses in the vehicle's rocker flange." *Vehicle* and *wheel* she understood; the rest took some investigating.

But when it came right down to it, getting the old tire off and the new one on wasn't so difficult. Not half as hard as roofing a house, really. All in all, the whole process couldn't have taken her more than an hour...once she'd stopped moping and gotten off her fanny.

Once her task was done, she rubbed her hands on her slacks and looked at her handiwork with pleasure. She couldn't wait to tell Cal about *this!*

HE WAS STUNNED.

But not in the way she'd apparently expected.

"What do you expect," he asked her, "a medal?"

Natalie stood before him, dirt smudged and grease stained and yet somehow more radiant than he'd ever seen her before, and frowned as if he'd just insulted her. "Don't you understand? I did it all by myself. No help."

"Natalie, you changed a tire. People do that every day."

"*I* don't," she argued.

He let out a huff of exasperation. This beat everything! If he'd ever needed evidence that Natalie was hopelessly spoiled and not right for him—and he found himself searching more and more desperately for such evidence every day—here it was. All she'd done was change a tire, but she was reacting to this accomplishment as if she'd just solved the riddle of the Sphinx. "Listen, I don't want to rain on your parade, but changing a flat is not something that's going to put you in the Emotional Maturity Hall of Fame."

"And what would you know about emotional maturity?" she shot back.

He lifted his eyes to heaven for patience. "Listen, can we not arg—"

"You're so crippled by one woman leaving you, you can't even accept an offer of love when it's handed to you on a silver platter!"

His jaw dropped in surprise. That word! *Love.* Last night he hadn't wanted to think that her suggestion meant what it did—that he was for her. God knows, Natalie was tempting enough as it was. The only thing that had been holding him back from being completely involved with her was the idea that she looked on him as nothing more than the flavor of the month—a whim.

But *love?* When had that happened?

He didn't have time to ask. Her castigation continued with a fury.

"You're so mired in the past, you're just going to let your whole life pass you by! You're going to be stuck up on this mountain and mope yourself to death."

He stepped up to the plate. "Now, wait just a cotton pickin' minute. Don't go playing Dr. Freud on me just because I'm less than impressed by your overnight transformation from a harebrained society dame to Miss Practicality."

"I never claimed to be either of those things."

"Oh, no?" His eyebrows shot up, and his voice a few octaves higher in fluttery imitation of her coming home this evening. "'Cal, Cal, you'll never guess what! I changed a tire!' I mean, good grief, from the way you swept in here this evening, I thought you were going to announce that the Winthrops had struck oil again."

Her cheeks blazed. "And to think that just yesterday I hoped I was finally getting through to you. Thank heavens I spoke to some people in town today! They warned me how emotionally choked off you are."

His first reaction was to be stunned. People in town had said that about him? Who?

Then he scoffed. Emotionally choked—what an idea! Who was more emotional than he was? Hadn't he suffered the local malady of heartbreak more obviously than anyone else? Didn't everyone understand what he had been through?

Apparently not.

Natalie turned and started snatching up her things.

"What are you doing?"

"Going home."

He crossed his arms, a smug grin pulling at his lips. "To Houston?"

"No! Down the hill, to my house."

He let out a sigh. "Natalie, you can't stay there."

"Better there than here. I don't want to impose on your hospitality another night."

"But what about the intruder?"

She shrugged. "He hasn't shown up again. We still don't know that it wasn't just a teenage prank. Anyway, I'm going with or without your permission."

"Oh, come on. Don't be childish."

She whirled on him with Winston in one arm and Junior in another. He almost pointed out that Junior was *his* cat, but her enraged expression stopped him. "So now you're adding childish to your unflattering description of me!" She tossed the kitties, hissing and growling, into the travel carrier. Then she grabbed the leashes and all hell broke loose. The dogs, conditioned by the sight of those thin nylon leads, began to dance and hop eagerly at her feet.

Cal came to her rescue by taking the leashes and hooking the dogs up to them. "Here, let me help you."

"Don't bother."

"The least I can do is help you get back down the hill."

"I can do it on my own," she insisted.

"I know you can, but I'll feel better if you don't."

Once again, Cal found himself loading dogs and cats and bird into his pickup and driving down the hill to situate Natalie in her house. Natalie followed in her own vehicle. Upon their arrival, Cal pushed open the door of the rickety old place, it was pitch-black inside. He stumbled across what someday might resemble a living room and struck a match.

Natalie, who had entered behind him, gasped.

When he looked up at the wall in front of him, his own breath seemed to momentarily fail him. On the wall was a message written in thick red paint made to look like dripping blood. It was short and frighteningly to the point. Two words.

GO HOME!

7

THANK HEAVENS SAM GOT there quickly, because if
he'd arrived a second later, Cal feared he might have
gone loco. He couldn't believe anyone had done this
to Natalie.

While they'd been waiting for the sheriff, Cal had
made Natalie stand outside with him. For one thing,
given what had happened, he didn't want her to be
alone for one single second. For another, every time
he looked at what someone had written on her wall,
he became madder than a stepped-on rattlesnake.

Unfortunately, out here in the moonlight, in the
chill of the night, Natalie looked small and cold and
grim. Staring at her, it was impossible to remember
that they'd just been fighting, or what it had all been
about. He just wanted to hold her. She kept her distance, though, and folded her arms protectively.

"Do you think it was the same person, Cal?"

He had no doubt of it. But who? Who around here
would be doing this to Natalie? He couldn't think of
a solitary soul.

Natalie shrugged and looked at him hopefully.
"Maybe somebody heard about the other incident and
decided to play a trick on me. Maybe it's not as bad
as it looks."

Cal crossed his arms and leaned against the old
beam supporting the porch rail. It squeaked, remind-

ing him that he couldn't lean against anything on this house too hard.

That was the damn shame of this. All Natalie had gone through, and for what? This silly house, without her help, would probably have expired of natural causes in another winter or two. Maybe they should have let it. Heck, maybe he should have offered to take the place off Jim Loftus's hands. Then Jim wouldn't have had the bother of the raffle and he wouldn't have had the bother of Natalie and the feelings she was stirring up inside him that he knew were better left dormant.

Not that he would probably have Natalie to worry about much longer. No doubt this little caper would collapse her idyllic country inn scenario once and for all—and who could blame her for turning tail and running after this? Not Cal, that was for sure. Seeing those letters made to look like something out of a horror movie nearly caused him to be physically ill, and their message wasn't even aimed at him. He could only imagine what Natalie must have felt like, reading those words.

Probably right this minute she was calculating how quickly she could skedaddle back to Houston.

"It's got to be the same person," he said, thinking aloud.

She frowned. "Why?"

"Because this wasn't exactly a copycat incident. Think about it. Last time whoever it was messed up your house. But this time, they came back and did one better—they left a message."

She nodded. "As if I didn't get their meaning the first time around!"

"Well, if their goal was to get you to leave, then to them it probably seemed as if you didn't get it."

Her lips pursed. "So in your opinion, this ghoulish person is just going to keep coming back until I take the hint and leave?"

"You know the old expression, 'persistence pays.' But the more times they come 'round, Natalie, the more chance they have of being caught."

She grunted. "That might be a comforting thought to a sheriff's department, but not to me. I'd rather not catch them and have them leave me alone, personally."

"Yeah, I can see where you might."

She smiled. Amazing that she could flash him a grin at a time like this. "But *you'd* rather have them be caught."

He shrugged. "I don't want you in danger…but yeah, it would be nice to catch the culprit."

She remained silent for a moment, studying him. When he had to look away from her, she mused, "You know, at first I was shocked when you told me that you used to be a lawman, but now I'm not. You can't stand the thought of people getting away with things, can you?"

He shook his head. "I believe in justice. A person shouldn't be allowed to do things like this."

"I agree. But my question is, given the strength of your feelings for right and wrong, whatever gave you the idea that you could walk away from your job?"

He'd been wondering the same thing himself since he'd been helping Sam. Connie had been dead wrong. Doing sheriff's work felt right to him, and it wasn't just a matter of him sleepwalking. He enjoyed the job. Much as he hated to admit it, this past year he'd felt a little rootless. It was the first time in his life since he'd started mowing lawns for people when he was just a little kid that he hadn't worked, and worked hard. Of course, he'd kept himself occupied, but that was different. Maybe that was why he had such a hard time understanding Natalie and her kind. One year of leisure, of pursuing just what interests he cared to, and he'd been on the verge of going bug crazy.

Of course, maybe that explained Natalie's own brand of nuttiness a little bit, too. She had spent a good deal of her adulthood aimlessly following whim.

Sam's cruiser turned off the road and lumbered up Natalie's driveway. Sam got out and walked up to the porch, investigating the dirt for more tracks, which Cal hadn't detected. Sam didn't, either.

Natalie greeted him enthusiastically and led him inside, pointing at the wall and explaining the circumstances under which they'd found the writing, including the part about she and Cal having a squabble. Apparently she didn't believe in hiding anything from the police!

Sam listened to her patiently, with only a brow or two raised Cal's way as she regaled him with the story of his less than satisfactory reaction to her ability to change a flat tire.

Then something caught his attention.

"You say you had a blowout coming up the hill?"

"That's right," she said. "It nearly scared the wits out of me—but if only I'd known what was coming I would have saved some fear for later!"

Sam chuckled. "I'd like to take a squint at your old tire, if you don't mind. Seems sort of strange that a brand spankin' new car like yours would already be having trouble, doesn't it to you, too, Cal?"

Cal frowned, realizing suddenly that he should have thought of this himself sooner. He and Natalie had become so embroiled in their personal squabble that he hadn't given the flat tire much thought as a menacing clue in and of itself.

Natalie led them down to her car. As she passed Cal's truck she checked inside for Armand, the kitten and Winston, who were resting quietly. The dogs they had let out; Natalie seemed to feel safer with the dogs out sniffing around, but Cal found himself looking nervously around the yard to make sure the pups were all safe.

Sam opened the trunk of her car and looked at the tire. Cal did, too, and shook his head at how obvious a slash job had been performed.

Even Natalie caught on. "Dr. Green on *ER* couldn't have made a cleaner incision."

Seeing the clean gash in the tire made Cal practically quake with rage. "Given these mountains, whoever did this had to know how dangerous it was."

Natalie gulped. "You mean...someone's actually trying to *kill* me?"

"Whoa there." Sam shook his head. "We don't know that for certain.

But what else could be going on here?

Natalie was stunned. "Who would want to kill me? I'm not even rich anymore."

"How many people know that?" Sam asked.

"As few as possible!"

Cal and Sam looked at each other. They weren't any closer to figuring this out than they were this afternoon, and Natalie looked as though she needed to get away from there.

"C'mon," he said. "Call the dogs and let's go home."

She looked at him with wide, beautiful eyes. "You mean back to your place?"

"Of course."

"But—"

"Forget that. You can't stay here, Nat."

He wasn't sure where the diminutive had come from, but once it was out, it seemed to suit her. And something in her face softened in response to the nickname. She capitulated and called for the pups, who came dashing off the porch in a heartbeat. They were all eager to get back to the warmth of Cal's house. Natalie got in her Volkswagen and started on her way back to the cabin.

Cal turned to Sam. "I'll drive down tomorrow morning and try to figure this thing out."

Sam nodded. "All right. And I'll do some snooping around town early. If her tire was slashed while she was in Heartbreak Ridge today, at least we'll know who was in town, and who might have seen something."

Of course. That was one thing about living in a town of sixty-four people. The suspect list for any given crime was bound to be a short one.

"THANKS FOR LETTING ME stay the night here, Cal." Natalie shook her head in wonder. "It seems as if I'm always thanking you for taking me in, doesn't it?"

"Don't mention it. It's nothing."

But Natalie knew better. This afternoon he'd seemed annoyed just by the sight of her. Now maybe he'd softened a little because of the second break-in, and because she'd been so frightened, but she didn't dare believe that he'd actually changed his mind about her. If it hadn't been for the mishap tonight, she would be sleeping on the hard floor of her place, and who knows if she and Cal would have even spoken again.

"It won't be for long," she promised him. She really didn't want to wear out her welcome this time.

"I didn't think it would be," Cal said, his lips a grim line.

So it was just as she thought. He was putting up with her, but still eager to be rid of her. "If I stayed down there, it might be a deterrent to whoever's trying to mess with me."

"You can't be certain of that."

"We'll find out."

Cal's eyes widened. "Don't tell me you're actually contemplating going back to that spook house!"

She blinked. "Of course."

"You mean to live?"

"Naturally. Where else can I go?"

"Back to Houston! I just assumed…"

She clucked her tongue. Didn't the man ever listen to her? "I told you today that I wasn't going back there. Anyway, I couldn't even if I wanted to. I have too much invested here now to leave."

And as she looked into Cal's blue eyes, she realized she wasn't just speaking of a financial investment. She had an emotional investment as well, in Cal Tucker. Hard as she'd tried to face their differences square in the eye, the unlikely mountain lawman appealed to her in a way no man ever had before.

He took a step forward. "You mean you intend to stay here permanently?"

"Good heavens," she said in exasperation. "Do I

need to tap it out in Morse code against that thick skull of yours? Yes, I'm going to stay here. Permanently. I have nowhere else to go. For better or worse, Heartbreak Ridge is my home now.''

"You must have people back in Houston who would take you in."

"No, I don't." She sighed, thinking about how shabbily most of her old "friends" would treat her if they discovered her reduced circumstances. The strangest thing to her now was that she could have ever considered that kind of shallow connection friendship at all.

Cal reached a hand out to her arm, startling her. She hadn't realized they were standing so close together...or had he moved in on her when she wasn't looking? "You mean that even with someone stalking you, you still want to live in that place?"

"Well, maybe not tonight..."

His gaze narrowed on her. "But why?"

At this point, it was hard not to scream. Maybe she would have, if his face hadn't been so adorably screwed up in an obvious effort to understand what she was telling him...over and over again. "Okay, one more time. Will you listen up?" She pointed toward the window through which they could just see the outline of her house. "That place is like Kansas was to Dorothy. My home. It's all I have."

The hand around her arm tightened, and his other hand lifted to touch her chin. "Not so, Nat."

Her heart hammered in her chest as she looked into his blue eyes. This was the second time he'd called her by that nickname. She swallowed, and tried to laugh. "You called me that before. I thought you meant *gnat*. You know, like the bug."

Those thick blond brows arched. "Do I look like I'm swatting you away?"

She glanced down at his arm tugging her toward him, then back up at his full lips and his eyes darkening with emotion. She felt her knees go noodly on her and put a hand on his shoulder for support.

"Actually, now it looks as if we're about to tango," she said, joking.

He ignored her stab at levity. "Did you hear what I said, Natalie? You're not alone. You have me."

The simple words, spoken so tenderly, were so unexpected that her lips parted in surprise. That, apparently, was all the invitation he required. His mouth descended on hers quickly but gently; the warmth of his lips felt reassuring, yet electric.

Natalie moaned and leaned into his chest, glad for the comfort he offered, the strength. How long had it been since they'd kissed? She wasn't sure now whether it was days or weeks; it seemed like a lifetime that she'd been stirred up with desire for this man, that he'd intruded on her waking and sleeping dreams. Now, seizing the opportunity, she clung to him as though this kiss would be their last.

She tried to memorize the imprint his lips made against hers, their exact warmth and the exquisite feelings they could create. His recently clean-shaven jaw now had a bristly shadow, and she traced her finger down it, memorizing its rough prickliness. She wanted to remember everything. Her relationship with Cal was so volatile, she felt as though she couldn't take one second for granted. Tonight they were kissing. Tomorrow different, more antagonistic sparks could fly between them. Tomorrow he might boot her back down the hill. Or she might just stomp down it on her own steam.

But she was just going to worry about tomorrow, tomorrow.

Cal pulled her up against him so close that she could feel every inch of their bodies touching, and there was no hiding his obvious desire for her. The feel of his stiffness pressing against her sent a thrill through her. She snaked her hands up around his neck, deepening the kiss.

"This is crazy," she whispered.

"Nuts," he agreed.

"I want you so much."

He held her tight. "I've wanted you ever since I first saw you. I wanted to lean up against that Volkswagen and kiss you."

"But you were so hostile!"

He laughed. "And you were so snippety!"

She shook her head, smiling ruefully at the memory. He'd looked so rugged, so imposing…so unlike any other man she'd known. Which is precisely what she still found so fascinating about him. "And now?"

"Now you can snip all you want. I couldn't let you out of my arms for a million dollars."

She tilted her head and lifted her lips to his for another kiss. This one was long, heated, and left no question in her mind how Cal wanted to spend the rest of the evening. Slowly he began peeling off her clothes. The look of desire in his eyes made her feel as if she were a present being lovingly unwrapped. It also made her feel, God help her, as if a volcano were building inside her. Her insides felt molten, irruptive.

"Cal?" her voice quavered as they stood entwined,

her clothes puddled at his feet. She felt awkward, just standing undressed in the living room.

He looked alarmed. "Are you cold?"

She almost laughed. *Cold?* She was about to combust! "No, but wouldn't we be happier taking this show into the next room?"

Without further ado, he swept her into his arms and carried her into the bedroom, placing her on the king-size bed as if she were a delicate package. But if she was delicate, it wasn't because she was made of fragile glass, but something far more explosive. Like a hand grenade with the pin pulled, she felt she could go off at any moment.

With that in mind, she sidled up against him and gingerly undid one shirt button at a time. Her efforts revealed such a perfectly sculpted chest that she was tempted just to sit back on her heels and gape at him as if he were the eighth wonder of the world.

His eyes burned into her. "What are you grinning at?"

A fluttery wave hit her as he reached out to touch her cheek. "I was just thinking of what a year of mountain living and rodent eating could do for the male physique."

He chuckled, and the sexy deep sound of it shimmered through her. "I was thinking of what a year of abstinence can do to a man's libido."

She blushed down to her toes. "So there's been no one since…" Speaking the name would be like dousing a blazing campfire.

He pulled her into his arms. "I haven't so much as thought of any woman but you, Nat. It's as if you've awakened me from a deep sleep."

From the feel of him pressing against her, he was

definitely wide-awake now. Every inch of him. She reached down and eased his zipper down over his swollen manhood, reveling in the feel of him, in her ability to bring out such a raw human response in a man who had been cut off for so long.

"I want you, Cal," she said as boldly as she knew how to put it.

He kissed her again, and she tried to put every iota of what she was feeling into that kiss. He reached down, teasing a bared nipple with his thumb until it was aching and erect. She let out a deep, almost painful moan.

He looked up at her with startled eyes. "Is something wrong?"

She shook her head. "Only that the night can't go on forever."

He grinned that sexy grin of his. "Well, sweetheart, we'll just have to stretch it out as far as we can."

And to the best of their abilities, they did. And all through the long night, Natalie savored every moment, storing each touch and caress into her memory. But as she finally drifted off to sleep at dawn, the sweetest memory of all was Cal's grin and his drawling voice when he called her sweetheart.

AT DAWN, CAL BELATEDLY crept around his house, tiptoeing over and around various snoring mounds of fur as he checked and double-checked the locks on all the windows and doors. *For Natalie's peace of mind,* he told himself.

But heck, who was he kidding? *He* was antsy himself. He'd lived all his life in a sleepy mountain town. Though he'd been a sheriff's deputy for years, the closest he'd ever come to serious crime was on *Kojak* and in Hollywood movies. Things like break-ins and stalkings just didn't happen here.

Until now.

He was scared for Natalie and for himself. Because he couldn't bear the thought of anything happening to her. Because, he feared, he felt more for her than was wise.

He stood in the bedroom door, looking at her silhouette as she slept, and he was filled with wonder at the long hours they had just spent discovering each other. Natalie had been warm, giving…loving. That last word filled him with more trepidation. Love was one thing he didn't want in his life. And yet…

Faint light beamed across the bed, making her seem almost achingly beautiful to him, like a dream. Her blond hair spilled across the pillow, and her wondrous body was only half covered by the tangle of sheets and blankets. But he didn't need to see it to remember every square inch of her beautiful body, so delicate and so perfect.

Something hitched in his chest as he looked at her. He knew that feeling well.

Part of him sent a plea up to heaven. *God, no— don't let this happen to me again.* Because to him, falling in love was inextricably linked with the heartache that inevitably followed it.

Then the other part of him—the same reckless part of himself that had led him to kiss Natalie last night— longed to jump into bed next to her and embrace her and all the love she could offer him. So what if she was flighty and unrealistic and everything he'd been trying to avoid for a solid year? Maybe the very reason she appealed to him was that she was flighty and unrealistic and bound to flee to Houston at the next sign of trouble.

All humans had their weaknesses. Some couldn't lay off booze. Some people craved chocolate and other rich confections. Other poor souls couldn't kick the nicotine habit no matter how many warnings the government slapped on everything. He wasn't any different. Only he couldn't seem to shake his attraction to Natalie. He wasn't even sure he wanted to anymore.

Natalie turned, smiling in sleep, so breathtakingly adorable that she managed to simultaneously arouse and beat down all his most deep-seated fears. She was everything he should avoid…and craved.

God knows his hometown had seen its share of star-crossed matches. Everyone here seemed to have a fatal love flaw. Maybe a weakness for fickle city women was simply his bane, his cross to bear. There was no fighting it, really. And why should he? So what if he was doomed to seek out only the most improbable people to fall in love with? What more could you expect from a man who'd grown up in a place called Heartbreak Ridge?

Or maybe, just maybe, all of Natalie's protests were sincere, and she really did consider Heartbreak Ridge her home now. Maybe the lady wasn't as fickle as he'd thought she was.

"WHOEVER IT IS BUGGING YOU SURE DON'T KNOW ZIPPETY-DO ABOUT PAINTIN'!" Howard declared in disgust later that morning as he inspected the house. "JUST LOOK AT THEM LETTERS—THEY'RE ALL DRIPPY!"

"I THINK THEY MEANT THEM TO LOOK THAT WAY, HOWARD."

"WHAT WAY? SLOPPY?"

Leave it to her handyman to dislike vandalism on account of its untidiness. Of course, Howard hadn't probably misspent his youth in movie theaters watching ridiculous slasher movies where this sort of thing was par for the course.

Considering the matter in that light, she turned and stared at the words again. They seemed less sinister than they had last night. Childish. But she couldn't forget that the same person who had done this might also have slashed her tire, and that hadn't been child's play.

"What on earth am I going to do?" she muttered to herself.

"PAINT OVER IT."

She hadn't thought Howard would have been able to hear her. But now that his common sense suggestion was out in the open, she nearly laughed at the logic of it. Of course! The longer this message was on her wall, the longer she would wander around in a funk of worry and indecision.

Also, the longer Cal would be obliged to extend his hospitality toward her. As appealing as that was to her, especially after their more than neighborly lovemaking last night, she didn't want Cal to keep her at his house because he felt sorry for her. Or because as long as she was having to live in his house she was a handy squeeze. She needed to know whether he was actually falling in love with her, the way she was falling for him. Or whether their physical relationship was just a playing out of some fantasy about the woman who had loved him and left him. Therapy for a heartbroken recluse.

She sighed. "YOU'RE RIGHT, HOWARD. I GUESS I NEED TO GO INTO TOWN AND BUY SOME PAINT."

"COVERING THAT RED'S GONNA TAKE A PRIMER."

She nodded. She only had a vague sense of what that meant, but she'd figure it out when she got to the hardware store. She was becoming adept at repeating Howard and Cal's instructions verbatim, like an immigrant working his way around a foreign tongue.

And there was something else she needed to tend to in town—something she'd decided to do while she'd been staring forlornly at her checkbook this morning.

She gathered her things and drove down to Heartbreak Ridge, trying not to let her mind wander too much toward last night. Though Cal's lovemaking had been the most wondrous experience she could have imagined, she kept reminding herself that theirs was not a relationship she could count on. Cal had been burned once, and now, despite the fact that he was slowly letting down his guard, one tiny piece at a time, he was still wary of her. This morning, no magical words of love had passed between them. He'd kissed her; they'd made love again. Then he'd told her he had promised Sam to meet him in town early.

And then he was gone.

Would things be different tonight when they met again? Or would having an entire day by himself to contemplate last night's turn of events make him regret what they had done?

Maybe, she thought, she shouldn't give him a whole day. She considered just dropping in on the sheriff's office.

At the hardware store, she learned more than she

ever wanted to know about primers, then she walked down the sidewalk till she reached Sam's office. She had never set foot in the place where Cal had spent so much of his time, but as she crossed the threshold, she felt almost as if she were walking on hallowed ground.

Till she heard a sharp laugh.

A short woman in overalls and cat glasses squinted up at her sharply. "Should have known *you'd* show up here sooner or later!"

Natalie blinked in surprise. It still stunned her that total strangers would know who she was. Then again, she'd never lived in a small town before. "I was looking for Cal. Is he here?"

The woman laughed again. "Cal? Is he ever here when we need him?"

Natalie didn't know how to answer. "Are you...Merlie?"

The woman stood and crossed to her with an outstretched hand. "Pardon my manners. We don't get much call to introduce ourselves to anybody around these parts. It's usually just the same old mugs wandering around town year after year. But you got your saddle on the right horse, anyhow. I'm Merlie Shivers."

"We have your kitten. Junior."

She shook her head adamantly. "Not mine. The last thing I need is another money drain like my Tubb-Tubb."

"Me, either."

The woman's lips turned up in a smile. "Yeah, Cal told me you were a soft touch."

Which is no doubt why she now had another mouth to feed.

"Do you know where I could find Cal right now?"

Merlie's expression was wry. "He and the sheriff told me that they were going to do some investigating—something that hasn't happened around here, by the way, since a box of Necco wafers disappeared from the candy display at the Stop-N-Shop checkout lane." She crossed her arms and nodded to the building across the street. "Their stated intentions to play Watson and Holmes notwithstanding, the best place to look for the dynamic duo is usually at the Feed Bag."

Natalie approached that establishment with some trepidation. She knew now that the diner was the nerve center of the town. When Cal had objected to her suggestion that they go there for dinner, she'd assumed he'd done so out of a desire for better food. Now she suspected that he'd really hoped to avoid gossip. She knew it for sure when she walked in, setting off a bell above the door, and was assaulted by the aroma of diner food—certainly no food could smell better than this.

She glanced around quickly and was disappointed to see that Cal wasn't here. Now she was in a pickle. Every patron in the place had stopped eating and talking to stare up at her; she couldn't just leave. Another whiff of the cheeseburgers frying on the grill and she didn't want to, either.

She edged down to the free booth at the back of the diner. In a moment, the man at the grill, an old fellow in a green cap leaned over the counter and peered at her. "Decided yet?"

Natalie looked around her, bewildered. Wasn't a waitress going to give her a menu and take her order?

Someone at the counter swiveled toward her and explained helpfully, "Jerry's too cheap to hire a waitress. Or print menus."

"But then, how...?" Her words faded when she

realized that a fuss would be pointless. "I'll have a cheeseburger and…do fries come with that?"

The fries at the next table looked great. She loved the crinkle-cut kind.

The diner burst into laughter.

"Everything comes with fries," the proprietor barked at her. "Even the fries come with fries."

She grinned. "Then the only other thing I'll need is a cup of coffee. Thank you."

She looked out the window, suddenly wishing she'd brought a book or a magazine with her. Come to find out, though, she shouldn't have worried about being lonely. In fact, the next moment she looked up, there was another couple sitting across from her. She looked into the man's face and nearly jumped out of her skin.

"Good heavens!" He looked so much like Cal, only slighter. And more clean-cut. Actually the words *Boy Scout* came to mind.

The man grinned, and the woman sitting next to him—a spiky-haired redhead in a loud zebra print shirt—explained the situation for her. "I'm Ruby Tucker, and this is Cody. Cal's brother."

"Pleased to meet you, ma'am," Cody said. His cheeks were rosy.

Imagine Cal having a blushing brother! Natalie thought in wonder. The idea gave her hope somehow; proof that there was civilization in his past somewhere.

"I came in here looking for Cal, actually," she told them. "Merlie suggested that I might find him here, but no such luck."

"You call the prospect of eating with that picklepuss lucky?" Ruby asked with mock amazement. "Then the gossip must be true!"

Natalie lowered her voice. "What gossip?"

"That you two are an item."

She wasn't sure she was ready to answer that. She suspected she should be denying it at the top of her lungs. But suddenly, the Boy Scout sitting across from her was wearing a dead serious expression, and she remembered that the whole bloomin' family had been lawmen—this one included—and he probably wasn't into evasiveness.

"Cody's worried about Cal," Ruby explained unnecessarily.

"I can see where he would be...having him up on the mountain all that time."

Both of them were frowning now. "Actually he's worried about *you* and Cal."

Natalie nearly laughed when she understood where this was all leading. They were afraid *she* was going to lead Cal down the garden path!

"Cal's been through a tough time," Cody explained. "And you—well, you're sort of like Connie. I don't know if he's told you about her."

"Well...I figured it out. Word gets around."

Ruby laughed. "Is this the gossipingest place you ever lived?"

Natalie smiled. "There was plenty of gossip in Houston, but of course there were enough people there to dilute it."

"I just want you to know that if you're intending on leaving, you should say so now. Cal doesn't need any more heartache," Cody warned.

So, Cal had a fierce little brother looking after him. She almost felt jealous. Who was looking after *her?* From the way things were going, she was the one likely to wind up heartbroken. Not to mention, there was another person out there on the loose who apparently wanted to kill her.

Before she could sort through the irony of someone warning her not to break Cal's heart, the diner's doorbell sounded off and Cal himself appeared before her. Her heart did an ecstatic flip at the sight of his smile of recognition, and when he came strolling over and slid into the booth next to her, she felt a pang of possessiveness. How could she possibly break his heart when she never wanted him out of her sight?

In the next second, he took a gander at who she was sitting with and let out a groan of dread. "What kind of powwow is this?" he asked suspiciously.

Cody laughed. "Don't worry, I wasn't telling her about the fifth-grade talent show."

Natalie's ears perked up and she swiveled on Cal. *"Talent show?"*

Cal rolled his eyes. "I'll tell you later. Right now, we have a lead."

Her mouth dropped open, as did the mouths of everyone within earshot. Jerry's head popped over the counter again. "You find out the identity of the tire slasher already?"

"No, but Althea said that she saw a gold car driving into town yesterday. Expensive looking, foreign make." His gaze honed in on Natalie.

She frowned in concentration, then gasped when she realized that the description actually rang a bell. "I did know someone with a car of that description…" And wouldn't you know it—it was the last person she ever expected to hunt *her* down. "Malcolm Braswell!"

8

BACK AT THE SHERIFF'S office, Sam didn't look convinced.

"What should I do?" Natalie asked, hysterical at the thought that her erstwhile accountant now wanted to take her life.

Sam frowned. "We can't be sure that Braswell is our man, Natalie."

"But if the car was as Althea described it—"

"That's a big if," Cal said. "Gold cars aren't exactly scarce in the world."

"They are in Heartbreak Ridge, though," she pointed out.

"That's so," Merlie agreed. "Scarcer than feathers on a frog. Especially foreign makes. If it weren't for the commercials during Tom Brokaw, I wouldn't know Lexus from linguini."

"But what are the chances Braswell would come after Natalie in his own car?" Cal asked. "He'd rent a car rather than risk being caught from his own license plates. Besides, if he took all your money, my guess is that he's bought a new car by now."

Natalie breathed only slightly easier. "I hadn't thought of that…"

The sheriff nodded. "Also, no offense to Althea, but we even have to take her memory with a grain of salt. She just glanced at the thing through her shop window—maybe what looked like gold to her was really tan, or yellow.''

''So what you're telling me is that you're no closer to figuring this out than you were yesterday.''

''Well…we've figured one thing out. A strange car drove through town yesterday while you were here. That suggests that whoever slashed your tire came from out of town for the privilege of doing so.''

''Oh.'' There went her hope that the incidents had just been the work of punk kids…the Necco wafer thief all grown up, say. Having the culprit be someone from her own past, with a motive for doing her harm, made the situation seem much more dangerous.

Cal escorted her out to her car. She needed to get back to the house, and Howard. But first, there was something else in town she needed to do—something that filled her with almost as much fear as thoughts of her stalker did.

''Be careful driving home,'' Cal said.

''I'm going to the Stop-N-Shop on the way. Anything you need there?''

He shook his head. ''Be careful, Nat. When I get home, we'll talk.''

She grinned. Fat chance. ''When you get home, I can think of much more stimulating things we could do.''

His lips pulled up in a slow, lazy smile. ''Me, too, but I was trying to be a sensitive twenty-first century type of guy.''

She looked horrified. ''Don't tell me you're trying to shake your caveman image at this late date. Prehistory becomes you so well!''

He puffed up proudly and let out a resounding ''Ugh.''

She laughed.

Cal looked around quickly to make sure that not too many people were staring through chinks in venetian blinds, and gave her what was meant to be a furtive kiss on the lips but naturally deepened into something much more delectable. She wasn't just joking when she said she insinuated that she wanted to make love with him the moment he got home. Desire churned inside of her, robbing her of logical thought.

Finally he had to propel her into her car. "We could get arrested for lewd behavior if you don't go now."

She nodded. She still had that errand to run. That one last test to see whether she had really progressed toward independence or not.

She said goodbye to Cal and made the quick trip to the other side of the small one-street town. On the grocery store's automatic sliding doors was a homemade sign whose two words made her heart skip a beat.

Help Wanted.

WHEN CAL EMERGED from the bedroom the next morning, showered and dressed to go into town to help Sam again, the sight of Natalie setting the breakfast table took his breath away. And not just because he could imagine her cheeks still flushed from their vigorous lovemaking of the night before. And not just because she was presiding over a table boasting a platter of pop-n-serve biscuits and sausages, though the appropriate feast was definitely a milestone in Natalie's culinary career.

No, what really caused him to freeze in shock was what she was wearing. She had on the bright yellow, tailored jacket and matching skirt that she'd been wearing the day of her arrival in Heartbreak Ridge. Her innkeeper's outfit, she called it jokingly once, although she hadn't worn it since he'd first seen her. And no wonder. It wasn't at all appropriate for fixing up a house. He wasn't dead certain it was appropriate for running a hotel, either. The outfit looked like *Vogue's* idea of what a businesswoman would wear, maybe, but somehow he doubted honest-to-goodness working women actually dressed like that.

"Do I look all right?" she asked anxiously.

He couldn't lie, nor could he help the grin that spread across his face when those honey-brown eyes met his. "Like a million bucks."

She sagged a little in relief.

His grin felt frozen on his face. What did this change of style mean? Only the worst possible explanations occurred to him. The other night's scare had been too much for her, so she was going back to Houston. Or their relationship was moving too quickly for her, so she was going back to Houston. Or maybe she was just going back to Houston.

"Guess what?" she asked.

He frowned. "You're going back to Houston?"

Her face screwed up in a perplexed expression. "No! I'm going to work."

Had the altitude gone to her head? "You can't paint in that."

"I'm not going to paint, silly. I got a job. In town."

His jaw dropped. "You didn't say anything about this before!"

"I wanted to surprise you."

She'd done that, all right. He looked her up and down again, wondering what she could possibly be dressed to do in Heartbreak Ridge. And now that he thought about it, he wasn't sure he was entirely comfortable with her running around in that outfit in town. The skirt was short with a slit up the thigh, giving whoever cared to look a mouthwatering view of her shapely legs. Under the jacket she was wearing nothing but a wispy silk shell that dipped low enough in front to give more than a hint of cleavage. And what position could she have secured in Heartbreak Ridge that would require her to wear a sexy designer getup?

"I don't recall any Help Wanted signs around town," he mused aloud, "except at the Stop-N-Shop."

A bright grin spread across her face. "That's my job! Isn't it great? I got it!"

She acted as if she'd landed a six-figure salary. Maybe she thought Doyle Stumph had potential workers beating down his door looking for employment, when the truth was just the opposite. The worker pool in Heartbreak Ridge wasn't much more than a puddle. Not to mention, becoming a Stop-N-Shop employee wasn't exactly a glamour position.

"Uh, Natalie…did Doyle tell you what you would be doing on the job?"

"Of course." She lifted her head proudly. "I'm going to bag groceries."

"In *that* outfit?"

She lifted her chin. "What's wrong with it? You just told me that I looked like a million bucks."

"Sure, but that was before…" He shook his head. "Have you ever bagged groceries before?"

"Of course not. I've never worked in the food distribution business in any capacity before, which I explained to Mr. Stumph right off. But I'm willing to learn.''

"Sure, but—"

She looked annoyed. "But what? You were the one who scolded me weeks ago for not going out and getting a job."

He couldn't say exactly why he was disturbed by this new turn of events. Maybe because he couldn't help thinking it was just a rich girl's whim. That she would tire of the job and quit it, just like he feared she would tire of her rustic life and go back to Houston. Or tire of her new rustic boyfriend and he would be left high and dry.

"What about the house? What about all the work Howard is doing?"

"I'll drop by this morning and tell him what needs to be done today, and he'll do it. Howard is trustworthy, Cal—you know that." She shrugged. "Besides, it's because I need Howard that I took this job. I don't have too much money left. This way, I'll take the money I make at the store and hand it over to Howard."

"That's not exactly getting ahead."

"No, but it's breaking even. That's better than I've been doing."

These were practical words coming from Natalie. He tried to believe that she was going to make an honest effort to stay here, follow through with her plans, and maybe even try to fit in eventually. But the change was just so hard to fathom! The baroness—a grocery bagger?

"Come eat your breakfast before it gets cold," she instructed, pulling out a chair for him. "You've got a hard day of vandal hunting ahead of you."

As she fluttered around the kitchen gathering silverware and pouring their coffee and slipping the dogs her sausages under the table, he marveled at how domestic a tableau they created. He could almost imagine him and Natalie going on and on like this…and living happily ever after.

From his cage by the window, Armand burst into a few words of song.

Both Natalie and Cal swiveled in the bird's direction.

"Well, I'll be!" Natalie exclaimed. "Isn't that the Hank Williams song you were trying to teach him?"

Armand repeated the phrase about making him weep again and again, but wouldn't spit out "Your Cheatin' Heart."

Natalie shook her head. "He has difficulty making the *ch* sound. It was the same problem when he was working on *La Traviata*. I'm sorry, Cal, I know it can be annoying to just get snatches."

And what a snatch! As Armand repeated the promise to make him weep, Cal suddenly wished he'd had the foresight to teach that damn bird something more upbeat.

Tonight maybe he'd start a bird tutorial on "Love Will Keep Us Together."

"TGIF!" Leila Birch exclaimed.

With three whole days of work under her belt, Natalie felt like a veteran already—and she had the sore feet to prove it. Nevertheless, she'd never felt so happy, so part of something, than she did at this job, and she beamed in camaraderie to hear the familiar phrase—albeit one phrase she'd never had call to use in her life before now.

"You said it!" she chimed in, leaning against the counter. Then, to make sure Leila knew she was hip to the lingo, she added, "TG!"

Leila laughed, setting off a small spontaneous outburst of mirth in Natalie as well. Somehow, life, which had seemed so bleak just weeks before, had conspired all at once to make her giddy with happiness.

Everything was different. The work on her house was going forward, and she was actually earning money to pay for it. She'd just received her first paycheck, too—sixty-five dollars and change for just two days' work. Incredible! She'd never imagined that anyone would pay her a dime for doing anything; if she'd known making money by the sweat of her brow would be so painless, she wouldn't have dreaded working so much all these years. She was actually having fun.

And for the first time in her life, she felt proud. Not just that Winthrop pride she'd always had, but pride in herself. All these years, her self-esteem had been tied to a checkbook whose balance she'd done nothing to create, or add to. It amazed her that she'd never understood that before.

But it wasn't just the money making her feel good. After three days of being on the job, she already knew everybody in town, and found that, once the ice was broken, people in Heartbreak Ridge were not only plenty friendly, but it was hard sometimes to get them to shut up. How could people say that life in small towns was boring? In the past two days she had learned of heartaches, gossip and scandal that would put *As the World Turns* to shame. For instance, Leila—the meek, pretty cashier she'd been standing next to for three straight days—had confessed at lunch that she had been in love with Cal's brother, Cody, for years, but that when he had married she'd set her sights on Ruby's brother, Lucian, only to discover later that it was another brother, Buck, whom she loved. Heartbreak Ridge strikes again! And Leila actually had asked Natalie's advice on what to do about this matter.

Imagine. People were already asking *her* for advice!

Now when she walked over to the Feed Bag for a cup of coffee on her break, people didn't yell over her, they yelled at her like one of their own. She was beginning to feel that she belonged.

And then there was Cal. She was beginning to feel *they* belonged, too—and that was the strangest, most miraculous happening of all. It seemed as if he was beginning to accept her for what she was, warts and all, which was amazing to her. More amazing, even, than finding herself gainfully employed.

At first she'd worried that she was really just in the throes of an incredible physical attraction. In thrall to lust. And she'd been right—she was in lust. Every time she caught Cal giving her one of his sexy looks, undressing her with his eyes, she felt the same raw desire she'd felt the first time they'd made love.

But there was also more than bedroom activity bringing them together. She liked working on the house with him, liked joshing him when he was in the middle of an earnest lecture about the appropriate way to patch Sheetrock, for instance. They usually broke into laughter every ten minutes while they worked. They'd even coaxed a few chuckles out of Howard.

But when they were home in the evening, listening to old LPs on the turntable and playing cribbage and backgammon…those were the times when she thought she was the happiest. They didn't have to clown or entertain each other. Sometimes they just lay on opposite ends of the couch sipping hot cocoa and reading those old tattered encyclopedia volumes of his. It sure as shootin' wasn't the glitter of Monte Carlo; it was better.

It was love, she was sure of it now.

Not that Cal had made any great confession of his feeling for her. He still called her the baroness and teased her for being a greenhorn. He was still wearing that emotional armor she sometimes feared she would never be able to pierce, no matter how much she loved him.

And wouldn't you know it, his reticence just made her want to love him all the more.

CAL SAW HER COMING OUT of the grocery store after her shift and crossed the street to meet her. It still shocked him to spy Natalie in Heartbreak Ridge. Not that she didn't belong there now…but he supposed he was a little jealous of having to share her.

What amazed him most was that she seemed to like being there. She took almost ludicrous pride in her job; every morning she painstakingly ironed her blue work apron—the one that read *Thanks for Stopping By!* On her breaks she hung out at the Feed Bag or window-shopped at the pharmacy. Or she would stop by the office and swap pet stories with Merlie.

Connie had never done any of those things. In fact, she'd never made the slightest effort to fit into his community. Yet Natalie was jumping into life in Heartbreak Ridge with both feet.

But would she tire of it sooner or later?

Cal took a deep breath. He was about to see if it was going to be sooner rather than later. He stepped forward and flagged her down before she could reach her car.

She flashed her million-watt smile at him. "Hey, you."

He felt temporarily blinded. Wasn't there some reason, at some point in time, that he thought she was something other than perfect?

Her brows drew together. "Cal?"

He shook his head, trying to clear it.

"Aren't you going to say something?" she asked him.

He grinned. "Sorry…I guess I was preoccupied."

"We've got to quit thinking about sex," she mused.

"Okay, how's this for something to think about. We've found your money."

Natalie's jaw dropped, and for a moment it was her turn to look frozen. "What did you say?"

"We had a guy in Houston work on tracing Malcolm Braswell. He found him. He's in the Bahamas."

She leaned against her Beetle, still stunned. Then, as the implications struck her, she frowned worriedly. "But if Braswell's in the Bahamas, then who is the tire slasher?"

"That, we don't know." Cal shook his head. "Look, I don't want you getting your hopes up too much, Natalie. Your money hasn't been recovered— but now that he's been located, there's a chance that we can do something. If threatened with enough litigation, he might buckle under and agree to return some of your funds."

She shook her head. "Amazing! Do you know what that would mean?"

Did he actually need a reminder of the fact that she would bolt at the first available opportunity? If he did, all he had to do was look into her eyes right now. They sparkled at even the remote possibility of getting her treasure back.

Of course, he couldn't say as he blamed her. A couple million bucks was nothing to sneeze at, and God knows he would probably be real happy to see it again if it were his. But hell. Just when he thought all was right with the world, they now had this issue gumming up the works again.

Because if Natalie had her money back, would she really stay here?

That rapturous expression in her eyes wasn't exactly reassuring.

She clapped her hands together. "Oh, Cal—I'll be able to do everything I've wanted to do!"

"Like what?" he asked. "Move to Paris?"

She frowned at him. "What?"

"You're not going to stick around here, are you?"

She put her hands on her hips. "What are you getting at?"

He shrugged. "Nothing. I just can't imagine you settling down here when you have the whole world to choose from again."

"But I have to stay here. I'm committed to Heartbreak Ridge now."

"Commitments can be broken."

A thunderous look crossed her face. "I can see you still have a very high opinion of me!"

"I think the world of you."

She laughed. "So much that you think I'd quit my

job, abandon my plans for the inn, abandon *you* at the drop of a hat?''

''At the drop of a million dollars,'' he corrected.

She let out a shriek of frustration. ''Why are we even talking about this? I don't have a million dollars.''

''But if you did...''

''Chances are no amount of threats will pry that money away from Malcolm Braswell!''

''That's a possibility,'' he agreed. ''But if in your heart of hearts, and under ideal circumstances, you would want to leave Heartbreak Ridge, you shouldn't be ashamed to come right out and say it.''

''Well I'm not saying it,'' she insisted stubbornly.

Of course she wouldn't. *Love makes people lie,* he reminded himself. Just like he'd lied a few weeks ago when he'd told her Mopsy's shedding didn't bother him when actually it drove him nuts. A few days without vacuuming and his whole house looked as if it were wearing mohair. But he'd fibbed because he hadn't wanted Natalie to try to go rough it in that house of hers.

And of course, now he really didn't notice the hair that much. And, God help him, he liked those damn dogs of hers. But maybe that was just part of this little honeymoon they were having, too. Maybe someday he would wake up and discover the dogs were driving him berserk.

''You're really something!'' Natalie exclaimed. ''Have you ever trusted anyone in your life?''

''Sure—''

''A woman?'' she clarified.

His mouth snapped closed. There was her answer. She rolled her eyes. ''I might have known. I could stay here twenty years and you'd still be expecting me to run back to Houston, wouldn't you?'' When he said nothing, she responded heatedly, ''What have I been for you, Cal? Therapy? Are you just using me to get over your Connie-phobia? Were you always planning for this to end?''

''I've never known a woman with staying power.''

''What about Merlie? She's been here forever.''

''That's different. That's a job.''

The expression on her face caused her blond brows to be raised high on her forehead. ''Is that so? Well then, I'll tell you what. I hereby declare it my *job* to be a thorn in your side until you croak, Cal Tucker. I will stay in Heartbreak Ridge and annoy you for years with my dogged stick-to-itiveness. I will defy every unfair stereotype about women lodged in that pea-size brain of yours, and I will taunt you with my roverlike faithfulness. And you know why?''

He almost smiled. Was she going to tell him she loved him? ''Why?''

She roared her answer so that the whole town could hear. In fact, when he looked up he realized that people were congregating in doorways, enjoying the show. ''Because I love to watch you suffer! It's incredibly entertaining to look at you writhing in doubt and suspicion—nobody else does it half so well! When it comes to heartbreak, you're Michelangelo. You've got it down to an art form!''

She flounced into her car and slammed the door, speeding out of town fast enough that her car trailed a whirlwind of dust.

Behind him he heard a laugh. Gritting his teeth at the familiar cackle, he turned and saw Merlie holding a bag of groceries. No doubt she and half the town had just heard every word that had passed between him and Natalie.

"Why don't you drive after her and give her a ticket, lunkhead?"

"Because I can't give out tickets, remember?"

She hiked the groceries on her hip and used her free hand to poke her glasses back up her nose. "Oh, that's right, Mr. Not-Ready-To-Go-Back-To-Work-Yet. You've just been hanging out around the sheriff's office every day because you're trying to help Natalie. But it looks to me that if you really wanted to help her now you'd go after her and tell her that you were sorry."

He put his hands on his hips. "Sorry for what?"

She rolled her eyes. "If you have to ask that, *Deputy*, then you don't know doodly squat about anything, especially women!"

Cal grumbled to himself as she walked away from him. What did he have to apologize to Natalie for? For his well-founded suspicions that she would leave if she had all her money back? That was just common sense, and yet Merlie and Natalie were jumping on his case for voicing the obvious. But if he didn't face facts and keep his guard up, then when Natalie drove out of town everybody would be laughing at him and telling him what a chump he was.

What was he supposed to do? Just trust her?

As the last question rang in his ears, he felt his face pale. Some gear seemed to have shifted in his brain. *Trust.* There was a concept!

As he walked, zombielike, back across the street, he started thinking Merlie had erred a fraction. He knew about women, all right. And yet in spite of all his suffering this past year, it seemed he still didn't know doodly squat about love.

9

NATALIE ZOOMED UP the mountain, hugging the hairpin curves like Mario Andretti. Greenhorn? Ha! She was as used to driving this road now as she'd ever been accustomed to slogging through congested Houston freeways. Yes, and she should have been used to Cal and his insulting lack of faith in her, too. But was she?

The hot tears on her cheeks answered that twenty-thousand-dollar question for her. Cal thought she was a Connie, and he would always think she was a Connie. And maybe that assessment of her personality had been correct not too long ago, but she had changed; the trouble now was that Cal hadn't.

Well, dummy, what did you expect—that you could come to a town named Heartbreak Ridge and find happily ever after?

She veered onto the turnoff that led to her and Cal's places, but when she got to the fork in the road instead of following the asphalt driveway that led to Cal's she jounced down the worn dirt path to her own house, hoping Howard would still be there. Intentionally or not, he could usually make her laugh, and she needed a little of that medicine right now.

Unfortunately she didn't see his truck. She parked her car and stared up at her house. Despite weeks of nonstop toil, work that she took pride in, she and

Howard hadn't made a whole lot of progress; the place was still a mess. Dr. Seuss couldn't have envisioned a more absurd monstrosity. And yet when she looked at it, she still saw that silly drawing of the graceful mansion with the beautiful shrubs that had led her to toss one hundred precious dollars into a cockamamy raffle. She still saw the dream that made her leave everything else behind.

She turned off her car's engine and sighed. The roof was fixed. A few rooms were livable. There was even running water—outside. There was really no reason why she and the pets couldn't move back in now. She'd really only been staying at Cal's for the past few days because she'd enjoyed being with him. But now that she knew that things, like the old song said, had gone about as far as they could go between herself and Cal, she might be wise to mosey back down the hill for a spell. Not to play hard-to-get, and certainly not to run away, she assured herself, but to give herself some emotional distance from the situation. Clearly she had fallen in love, while Cal hadn't.

Hadn't *yet,* she dared to hope.

She got out of the car and wrinkled her nose. Something seemed strange. There was the faint odor of smoke in the air. She strode toward the porch a little more quickly, her prickling apprehension growing when she noted that the door was slightly ajar. What was going on? Had Howard run into trouble? God knows, just thinking about the antique wiring in this place scared her.

Her panic in full-sail now, she sprinted over the threshold and took the rickety old stairs two at a time. At first she thought her feet were making an incredibly loud echoing racket, until she reached the first landing and realized that there was no echo—just another pair of feet! She almost rammed smack into someone. She yelped and looked up, stunned to find herself face-to-face with the last man she ever expected to see in Heartbreak Ridge.

Jared Huddleton!

She gasped and said his name, stunned to be faced with her handsome, well-groomed ex-fiancé in the dingy surroundings of the house for which she'd abandoned their wedding. "What are you doing?" she asked, breathless. It was the only question she could spit out.

His eyes glittered. "I could ask you the same thing! Taking off from work early these days?"

He knew she was working? He'd been spying on her?

Of course he had, she realized. The vandalism, the scary writing. He'd done all of it. Had he been watching her all these weeks? Why?

Trying to keep her head clear, she concentrated on what he was saying to her and shook her head frantically. "I just left early today." But of course Jared hadn't come here to discuss her work schedule. Fingers of fear began to take hold of her throat, making speech difficult. "Jared…all this time…it's been you here, trying to scare me?"

He scowled at her. "Dumb me, I didn't realize till last week that you had a shoulder to cry on. I bought into your explanation that you were ditching me and going in for this inn scheme because you wanted to 'find yourself' or some such nonsense."

"I did!"

He sneered. "And in the process you just happened to 'find yourself' a squeeze up the hill?"

He was getting angry now, and she knew instinctively that was one thing she didn't want. Plus there was a gray haze coming down the stairs that made her quake in fear. She attempted to dash around Jared to see what was happening, but he blocked her.

"Why are you doing this?" she said, her tight voice practically a shriek.

"Because I wanted you to come home, Natalie. Back to Houston. Back to me."

And to think that back in Houston she'd thought he was overly suave! Right now his powers of persuasion seemed far from cool. "And *this* is your way of wooing back a woman? Scaring her half to death?"

He looked irritated, and she guessed immediately that she'd taken the wrong tone with him. He grabbed her arm and squeezed hard. In that moment, she knew. The man was a serious psycho. "I wouldn't know about winning a woman back because no woman's ever dumped me before, Natalie."

She willed herself to at least appear calm, though her heart flapped uncontrollably in her chest and it felt as though the circulation had stopped in her legs. "Believe me, Jared, what I did was for the best. Our marriage wouldn't have worked."

"You never gave me a chance!"

"*You* weren't the problem," she assured him. "It was me—I was wrong to have led you on. I…" She took a deep breath and admitted her deepest shame. "I was broke, Jared. Desperate. I was going to marry you for your money."

Oh God, she thought, *now he's really going to kill me.*

But he didn't. His crystal-clear blue eyes widened almost to popping, and the grip on her arm suddenly released. Natalie felt as though she might collapse, yet stood amazed when Jared started laughing. And not just a sneering laugh or a chortle, either, but a full-fledged belly laugh. In fact, he let out something like a howl as she gaped at him.

"What's so funny?" she demanded.

"You! Broke!" He gasped for breath. "Marrying me for money—" another breath "—when that was the reason I was marrying *you!*"

She hardly knew what to say. Jared Huddleton, a fortune hunter? She couldn't believe it—when he'd moved to Houston he'd seemed so charming, so well-off, so urbanely unemployed. And yet, that's probably how *she* had seemed, using up her last nickels so no one could tell how poor she was becoming.

She almost felt like laughing herself, except that there was smoke coming from the second floor. What did he plan to do, burn the house down and her with it?

"Jared, what have you done?"

He wiped a mirthful tear from his eye and looked up almost casually to the top floor. "A last-ditch effort to smoke you out, dear. I meant for you to find the place a cinder. I didn't know you were coming home early today."

But now that she'd caught him in the act of arson, what was he going to do, kill her? She felt her whole body tense, waiting for him to pull a knife or a gun or simply toss her backward down the stairs like in a movie. Instead he pushed her all right, but against a wall. Her head cracked against the old plaster, stunning her momentarily. When she looked up again, he had taken off running down the stairs himself.

She watched him flee from the house and wondered

briefly what the hell he was going to do next. But she didn't really have time to contemplate the matter. Instead she sprinted up the stairs and dashed around the bedrooms. Still she couldn't find the source of the smoke. Then, suddenly she looked up to the stairs leading to the attic, where smoked billowed out in angry clouds. Flames licked at the top of the narrow stairwell.

As she realized what this meant for her roof, she suddenly felt like screaming. They'd just finished it, and now it would be ruined! All their work—hard, backbreaking dangerous work—would be for nothing!

Well, not if she could help it!

She spun on her heels and flew down the stairs and ran outside. Howard had installed an outside faucet, and she hooked up the water hose she had bought in town, turned on the water to full blast and dashed up the stairs. The hose didn't reach all the way, but she aimed up the stairs and sprayed as much as she could. As the water met the heat, the smoke seemed to increase, and she had to pull her T-shirt up over her face to block out the smoke so she could keep breathing. Even so, she still felt a little woozy, but damn it, she was not leaving her house till this fire was out!

AS HE DROVE HIS TRUCK up the mountain at a crawl, Cal practiced saying "I'm sorry." They weren't words that seemed to fall trippingly off his tongue. In fact, when he caught a glimpse of himself in the rearview mirror, he jumped back in his seat in shock. His face was twisted into a painful-looking contortion, as if his lips were being forced to form torturous syllables.

He tried "I was wrong" but the results were even worse.

He was working on a simpler "forgive me" when he found himself almost colliding with a set of oncoming headlights. The jerk had on his high beams, nearly blinding him. Cal threw on his breaks and spun around to look at the car that had nearly run him off the road. A gold Mercedes jounced around a tight corner.

Gold. *Mercedes?*

Without thinking, Cal swung into action. He spun the truck around and raced down the hill after Mr. Mercedes, yelling curses at the truck as he went. Was the guy fresh off another attack on Natalie's house?

The thought made him push the pedal to the metal until he was right on the guy's bumper.

Damn! What he wouldn't do to have flashing lights and a siren right now. Not that this jerk would necessarily stop—he seemed perfectly willing to get them both killed—but right now Cal had absolutely no way to force the guy to stop except by using the truck to block him. Which he proceeded to do. He drove his vehicle alongside the Mercedes in a straightaway, and signaled at the driver to pull over and stop. To no avail. The character wasn't even glancing over at him. Instead he was barreling down the hill, his gaze pinned on the road like a man possessed.

But Cal was possessed, too—possessed with the desire to wring the man's neck. If he'd harmed one hair on Natalie's head…

In a move that he'd hoped never to see outside of

The Dukes of Hazzard reruns, Cal accelerated the truck to pass the Mercedes then jackknifed quickly and gritted his teeth. He heard the terrible squeal of tires, then the more awful sound of metal crunching against metal. A quick explosion followed and threw him back against his seat—his airbag deploying. When it was all over, he hopped out of the truck feeling rattled but unscathed and went to check on the other guy.

A white male in his thirties with brown hair sat staring straight ahead at the side of the truck he'd just hit. He looked stunned. Cal wasted no time opening the driver-side door, tugging him out and trying to shake some sense into him.

"Who the hell are you?" he demanded. "What are you doing driving down from Natalie's like a bat out of hell?"

At the mention of Natalie's name, the guy blinked. "She'll be okay."

It was all he could do not to scream. "Damn straight she'll be o—" A shiver prickled up his spine. "What do you mean? Did you see her?"

"I didn't do anything, it was an accident," the man blabbered. "We just argued, then I left."

"Argued about what?"

The man squinted. "It's a private matter."

The cool tone the jerk used was enough to send Cal over the edge; he was walking a tightrope of control. "What's your name?"

"Jared."

That almost tore it. *Jared*—the fiancé! So that's who had been bothering her, scaring her, vandalizing her house. Hell hath no fury like a millionaire playboy scorned, he supposed. The most galling thing about the realization was that Merlie had been right all along. She'd told them from the beginning that she suspected the boyfriend.

But back then he'd assumed that any man would be glad to be rid of Natalie.

Now his words came back to haunt him. Where was Natalie? Was she okay?

Before he could throttle the man to get the information out of him, flashing lights approached and stopped at the roadblock he'd created. Sam jumped out of the car.

"What the heck happened here?" he asked as he approached.

Cal frowned at his uncle. "I caught this guy speeding down from Natalie's—gold car, foreign make. And get this, he's Natalie's jilted fiancé."

Sam nodded and pulled the handcuffs off his belt. "Okay, cuff him and throw him in the back of my cruiser. We've got to clear this road to let the fire trucks through."

Fear froze Cal in his tracks. "Fire trucks?"

"Old man Withers saw a plume of smoke coming from the old house on Heartbreak Ridge. Natalie's house."

Cal didn't stop for more explanation than that. Handing Huddleton over to Sam, he jumped into his truck and wheeled it around—toward Natalie's.

His heart was pounding like a jackhammer. He couldn't make his old bucket go fast enough, though he was already screeching around corners, the big tires spitting up dirt as he accelerated.

He wanted to scream at all the precious time he'd wasted yammering with that jackass ex-fiancé of Natalie's when he should have headed back up the mountain the minute he suspected something fishy. He should have known she was in trouble. He gritted his teeth as he pulled off the road and saw the flames licking the dark sky.

He didn't even remember braking the truck. For all he knew, he might have jumped out of the thing while it was still running. It could roll right off the mountain for all he cared. *Where the heck was Natalie?*

He'd expected to find her outside, running around with that water hose of hers, but he didn't see her. Unfortunately he did see the water hose, and it led him right into the smoke-filled house.

The second he walked through the door it was as though he stepped through a threshold of heat and smoke. Waves of hot acrid air hit him, nearly blowing him back through the doorway, but he pushed forward, following the hose. There was no time to waste. If she'd been in this house for long, there was no telling what shape he'd find her in.

"Natalie!" He hollered her name as he ran up the stairs, and tried not to panic when he received no answer. *She's going to be okay,* he told himself. There was no way he was going to let anything bad happen to her. Finally he saw her, a slumped form in the hallway of the second floor, lying in a puddle of water that had cascaded down the stairs. He ran forward, grabbed her arms and hoisted her over his shoulders.

He nearly buckled with relief when he heard her let out a cough. He had to get her out into the fresh air, out of the smoke. A snippet from his police training came back to him. *Most victims of fire die from smoke inhalation.*

But Natalie wasn't going to die. He wasn't going to let her.

WHEN NATALIE'S EYES fluttered open, she was in a completely strange place where everything was hushed and downy white. She considered the possibility that she'd died and gone to heaven, but she changed her mind quickly when the face of Merlie Shivers appeared no more than six inches from her own face, peering down at her through rhinestone-rimmed glasses.

Not exactly the face of an angel, Natalie decided.

"It's okay, girls—she's coming to!" Merlie exclaimed.

Natalie blinked again. Coming to? How long had she been out?

She felt embarrassed, not to mention a little silly. What had happened? She'd never fainted before! She felt like apologizing, but to whom? Was Cal here?

Suddenly, two more faces appeared over her, squinting down at her with the same rapt relief as Merlie. One was Shelby Weston, her red locks spilling forward almost into Natalie's face. The other was Cody's wife. Ruby, she remembered.

Hey, she couldn't be too badly off if she could remember the names of people she'd only met a couple of times!

"Well for pity's sake don't wake Cal yet," Ruby said after giving Natalie an objective squint. "She looks like death warmed over."

Cal? Natalie's pulse skittered like a rodent's. Was Cal in the hospital? Was he okay?

Shelby punched her sister-in-law. "Don't say that! What if she can hear you?"

Natalie smiled, but doing so made her feel as if her entire face was going to crack.

Merlie put her hands on her hips and frowned at

the other two women. "She probably doesn't care one whit about how she looks. DO YOU?" When she addressed Natalie directly, she raised her voice, reminding Natalie of Howard. "CAN WE GET YOU ANYTHING?"

Natalie, suddenly realizing she was parched, licked her lips.

"Some of that Chap Stick for her lips," Shelby instructed.

Natalie waited patiently while her three nurses smeared goop on her lips, then she cleared her throat with effort. "Water…" She wasn't sure if the word came out right; surely no one since Helen Keller had had such a difficult time spitting out that one elemental word.

But from the delighted reaction of her audience, she had scored. "Did you hear that?" Ruby asked gleefully.

"She wants water!"

Merlie disappeared and she heard the wonderful sound of something being poured.

After she sipped the water Merlie brought to her, she was able to speak more easily. "Have I been here long?"

"Just overnight, hon."

Overnight! She tried to think back—the fire. She'd just been getting off work then. The confrontation with Jared spiked at her memory, but after that her mind was a blank. What had happened?

Then she remembered. The fire! She'd been trying to save her roof when she'd gone out like a light. One minute she'd been her own one-woman volunteer fire department, the next minute she'd been history.

"Who found me?"

"Cal," Merlie said. "He found you and pulled you out of the house."

"But he's okay?" She wanted that clarified.

All three heads bobbed.

"He stayed up with you all last night," Shelby gushed, "but Sam made him go back to the sheriff's office this morning to clean up and change clothes. He came back about an hour ago and passed out on a gurney in the hallway. No one has the heart to wake him."

Cal saved her life? More interestingly, he'd kept a bedside vigil all last night? He must have been some kind of worried.

She couldn't stop her pulse from racing. Why? Why would cranky heartsore Cal be all balled up with worry about little ol' her?

She grinned, and pushed herself up. "*I* have the heart!"

Three disapproving frowns met her action. "Honey, you'd better stay in bed," Merlie warned. "You've got a concussion."

She paid them no heed, swinging her legs off the bed and sitting up. "I've never felt better!" Her head was pounding, she smelled like a used ashtray and the "gown" they'd put her in was definitely lacking in the style department—for one thing, it had no back— but she was beyond caring. She jumped off the bed and hurried toward the door.

"Wait!"

The three women charged after her.

"You can't go out like that!" Merlie hollered.

Ruby, ever practical, ran after her with the top bed-sheet she'd just torn off the bed. "Here," she said, draping it over Natalie's shoulders.

Natalie swept out the door and was stopped cold by the sight that greeted her.

Cal. *In uniform!* In the old days, she might have been tempted to make a crack about the Boy Scouts or Barney Fife, but today, after what they'd been through, after what he'd done for her last night, the sight of him clean-shaven, propped upright on a gurney with his head falling forward in sleep and wearing his tan, pressed uniform nearly brought tears to her eyes.

She came right up to him and pressed a kiss against his forehead.

He let out a quick snort and bolted awake. It took him just a split-second to focus on her. A fleeting ear-to-ear grin dissolved into worry. "You shouldn't be up! What are you doing here—you should be in bed."

"So should you," she said, taking his hands in hers.

As she gazed lovingly into his eyes, the wariness she'd seen in them just last evening seemed to melt away.

"Natalie—I was so worried. We caught Jared."

"Good," she said. "But I don't care about Jared."

His face screwed up in puzzlement. "Don't care?"

"I knew he'd be no match against a crack team of cops like you and Sam."

He laughed. "Oh—your dogs are fine. The cats, too. Merlie fed them last night and she checked on them all this morning."

"I wasn't worried about them."

He tilted his head. "Well then, what else can I tell you?"

She smiled. "You can start by telling me how you are. And where you got those clothes!"

For a moment, she detected a blush in his cheeks. "It's my old uniform. Sam had it down at the office. If I was going to come back to the hospital, it was quicker going there than back home."

"Why were you so eager to get back here?" she asked. "Did the doctors want to check you out?"

He frowned. "No, of course not. I just wanted to be near you."

She grinned. "That's what I was hoping you'd say!" And with that, she jumped up on the gurney with him.

He looked almost shy. "Your house, Natalie...you won't be happy when you see it. The roof is a mess."

She sighed. "Well, at least I know how to fix it now."

Cal blinked. "Fix it? You mean you *still* want to try to make a go of that place?"

She laughed. "Cal, is there any part of the word yes you have trouble understanding?"

"But why? The place is a mess. If you got your money back you could—"

She didn't even let him finish. "Fix it up better. After all, even if the hotel flops, I think it will be a nice house to raise our kids in."

He did a double-take. "Our kids?"

She crossed her arms, which were all tangled up in the sheet she had draped over her. "That's right. You got a problem with that, Deputy?"

Cal shook his head, that million-dollar grin spreading from ear to ear again. "Maybe I should ask you to marry me."

She tilted her head. "Are you sure? The six weeks isn't up yet, if you recall. You'll lose your hundred dollars."

"But look what I'll be gaining." He pulled her into his arms. "No kidding, Nat. You really want to marry me?"

She nodded.

"Even though I'm nothing but a small-town deputy?"

"And an almost graduate of the University of Britannica," she reminded him.

"And what about Heartbreak Ridge? We'll be starting our marriage with the town curse over us."

"How can a town be cursed when it's seen three happy marriages in the space of a year?" She drew up to her full height and imperiously swung the sheet over her shoulder. "As the town's only unofficial baroness, I hereby declare the Heartbreak Ridge love curse over."

He pulled her into his lap for a long, lingering kiss. When they came up for air, he grinned at her. "I wonder if it will work."

"Our marriage?" Surely he wasn't having doubts already!

"No, your proclamation."

"There's only one way to find out," she said.

His dark blond brows arched in interest. "How?"

"If we make it to our silver wedding anniversary, then we'll know my decree worked."

He scoffed. "Twenty-five measly years? Is that the best you can wish for?"

She grinned. "What would you say?"

He drew her into his arms, not caring how many of the hospital staff stopped to gawk at them. Natalie didn't care, either. She was too happy—and too eager to taste those lips again.

"I say let's go for the gold, baroness. Fifty years or bust!"

Epilogue

CLARICE BIDDLES of River Oaks, Houston, stood on the graceful front porch of the Heartbreak Ridge Inn and looked around in wonder. "What a beautiful view!" she exclaimed to Jim Loftus, a local businessman taking advantage of the Inn's hospitality for the afternoon. They both held mint julep glasses in their hands as they stared out at the impressive landscape.

"Yep." Jim's jowly face was flushed with satisfaction, and julep. "I always did know that this place of mine would make a fine hotel."

"*Your* house?"

He looked at her with raised brows. "Didn't you know? Oh, sure, I got the ball rolling on this project. Sold the place to Natalie for a song, but then I just didn't have the time to spend on it..."

"And what a house—a perfect gem!"

Natalie came out the front door and heard the tag end of the conversation taking place on her porch. Jim Loftus, who had been coaxed away from Honolulu only by Natalie's long-distance promises that she bore him no ill will, was a regular at the Inn now. He usually came by for breakfast or happy hour to boast about how well the hotel had turned out. He was irritating, but Natalie could laugh at him. After all, everything *had* turned out well; how could she resent

Jim anymore when his swindling her had resulted in her getting everything she'd ever wanted?

"There are some of those little muffins you like, Jim, fresh out of the oven. You should go grab some."

Jim broke into a bigger grin. "Don't mind if I do!" He scurried off to sample the goods, leaving a very interested Clarice in his wake.

"My…" she said, watching Jim's lumpy retreating figure with open interest. "He seems very well-off. Is he a bachelor?"

"Yes, he is," Natalie said, trying her level best to hold back a shriek of laughter.

Clarice clasped her hands together and leaned confidentially toward the woman she still considered one of her oldest and dearest friends, even after a year and a half of not speaking to her. "I must say that I was worried about booking myself into a place called Heartbreak Ridge Inn…one thinks of Heartbreak Hotel, and then one thinks of white sequins and black velvet paintings."

"One does?" Natalie grinned.

Clarice clucked her tongue. "Well naturally. All those tacky Elvis things."

Natalie smiled patiently. "The town of Heartbreak Ridge predates Elvis."

"I suppose some things do," Clarice said absently. "Anyhow, I never expected to find interesting men here. Or at least wealthy single ones. Natalie, there are just no good men in Houston anymore!"

Clarice sipped her mint julep and gave Natalie all the gossip about their friends back in Houston. At length. Natalie listened to the tales with waning interest. True, she was as fond of juicy tidbits of gossip as the next person, but whereas she might have been consumed with interest in what Clarice was saying a few years ago, now she had other, more important matters consuming her attention. Her inn, more successful than she could have dreamed, was a full-time job and more. Thanks to her investing in advertisement in state publications, there was rarely a room free on weekends, and even with help Natalie always felt as if she were two chores behind.

But she still took time out to play. That was one thing Cal insisted on. They had as yet forty-eight years to go to break the Heartbreak Ridge curse, and until that time, they intended to stay as fresh as newlyweds...with maybe just a few spats thrown in for good measure.

Luckily, the one thing they didn't have to worry about was money. Malcolm Braswell had been caught trying to sneak back into the country and was prosecuted on multiple counts of theft. True to Sam and Cal's predictions, in return for a lighter sentence, the accountant had forked over a considerable percentage of what he'd stolen. With that money, Natalie had fixed up her place and opened its doors last summer. And she still had enough left over for security...and maybe a few college funds.

"And oh, my," Natalie rattled on, "wasn't that something about poor Jared? Getting married in jail— to a prison guard!"

Natalie laughed. She could only assume the guard was well fixed...or that Jared thought she was.

Clarice shook her head. "I guess you never can tell about people, can you? You think you know them and..." Something in the yard caught her eye and she let out a delighted cry. "Oh, look!" Howard was pushing a wheelbarrow slowly up the hill toward the house. "What cute rustic little people you've hired!"

Natalie grinned. "I was going for an authentic look."

Howard frowned at the newest guest. He was always appalled that they'd worked so hard to provide temporary housing for such unworthy people. One glance at Clarice's tan silk pantsuit and strappy high-heeled sandals and he looked as if he'd sucked on a sour pickle.

"Howard, this is Clarice Biddles. We were sorority sisters in college."

"YOU MEAN TO TELL ME SHE WENT TO COLLEGE AND SHE'S STILL DUMB ENOUGH TO BUY SHOES LIKE THAT?"

Clarice's jaw dropped, and Natalie bit her lip trying not to laugh. She was about to try to usher Clarice inside when the sound of hoofbeats pricked up her ears.

As Cal rode into view, her heart did an elaborate pirouette in her chest. He might be wearing his uniform, but he still had the long hair, the deep tan and the dazzling blue-eyed gaze that had first taken her breath away. He took it now as he galloped toward her.

"Oh, my!" she heard Clarice exclaim, her gaze taking in Cal appreciatively. "Who is *that?*"

Natalie grinned. "More rustic local color."

"A lawman right on the premises?" Clarice said admiringly. "That would be handy!"

Howard just looked irritated. "*I'M* THE HANDY-MAN. HE'S JUST THE HUSBAND!"

Fortunately Cal didn't give Natalie the opportunity to make introductions. He thundered up and, barely stopping, swept Natalie up behind him on the horse. She heard Clarice let out a gasp of surprise.

"Busy?" Cal asked, pressing a kiss to his wife's lips.

The kiss lingered longer than either of them intended.

"Not so busy that I can't stop to be abducted and ravished."

"Your wish is my command, baroness."

Natalie, feeling as she always did these days that she had the world on a string, let out a whoop of delight as they galloped happily into the sunset.

Keepsake Cowboy

CARRIE ALEXANDER

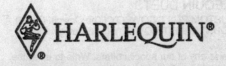

TORONTO • NEW YORK • LONDON
AMSTERDAM • PARIS • SYDNEY • HAMBURG
STOCKHOLM • ATHENS • TOKYO • MILAN • MADRID
PRAGUE • WARSAW • BUDAPEST • AUCKLAND

Dear Reader,

It simply wasn't possible for me to write a trilogy
like THE COWGIRL CLUB without including an
inherited ranch. This being Duets, however, my
take on the traditional ranch story is slightly askew.
Or, as Laramie Jones says after arriving at the Lazy J,
"Everything here is inside out and upside down."

While Laramie's cowgirl enough to handle the
world's slowest barrel racer, an impotent rooster and
a visit from her mother, her two new roommates—
broken-down rodeo cowboy Jake Killian and a nasty
brute named Goliath—are another matter. Does
Laramie earn her spurs? Will Jake and Goliath ever
bond?

Turn the page and find out!

Happy reading!

Carrie Alexander

Books by Carrie Alexander

HARLEQUIN DUETS
25—CUSTOM-BUILT COWBOY (The Cowgirl Club I)
32—COUNTERFEIT COWBOY (The Cowgirl Club II)

Prologue

Laramie Jones swung open the door to her studio apartment on the second floor of a narrow Brooklyn brownstone. Grace Farrow and Molly Broome stood in the hall, smiling expectantly.

"Welcome to the ranch," Laramie said, after an awkward pause. Even though she'd lived here for a year—since she was nineteen—this was the first time her two best friends had visited. They'd all been busy with college classes, but now that summer had come they were ready to resume their more frivolous Cowgirl Club activities.

Grace burst inside and twirled around the room. She was as colorful as ever, from her curly copper hair to the lime green jeans no other self-respecting Manhattanite would dare attempt. "Laramie—cowgirl! Where's all your furniture? Don't tell me you've been ripped off!"

The banter was familiar. Laramie's shoulders relaxed. "Whaddaya mean? I like it this way."

"Of course you do." Molly, a curvaceous brunette dressed in a plain blouse and khaki walking shorts, gave Laramie a warm hug before stepping into the nearly empty room. She confronted a low, tightly upholstered daybed. "Then again, a few pillows wouldn't hurt…"

"And candles," Grace piped, inspecting the austere galley kitchen.

"No pillows. No candles." From the open doorway, Laramie's glance traveled up the twisting steps that led to her mother's rented room in the attic, where she and her gang of loonies had gathered for their daily ritual of praying, chanting and meditation. A familiar odor seeped out from beneath her mother's door: incense, essential oils, potpourri, plus three kinds of cigarettes—clove, Camel and cannabis.

"Thanks, but no thanks." Laramie closed her door. "I relax my guard to let in one frill and next thing my mom will attack the place with batik wall hangings, buddha statues and incense burners." In the past year on her own, she'd learned to find her own serenity in silence, clean lines and empty space.

Grace straddled a hard wooden chair. "And how is Sana Shakira?" she asked with a teasing lilt, referring to Laramie's mother's temporary Arabic name.

Molly perched on the daybed. "You mean Glory Warrior." The running-with-the-wolves period.

Laramie shook her head. "These days, my mother's calling herself Sunshine Destiny. And she swears she's thriving, now that she's discovered macrobiotics."

"Goodness." Molly's smile was accompanied by a cute dimple. "And here I was going to suggest a barbecue blowout for our first Cowgirl Club meeting of the summer."

"Sounds good to me." Though Laramie had grown up on a vegetarian diet supplemented by holistic medicine and spiritual cleansing, she'd been rebelling with the occasional Big Mac or red-hot spare rib ever since.

"Followed by a long horseback ride through Central Park." Grace was always eager to give her riding horse, Dulcinea, the Cowgirl Club's official equine mascot, a good workout. "Dulcie was terribly neglected during spring exams."

Laramie sat beside Molly. "So was the club."

They'd started the Cowgirl Club a decade ago when they were ten, more interested in ponies than cowboys. Although that had changed, so far none of their boyfriends had come even close to cowboy standards.

"Say, guys? I've been wondering." Laramie's throat tightened, but she kept her voice noncommittal. "Now that we're twenty and in college, are we too mature for the Cowgirl Club?"

Although Laramie felt she had to ask, she found herself holding her breath, fearing the answer. For her, the Cowgirl Club had always been something more significant than horseback riding and John Wayne movies. It had been a way to keep her mother's stories of her long-lost cowboy father real rather than fiction.

After a silence, Molly said, "Well, my and Grace's trip out west during spring break was a major disappointment."

Grace twirled one of her corkscrew curls. "Our tour group was thick with balding middle-aged white guys who'd taken City Slickers way too seriously."

"And New York's not exactly teeming with cowboy possibilities, either," Laramie said, to agree. Of course, she didn't intend to stay in New York forever. One day soon, she would return to the namesake city of her birth. She'd find her father. She'd put down roots.

Molly nodded. "That's right. We should be practical. I've got a summer job at the bagel shop, Grace has her brother's wedding, you've got both work and…" She pointed at the ceiling.

"Sunshine Destiny," Laramie said with a sigh. Her mother needed looking after, else she'd take it into mind to quit her recent incarnation as a part-time book shop clerk and hitchhike to Backwater, Oklahoma to worship at the site of the latest weeping Mary statue or wacky UFO sighting.

Another silence ensued.

Laramie closed her eyes, trying to prepare herself. When the whoosh of Mrs. Kovacs flushing her john next door drowned out the faint sounds of chanting and Indian sitar music that floated down from the attic, she blurted, "So. We're agreed. It's time to quit."

Grace shot up. She flapped her arms in distress. "Quit the Cowgirl Club!"

Molly gripped the edge of the daybed. "Quit the Cowgirl Club?"

Laramie looked at them, certain of her own dedication to the club, less sure of theirs. "Yes," she said. "Quit…" She could not continue.

"No way," Grace said. "No freakin' way!"

"We've only just begun to barbecue," Molly vowed.

Immense relief washed over Laramie. She reached for the worn black Stetson that had been her talisman for as long as she could remember. It was proof of her father's existence, perhaps of his love. *Wait for me, dad, wherever you are. I haven't forgotten you. Someday, somehow, I'm coming to Wyoming.*

She put on the hat and grabbed Molly's hand, then reached for Grace's, too. "Cowgirls," she said with a wide smile, "one and all."

"Cowgirls," Molly repeated, beaming.

Grace flung back her head. "Yee-haw!"

1

THE MAN WAS A GENUINE COWBOY.

Laramie Jones pressed her lips together; the room was so silent the resulting small click of her teeth was audible. She grimaced and shifted on the sofa cushion, crossing her legs, running a palm along the seam of her slim black skirt to check that the side slit wasn't showing too much thigh. Not that the cowboy was looking or listening.

He was sleeping.

Laramie glanced at the lawyer's closed office door, behind which a full-figured, sixtyish secretary had disappeared five or ten minutes ago. After Laramie's long flight from New York, which had included connections in Chicago and Denver and a lengthy landing delay at the Laramie, Wyoming, airport, she should have welcomed the breather. She should have caught a few winks herself.

Hah. Not with *him* in the room.

This was a fine howdy-do. It either had to be the cowboy slumped across from her or the prospective meeting with Buck Jones's lawyer that was giving her the goose-bump heebie-jeebies. Frankly, as shocking as the news about Buck Jones had been, her money was on the cowboy. Though his weren't the first pair of cowboy boots and tight-fittin' jeans she'd spotted in her short time in Wyoming, they were certainly the most…the most…

Laramie touched a fingertip to the indent above her top lip.

Let's be blunt, cowgirl. His were the most provocative. By a country mile.

Whatever that meant.

Country or city, she'd walk a mile in strappy stiletto sandals for a glimpse of this man in chaps. She'd walk even farther to see him on a bucking bronc, but of course she was slightly nuts when it came to cowboys. Ever since her friends Grace Farrow and Molly Broome had gone west and roped their men, as it were, Laramie had become even more intent on fulfilling her own cowboy destiny.

She recrossed her legs, unusually fidgety.

Psychologically, she was skating on thin ice. Who knew how badly her long inner search for a mythical cowboy father figure had messed with her head? Pile on fifteen years with Grace and Molly and their rootin'-tootin' Cowgirl Club and, sheesh, let's face it, she was obviously not dealing with a full deck when it came to her limitless desire for all things cowboy.

Nevertheless, Laramie had to suppress a shiver each time she looked at the bronco-busted cowboy sprawled across from her. Her reaction didn't feel like a head trip. It felt like one-hundred-per-cent pure physical attraction.

Suddenly the cowboy spoke from beneath the beat-up straw hat that covered all but his five-o'clock shadow. "Never seen a cracked-up rodeo cowboy, have ya, Miz Jones?"

For one excruciating instant, Laramie was paralyzed. Then she gave a toss of her head and continued her perusal even more blatantly. "Is that what your style is called?"

She dragged her gaze up the worn denim molded to his crossed legs, past the tarnished rodeo buckle, over the crumpled shirt, bandages, bruises and raw scrape on his chin. One side of her lip lifted with a ladylike distaste that was entirely manufactured. The cowboy's insolent drawl had pricked at her composure even more than the strong sense of animal attraction…and she didn't like it.

She sniffed. "I wondered."

His shoulders shifted negligently. "You and your fancy New York designer labels ain't got nothin' on me."

"And for that we remain ever so grateful."

The cowboy raised a hand and slid the straw hat back a few inches so he could peer out at her. "You don't like it, send in the fashion police."

"I'm afraid their jurisdiction doesn't extend this far west." She flicked a piece of lint off the sleeve of her loosely draped Donna Karan top—an outlet store bargain, but he didn't have to know that. "More's the pity."

Deliberately he took his own good time to do a retaliatory once-over. His full, sexy lips formed a teasing grin. "Miz Jones, you're one long cool drink of water."

Though she'd held herself still for the inspection, his continued use of her name made her clench her hands and narrow her eyes. "Do you know me?"

"Nope. I knew Buck Jones."

The man who might be her father. Laramie's hollow stomach folded in on itself. She'd assumed the cowboy was here on another matter. "You're not…"

"Jake Killian," he said. "I'd stand to shake, Miz Jones, but it'd take a crane to hoist me off this chair."

She uncrossed her legs and sat up straight, poised on the edge of the couch, her palms placed over her kneecaps. Why was she breathing so heavily? Why was her heart pounding so hard?

"Buck's your…" She swallowed. "I don't understand what your relationship was to Mr. Jones."

"Me, neither."

His throwaway tone was frustrating. "But you did know him?" she pressed.

"Twelve, thirteen years ago, he was my stepfather. For the blink of an eye." The cowboy tilted up the brim of his hat and she saw his eyes, crinkled at the corners, too dark to decipher. "And you, Miz Jones?" he asked, drawing out the *z* in a way that was intentionally vexatious. "I take it you're a relation?"

"Perhaps." She could be as circumspect as he.

"I hear you're from New York City."

"More or less."

"Got a round-trip ticket?"

Her brows rose. "Is that any of your business?"

He shrugged. "Seein' as how we're partners…"

"Partners," she repeated, startled. But of course he was right. According to recent correspondence and telephone calls from the lawyer, Robert Torrance, she and Jake Killian were Buck Jones's heirs, fifty-fifty. Whoever this man was, whatever his apparently downtrodden circumstances, he'd been as important to Buck Jones as she, the long-lost daughter.

Laramie Jones, a stranger estranged, and Jake Killian, cracked-up rodeo cowboy, were full partners in Buck's legacy, a ranch called the Lazy J.

Good God.

"Actually, your being a city girl should work out just fine." Jake cut the air with the side of his hand. "Let's keep this simple. Sell out, split the profits down the middle. No complications." His dark lashes flicked at her. "No grief."

Laramie's tone turned to ice. "It might be better to wait until after we've seen the lawyer before you begin counting up your share of the proceeds."

Jake—for now, she preferred to think of him as "the cowboy"—was not bothered. He stretched, moaning softly, then interlocked his fingers atop the rodeo buckle, momentarily drawing her attention to regions below his belt. "So you've never seen the Lazy J?"

Her gaze rebounded to his face. "No, I have not."

He chuckled. "I want to be there when you do."

Laramie was confused. What was he insinuating? Was the ranch a showplace? A wreck?

Probably neither, she decided. Which was okay. Just about anything in between would suit her fine. And her so-called partner could stuff his sell-out scheme where the sun don't shine, as they said in this part of the country.

After twenty-five years, Laramie Jones was heading home, a stranger no more.

Of course, that would make this Jake person her actual partner. Which was…an irritating prospect. But not as irritating as it ought to be, considering his cold-hearted, uncompromising attitude.

Laramie studied his face. It was a good face. Very masculine. Handsome, even. Certainly not as beat-up as the rest of him, aside from the scrape on his chin. However, there were flaws. There had to be. The bump on his nose, for instance. It was huge. Such brown skin must be leathery to the touch. Even though he was probably in his early thirties, he already had laugh lines and crow's feet—sun damage, for sure. His lips were *too* full. And that bristly, unshaven look didn't cut it with her. What was it with cowboys? Didn't they know that disposable razors were a dime a dozen?

Laramie looked away, avoiding the teasing glint in the cowboy's dark eyes. The heebie-jeebies were back, so she studied the office with a concentration that was intense. Old yellowed wallpaper, a beamed ceiling, parchment lamp shades with rawhide stitching, furnishings made from sturdy oak. The scent of stale cigar smoke hung in the air. An expensive beaver-pelt cowboy hat hung on a rack near the door.

She broke the silence with an abrupt question. "Aren't cowboys supposed to remove their hats indoors? In the presence of a lady?"

"Been reading the cowboy handbook?" Jake swept off his battered straw hat with a conciliatory nod. "'Scuse me, Miz Jones. I must have been sleeping on my manners when you arrived."

His hair was thick, dark, wavy. A bit too long and uncombed, but she liked it that way. Cowboys and blow dryers were not compatible.

"Did Buck Jones wear a hat when you knew him?" she asked suddenly. "A black Stetson?"

After a moment, Jake nodded. "Yeah, he always wore a black Stetson. Kinda his trademark." He gave an amused harrumph. "Buck fancied himself a bad guy."

"But he wasn't." Laramie was fearful of discovering that her father had been a dishonorable man.

After all these years, how could she compromise her grandiose cowboy hero image with an ugly truth?

"No-o-o," Jake said slowly, as if he had his own expectations to contend with. "I wouldn't say Buck was a bad guy."

Laramie's relief was such that she missed the cowboy's hesitation. She was about to ask more when the door to the inner office opened and the bespectacled secretary emerged, followed by the lawyer, Robert Torrance. "Sorry to keep you waiting, folks," he said, coming forward with his hand extended. He was a small, skinny man in a big, broad-shouldered suit, even younger than she'd expected. *His* chin was barely touched with peach fuzz, so he had an excuse for going unshaven.

The secretary took charge of introductions. "Bobby, this is Ms. Jones."

"Laramie," she said, and he said "Laramie" in agreement. They shook, Robert Torrance overcompensating for his pip-squeak voice with a grip that was a shade too strong.

"And you already know Buck's stepson," the secretary continued. She smiled at Laramie, woman-to-woman, her eyes twinkling behind thick lenses. "Did you two introduce yourselves after Jake woke up from his little catnap?" Laramie nodded, responding with an answering smile despite herself. *Ain't that man one fine hunk of cowboy?* seemed to be the secretary's underlying message. How could Laramie not agree?

"Jake Killian! It's been a long time." The young lawyer offered his hand, not quite as eagerly as he had with Laramie. She understood why. Even bandaged, the cowboy's hand looked rough as sandpaper and strong enough to crush a lump of coal into a diamond.

Jake shook gingerly. "Bobby Torrance? I was expecting your father."

Bobby's expression turned sorrowful. "Dad passed on two and a half years ago. Stroke. I took over the business right after I passed the bar."

"And he's doing a fine job," the secretary said, all motherly encouragement, though she resisted patting the young lawyer's sandy-colored curls.

"Really. Well, sorry to hear that. About your dad." Jake tapped his hat against his thigh. "Hell, Bobby. Last time I saw you was in Little Britches rodeo—you were no bigger than a mosquito, gettin' bucked off that scrawny mustang...."

Bobby Torrance laughed uncomfortably. "I guess that's why I went on to law school instead of the rodeo circuit."

Jake touched the red scrape on his chin. "Smart boy."

Bobby scowled doubtfully. His face cleared when he turned to his other client. "Laramie Jones—now, you were a tough person to get a hold of. I had to hire an investigator and even she took a month finding you. New York City was the last place Buck expected your mother to take you."

Laramie's heart skipped a beat. "Buck Jones was...looking...for...us?" she said faintly. "For me?"

The young lawyer swallowed; the bolo tie cinching his collar bobbed in sync with his prominent Adam's apple. "I dunno what, if anything, he did about finding you when he was alive. But he came to me a while back to make out a will, naming you and Jake.

He gave me what he knew about you, Laramie. Which wasn't much, I have to say. He wasn't even sure of your surname.''

Neither was I, Laramie thought.

"When Buck passed on a couple of months ago—"

"Cancer," the secretary mouthed, patting Laramie's shoulder.

Bobby continued. "I reviewed the terms of his will and initiated a search for both of you. I knew where Jake was, more or less—it was simply a matter of catching up with him. But you…" The lawyer shook his head. "Buck had me looking for a Laramie Vogel, or a Laramie, er, Lightbringer, I believe. That you'd be going by Laramie Jones didn't occur to him."

"My mother doesn't believe in conventional names," Laramie murmured. Years ago, when prowling through boxes of junk stored in the back of their van in preparation for another move, she'd come across papers that identified her mother as Patricia Ann Vogel. Even at eight years old, Laramie had known that her mother would never be like other mothers. She'd never answer to Patty Ann.

"She'd started calling herself Bringer of Light around the time that I was a baby," Laramie explained, recalling the personal history that, though sketchy and unreliable, was still her only link to her father. According to her mom, they'd lived in a teepee in Arizona for the first three years of Laramie's life— Bringer of Light's Native American period. "I've never been sure where the Jones name came from, myself."

"Gosh." Somewhat awkwardly, Bobby took her hand in a comforting gesture. "I do wish we'd found you sooner. I'm sorry you missed your father's funeral.''

Laramie paused. Hearing the man, Buck Jones, referred to as her father gave her a start. Perhaps she carried his DNA, but now that he was dead he would forever remain a stranger. As would she. Unless the ranch proved to be a true home.

"I appreciate that." She gave Bobby's fingers a brief squeeze in thanks; the young lawyer turned beet red. "I understand that it couldn't be helped." She aimed a sidelong glance at the cowboy who'd been Buck's stepson. "Did Jake make it, at least?"

"'Fraid not," the cowboy said easily, answering for himself. "I was in Vegas."

"We arranged for a nice funeral," Bobby said quickly.

"In your initial letter you wrote that there's no other family except a distant cousin," Laramie said. "I'm glad Buck's friends could attend, at least."

The lawyer shifted. "Er, sure..."

"I was there," the secretary said helpfully.

Bobby nodded. "We sent flowers."

Laramie turned, her brows rising. "Jake?"

He shrugged. "The Buck I knew wasn't much interested in flowers."

Her father must have been a rough, gruff cowboy, Laramie told herself. A loner. From the sound of it, he didn't have need for either family or close friends. Still, he'd wanted to find her.

Just not, apparently, while he was alive.

Her sense of disappointment was growing. She tried to push it aside, toward the vast and empty gulf of unanswered questions and hopeless dreams. This hollow space inside herself was something she'd learned to live with. Only now, when her hopes had risen only to be dashed once more, was she keenly aware of how empty it could still make her feel.

"Let's go to my office," Bobby Torrance was saying, "and discuss the terms of Buck's will."

The Lazy J, Laramie said to herself, latching onto the ranch like a life preserver. She still had the Lazy J. One way or another, she would find her answers. She would make herself a home.

BABY BOBBY TORRANCE droned on for fifteen minutes, flashing every fancy legal term he knew in an effort to impress the long-legged beauty seated beside Jake. Not that Jake blamed the boy. As women went, Laramie Jones was the kind of hot-blooded filly a cowpuncher didn't come across too often, particularly in the wilds of Wyoming. And Idaho. Utah, Nevada, Arizona, New Mexico…

He'd been there, he'd done 'em all. But no one like her.

It was a shame their acquaintance would be so short. In fact, Jake wouldn't be here at all if he hadn't needed a temporary hideout. The Lazy J would have to do, even though he'd once sworn that he'd rather tear his own cast off with his teeth than return to Buck's schizophrenic petting zoo.

What the hell. He'd already done the cast thing. In Houston. A big-time event. The bull-riding purse had been too healthy and the newly crowned rodeo queen too tempting to let a one-week-from-mended wrist fracture stand between him and rodeo cowboy glory.

But that had been the good old days. Before he turned thirty and realized he was feeling his injuries long after the dust had settled in his rearview mirror.

Jake tuned back in, even though listening to Baby Bobby gave him a pain—one thing he didn't need right now. His nap in the reception area hadn't done him much good in that regard, either. He felt stiff and sore and altogether crushed—something to be expected, considering that only yesterday he'd been stomped on by a bull named Black Tornado. Black Tornado was the terror of the rodeo circuit, worth major prize money to the contestant who could stay on his back till the buzzer.

Jake had been a fraction of a second away.

Turned out one hell of a lot could happen in a fraction of a second.

Like wrist sprains and pain pills and double shots of whiskey and very bad decisions to play poker with the Naylor brothers, who were dishonorable enough in the rodeo arena, but downright crooked when it came to cards.

"Jake, you with us?" Bobby asked with an indulgent glance.

Jake's wrist was on fire and his entire body felt as mangled as roadkill, but he managed to nod without wincing. He was with them as far as he wanted to be, having gathered that Laramie—odd coincidence, that name—truly was the daughter Buck Jones had never told anyone but his lawyer that he had. From the tenor of her questions, she knew next to nothing about Buck, even less about what she was inheriting.

She cut Bobby off midbequest. "What about the ranch?"

"The ranch? Oh…Buck's place." Bobby was smiling as he shook his head. He glanced at Jake to share the joke. "Aw, shucks. Wouldn't old Buck have loved hearing the Lazy J called a ranch?"

Jake's amusement was fleeting. "Yep."

Laramie frowned, looking from one to the other. "It's not a ranch?"

Bobby flipped through papers. "Well, there's a ranch house and, yeah, there's a piece of land that goes with it. The deed is in a safety deposit box. You and Jake share the place equally, same as everything else."

"You mentioned livestock."

"The animals have been a problem. I hired a neighbor boy to care for them since Buck's death, but I'm afraid the situation's gotten rather hairy." Bobby glanced again at Jake. "Do you remember Goliath?"

"Goliath's still kickin'?" Jake said, thinking, *Oh, sonovabee. Goliath.*

"Meaner than ever."

Laramie blinked. "Who's Goliath?"

"Buck's stallion," Bobby answered. "In his prime, Goliath's stud fees brought in a pretty penny. Buck could have sold him for a good chunk of change, but he wouldn't even entertain offers. He claimed the horse was the only friend he'd ever had who didn't expect anything of him."

Jake was taken aback for an instant, recognizing the concept. Then he smirked. "The man was sentimental. Soft." *Nothing like me.*

"Sounds more like loyalty," Laramie commented, shooting darts at Jake with her darkly luminous cat's eyes.

He only shrugged. "You'll see."

"There's also another horse," Bobby added. "A quarter horse that used to be a champion barrel racer. Buck had registration papers on both."

"A barrel racer," Laramie said in wonder. She

touched a palm to her high forehead, brushing back
a strand of the black silky hair that was gathered into
a loose knot at her nape. Stray wisps caressed her
neck, which was long and graceful, white as a swan's.
Jake imagined his rough brown hand there, gentling
her to his touch.

"A *retired* barrel racer," he heard himself say ruthlessly. He, who'd just risked his hide and his reputation to keep his own horse—a buckskin mare he'd
raised from a filly—out of the hands of the dirty,
stinkin' rotten cardsharps who'd taken advantage of
his recent incapacitation. "Good for nothing except a
feed bill."

Laramie's lips pursed with agitation, but she barely
spared him a glance. "You're a hard man, Mr. Killian."

"Yep," he said, not bothered. Lucky for cool,
sleek, butter-wouldn't-melt Miz Laramie Jones, she
didn't know how right she was.

"I can't imagine that Buck wanted us to be partners
in the ranch."

Jake said nothing, his expression flinty. Hell, she
could have the ranch for all he cared. So long as he
had a few days, a week, maybe, of reprieve. Once he
was up to snuff, he was out of here.

Baby Bobby's face was a dull red. "As a matter
of fact..." He cleared his throat. "My feeling is that
Jake was named mostly as a fallback position. In case
we couldn't locate you, Laramie. Buck didn't want
his property to revert to the state and be sold piece-
meal."

"That sounds about right," Jake muttered. So he
was Buck's convenience, huh? Well, Buck was his,
too. Good thing he hadn't gone and gotten all sloppy

over the man's parting gesture. Good thing he hadn't started believing that his temporary stepfather might have either remembered or cared.

"Then Buck's wishes were that we don't sell," Laramie said, pouncing on Bobby's words with a triumphant so-there for Jake.

He rolled his eyes. Aw, hell. Buck's bastard daughter was going to get sentimental about the old man.

"There's no provision in the will against it," Bobby said, and Jake was sorry that he'd been thinking of the young lawyer as Baby Bobby Torrance, the whiny little mama's boy he remembered from thirteen years ago. If the red tape of the situation got complicated—and Jake was figuring Laramie for an awfully complicated woman—Bobby might be an important ally to coddle.

"I want to see this ranch before I make up my mind about how to proceed," Laramie said, looking like a woman who was quick and firm about her decisions.

Jake didn't bother getting worked up over their potential conflict. One glimpse of the Lazy J should upset her applecart but good, without any shoves from him.

"I'll be glad to take you," Bobby offered, his voice rising to a squeak of willingness.

"I can do it," Jake insisted, finding that despite his age and assorted ills he could get to his feet pretty darn fast when he wanted to. "I'm heading that way, anyhow. Gotta hang my hat somewhere for a few days."

Laramie looked dismayed. "But *I* was going to stay there."

Jake shook his head. "Believe me, Miz Jones, a gal like you would prefer a nice clean hotel."

"A gal like me?" She crossed her arms, turning her shoulder to Jake while she addressed Bobby. "I'll be staying at the Lazy J. I don't care how rustic it is."

Jake snorted. "Rustic? That's not how I'd put it."

"I'll get the keys," Bobby said, neatly removing himself from the conversation.

Laramie stared into space, her chin jutting. "I don't believe the ranch is as bad as you're making out, Jake. So you can just forget about scaring me off. The Lazy J is my legacy. I mean to do it justice in a way that would make my father proud."

Legacy? Justice? Pride? For an offspring of Buck Jones's, the woman had some high-falutin' ideas. Jake was almost sorry that her comedown would be so harsh.

"Fine by me" was all he said. "We can be room-mates. For the duration." Which was sure to be short, on at least one of their parts. Mixing a transplanted woman with grand expectations, a broken-down ro-deo cowboy with none, and the god-awful abode called the Lazy J was a sure recipe for disaster.

"SO YOU LIVED WITH BUCK more than a decade ago." Laramie fastened her seat belt, then gazed steadily at Jake while he drove from the law office's small lot. Her eyes were hidden behind dark sun-glasses. "That's a long time. And there's been no contact between you two since?"

He knew she was only trying to figure out his place in the scheme of things. All the same, he'd never taken kindly to being put on the spot. "Did I say that?"

"Your lack of feeling certainly implied it."

"So sue me. Buck and I weren't close. We liked it that way." After a minute, he relented. "I left town when I was seventeen. Buck's marriage to my mother was already rocky. She moved on three, four months later. Since then, I've seen Buck a handful of times—always by chance when I was competing in local rodeos. I never knew he was sick."

"Yet you were named in the will. Buck must have placed more importance on your relationship than you believe."

"You heard what Bobby said."

"I don't buy it. You were always going to be a full partner, whether or not I was found. Seems meaningful."

"Does that bother you?" he mocked. "Are you worried that Buck gave me the legal say-so to horn in on your vast inheritance?"

An odd expression flickered across her face. "It's not the value of the property I care about."

"Good thing," Jake said grumpily as he slowed for a stoplight. He forgot and clenched his fingers on the wheel; searing slivers of pain shot toward his right elbow. *Holy hell.*

He gritted his teeth. It was Laramie's fault. Her questions were getting to him, distracting him, prodding at what had been his complacent psyche, bringing up old resentments that were better left buried.

He glanced quickly at her before turning wide through the intersection, proceeding cautiously because of the horse trailer hitched to his truck. He was always careful with precious cargo...precious female cargo, back *and* front. One valuable mare, one extremely fine filly.

Bother that she was, Laramie looked good sitting

beside him. If out of place. Other than her height and black hair, he saw little trace of Buck's blood in her. She was tall and slim, with legs up to her neck, or so it seemed when they were fully displayed by her short tight skirt, folded and tucked so enticingly inside the cab of his pickup, set off by a pair of black suede high heels that had probably never before stepped off a city sidewalk.

"Say, New York. I hope you brought more suitable clothes than what you're wearing." He'd stowed her one small suitcase and leather-banded hat box in the back. At least she traveled light.

"I know how to dress, thanks." Her voice was soft and full with self-mocking humor. "Appearances to the contrary, I'm not your stereotypical city girl stumbling around the countryside in designer silks and three-hundred-dollar shoes. In fact, I'd have changed into something less practical, but by the time my plane landed I was more concerned with keeping the appointment with Bobby." She lifted her shades and gave him a sassy wink. "If I'd known that my choice of wardrobe would irritate your tender sensibilities, *cowboy...*"

His gaze had strayed to her legs. He redirected it toward the road with a snap of his head. "Oh, don't mistake me. I'm not complaining."

"No?"

"You can go bare-legged, for all I care." If she went bare-legged, he'd care. One heckuva lot. "Just don't give Baby Bobby Torrance a heart attack if you do."

"Baby Bobby?"

Jake grinned. "The name says it all." *Sorry, Bob, but all's fair.*

"I'll bet you were his tormentor, once upon a time."

"I was bigger, stronger, older. It's the law of the jungle."

She flexed her jaw, sliding one smooth, rose-colored lip against the other in a way that was unintentionally provocative. "You look utterly lawless to me," she drawled, after a long stare at his obvious injuries and torn, wrinkled clothes. She shook her head over his unpoliced appearance, her intentionally prissy expression making him laugh.

She was a pistol. He liked women who had the stuff to challenge his ego rather than stroking it, cuddling up to him, bleating like baby sheep, looking for him to take over their lives.

He'd raised a sheep once, in 4-H. Then his mother had lost her job and gotten interested in a new man and they'd moved away just weeks before the big county fair—the first of many such disappointments. One he hadn't thought of in twenty years. And didn't care to revisit for another twenty. There was no use for it.

"What happened to you, anyway?" Laramie asked. "Maybe you should be checking into a hospital, not a ranch."

"Just the usual bruises and scrapes. Always looks worse than it feels." Turning the wheel gave him another piercing pain that said otherwise. His oft-injured wrist couldn't take the beating it once had. "I've got pain pills in my shirt pocket." Maybe she'd fish one out for him.

"The way you've been wincing, you'd better up the dosage."

"I tried that last night. And paid for it."

She gave him another sidelong look.

"I was stoked," he admitted. "Got myself into a fixed poker game with the wrong cowboys. Now the Naylor brothers are after my horse." Man, she was going to think the worst of him. Why her opinion should matter to him, he couldn't say.

"What do you mean?" She sounded alarmed. Being a city girl, she probably expected a showdown at high noon.

"Don't worry about it." *I will.* "There's no way Reggie and Rusty can trace me to the Lazy J." 'Cause no self-respecting cowboy would set foot on the place.

"Reggie and Rusty Naylor?" she said, putting together the names. "They sound harmless enough."

"Yeah." Jake shifted uneasily onto his left buttock. His right side was one long, ugly bruise, too tender to touch. Black Tornado's handiwork. Unfortunately, his left side was nearly as sore. The "harmless" Rusty Naylor had sucker-punched Jake in the kidneys while Reggie swung a chair at his ribs. Just another fun weekend at the rodeo.

"Well, you don't look good," Laramie said. Worriedly, he thought, till she added, "Just so you know, I'm no Florence Nightingale. I didn't come to Wyoming to nursemaid a cracked-up rodeo cowboy."

"Don't fret, New York. I wouldn't dream of asking." Okay, he thought, that's plain. She's not interested. Then why did she keep looking?

"Aren't there any friends or relatives who can take care of you?"

"Nope. It's just me and Lar—my horse."

They rode in silence for a few minutes before Laramie mused out loud, "Buck must have been the same way." Her expression was distant, dreamy. "I can see him, alone on his ranch, one man against the elements...." She came back to the present and looked expectantly at Jake, obviously hoping he'd concur.

He was uncomfortable, no longer so willing to be the bearer of bad tidings, despite her lack of sympathy for his injuries. "Buck was a lone wolf, sure," he said, aware that the words were misleading. Apparently Laramie had built up a romantic image of her father as the last of the old-time cowboys. "He didn't go in for socializing."

"But he was married, for a time. What's your mother's name?"

"Iris Porter. She lives in Miami with her latest husband." Number Five.

"What about your father?"

"Long gone."

His tone put a halt to Laramie's curiosity. They'd driven through the streets of western Laramie and were coming to a more open area. The landscape was marred by an ugly, sporadically achieved housing development of seventies vintage. Rundown split-levels fought against a terrain of sweeping meadows and pockets of pine and aspen. It was all that Jake remembered, except that the surviving trees had grown taller and spread, softening the scars of suburban sprawl.

"Take me to the country," Laramie murmured, looking out the window. "I want to see Wyoming at its best."

He slowed the rig. "This'll have to do for now."

"This?" She chuckled. "I don't think so."

"You wanted to go to the Lazy J." Jake stepped

on the brakes and pointed past the windshield. "There it is."

Laramie took off her sunglasses. Her head swiveled back and forth in confusion. Disbelief. She stabbed impatiently at the toggle that rolled down her window. "Oh, come on, Jake. That's not…"

"Yep. This is it."

"This is it?" She was as stupefied as he'd expected.

"This is it," he echoed.

"This?"

"This." Slowly Jake turned the rig into the driveway, easing over the ruts and grooves to protect his horse from jostling. He cut the ignition and stared at the house and surrounding property that had received all of Buck's lavish attention. It seemed that the past decade or so of wear and tear had been equally hard on all of them. The place was even worse than Jake recalled, but that fact made him sad now, not triumphant. Buck was gone. In his absence, his home was revealed to be shabby and unwanted. Jake—such a saddle tramp that he didn't have even an address to call his own—couldn't find it in himself to gloat.

It was with a certain consolation that he touched Laramie's arm and said softly, "Welcome to the Lazy J, Miz Jones."

2

EVEN THOUGH LARAMIE didn't want to believe it, there was a sign that said so. A wooden plaque swung from a crooked post, its woodburned letters proclaiming the truth. This was, indeed, the Lazy J.

She stepped from the truck, dumbstruck.

It was a ranch house, all right. A 1970s split-level ranch house complete with blue asphalt shingles, peeling white siding, red trim and shutters with star cutouts. There was a brass eagle above the double garage door, state and American flags hung on poles that jutted from either corner, wagon wheels lining the driveway. The spokes were painted to suit the theme, alternating red, white and blue like a candy-striped barber's pole.

"I should salute," she said. *I should faint.*

Jake reached through the open window of the truck and pulled out his straw hat. He set it at a cocky angle on his head, untroubled by the spectacle. "Check out the yard."

The lawn was a flat expanse of sod, unbroken by bush, tree or flower. Instead it was crowded with a tacky collection of lawn ornaments: multicolored spinning pinwheels, molded plastic deer, bobbing fishermen, flat wooden cutouts of the backsides of bent-over ladies showing their polka-dotted pantaloons. Ceramic gnomes and wooden toadstools populated the shady spot near the covered entryway. A life-size fiberglass horse was set beneath the picture window, decked out in full western saddle and bridle—vinyl version—one rein looped around a hitching post. Heigh-ho, Silver.

"I don't understand." Laramie spun in a circle, her palms upturned. Though the property was bordered by a split-rail fence, she didn't see any livestock other than the synthetic. "Is this a joke?"

"If so, Buck wasn't in on it."

"The Lazy J isn't a ranch...?" *Just a ranch house.*

"No one but you ever said it was."

She flushed. "You could have warned me."

Jake shrugged. His glance skipped over the whimsical decorations. "There are no words."

Her shock was starting to wear off. "You're a funny guy, huh?" Had he been laughing at her all along? "Playing a backhanded trick."

He set her suitcase and hat box on the cement steps that led to the front door, then slowly turned to face her, sliding his hands into the back pockets of his jeans. "I'm sorry that you're disappointed, but it wasn't my doing. The truth is, Buck Jones wasn't who you—"

"Don't bother now," she snapped. "I'll find out on my own." Her eyes welled and she slammed them shut, fumbling for the sunglasses she'd tucked into her waistband. Dammit. She didn't cry. She didn't snivel.

No—she lost her grip and cut into people who didn't deserve it.

"Look," she muttered at Jake, "I'm sorry. You're right. It's not your fault. It's just that I've been hoping for years that my father was someone I could be proud of…." She jammed on the glasses and looked again around the yard. Dark lenses didn't help. It was still gaudy and tacky and carnival cheap. Suburban bad taste elevated beyond kitsch to full-flung horror, lacking only ropes of flapping flags or glittery fringe—the kind county fairs and used-car lots used—to set the whole thing off.

She blew out a noisy breath. "Okay. Having bad taste isn't a crime. Neither is living in a subdivision. So the Lazy J's not a ranch." Her heart wrenched for the death of that dream, but she went on. "So Buck wasn't a cowboy. So what?"

Jake, suspiciously silent, looked down at the heel he was scuffing against the pavement.

Laramie clenched her jaw. "What?"

"Uh…there's more."

"The animals? There are real horses, aren't there, not just fiberglass replicas?"

"Sure, they're real. If the place hasn't changed since the last time I was here, there'll be an entire zoo in the backyard."

"A zoo," she echoed.

Jake rubbed his stubbly chin. "As I remember it, Buck bought this house new from the developer. There were supposed to be close neighbors on both sides—" he gestured, pointing out the empty lots "—until the developer declared bankruptcy. Buck purchased several extra acres at a discount, then found out that because of a badly written zoning law, the extra land allowed him to keep stock on the premises. By the time I lived here, he had chickens, pigs, sheep and, uh…." An odd look passed over Jake's face. "And Goliath."

Laramie was beginning to get a sense of how the

wind blew. She crossed her arms in preparation, resigning herself to it. "I take it Goliath is the Clydesdale who lives in the garden shed."

"Opposite extreme," Jake said, but she'd had enough. She brushed past him on her way to the front door, keys in hand. The inside couldn't be worse than the outside.

She was wrong.

The first thing she saw was orange shag carpeting, thick with grime, sprinkled with chaff. There was an odor. A distinctly bring-the-wheelbarrow-and-pitch-fork odor. She covered her nose and mouth. Jake, coming in behind her, let out a whistle.

An archway on the right opened onto the living room. Its picture window looked out over the front yard menagerie. The walls were paneled with rough brown barn siding—suiting the barnyard stench—and hung with 3-D and paint-by-number artwork. An enormous emerald-green vinyl easy chair was plunked before a big-screen TV. Bowling trophies lined the mantelpiece of a synthetic brick nonworking fireplace flanked by ceramic dalmatians.

Laramie went back to the foyer and followed the odor toward the kitchen. This room was clean, more or less, except for a filthy floor. No dishes in the sink or rotting food in the fridge. "Is there a dog?" she called to Jake, having noticed an opening cut into the back door, like the ones for pets. The flap was sized for a sheepdog.

"Couldn't say," he said, coming into the kitchen from another direction, "but I found the source of the stench. The dining room needs mucking out."

Laramie cupped her ear. "Did you hear that?" A

clip-clopping of hooves came from the porch tacked to the back of the house. "That's no Clydesdale."

"Meet Goliath," Jake said, just as a miniature horse nosed past the doggy door. Goliath came into the kitchen with his teeth bared, ears flattened against his neck, tail swishing in agitation. White-rimmed eyes glared out from beneath the forelock of a thick, frizzy mane. By all appearances, a bad-tempered little beast.

While Laramie was cautious, she wasn't particularly alarmed. How could she be? The horse barely came up to her thigh. She stepped closer despite Jake's warning and held out her hand. The miniature horse, a brown-and-white piebald, snorted warm air into her palm, its ears pricking with interest.

"Hey, Goliath," she said. Everything was backward on the Lazy J. Next she'd meet a goose who laid wooden nickels.

Jake circled the room. "Watch out. He's mean."

"He's lonely." Laramie rubbed the tiny stallion's bristly nose. She gave Jake a look. "Here I thought you were a bronc buster and it turns out you're scared of a cute little pony...." She bent to stroke Goliath's shoulder. He rubbed his bony head against her thigh. She angled toward Jake so he could see how easily she'd tamed the savage beast. "This little guy wouldn't hurt a—"

Without warning, Goliath's teeth sank into the fleshy part of her hip. He chomped down viciously.

"Eeeyahhh!" Laramie bolted upright, howling with pain. Jake beat the horse away from her with his hat, swatting at Goliath's snapping teeth. Goliath wheeled around and kicked out with his tiny hooves, tattooing them against the kitchen cabinets when Jake slid aside as gracefully as a matador.

Swearing passionately, Laramie scrambled out of striking distance. Fiery pain radiated from her buttock. The ignominy was worse. She could feel her face heating up.

"G'wan," Jake shouted, and gave the miniature stallion a slap on the rump. "Get going!" Goliath bolted out the doggy door. Jake jammed a kitchen chair under the knob, blocking the horse's ingress.

He approached Laramie. She put up her hands to ward him off, but he kept coming, turning her with gentle insistence. "Let me see."

"I'm okay. It was just a nip." She was in agony.

"Your skirt's torn." Jake prodded her hip. "He broke the skin."

She said a rude word, then apologized. "Sorry."

"I've heard worse." He knelt at her side for a closer look.

"How bad is it?"

"Let's see." He gripped her skirt at the side slit and with a sudden wrench tore it up the seam—as high as the elastic on her French-cut panties.

She let out a yip and slapped his hands away. "What do you think you're doing?"

"It was ruined, anyway," he said mildly. She flinched when he inserted a finger into a small tear in her expensive silk hose. They split easily, all the way down to her knee, leaving her feeling naked, embarrassed and perhaps a bit turned on. She wondered at his efficiency. Either he was a practiced medical technician or he was very adept at removing women's clothing. Guess which, she thought.

"Don't worry," he said. "I have experience."

"That's what I'm afraid of." Her tone was wry.

He shot her a glance. His eyes were brown, warmer and kinder than she'd have believed possible thirty minutes ago. Also rather amused. "I promise I won't look...in that way."

"Oh, I'll bet."

His hands brushed her bare thigh and for a moment she forgot her pain and humiliation. "Seriously," he said, "this bite needs medical attention."

He pressed; the throbbing pain increased. "Unh." She grunted and put her hands on the kitchen table, bent at the waist, trying to relax her taut muscles. "Will I need a rabies shot, doc?"

"Goliath may be feral, but he's not diseased. I'm going to see if I can find a first-aid kit. Don't move."

She did, of course, as soon as he left the room. Leaning sideways, she checked out the situation. The bite was red and sore, already slightly swollen, but not as serious as she feared. It was her state of undress that was alarming. Her left flank was more or less naked from the waist down. No matter how efficient Jake might be, he was also male. She knew darn well he'd noticed.

She tried to pull the tattered remnants of her skirt together, tucking the shredded ends into her waistband. The hose she stepped out of, after kicking off her shoes. Immediately she slipped the suede pumps back on; the floor was too dirty for bare feet.

Jake returned with a sterile pad, bandages, hydrogen peroxide and a tube of salve. "All set." He pushed her skirt aside again, giving himself plenty of clear access. Despite the warm May day, Laramie's exposed skin prickled into gooseflesh. "Get ready," he warned. "This is going to sting."

"Isn't this the part where you give me a bullet to bite on?"

He chuckled. "Bend over and grab hold of the table."

"Said the proctologist."

"You've got a smart mouth." He uncapped the hydrogen peroxide.

"Oh, hell," she said, already wincing. "Can't you distract me?" Her thigh twitched when he pressed the soaked pad to the bite mark. The pain was sharp. She clamped her hands on the table, sucking air through her teeth.

"Will this do?" Jake slid his left hand up the inside of her thigh.

She went up on tiptoe, her eyes and mouth opening wide. Jake was not deterred. His callused fingertips played across the smooth skin of her inner thigh like a pianist doing scales. The sensation was delicious…and alarming. It was certainly distracting.

"Jake," she said, meaning to warn him, but finding that her voice came out so husky his name sounded like an invitation to continue. She squirmed.

"All done." He removed his hands, leaned back on his heels. She was left with only a pulsing soreness…and a lingering sense of desire deferred.

"That was…" Her mouth was dry. "Um, thanks."

"Any time."

She met his eyes. They glittered with promise. "I meant for the first aid," she whispered huskily.

His smile was charming in a roguish way. "So did I."

They both lied.

"You make a pretty good Florence Nightingale," she said, trying to be brusque but aware of the irony.

She fiddled with the first aid supplies. Jake got slowly to his feet, grimacing in a way that made her heart flip-flop with all kinds of girlish nurturing tendencies that suited her friend Molly way better than herself.

Then again, Jake didn't expect it of her, and it felt good to surprise him. He flinched when suddenly she dabbed the disinfecting peroxide on his chin. "Hey." His eyes sought hers. "I thought you don't practice medicine on cracked-up rodeo cowboys."

"Quid pro quo." She swiped the raw scrape liberally, letting a smug little smile surface. "Stings, doesn't it?"

He laughed. "I don't know who's meaner, you or Goliath."

HOME SWEET HOME.

While Jake meant it sarcastically, he couldn't shake an oddly comforting sense of déjà vu. Unless he counted yearly motel check-ins during his cross-country loops of the rodeo circuit, it wasn't often that he revisited a place where he'd once lived. There was the time he'd driven by the house in San Antonio where stepfather number one—Dr. Tom Garrity, the worst by far—had lived, but that had been a mistake fueled by a long-delayed need for retribution. Luckily for both Jake and his stepfather, the doctor was no longer in. Kids' bikes and a bright plastic playhouse had added a dash of lively color to the familiar gated courtyard—something strict Dr. Tom would've never allowed. By morning, Jake's resurgent anger had once again burned itself out, leaving only the bitter residue that was always with him, but that he had learned to ignore.

Maybe, then, it wasn't so strange that his dusty old

bedroom at the Lazy J should produce more pleasant emotions. Buck had not been a model dad, but at least he'd never blatantly mistreated his stepson. Jake fingered the old sleeping bag that was laid out on the bed like a comforter, remembering how Buck had kept his cool even when adolescent highjinks had gotten Jake delivered to the Lazy J in the back of a police cruiser at 3:00 a.m.

Like he'd told Laramie, Buck wasn't a bad man. Just a shlub.

Jake threw his duffel on the narrow twin bed and took another look around. Who else but a shlub would hang cowboy wallpaper meant for a ten-year-old in every bedroom and bathroom in his house?

Grounded to the Lazy J, stuck with nothing but zoo duty to occupy his teenage energy, Jake had spent hours sprawled on this bed with grunge rock pounding through his earphones while he stared at wallpaper decorated with bucking broncs and lariats and tiny cowboys wearing chaps and spurs. The seams in the paper didn't match—ten gallon hats met equine hindquarters, bowlegged cowboys were split up the middle. One strip near the door had even run in the wrong direction.

Looking at it, Jake suddenly recalled every mismatch, every upside-down cowboy. With a degree of fondness, apparently. Surprising.

He rubbed the back of his injured wrist against his abdomen, absurdly pleased to discover that he wasn't as hard and dry as an old wrung-out washrag after all. He could still be stirred, pleased, surprised.

Miz Laramie Jones was certainly a surprise. A slick, shiny package, attractive, but unexpected. Misdelivered.

Definitely misdelivered.

Buck's daughter?

"Buck, you old devil," Jake muttered. It was another surprise. The man had actually managed to climb off the back porch once or twice in his lonely, sedentary life. Once long enough to meet and marry Jake's mother, Iris—no great accomplishment there, since it was a feat shared by four other men—and at least once to impregnate Laramie's mother.

Jake shook his head. The two women must have seen something in Buck that he hadn't, which was simply a tall, dark man with a placid countenance, a beer gut and a lazy-ass cowboy delusion. No more, no less.

Pity Laramie, the rancher's hopeful daughter. She was looking for a whole lot more.

Jake felt that he should explain, but it wasn't any use unless she was ready to listen. He knew very well how blind women could be when their sights were set elsewhere. Hell, he thought, scowling at his sorry hungover self in the round bureau mirror, how many times had a woman looked at him instead of listened to him, believed his kisses instead of his words of warning? They convinced themselves that he'd still be around in the morning. And inevitably called him a heel when he left exactly how he'd told them he would.

Jake swore silently to himself. He damn well better make sure that he was straight up with Laramie from the start. For both their sakes.

Hello-I-must-be-leaving he could handle. It was the smooth feel of her inner thigh and the promise in her finely tuned responsiveness to his touch that sent him in search of Buck's secret stash of Jack Daniel's. A little hair of the dog never hurt.

JAKE KILLIAN WAS A PLAYER.

Not exactly a smooth operator, Laramie decided as she finished changing into jeans and a plain white T-shirt. But an operator nonetheless. She figured he played his ma'am-I'm-just-a-lonely-ole-brokedown-cowboy shtick like a violin. Unfortunately, she was susceptible. *Highly* susceptible.

She plopped onto the bed to pull on her boots, forgetting about her injury until a stabbing pain reminded her that she'd been bitten on the butt by a stallion no taller than a yardstick. "Ouch." She cringed, remembering. "Oh, cripes, Goliath." She'd have to take over his care. And there was another horse, full-size, presumably. What else?

Livestock, Bobby Torrance had said.

A zoo, according to Jake. Which was probably more accurate, by the looks of it.

Laramie gazed around her. This had been her father's bedroom. The king-size bed made of sturdy log ends didn't surprise her. Nor did the equally king-size TV on the opposite wall, the cheesy collections of beer bottles and horseshoes or the 3-D print of a cattle drive.

The rollicking-cowboy wallpaper raised her brows. It belonged in the bedroom of a child, not a man. She wondered about Buck's state of mind. Had he recognized reality or had he created his own whacked-out version, same as her mother?

Laramie bit a fingernail. Perhaps her expectations of a mythical cowboy and idyllic ranch had been more romantic than plausible, but was she wrong to have wished for a taste of a normal family life? She thought of her friend Molly Broome, fellow founding member of the Cowgirl Club. She'd always envied Molly's stable nuclear family and their home in the Connecticut suburbs. Molly, naturally, had believed herself to be boring and Laramie to be the lucky one, with her kooky mother and adventurous upbringing. The grass was always greener…

Molly lived in Treetop, Wyoming, now, where she ran what she called the creature-comforts side of a struggling dude ranch. Even though Laramie knew that Molly was gnashing her teeth over both the tangled finances of the rundown ranch and a long-distance relationship with her fiancé, Secret Service agent Raleigh Tate, she no longer had reason to cast an envious eye at anyone else's grass. Certainly not Laramie's. Both of her sister cowgirls were going to get a good giggle over the revelation of the Lazy J.

Needing to talk, Laramie reached for the phone by the bed. The line was dead.

She replaced the receiver slowly, her eyes drawn to the bedside table. To a small framed photo, in particular.

She picked it up, her chest filling with emotion.

Buck Jones hadn't chosen to seek her out while he was alive; there could be a hundred reasons why not. But at least he'd wanted her to have his house and his animals. And he'd kept her baby photo beside his bed as a reminder.

It was just a snapshot, faded with time. A woman held a baby up to the camera, mountains blue in the background. Laramie's mother, young and slightly plump from pregnancy, wearing a poncho, squinting into the sun. And herself, surely herself, in a tiny but still oversize cowgirl costume, the white fringe of the little skirt dragging across her bare toes, a hat—the familiar black Stetson—perched precariously so that it didn't envelop her bald head. The frame was an inexpensive dime-store job, sporting the legend Daddy's Li'l Cowgirl.

"Buck. You remembered me." A tear fell onto the glass and Laramie wiped it off, sniffling. She didn't cry. She didn't cry.

Another tear slid down the side of her nose.

For once there was no denying it. She was crying. For her father. For her mother, for herself. For the family that they'd never had.

JAKE COULD TELL that Laramie was feeling fragile by the way she stomped out of the master bedroom, retrieved her sunglasses from the kitchen, shoved them in place, and said, most snappishly, "Show me the zoo."

"Okay. First I need to unload Laramie." She looked puzzled. "I meant my horse," he said, remembering too late that she still didn't know that Buck had used her name twice.

"Fine. I'll help."

He hesitated, his eyes tracing her slender curves. Wouldn't you know, she was just as attractive in a T-shirt tucked into faded jeans as she'd been in her fine-feathered city clothes. Her hair was now loose, hanging straight to her waist, but it was the old black cowboy hat that tweaked his curiosity. "Nice hat."

"It was a gift from Buck," Laramie said as they went outside. She cleared her throat. "From my dad."

"So you did have contact with him?"

"Only in my imagination."

"Sometimes that's a better deal for all concerned."
Jake opened the back of the horse trailer. "High expectations are rarely met."

She flicked her chin at him. "You're a glass-half-
empty kind of guy."

He patted the equine Laramie's rump as he climbed
into the trailer. The mare's long black tail swished
companionably. "My glass is usually completely
empty. I've drunk the contents."

"Your *shot* glass," the human Laramie said as-
tutely. She peered into the dim interior of the trailer.
"Nice horse." He backed out the buckskin mare.
"What's her name?"

Here we go. "Laramie."

"Yeah?"

"Not you. That's the mare's registered name—
Lady Laramie."

Laramie put her hands on her hips. "You're pulling
my leg."

Jake glanced at her. If he touched her legs, it
wouldn't be for the purpose of a joke. No-siree, he'd
be stripping them down and pulling them up so they
could wrap around his hips as he sank into her lovely,
welcoming body....

Stop now, he told himself. Keep this situation as
uncomplicated as possible. Hello, goodbye, same as
always.

"The name was Buck's idea. Lady Laramie was
my present from him and my ma the only Christmas
we all spent together. They didn't know that giving a
green-broke filly to a wild kid was asking for trouble."

"Hmm. Maybe they were wiser than you knew."
Laramie took off her sunglasses. A frown line carved

a notch between her winged brows. "Looks like at least the *horse* turned out okay."

"I found a trainer. He tamed both of us." Jake slapped the mare's shoulder. "It took with Laramie."

"Buck wasn't a horseman?"

"Goliath was all he could handle."

She seemed skeptical, as if Jake's opinion couldn't be trusted. "Bobby Torrance mentioned a retired barrel racer."

Jake shrugged. "S'pose it's possible. Let's go see."

They led his horse around the side of the house. "Either Buck named your horse after me or we were both named after the city," Laramie mused. "I don't know if I should be insulted, complimented or confused."

"Maybe it was just that Buck had a sorry lack of imagination" was Jake's suggestion.

She slowed her steps as they rounded the corner. "Does Goliath attack on sight?"

"Naw. He prefers to get you when your defenses are down."

"Yeah, thanks for the warning." Through her jeans, she fingered the swollen lump on her hip.

Jake looked away. The backyard zoo had grown wild in his long absence. The corrals and sheds were still standing, but that was the best that could be said for them. Rust and weather and weeds had attacked without mercy. The chicken coop leaned to the right and the hog shed leaned to the left. The horses' three-sided shelter was seriously swaybacked. A few scrawny chickens pecked at the ground while a despot of a rooster stood guard over a dented water pan, now and then running off thirsty fowl with a mean snaking of its beak. A supersize hog lolled in the dirt of another enclosure, snoring, with its bulk pressed to the side of an empty feed trough. Ten years' worth of unwieldy discards like oil barrels and rusted lawn mowers completed the ugly picture.

Lady Laramie pulled against her halter, crowding the fence that butted up against the house. She whinnied excitedly. The bay horse that had been lazily grazing in the pockmarked pasture flung up its head and trotted toward the fence, whickering in response.

Suddenly Goliath shot out from behind one of the sheds, bushy tail churning like a propeller. The miniature horse snapped at the bay, driving it back. Satisfied that dominance had been established and his Napoleon complex reinforced, Goliath trotted over to greet the new mare, his head held high. Lady Laramie, no fool, backed away from the fence without Jake's prompting.

Goliath put his head through the middle row of rails for a sniff, his nostrils working like a bellows. He stamped a hoof and squealed, setting off the hog, who roused itself and started grunting for food.

Laramie shooed her hands at Goliath. "Nasty little brute. Get away."

Lady Laramie chuffed air through her nose and shook her dark mane, possibly in agreement. Unlike her namesake, the mare knew better than to succumb to the savage beast's entreaties.

Jake was tracing the maze of fencing, a patchwork job of chicken wire, barbed wire, rails and peeling planks. The horses' enclosure ran right from the back porch to the small pasture beyond, but there was a gate beside the chicken coop that when closed would keep Goliath near the house and away from the other horses. For shelter, the minibeast would have to make do with the back porch. No more house privileges.

Once Goliath was safely segregated, much to his displeasure, the other two horses snorted their acquaintance and soon settled down to graze. Frustrated, the small stallion grabbed hold of the gate with his yellow teeth and rattled it vigorously. When it didn't yield, he beat the chicken coop with his back hooves; the birds squawked and flapped in distress. The hog continued grunting, regular as a metronome.

Jake was hit with another distant memory, less pleasant, more raucous. "This place was always noisy," he growled. "You can see why I call it the zoo." He glanced at Laramie, who leaned against the fence with a startled look on her face. "Some inheritance, huh, New York?"

She touched the earpiece of her sunglasses to her bottom lip. "It's not what I'd imagined, I'll grant you that."

"So we're in agreement?"

She cocked her head at him, brows raised.

"You don't belong here." A shadow fell across her face, and he quickly amended, "I meant that you don't belong in a place like this. It's—" he shrugged, hoping she'd be reasonable "—beyond hope."

"My father thought otherwise."

"Buck Jones was a crackpot."

Laramie put her elbows on the top rail and rested her chin on her hands. She gazed over the ramshackle backyard zoo with a hint of a smile turning up the corners of her wide mouth. "Then you shouldn't be surprised that as Buck's daughter I'm just crazy enough to continue his legacy."

3

"I'M DEAD ON MY FEET," Laramie said, even though sitting across a restaurant table from Jake, with his gaze continually brushing her face, her hands, her hat, was giving her the heebie-jeebies. Again. *I'm in Laramie, Wyoming, at last,* she told herself, working at staying cool, her hands clasped in her lap. *I'm at dinner with a genuine cowboy.* That was worth a few shivers, right there.

"I'm dead *off* my feet," Jake said, slumping. He rested his head against the vinyl booth but continued to watch her through half-closed eyes.

Laramie deliberately looked away so her concern—and consternation—wouldn't show. The downtown restaurant they'd chosen was unpretentious, a large, clean, noisy, them's-good-eats kind of place. There were quite a few cowboy hats and boots and snug, faded jeans scattered at the counter, tables and booths. Quite a few good-looking bodies filling them out, too. Somehow, though, she'd lost interest.

Try as she might to distract herself, her attention kept returning to Jake. At first, she'd been all set to dislike him for his stand against Buck and the Lazy J. Then she'd begun noticing little signs that suggested he wasn't as callous as he acted. At times, when he mentioned Buck, there was the slightest hint of real feeling in his eyes—regret, she discerned.

Also, he'd bandaged her Goliath bite, his touch gentle and deft; he'd helped her scrape out the dining room and pull up its rotting carpet; he'd spoken to the teenage boy who'd been caring for the menagerie, then done what he could to improve the rundown backyard pens. A man who put an animal's comfort before his own couldn't be all bad.

Jake was pale under his tan. Pain had etched tiny lines around his mouth. "You did too much," she said. "You should be home in bed."

He tried to look suggestive, but was too tired to put much oomph in the effort. "Is that an offer, New York?"

"Simply an observation." Her tone was clipped. "Sheesh—men! They never know when to stop. It's obvious you're done in, Jake. Give it up."

He smiled lazily. "Thought you wanted to do up my bed with hospital corners, is all."

"Don't get ideas just because I cleaned your scrapes and cuts and changed the bandage on your wrist. New Yorkers are notoriously hardhearted."

"Just my luck. I'm partners with a regular Nurse Ratched."

"It's okay. I don't do lobotomies." A waitress approached with their drinks. "But you'd better keep an eye on Goliath. Bend over within striking distance and he'll crack your skull in an instant."

"Or attack the other end," he reminded Laramie, giving the middle-aged waitress a languid smile that put a flutter in her lashes and a spring in her step.

He's kind to animals and women who work their butts off for tips, Laramie thought. That tore it. She *had* to like him.

She'd ordered an iced tea, Jake a beer. She glanced

at the pill bottle he'd set on the table, but withheld comment on the advisability of mixing liquor and prescription medicine.

The tea was pleasantly tart. "Buck's neighbor sure looked relieved to hear that we'd arrived."

"Goliath had the boy terrorized. He was afraid to get close."

"And that's why Goliath had free reign over the house?" She wrinkled her nose in distaste. Aside from the manure in the dining room, they'd discovered that the bathtub had been serving as a water trough, with a magazine holder and chewed-up dishpan doubling as hayrack and oat bucket.

"Nope. From what the kid said, Buck had taken to keeping Goliath inside the past few years. After his death, the situation slid downhill to squalor."

Laramie frowned. "I guess Buck *was* a crackpot."

Whether or not from concern for her feelings, Jake chose his words more carefully this time. "He was an unusual character."

"Not a cowboy."

"He admired cowboys. He loved to watch old *Gunsmoke* reruns."

"Okay," she said softly. Things were what they were. She'd have to accept that. "I'm just not sure I can believe that Goliath was his closest friend."

"Maybe it was a King Kong-Fay Wray thing. I remember Goliath being difficult, but not completely unredeemable." Jake shrugged. "Tell you what. Tomorrow, I'll wash and groom him, then thoroughly check him over, even if that means I have to rope and hog-tie the little beast. There could be a physical reason for his ill temper. Bad teeth. Thrush. Whatever."

"Is that smart? At the moment, you appear outmatched."

Jake flexed his fingers. "I've got one good hand." His brows inched upward as he engaged her eyes—with enough oomph this time to shiver her timbers. "I can do a lot with one good hand."

She firmed up her lips, ignoring the insinuation even though her face felt all hot and tingly. "In that case, I'll sell tickets."

He laughed. "What does a front-row seat at a three-ring circus go for these days?"

"You're no clown." A flash of a grin. "An amateur lion tamer, perhaps."

"Hey. I'm no amateur, either." He tilted back his head and swigged beer.

She grew serious. "You'd better tell me about those Naylor brothers you mentioned. I want to know what to be on the lookout for."

Jake waved off her concern. "They're just a coupla tough nuts. Every time they lose an event, they set up a poker game to win back the rodeo fees they'd paid out. There's always some poor sap willing to be cheated out of his winnings."

"And this time you were the sap?"

His pallor darkened. "Guess so." He shifted uneasily, took another long drink. "Like I said, I'd popped a few too many of the pain pills. Some of my buddies tried to warn me off, but I was in a bad mood. Wrangling with Black Tornado can do that to a guy."

She shook her head. "Black Tornado?"

He indicated his bandages. "The bull who mistook my hand for the ground."

"Ah."

"Anyway, my losses started piling up. Then I got

a pair of queens.'' He shook his head. "Hell, I shoulda known the Naylors were settin' me up. But I wasn't thinkin' too straight, so I..." He ran a finger along the wet beer bottle, then said in a low voice, "I put up my horse."

She blinked in surprise. "That was really dumb."

Although he made a no-big-deal shrug, he looked totally disgusted with himself. "Rusty had a full house—surprise. I accused him of cheating. We got into a little tussle." He stroked his ribs. "Next thing I knew, I was waking up in my motel room at dawn. The letter from Bobby Torrance was on the night table. Since I was in no shape to wrangle with the Naylors over possession of my horse, I collected Laramie and headed out to Wyoming. By the time I'm healed, I'll have thought of a way to settle my score with the Naylors." He picked up the beer bottle, put it down again, shook his head and said with a certain put-on belligerence, "Those no-good double-crossin' card-sharps ain't gettin' their dirty hands on my horse."

Laramie thought over his story, suppressing the scolding that sprang to mind. Buck and Goliath, she thought. Jake and Laramie...Lady Laramie, that was. She might not be an authentic cowgirl, but she knew enough to never come between a cowboy and his beloved horse.

She cleared her throat. "Then your interest in the Lazy J is...?"

"I have no interest in the Lazy J."

"Except as a temporary pit stop."

"I'm a saddle tramp, darlin'. I like the open road. The only home I want is my truck, saddle and horse."

"If that's truly the case, do you mind if I make a suggestion?"

He lifted the bottle. "Go ahead."

"Your story's not a pretty one. It seems obvious that if you want to continue as you are, you have two choices." Jake sat up, his expression alert. Ah, she had his attention. For emphasis, she closed her fists and rapped them on the table. "You can give up drinking." *Knock.* "Or you can give up gambling." *Knock, knock.*

Jake was momentarily taken aback. Then he relaxed into a slump again, his mouth twisting into a lopsided grimace. "My, my, aren't we self-righteous."

She shook the slender brown bottle of his pain pills. "I'd suggest quitting the liquor. Unless you want to put yourself into a coma."

He blinked but said nothing. She could practically see him weighing the options. At least he was taking her seriously.

"You're right," he said suddenly. Without ceremony, he picked up the beer bottle and upended it over a potted plant set on the windowsill beside their booth. The scent of the yeasty brew thickened the air as he shook out the last few drops. "There you go. I quit."

It was Laramie's turn to be taken aback. "Well, good," she said awkwardly, trying to figure out what had just happened. Jake didn't look like the kind of man who took advice. Then again, there were those little signs....

She regarded him with a softening expression, her initial attraction to him beginning to deepen into tenderness. Which did not mean, she reminded herself, that she was going to forget the short-term aspects of their situation. She didn't need another man in her life whose main intention was being *out* of her life.

Fortunately, Jake was quick to cut back her swelling sentiment. "If you're thinkin' all it took was the love of a good woman to set me straight..." His face was a scowl, his voice a growl.

She blanched. "God, no. What's love got to do with it?" *Okay, cowgirl, get ahold of yourself. This isn't a dreadful penny novel about a temperance fighter and an unrepentant outlaw.* "I'm just concerned about my share of the Lazy J. You might decide to gamble away your half of the inheritance, and then where'd I be?"

Though Jake nodded, he didn't look entirely convinced that her intentions had been self-serving. Smart man. "There's a thought," he said, brightening. "How'd you like the Naylor brothers for roommates?"

She tossed her hair, nonchalant if it killed her. "Only if they're neater than Goliath."

JAKE AND LARAMIE WERE eating steak and salad, respectively, and comparing peripatetic pasts—a lot of similarity there—when a perky, curvy, smiling blonde arrived at the table. Her lips matched her nail polish and she wore a flattering yellow print sundress that revealed lovely tanned shoulders and lots of leg. By comparison, Laramie felt like a ranch hand in jeans and her well-worn hat.

The woman squealed, the heels on her sandals clicking on the wood floor as she scurried toward them, hands extended. "Jakey!"

Jake didn't wince, the way Laramie expected he would. Instead he looked up and smiled. "Helen."

Helen? Laramie thought. The woman deserved a pom-pom girl name. Debby. Suzie. Candy, Sandee, Randi.

Helen hugged Jake around the shoulders. Gingerly. "Been rodeoing, I see." She chucked him under the chin. "When did you get to town? Why didn't you call me?" She glanced at Laramie. "Oh-ho-ho, so she's why!"

Laramie raised her brows, not risking comment until she figured out the dynamic. Old girlfriend, maybe, old friend for sure.

Helen bopped Jake with her hip so he'd slide over. "This one's different, Jakey—gorgeous, but probably not a rodeo queen. You're a barrel racer?" She was studying Laramie, evaluating her with sparkling green eyes.

Laramie shook her head. "I'm not—"

"A heeler?" Helen wound an arm around Jake and gave him an affectionate squeeze. "Don't tell me our boy here has actually taken on a female roping partner! Other than Laramie, of course. How's Laramie doing, by the way? Won any events lately?"

"Ask her yourself," Jake said, indicating the other Laramie.

Helen batted her lashes. "Huh?"

Jake was nearly droll. "Wanna neigh for us, Laramie?"

"Stop it," she said, then looked at Helen. "He's being funny. My name is Laramie. Laramie Jones."

Helen's lips formed an O. "That's weird. Because Jake's horse—"

"Also Laramie. I know."

"Jones?" Helen was quick. "Any relation to Buck Jones?"

"As far as I know, I'm his daughter."

"Holy cannoli!" Helen grinned at Jake. "Imagine, Jakey, you've got a sister."

"We're not kin," he said with seemly—or maybe unseemly—haste, looking alarmed.

Helen's mischievous grin switched over to Laramie. Her glee was apparent as she caught the tip of her tongue between her teeth. *I knew it, I knew it!* her dancing eyes seemed to sing. *Jake and Laramie, sitting in a tree, K-I-S-S-I-N-G...*

If that was going to be the case, Helen knew more in three minutes than Laramie had figured out after a full day.

The blonde gave Jake another squeeze, then extended her hand across the table to shake with Laramie. "Jakey was my high-school boyfriend for all of three weeks, but don't you worry about me horning in. We're just friends now. I've got a guy—a cop. He's the jealous type, and he'd pound Jakey into the ground if there was *anything* at all between us."

"Hey," Jake said in protest.

Helen shushed him. "Nice to meetcha, Laramie. You want the dirt on Jakey, come on by and visit me at the branch library. Traffic's real slow midmorning—we can chat. I'll give you all the gossip on our boy's secret past. Did he tell you about getting suspended for setting Goliath loose on the football field at halftime of the homecoming game? By the time the tuba players corralled the little guy, most of the brass section had bruises shaped like horseshoes!" With a happy wave, she departed in a swirl of yellow daisies and sunflower perfume.

Laramie watched until Helen joined a burly fellow with a crewcut, then settled back in the booth. Jake skillfully evaded her gaze. "So," she said. "The first old girlfriend pops out of the woodwork. Wait—don't say anything. I'm trying to picture Mr. Cynical pulling high school pranks."

He looked sheepish. "It wasn't really me. I gave 'em Goliath, is all. And he was supposed to be sicced on the opposing team, not the marching band."

"How come you weren't playing football?"

"I wasn't at the school long enough for team sports. Besides, I prefer getting beat up by creatures with four legs."

She shook her head. "It must be the testosterone that makes men do crazy things like playing football and riding bulls."

"And the estrogen that makes women applaud them for it."

"Spoken like a cowboy who's fended off his share of perky blond cowgirls." Laramie's eyes narrowed as she replayed Helen's stream of tidbits. "Three weeks, hmm? Is that your limit? Do you think your injuries will be healed by then?"

"More like three days."

"I see. Shall I consider myself on notice?"

He shrugged and stabbed a bite of steak, taking the turn of their conversation much less seriously than she. "If you like."

Laramie wasn't full, but she couldn't eat another leaf. She sat in silence and studied Jake as he unconcernedly poked at a baked potato. She was thinking, *Yes, cowboy, I'd like to know exactly what to expect from you,* but trying to accept that it would never happen. Her emotional responses were out of control...and not entirely because of her loss of the stranger who'd been her father. Knowing that Jake was already plotting his departure had set her unexpectedly off-kilter.

She would have to find her bearings. Because, sad excuse for a ranch though it was, the Lazy J was still most important to her. For Jake, it was an unloved piece of his past. But for her...

It was the future.

Just not the one she'd dreamed of.

"BUT YOU SAID YOU HAD no interest in the Lazy J!" Laramie slammed into the split-level ranch house, turned right, glared at the ugly green easy chair that sat like a puffed-up bullfrog in the center of the living room, and then strode off in another direction. With her long black hair flying free, she galloped down the short flight of steps that led to the lower level and disappeared into what had been, in Jake's day, the game room.

It still was. The pool table and jukebox took up most of the space, but to one side there was room for a bar and three stools fashioned from beer kegs. Laramie stood at the light switch, making the overhead lamp and neon beer signs blink on one by one.

Jake idly picked up a cue stick. "I couldn't care less about the Lazy J. That's why I want to sell it as soon as possible."

She crossed her arms. "You're not the boss."

"Neither are you."

"Okay, then—we're agreed. We're partners."

"Temporarily."

"Three measly days," she stressed, making it sound like three minutes.

He sniffed a square of blue chalk. "Maybe more." He could concede that much.

"Three weeks?"

"Laramie..." *Laramie, beautiful, fierce Laramie.* "Why on earth would you voluntarily spend three weeks of your life at the Lazy J? You can see at a glance that this place isn't worth the hassle."

She prowled the edges of the room, avoiding the pool table. Beneath drawn brows, her eyes looked black as bottomless wells. "Buck didn't want the place sold."

Back at square one. "There's nothing else to be done with it."

"I'll *live* here."

He muttered an oath, not imagining that she could be serious.

"I can make it work."

"You're not that naive." He slammed a cue ball onto the green felt and shot it ruthlessly into a corner pocket. The racket of it ricocheted through their tense silence. "What are you going to do?" he said at last. "Sell lawn ornaments? Chicken farm? Breed baby Goliaths?"

Laramie flung herself onto one of the keg stools. "I don't expect to make a living from the Lazy J." She drew the brim of her Stetson low over her forehead. "But there's no reason it can't be..." She hesitated, searching for words.

"Restored to its full glory?" he suggested, sounding so sarcastic even he got a sour taste in his mouth. Though the slight, nearly undetectable quiver in Laramie's voice wrenched at his resolution, he knew it was best for her to face facts. In the end, the straight story hurt least.

He tossed down the cue stick. "Here's a hot bulletin, New York. There ain't no glory in shoveling chicken shit.''

She made a choking sound, her face hidden. "Umph."

He pressed the knuckles of his good hand into the felt. "Aw, Laramie, don't cry."

She ducked even further beneath the hat brim. Her shoulders shook. "How can you...be so...mean?" she sputtered.

His eyes narrowed as he walked toward her. He put his palm between her hunched shoulder blades and felt the tremors that gripped her. Surprise shot through him. "Hell, woman—you're laughing!"

She sat back, tossing off the hat so he saw the merriment in her dark eyes and wide smiling mouth. "Jake, that was wonderful. Can I quote you?" She squared her shoulders. Raised a finger in the air. "'There ain't no glory—'" Her laughter interrupted the pronouncement, much to his relief.

"Okay, okay," he said. "Call it what you want. It's still true."

Her face grew softer. "I'm not looking for glory, Jake."

"You've got some crazy, mixed-up notion that you're honoring Buck by continuing his...his..."

"Legacy?"

He threw up his hands. "If the Lazy J's a legacy, I'm a little girl with a curl."

And when she was bad, he thought out of nowhere, imagining how good Miz Laramie Jones would be at being bad...very, *very* bad....

Fortunately she had no idea what turn his thoughts had taken. "Well," she said, speculating, "you *are* horrid."

With a small private laugh, she got to her feet, her lithe form elongating into a catlike stretch. Her arms reached toward the cottage-cheese ceiling. "I'll make you a deal." She came down off her toes. "Better yet, a wager."

His gaze followed her like a string on a kite as she slid, loose-hipped, around the corner of the bar. "Remember dinner?" he said. "You told me to give up liquor and gambling."

"Ah, but you chose liquor, didn't you?" She poked through various drawers and cupboards until she found one that held a stack of games, Monopoly, Yahtzee and the like. "Here we go. What's your poison? Dice or cards?" Answering herself, she glanced at him through a skein of jet-black hair as she reached into a drawer. "Cards. Definitely cards."

"What's this?" he said warily when she slapped a deck of well-used playing cards on the surface of the bar. "I've already wagered my horse. Now you want me to put up my half of the Lazy J?"

"My proposal isn't as risky as the Naylor brothers'." She shuffled. "A simple cut of the cards. You win, we sell right now—get a Realtor out here tomorrow morning. But if *I* win…" She flipped her hair off her face. "If I draw top card, I get a month on the Lazy J. One month to make something of the place. To clean it up, turn a profit. Now, I'm not talking big money—that's obvious. I just want the chance to try. I think Buck would like it if at least one of us *tried.*"

"And what happens then? If, by some stretch of the imagination, you succeed?"

"I'm sure we can come to a mutually acceptable compromise. If I have to, I'll find a way to buy you out.'' She tapped the cards on the bar. ''What do you say?''

He shrugged. It was no skin off his nose, either way. She was nuts, of course. Loony as a billy goat hopped up on the first green grass of the spring. ''I'll cut.''

He did so, then lifted off the top card. Ten of clubs. Not bad.

She rubbed her hands together before drawing the next card. With neither coy hesitation nor peeking, she flipped it over. Her smile told the tale before he'd even looked at the card. He did, anyway.

Queen of hearts.

Laramie crowed. She clapped her hands in the air and did a shimmying, twirling victory dance. Jake, who didn't feel the loser considering the circumstances, watched with not a little appreciation until she swung around to face him. He sobered then, scowling at her card as if having to do time in proximity with a leggy dark-haired beauty was something he dreaded.

''Queens are my downfall.'' He bent the card in an arc between his thumb and index finger and, with a snap, shot it across the room. ''So be it. You win.''

She'd come to a standstill, realization dawning. Her expression was comical. He could almost hear her count up the toadstools and whirligigs, the roster of live animals versus synthetic. The sagging fences. The noise. The manure. ''Umm...yeah,'' she said. ''I win.''

''Have fun with Goliath.'' He shifted, as if to leave.

Her eyes widened. ''Wait a minute, Jake. I'm not—'' She reached over the bar and grabbed hold of his arms with both hands. ''You don't have to move out, you know. I mean, I could probably use the help.'' She was almost pleading. ''And you need the, uh, break, right? The Naylor brothers might be looking for you. And Lady Laramie. You're safe here.''

His elbows were on the bar. He leaned closer, inhaling her spicy, exotic perfume. ''Yeah, I suppose I can stay. Long enough to see that Goliath doesn't have you for lunch, anyhow.''

Her smile flickered uncertainly. She might have pulled away, but Jake had closed his hands over her elbows; their arms were intertwined. ''I'd appreciate your...guidance,'' she said, her voice so low and husky it eased its way deep inside him. ''If you'd be so kind, that is. I know you're hoping I'll fail.''

There was no question in his mind that she'd fail. Not because of incompetence, necessarily, but because all she had was the Lazy J to work with.

''I'm not completely hardhearted.'' His thumbs brushed back and forth over the soft skin of her inner elbows. Her lashes lowered, screening her responses except for a small, involuntary purring sound of pleasure that reverberated in his spine. ''But you've got to know you're working with worse than nothing.''

''There's, hmm, there's the quarter horse.'' Her face moved closer to his. But not close enough. ''A champion barrel racer. I could...''

He slid his good hand up her arm, taking his time, nice and slow, letting her know that she had plenty of opportunity to retreat but that she'd be missing out on an experience if she did. Laramie, no shrinking violet, pressed herself even tighter against the bar that divided them. Her breasts were nicely rounded against the taut fabric of her T-shirt, drawing his gaze but not his hands. Not yet.

His fingers brushed beneath her jaw. The nearly silent scrape of the callused tips on her fine white skin was surprisingly erotic. She exhaled softly and stretched her neck, reaching to meet his touch, her face tilted.

Close enough.

They kissed. Rather, he lightly—incredibly lightly—touched her lips with his and she sighed and shivered and *then* they kissed. In the heat of their clinging mouths, her lips opened like a rosebud, soft petals unfurling, her tongue quick and velvet, there and gone.

He held her face in his hands. His fingertips pressed beneath her slanted cheekbones, feeling the warmth that rose off her skin like sun-baked river stones. She tasted sweet, spicy, mysteriously female, completely unique.

He'd never kissed a woman like her, like this.

"Jake," she murmured, her voice rasping against his melting senses. He felt her open her eyes and he closed them with pattering fingertips, the flutter of her lashes the softest thing he'd ever felt. But something had changed. Their kiss became more firm, less wondering, a kiss that had an ending rather than a promise, a tangy bite rather than a sweet, slow exploration of desire.

He said, "Aw, Laramie," and withdrew only an inch, angling his forehead against hers. Her lidded eyes moved beneath his fingertips. Gracefully she tangled her fingers through his and brushed her lips over his knuckles. A gesture of consolation.

He clenched his jaw, battling the urge to catch her up in his arms and kiss the bejesus out of her as if hot passion would solve their dilemma. In his heart, he knew it wouldn't do any good.

Tomorrow, she'd still be a woman he had no business wanting.

And he'd be exactly the kind of man she didn't need.

After a while, Laramie turned her face away from his. Her eyes were still closed when she whispered, with a small catch in her voice, "What are we doing?"

He couldn't answer because he didn't know.

4

NO NEED FOR KISSING.

Although Laramie had run the refrain in her head all morning, it still wasn't convincing enough.

No need. She shoved the rusty barrel with all her might, her face contorted. *For kissing.*

K-I-S-S-I-N-G...

"Stop it," she said, and the barrel obediently did, rolling to a halt against a hillock of tall grass. The small pasture that passed for Buck's backyard was lumpy and weedy—as unkempt as everything else on the suburban farmette. There was little wonder how the Lazy J got its name. Buck Jones must have had a sense of irony and at least some amount of self-awareness.

Laramie upended the barrel, then put her hands on her hips as she lifted her face to the sun. The sky was expansive, the clouds a billowing mass of dreamland castles.

Her mother, presently known as Rainbow Miracle—née Patricia Ann Vogel—was well acquainted with building castles in the sky. Her stories about Buck Jones had always started the same way, like fairy tales: "He was a tall, handsome cowboy..." Only the happily-ever-after was lacking. Now, though, it seemed clear to Laramie that the entire thing was just a pretty fiction spun by a woman whose head was forever in the clouds.

Which was no less than Laramie had told herself to expect. She kicked the tuft of grass. Why was she so disappointed?

Because hope, like weeds, springs eternal.

The back door to the porch creaked open, then slammed shut. Goliath's hooves clattered across the wooden porch, followed by Jake's shout. "G'wan!" They had engaged in an ongoing war over possession of the porch.

Goliath must have lost. There came a thud and a splintering crack. Laramie cringed, betting that the little horse's hooves had just taken another chunk out of the lattice that framed the porch. The pig began its pathetic grunting, the chickens to squawk. One of the sheep that shared the pasture gave a token bleat.

Laramie listened for the sound of the gate before she turned. No need for kissing, she told herself once more as she watched Jake approach with a cocky loose-limbed walk that was everything a cowboy's rolling gait should be.

Jake looked good. Stronger and healthier, his eyes clear and his chin shaven. Snug jeans rode low on narrow hips and she was reminded of the Cowgirl Club's motto, something she and Molly and Grace had thought up in one of their schoolgirl rhapsodies over the way life should be—and would be if only they could live it out west.

Straight talk, hard work, open skies, tight jeans.

It shocked Laramie to realize that, at least for the moment, she had it all. She put her hands to her head in disbelief and felt the heat of the sun absorbed by her dark hair. By mistake or not, temporary though it may be, she'd achieved her dream.

Jake snagged her hat off a fencepost and popped it onto her head. "Dazzled by the sun? Or just Buck's landscaping?"

"I was thinking—oh, nothing." She blinked. "You look…healthy." Her lips pursed. "No hangover?"

He tipped the brim of his straw hat. "Thanks to you reading me the riot act, Miz Jones."

There you go, thought Laramie. Straight talk.

"What's up?" Jake squinted at the two old barrels—one dented and half eaten by rust, the other wooden and growing mold—and the galvanized tin washtub she'd positioned at roughly equidistant, triangular points in the fenced pasture.

"It's for practice." She drew a design in the air, approximating the standard pattern run by barrel racers. "The cloverleaf pattern."

"I see." His features twisted with suppressed amusement. "And the washtub? An unusual choice."

"This is a make-do operation."

"Uh-huh."

"Laugh if you want to."

He let out a shout that set off the porker and the chickens again.

"Not *that* loud," she said, pretending insult.

"You're never gonna make it to the rodeo circuit, darlin'."

"We'll see." Chauncey, the bay quarter horse gelding that had supposedly been a champion barrel racer, had grown fat and placid during his hiatus on the Lazy J. He was healthy, however, and at sixteen not too old for a comeback. As far as Laramie could tell, there was no reason she couldn't work the horse into shape, enter a few local competitions and carry the Lazy J banner into glory.

Or, in a pinch, second place. Even third. She wouldn't quibble. Any ribbon at all would be a triumph. Jake would have to admit that the Lazy J was not entirely hopeless.

"Can I use your saddle?" She'd already haltered and groomed the gelding, but Buck must not have ridden because the only tack she'd found was the really tacky gear strapped to the fiberglass palomino in the front yard. "That is, if you think it will fit old barrel-gut, here," she qualified, sliding a palm over Chauncey's rounded midsection. His tail swished contentedly.

"Sure. I'll get it." In moments, Jake was back and together they saddled and bridled Chauncey. The horse put up a mild resistance to taking the bit until Jake clamped a hand on his nose. Then his head lowered obediently and there was no more trouble, save the racket made by Goliath as he butted against the gate.

Laramie mounted under Jake's watchful eye. Unlike Grace Farrow, who'd taken lessons and competed since she was eight, Laramie was not a highly skilled rider. Thanks to summers at camp and subsequent Cowgirl Club horseback outings, though, she was fairly comfortable on horseback. She had confidence, and Chauncey did not appear to be a difficult ride.

Jake, holding his mare's halter, looked doubtful, even though her failure would be his triumph. Perhaps he was worried about his saddle.

For ten minutes, Laramie and Chauncey circled the pasture at a rather sedate walk and trot, testing each other out. Laramie waved at Jake when they jogged past his position. The gelding was lazy and out of shape, hardly a horse to buck or run away with her. In fact, she had to apply her heels frequently to keep him in a trot.

Surely a fifth- or sixth-place ribbon would be adequate.

"What were you the champion of?" she asked Chauncey brokenly as she jounced up and down in the saddle. His trot was slow but rough, although that could be the bumpy terrain. "The merry-go-round?"

"We're going to lope," she called to Jake when they'd circled around again, and he said, "Go for it." He was leaning against the fence, his expression noncommittal. Not really smiling, but no longer worried, either.

A spurt of I'll-show-him spirit gripped her. She set her hat firmly on her head and cued Chauncey to lope. The gelding's head bobbed a couple of times—and that was it. She pressed her right heel behind the saddle girth and clucked in encouragement. "Come on, Chauncey. Jake and Lady Laramie are watching. Let's impress them."

Chauncey's ears twitched as his pace changed. To a walk.

"Okay." Laramie twisted in the saddle and waved at Jake. "Here we go!" she called, and drummed both heels into her mount's sides. Chauncey let out a grunt and moved into a trot, going slightly faster than before, but still not what anyone would call speedy.

"Go-go-go-oh-oh-oh," Laramie said, squeezing her knees, working her heels, flapping the reins. She took off her hat and slapped it down on Chauncey's hindquarters and finally he stepped up into a lope. For three strides. Then it was back to the bone-rattling trot.

"Need spurs?" Jake yelled as they circled past him again. He'd put his hand up to his mouth to yell, but that didn't hide his smile. It was, she imagined, a gloating smile. A let's-cut-to-the-chase-and-call-the-Realtor-right-now smile.

Laramie wouldn't stand for it. She wouldn't walk or trot for it, either.

"Heyah!" Without warning, she let out an ear-splitting yell and dug her heels into Chauncey's ribs, slapping the loose ends of the reins against his neck for good measure. Hey—it worked for movie cowboys.

The gelding flung up his head and with a supreme effort took off at a rollicking, gallumphing lope. Laramie kept her legs clamped tight around his heaving sides, urging him faster. After they'd cantered past the barrels and the washtub, she made a wide turn and brought the horse around again, aiming him for the first barrel. Since she didn't know how long Chauncey would keep up the gait, they were going to have to show Jake their stuff on the first go-round.

Chauncey slowed drastically for what was supposed to be a hairpin turn around the first barrel. The hairpin became more of a hairbrush, but they made it around and continued across the pasture toward the second barrel, dodging one of the sheep along the way. Laramie drummed the horse's sides like a bongo. By now, Chauncey was immune. He slowed even more, dropping down to the vibrating trot as they made another wide turn and headed for the wash-tub.

Sunshine glinted off the lip of the discolored tub.

Chauncey's ears flattened and he came to a dead standstill, regardless of Laramie's commands. Apparently he was still enough of a barrel racer to know that something wasn't right. He snorted at the washtub, identified it as an object as inert as himself, then walked calmly past it, clearly intending to continue on to the tasty grass beyond.

Laramie tugged at his heavy head with the reins, slowly reeling him around so they were facing home. Chauncey—blast him—paused to dip his nose into the washtub, slurping at the inch of rainwater it held.

Her groan was pure embarrassment. If this had been a rodeo and there'd been a stopwatch on her and Chauncey, their time would have qualified them for something like sixteenth place out of fifteen, having surrendered a spot to the rodeo clown—who could have cartwheeled around the barrels faster than they.

Still, there was no reason they couldn't finish in style. Lazy J-style, granted, but style nonetheless.

"Let's bring it home," she said, applying her heels once more. Chauncey lifted his dripping nose out of the washtub and obediently plodded toward Jake and Lady Laramie, kicking up to a trot only when the buckskin mare whickered her welcome.

"Whoa," Laramie said, tugging on the reins. As if stopping was a problem. Chauncey quit even before they'd reached his new girlfriend—he was a gelding, after all—and dropped his head to graze as if such strenuous exercise required his immediate nourishment.

Jake didn't laugh. But he did click an imaginary stopwatch and say, "Five minutes. Not bad, New York. With practice, I bet you can whittle it down to four."

Laramie swung her leg over the saddle and slid off. Her face was flushed, so she took off her hat and wiped her forehead, pretending it was the heat that had gotten to her. "This was only our first attempt." Her chin tilted regally. "By next week, we'll be...we'll be..." She gave up with a roll of her eyes. "Okay, we'll still be rounding the first barrel. Good barrel racers do the cloverleaf in, what, something like twenty seconds?"

"Something like."

She sighed. "Twenty seconds isn't even enough time for a call to action to travel between Chauncey's brain and his hooves." She patted the horse in consolation. "No offense, barrel-gut."

"Now you know," Jake said, being pretty decent about it. "The horse was retired for a reason."

Laramie loosened the girth and lifted off the saddle, letting Jake take it from her when he offered. Normal horses required a cooling-down period after a workout, but in this case she could safely skip that step. Chauncey, by definition, was his own cool-down.

What kind of man was her father to buy a way-past-his-prime barrel racer? She could go two ways on that: one was that Buck had been duped, the other that he'd been generous and kind—Jake would say softhearted—in giving a retired horse a home.

Laramie decided on the latter. Whenever possible, she was giving Buck the benefit of the doubt.

Jake put his hands on her shoulders from behind. "Tomorrow, maybe you'll try the spurs."

She nearly leaped out of her boots. "After that debacle, what makes you think I haven't given up?" She swung around, twisting out from beneath his touch. They hadn't yet talked about last night's kiss and she wasn't sure that she wanted to. The attraction simmering between them was the kind that defied definition. It was simply...instinct. Dumb, blind instinct. Earthquaking, yes, but not the kind of solid base on which to build a lifetime love.

No way was she going to fall for the first handsome, charming, unbelievably sexy cowboy who made her squirm in her boots.

Jake answered. "You've got a stubborn streak, New York. I don't figure you for a quitter."

She ignored how that applied to him personally and focused on the Lazy J instead. "What am I fighting for?" She gestured at the seedy grounds and rundown ranch house. "Is anything here worth it?"

"Maybe what you want is intangible."

Jake spoke offhandedly, then turned to unbridle Chauncey, giving Laramie time to adjust. His insight startled her. What could he know about her longing for a real home? Despite the similarities in their backgrounds, they'd grown in opposite directions.

She wanted roots.

Jake wanted wings.

That said it all.

With an impressive cool, she told him, "I'm not sure what you mean."

He gathered the dragging reins in a loop. "Just that the Lazy J itself isn't really what you came here to find."

"Why not? It's my inheritance," she insisted, though he was right. She'd wanted to know her father. She'd wanted a keepsake of the heart, not a piece of property that thus far held no real meaning for her.

She couldn't concede the point so soon. "Buck is

gone. The Lazy J is all I have. And you, Jake, are not going to confuse the issue. We still have a deal."

He looked at her from beneath his hat brim, then flipped his bandaged hand in surrender. "Absolutely."

His smile was so unbothered it bothered her. And why that should be annoyed her even more. He had every reason to smile. After the show she'd put on with Chauncey, he must figure it was safe to total up his share of the estate sale. Any talk of intangibles was meant to distract her.

And that went for kissing, too.

No need for kissing, she repeated once more, even though as Jake walked away her gaze lingered helplessly over the rear end view of his very much Cowgirl Club-worthy tight jeans.

Drat that mantra.

LARAMIE HAD ARRANGED for the telephone to be turned on, so the first thing she did after a quick shower and change of clothes was to call Molly Broome. She was feeling defeated, and Molly was good at consolation. However, Molly was also a busy lady. It was high season at the Triple Eight dude ranch, and according to Sharleen Jackleen, the newly promoted housekeeper, they were fully booked and Molly was out buying supplies for a Saturday barbecue for fifty. Laramie left a message she wasn't sure Molly would get—Sharleen broke a nail midway through the transcription—and then she telephoned Grace.

Grace Farrow McHenry lived on Goldstream Ranch with her husband, Shane. Shane was the tall, rugged, quiet type, a cowboy custom-built to meet every one of the Cowgirl Club's standards. Lightning quick, Grace had snatched him up long before Molly and Laramie were up to speed, and rode with him out of Manhattan on a trail of cowboy kisses and tiny green feathers.

It was seven rings before Grace picked up, breathless. "Am I interrupting?" Laramie asked, thinking that after five months of marriage, Grace and Shane still qualified as newlyweds—particularly since his mother and sister had recently moved off the ranch.

"Just doing the hokey-pokey," Grace said.

Laramie's brow furrowed. "The hokey-pokey? Is that what you and Shane are calling it these days?"

Grace chuckled. "Sorry to disappoint. I meant the real hokey-pokey. It's a long story, but to keep it short I'll just say that there are a group of day-care kids here for a tour of the ranch, and first I had to talk Shane into coming down from the high pasture to do his Cowboy Shane act, and then we had the water-trough disaster and the pitchfork incident, and so a corral hokey-pokey was our last resort. Needless to say, I'm rethinking our decision to try and get pregnant."

"Whew."

Grace let out a shriek. "But what about you? I nearly forgot you're in Laramie! Omigosh—what's your father's ranch like?"

Laramie swallowed. "It's not exactly a ranch."

"But you said..."

"It's a ranch house, suburban Brady Bunch-style. Only worse. There are lawn ornaments and shag carpeting, bowling trophies and, oh, boy, the backyard. You will not believe the backyard." Laramie was sorry she had to pause for breath. Grace's chatterbox mode had its advantages—getting all her complaints out in one fell swoop was liberating. "There are sheep and chickens and a pig—all squeezed together in a couple of cruddy acres. And there's Goliath. He came in the doggy door and bit me on the butt—"

"Wait!" Grace interrupted. "What's Goliath? A...what do you call those big dogs? A doberman?"

"Worse," Laramie said blackly. "He's a miniature horse. Jake is outside wrestling with him right now and..." She leaned over the kitchen counter and lifted a corner of the dingy curtain. "Ouch. Goliath just kicked him in the kneecap. Maybe I should go and help."

"Don't go! I have to know! Who's Jake?"

"Jake is..." Laramie had to stop and line up her thoughts, because every time she thought of Jake her synapses misfired, resulting in touch-me-kiss-me-lick-me endorphins shooting toward various parts of her body. This was very nice for her body, but very bad for her brain.

"Actually," she admitted, "Jake is the reason I'm calling. Even the Lazy J's been reduced to second place."

"Hold on. I've gotta sit." After a muffled thump, Grace came back on the line. "You've knocked me off my feet, cowgirl. Now, who's Jake? And what the heck's a Lazy J?"

Laramie kept an eye on the activity outside as she explained about Buck Jones's misbegotten legacy and the rodeo cowboy who was included in the package.

After she'd finished, Grace was silent for a moment. "And this is not pleasing you because...?"

"Well, the Lazy J's a dump. And Jake's halfway out the door. There's no future in either of 'em."

"Cowgirls make their own future."

"It's not that easy."

"Whoa, tell me about it—I survived the winter that defines the phrase *when hell freezes over!* Or tell Molly, for that matter. Did you know that she's thinking of buying the Triple Eight from Cord Wyatt? After that whole counterfeiting scam, I guess the ranch got sort of infamous, and now Mol's up to her ears in reservations. She's going to convince Raleigh to quit the Secret Service and go partners with her. And *that's* what I mean about making your own future."

Laramie gulped. "Grace, that's all well and good for you two. You have real ranches to work with, and men who are at least halfway amenable. All I've got…" Her voice trailed off again. Jake was straddling Goliath, squeezing the tiny horse's neck between his thighs as he held on to his head with one hand and with the other pulled back Goliath's lips to examine his teeth. Goliath was resisting with all his might, his hocks practically in the dirt, his bushy tail whirling up a sandstorm.

"Has he kissed you yet?" Grace asked with sly precision.

Laramie's mouth went dry. She dropped the curtain. "I should let you get back to those kids before there's a hay mow massacre."

"Oh, no, no, they're fine. They've got two teachers and Shane threatened the troublemakers with lassoing. Really—I can talk."

"Well, I can't," Laramie said quickly when Jake stomped on the porch outside the back door. He was beating dust out of his jeans. "I've got to go. Jake's coming inside—"

"Oooh, put him on the phone!"

"Absolutely not." The door opened and for a moment her mind went blank. She turned too fast, getting wound up in the phone cord she'd stretched across the kitchen.

In her ear, Grace said cozily, "Then you've got to tell me about the kiss."

Laramie lowered her voice. "I can't talk."

"You can answer. Was it hot?"

"Mmm, no, not exactly…"

"Then was it sweet?"

"Yeah." Laramie could feel Jake's gaze on her, but she refused to look at him. "Sort of."

"Now, that's interesting. From what you said, he sounds like the kind of cowboy who'd grab a woman and kiss her soundly enough to overwhelm all objections. Don'tcha think?"

"I can't think," Laramie said desperately. She sneaked a peek at Jake. He was washing his hands at the kitchen sink and aiming quick, interested glances at her over his shoulder.

"A girlfriend?" he asked when he caught her looking.

She smiled vacantly. *He knows we're talking about him,* she thought first, which was quickly followed by the realization that he had her acting like a giggly schoolgirl—something she'd never been.

"But since he didn't do that," Grace continued, oblivious, "the man must have unplumbed depths. And you're the lucky cowgirl who gets to do the plumbing!"

"I'm no good with a wrench." Hah! Let Jake try to figure that one out.

"Break out the serious tools. You've got a killer bod. Use it, cowgirl."

Laramie spun to unwind herself, then stretched the cord as far as she could in the opposite direction so that she was standing around the corner in the foyer. "Grace!" she whispered urgently. "I'm not interested in seducing him. What's the point? He's still going to leave—he's made that clear."

"What's the point?" Her laugh rang hollow. "Oh, Laramie, hon, you've lost your way. I'm going to have to call an emergency session of the Cowgirl Club." Grace started calculating miles and speed limits and the odds of convincing Molly that she should leave the dude ranch in Sharleen's incapable hands. Both Grace and Molly lived near Treetop, a small town tucked amid the eastern slopes of the Rockies, a couple of hundred miles away from the capital city of Laramie.

"I'll call you back to set something up," Laramie said once she'd managed to break in. They said goodbye and she sidled into the kitchen with the receiver, only to find that Jake had gone back outside. Which was a good thing for her thought processes.

But not so hot for her killer bod.

"SHE DOESN'T WANT ME," Jake said, out on the back porch. He'd given Goliath the heave-ho and gingerly lowered himself onto the ratty old upholstered bench that hadn't been moved in more than a dozen years. The colorless fabric was torn into long frayed strips, revealing gobs of stuffing. "You hear that, Goliath? She doesn't want me."

The miniature horse ripped out a pocket of dandelion weeds and chewed with a sullen look in his eyes.

"Least not in the kitchen," Jake qualified a minute

later. The bedroom was still an option. He just couldn't figure where a wrench fit into the deal.

Laramie switched on some music inside the house. Female-type stuff. Had to be her own. All Buck had in the house was old Johnny Cash eight-track cassettes.

Okay, fine. Laramie and he were a no-go. Or ought to be.

He would do the smart thing, for once in his life. Soon, he'd be physically up to snuff. He'd call up some of his rodeo buddies, scout out the territory vis-à-vis the Naylors. Lady Laramie could be stashed on a friend's ranch while he went to confront them. A bet was a bet, and a Naylor was a greedy sonovabee. They'd take cash. It pained Jake to pay off a cheater, but he couldn't risk the Naylor brothers showing up at the Lazy J. Luckily, he'd saved a healthy percentage of his rodeo winnings. He could afford his own stupidity.

Next, he'd sign over his half of Buck's place. Laramie would be glad to see him go, except maybe in that small part of her that kissed him with such a sweetly lusty affection.

Lust he could handle. But sweet affection?

Reason enough for him to get out now.

"It's the smart thing to do," he told Goliath, who was standing with his head low, breathing sour dandelion breath. "You don't have to look at me that way."

5

As Laramie figured it, Helen Olney was the reason Jake had insisted upon accompanying her to the library. Either he wanted to revisit his former flame or he wanted to vet the conversation. Tales of gushy first kisses and teenage pranks could be damaging to his precious reputation as a rough, tough rodeo cowboy.

She smiled to herself. As if seeing him take one in the kneecap from a miniature horse hadn't already done enough damage. Not to mention how un-tough he'd looked, stumbling to the bathroom at 6:00 a.m. with bed head and pillow creases and boxer shorts that hung nearly to his knees. She'd have snickered over the sight if not for the yellow-and-purple constellation of bruises that mapped his body. She couldn't tease a man who…well, who took it like a cowboy.

"And here you are," Helen said cheerfully, rising to greet them. The branch library was on the small side, but its rooms were airy and bright, filled with neat rows of books, computers, colorful posters and other decorations. At the moment, there were few patrons, so Helen indicated that they could speak freely.

"Took you long enough to get here," she scolded. It had been two days.

Laramie wasn't sure if the blond librarian referred to herself or to Jake. As he was doing his reticent cowboy thing, she stepped forward and shook Helen's hand. They exchanged hello-how-are-yous. "I had to drag Jake in here, kicking and screaming," Laramie said, tongue in cheek. She shot him a sly glance. "Is there something in his past he's trying to cover up?"

Helen was game for a round of male-ego tweaking. She tapped a pumpkin-colored nail against her chin. "Hmm. I remember a particularly embarrassing original poem he was forced to read out loud in English class. What was it called, Jakey? The Rime of the Ancient Gunslinger?"

"No worse than your ode to Mel Gibson." Jake caught the nape of Helen's neck and hauled her toward himself with a rough affection that was brotherly rather than romantic. Or so Laramie hoped.

Helen leaned companionably against his chest. "Aah…the Mel years. I remember them well. I believe I compared Mel's eyes to a deep river and his voice to a violin and his…his—"

"Naked behind," said Jake.

"That would be a ripe apricot," Helen confessed, sotto voce, with a wink at Laramie.

She was still weighing their easy camaraderie. "Are you certain it's Mel you memorialized?"

"Oh, yes. It was definitely Mel." Helen reached around and squeezed Jake's posterior. "This one's too hard. Not nearly ripe enough."

He gave her a gentle push. "Bold wench. Keep away."

Helen opened her arms and rounded on him. "You know I love my Jakey!" A big hug. "Even though I don't see you nearly enough." She glanced at Laramie. "My sweetie, Karl, and I attend lots of rodeos. Have you ever seen Jakey in action?"

"Only with Goliath."

Jake's grin warned Laramie he was about to turn the tables. "Speaking of ripe apricots…"

Helen's mischievous glance darted from one to the other. "Oopsie. Has someone been sampling forbidden fruit?"

"Oh—no," Laramie blurted. "Not Jake."

"I don't bite," he said. "Usually."

"It was Goliath." Laramie wanted the record set straight. "He…well, he bit me."

"On the apricot," Jake said, and Helen giggled.

"It was nothing." Laramie made a face. "A suitable welcome to the Lazy J, I suppose."

Helen nodded. "I've seen Buck Jones's house."

"That's why I'm here." Laramie disregarded Jake's pained expression. "Do you have any, uh, how-to books about sheep shearing?"

"Sheep shearing?" Helen was as skeptical as Jake.

Laramie maintained her cool. "I'm taking care of business at the Lazy J. There are two enormous balls of dirty cotton batting waddling around the backyard corrals. They've got legs, so I think they're sheep."

"I'll see what I can come up with." Helen bustled off, a bright spark in an orange top and black skirt, her steep heels clacking on the stone floor. She was one of those women whose every movement was accompanied by jingles or swooshes or clickety-clacks. Laramie was not.

"I could also use information about chickens," she called. Jake grumbled as he eased himself onto the edge of one of the reading tables, so she smiled and said, "Pigs, too."

Helen frowned over her terminal. "Have you tried the county extension office? They have pamphlets."

She tapped keys. "I'm not finding anything on sheep shearing, specifically, but how about a good general book on farming? We've got one, although it's thirty years old. The methods may be out of date." She disappeared into the stacks. "We don't have the budget to replace books as frequently as I'd like."

"That sounds fine, Helen. I'm not trying to establish an agricultural showplace." Laramie raised her brows at Jake and added, so only he'd hear, "All I've got to do is win one little bet."

"Why not save us both the trouble," he complained.

"It's no trouble." At least not much. While she might have brushed up on her barrel-racing techniques as well, after a second day of futility she'd given up on the idea of bringing home the glory on Chauncey. Presently her hopes were pinned on the sheep and chickens. If they could produce a little wool, a few measly eggs…

Helen arrived, carrying a small stack of books. "Here you go!" She blew the dust off a heavy tome and handed it to Laramie. "That's the dreary technical stuff. I also found you a paperback—*Farming on Ten Acres or Less*. There's a section on livestock. And here's one more—*From Birth to Bacon: Twenty Easy Steps for Raising and Slaughtering Hogs*."

Laramie choked. "Oh, no, I don't think…"

Jake stepped up to lay claim on the book. "That's exactly what we want. Thanks, Helen."

"Jay-ake. I am not going to—" Laramie shut up when she saw that he was teasing her. She snatched the offending book out of his hands, certain that eating Buck's pets would not win her any points in her effort to earn her father's posthumous favor.

What would? It might help if she knew what his vision for the Lazy J had been in the first place. She considered Helen and her voluble expansiveness. Then she considered Jake, and his taciturn pessimism.

"Can I check these books out without a card?" she asked, calculating her next move.

"Sure. I'll give you a temporary card." Helen got busy with the paperwork, entering Laramie's vital information into the computer as they talked. "Are you planning on living here in Laramie? If so, we might as well fill out the form for a permanent card while we're at it."

After a glance at Jake, who'd been slowly backing toward the door but had halted to hear her answer, Laramie shook her head. "Let's hold off on that. I haven't made a decision."

Helen handed over the rather permanent-seeming farming books without comment.

Laramie hesitated. "I'll be with you in a minute, Jake."

He took the hint, said goodbye to Helen and departed.

Laramie listened to be sure he'd left, then asked Helen, "Did you know my father, Buck Jones? I'm hoping to find out anything I can about him."

"Sorry, I can't help. Jake wasn't the come-on-over type, so I never met his stepfather. And Buck must not have been a reader, because he never came to the library."

Laramie sighed. "He didn't seem to have many friends, either."

Helen cocked her head, making the big wooden beads of her dangling earrings click. "What does Jake say?"

"Not much."

The librarian laughed. "Yeah, that sounds like Jake. His is the original stiff upper lip."

"Even in high school?"

"Especially in high school."

"I can't seem to get a handle on either of them." Strike that. She hadn't meant Jake's lips—those she'd already taken on a test drive and they'd handled fine. "Jake and my father, that is."

Helen agreed. "Men are complicated creatures. The way they suppress their emotions, we women may never figure out how their minds work."

Sounds from the entrance made both women glance that way expectantly, but it was a pair of library patrons, an elderly couple wearing matching glen-plaid golfing outfits. Helen greeted them by name, then directed the woman toward the new Danielle Steel.

Laramie picked up her books. "I should let you get back to work." She hesitated again. "You seem to have your finger on the pulse. Can you think of anyone who might have been on friendly terms with Buck Jones? Anyone at all?"

The man in the plaid knickers looked up from his newspaper. "Did you say Buck Jones?"

Laramie's hopes rose. "You knew him?"

The old man waved the wooden wand that held the paper. Pages rattled. "My daughter lived across the street from the nut! Imagine! Ruthann had to look at that horrible, horrible house every time she opened her curtains or stepped out the door. Buck Jones was an awful man. He fought the lawsuit tooth and nail. Nearly gave Ruthann an ulcer. Horrible!"

Laramie gulped. "There was a lawsuit?"

"The neighbors tried to force him and his junk and

all those smelly animals out of the subdivision.'' The golfer shook his head. ''Didn't work. Jones wouldn't budge and the dang lawyers couldn't make him even though the case dragged on for years.'' The man went back to his newspaper, muttering beneath his breath about the decline of neighborly manners.

Laramie might have asked more, but she wasn't sure she wanted to hear the answers. It seemed that Jake was right. Buck had been a crackpot. A bad joke. And now, whether out of stubbornness or misplaced pride, she was picking up the gauntlet.

''Jake wants to sell the house,'' she told Helen as they walked to the door.

''And you don't.''

A shrug. ''I guess I'm my father's daughter.''

''You're keeping the windmills? The gnomes and trolls? The bobbing fisherman and plastic reindeer?''

''Heavens, no. I'm not that far gone.''

''Then would you mind if I took them?'' Helen seemed quite eager for a woman who matched her shoes and nail polish to her outfits without flaw.

''Whatever for?''

''For that.'' Helen swept a hand at a notice affixed to the bulletin board near the entrance. In bold red letters it announced an impending weekend festival of epic proportions, something called Rodeo Days. ''Rodeo Days is a street fair, rodeo competition, parade and bake sale all rolled up into one. Proceeds benefit the library and other neighborhood charities. I'm in charge of the Saturday morning flea market, and I just know that your father's collection of kitsch will sell like hotcakes. People love that kind of stuff, the cheesier, the better.'' Helen slapped a hand over her mouth. ''No offense.''

Laramie offered a wry smile. "None taken." A touch of guilt squirmed in the pit of her stomach, but her loyalty to Buck could extend only so far. "You can come and collect the stuff right out of the yard any time you want. I doubt that Jake will object. Apparently there was no love lost between him and Buck."

"Oh, I don't know. You have to understand that when Jake moved to town, he was just sixteen and sort of wary and wounded. Buck left him alone, which was what Jake needed right then. He didn't trust a soul, and certainly not another stepfather."

"Why was that?"

Helen's features tightened with concern. "How long have you known Jake?"

"A matter of days." *But I've wanted to meet him all my life,* she admitted to herself, and then was startled to realize that it was true. In her heart of hearts, it was true. And that could lead to only one thing.

Danger: Heartbreak Straight Ahead.

"Is that all?" Helen blinked, disconcerted. "You two seem so natural together. I thought..."

"We're barely acquaintances," Laramie said. A lie. She didn't French-kiss acquaintances.

"Maybe it's because you're so alike."

That again. "We're also very different."

Helen paused to consider before continuing. "Okey-dokey. Since I know how closemouthed Jake can be, I'm going to clue you in on what little I know. See, Jake was always a tough nut to crack. When he started school, I tried to be friends, but it was two straight weeks before he'd even return my hello. He was like a wild animal—I had to win his trust gradually, over time. But something told me it was worth the effort." She grinned. "And it wasn't only that he was already the cutest cowboy this side of the Rockies."

They had moved out into the enclosed entryway. Laramie glanced past the short flight of steps and through the glass doors. Jake was waiting for her outside, pacing back and forth on the sidewalk. If he'd had a tail like Goliath, it would have been switching.

"What is his problem?" she asked softly.

Helen had turned solemn. "He'd been abandoned by his real father at six and then mistreated by a subsequent stepfather. Pretty badly, I guess. Jake would never go into details. He'd even run away at some point, but came back again, to protect his mom, I think. Their life was better with Buck. Jake might not admit it. But I know. I saw the change in him... eventually."

Laramie's emotions were mixed. She was concerned for Jake, appalled by his mother's choices, riddled with outrage that no one but Helen had offered aid or friendship.

Unless Buck's hands-off approach had been as helpful as Helen believed. To be blunt, though, she wondered if Buck had done nothing simply because that was what he always did. Certainly he'd shown even less parental interest in herself.

"You could say that Jake's been running ever since," Helen concluded. "I've never known him to stay in one place for very long."

Laramie drew her gaze over Jake's hardened features. "To make a home, you must first feel safe."

"Exactly," Helen said. "You know firsthand?"

"In my own way."

"Then you may be just what Jake needs."

Although there was no longer any point in denying her romantic interest in the cowboy, Laramie wasn't ready to go quite so far. "Maybe, maybe not. He seems pretty determined to keep things as they are."

Helen patted her shoulder. "They all are. If men ran the world, we'd still be living in caves, listening to them grunt about how marriage and material comforts are for sissies." Helen let out a little sigh of her own. "I keep telling Karl it takes a real man to commit, but he's not getting it."

Laramie nodded as if she knew. "Nothing turns men to mice faster than the *m* word." In actuality, the closest she'd come to marriage was being a bridesmaid at Grace's wedding.

She eyed Helen. "Can I ask you one more question?"

"Sure. I'm the information lady."

"Why do you call him Jakey?"

The stylish librarian smiled, pleased with herself. "Oh, gosh, that's just 'cause he hates it. Kinda puts him in his place, you know? Reminds him that he wasn't always the rough-stock rider all the cowgirls swooned over." She paused to consider Laramie's hat, boots and jeans. "Which reminds me…" She clickety-clacked back into the library.

Jake opened one of the glass doors and poked his head inside. "Can we get out of here now or do you have to hear about my every teenage blunder?"

"What makes you think we're talking about you?" Helen retorted, returning with a clipboard. "As it happens, I was about to sign Laramie up for the Rodeo Days cowgirl competition."

Jake's scowl changed into an expression that approached delight. Which didn't bode well for Laramie, even though seeing his eyes light up had given her a pleasurable jolt.

She girded herself. "Do I dare ask?"

"It's perfect for you" was all Jake would say as he climbed the short flight of steps, favoring his right side. To Helen, he added, "What are you waiting for? Sign her up."

Helen brandished a pen.

"Wait a minute," Laramie said. "What is the cowgirl competition?"

"It's part of Rodeo Days. A really fun event. I've entered myself and Karl. You don't have to be an honest-to-goodness cowgirl, of course. In fact it's better if you're not—"

"You've entered Karl?"

Helen nodded with enthusiasm. "In the cowboy competition. They run simultaneously. The winners preside over the Sunday parade on horseback."

"I'm not much of a rider," Laramie warned, thinking of Chauncey.

"Can you ride a rocking horse?" Helen's eyes were dancing with secret amusement. Even Jake was trying not to smile too broadly as she nudged him, muffling her laugh behind the clipboard. "Can you sit in an outhouse? When it's on wheels? And moving? See, the cowgirls sit in them and the cowboys push them down the street...."

"Yeah, I see," Laramie said, although she didn't. Not really. Country folk had strange methods of entertainment.

"We're always looking for new contestants," Helen pleaded. "The more the merrier."

"Sign her up," Jake urged. "A cowgirl from New York is sure to be a real crowd pleaser."

"New York! This is getting better and better." Helen proffered the pen, smiling hopefully, her pert nose crinkling across the bridge.

"Okay, I'll do it." Laramie aimed a challenging stare at Jake, who was far too complacent to suit her. "If Jake will do it, too."

"Fabulous." Helen handed over the clipboard. "A two-for-one deal is perfect since the competitors have to pair up, anyway."

"Now, hold on," he said.

"You chicken?" Laramie squinted like a gun-slinger at high noon. She scribbled her name on the sign-up sheet and then thrust the clipboard at him.

"I'm not even going to be here," he protested.

"The competition's in ten days. You promised me four weeks."

Helen looked interested.

"I can't waste my time on—"

"It's for a good cause."

Helen nodded eagerly.

"I'm still healing—"

"Three days, you said. Or was that just bragging?"

Helen stroked his bandaged hand, cooing with sympathy.

Laramie's chin jutted. "That's okay. I saw Bobby Torrance's name on the list. He can be my partner."

Jake couldn't sign fast enough.

"THE LAZY J SEEMS TO BE a hotbed of sexual dysfunction." Laramie slapped shut the farming book she'd been consulting and leaned back against the porch railing. With a desultory grace, she stretched her legs across the steps lengthwise, crossing one over the other.

Jake's eyes traced the long curved lines of her legs, displayed to fine advantage in denim cutoffs and sassy red cowboy boots. After only five days in Wyoming, she'd acquired a glowing tan, not just on her legs but on every inch of skin that he could see, which, between her shorts and her tiny red-and-white-striped tank top, was quite a lot. Enough to prove that he, at least, was suffering no dysfunction whatsoever.

"Perhaps a *hotbed* is not the proper word to use, considering." The corners of her wide mouth lifted briefly with amusement. She glanced sidelong at Jake, lashes lowered. "You think?"

"My bed's cold. How's yours?" Since their kiss, they'd been circling each other warily, afraid to get too close, not yet ready to go too far.

She fanned her face. "It's eighty-eight degrees. How cold can a bed be?"

Pretty darn cold. "When it's dysfunctional..."

"I was mainly talking about the rooster." She glanced at the grazing horses—the buckskin mare, the bay gelding. "Chauncey's condition is beyond dysfunction."

"If you're looking for candidates—" Jake indicated Goliath, who was engaged in his favorite pastime, worrying the gate that separated him from Lady Laramie. "Acute frustration can be torture." The little horse whinnied at the mare, who turned, ignoring him, her tail swishing idly across her lustrous golden hindquarters.

Goliath whipped around and charged across the small sandy pen, bucking, kicking and generally raising fifty kinds of hell. Jake had to sympathize.

Laramie drew up her legs defensively, leaning forward to wind her arms around them. Her silky black ponytail slipped across her shoulder blades. A skinny strap no more substantial than a piece of string slid down her bare arm, drawing Jake's attention to the smooth S curve of her armpit and left breast, flattened against her thigh. He nearly groaned out loud, the need to touch her pulsing in each one of his fingertips.

"Keep away from me," she suddenly said, and he clenched his hands. But she was talking to Goliath, who'd settled down to nose at the grass that grew long near the porch. His eyes rolled at Jake and Laramie, showing white around the edges. Although Goliath was still irritated about losing his passage into the house, they'd settled into an uneasy agreement of mutual antipathy.

"I thought I'd expand the flock, but according to the book, the rooster's failing in his duty," Laramie groused as she kept a cautious eye on Goliath. "The eggs won't hatch."

Jake watched the rooster chase the speckled hens around their enclosure. Every now and then, in a flurry of pecking and flying feathers, he caught one. "The spirit seems willing."

"Pfft. Either that bird is shooting blanks or the equipment has failed and he's too dumb to realize it." She cast an accusing glance at Jake, whose only crime was being at hand. "Just my luck. Buck owned an impotent rooster. What earthly good can a limp bird do me?"

"I don't dare imagine."

"There must be something…" Her eyes narrowed. "Do you think they make Viagra for barnyard fowl?"

"I couldn't say."

"*Playbird of the Month?*"

"I wouldn't know."

She reached out and slapped his boot. "You're no help."

He relished even that. "Well," he said, silently berating himself for being so desperate for a woman's touch, "there are still the sheep."

She brightened. "I found a pair of clippers. And Helen dropped off an instructional 4-H pamphlet when she came to collect the flea market junk."

Jake nodded. He'd trundled a creaky wheelbarrow around the yard after the two women, collecting several heaps of the useless lawn ornaments.

"Still…" Laramie tugged on the hem of his jeans and damn if his senses didn't leap. "I have to admit the shearing process intimidates me. What if I zip when I should have zapped and accidentally draw blood? Will you help?"

"That's not how our deal works."

Laramie threw back her head, nostrils flared. "So you're just going to sit on that bench and watch while I do all the dirty work? Talk about dysfunctional!"

It took an effort to maintain the lackadaisical demeanor he'd adopted for the duration. "I'm taking Buck's role in your Lazy J re-creation. As he always said, someone's got to hold down the porch."

"Then I'll do it on my own." The words were brave, but she paused expectantly.

While he admired her grit, Jake didn't jump in to volunteer. She had it right—she was on her own. And would be the stronger for it. He knew from personal experience. Just as he knew that Buck Jones was no one's cowboy hero, and that the Lazy J could only continue to deteriorate, regardless of Laramie's spunky efforts.

"First thing tomorrow," she promised under her

breath, and he was reminded that despite her easy adjustment to the tranquillity of rural life, she was only a pretend cowgirl from New York City—far removed from the earthy practicalities that ranchers and farmers dealt with every day.

"There's always the pig," he said.

"Forget it!"

"From birth to bacon..." Lord, he was mean.

She stood and hefted the heavy farming book over her head. "Suggest that again and I'll batter your skull with all ten pounds of the *1970 Agricultural Yearbook*."

"Watch out, Laramie. Goliath's sneaking up on you."

She shot up the steps as if he'd lit a fire beneath her tail. When—halfway through the door—she looked behind her and saw that the spotted horse had simply returned to the gate to moon over the equine Laramie, she came back out and dropped the book in Jake's lap. He said, "Oomph," and she spun on her heel. The door banged shut behind her like a gunshot. The impotent rooster crowed, setting off the squabbling chickens and grunting hog.

Recognizing that he was inviting trouble, Jake set aside the library book to follow Laramie inside. Life on the road being what it was, he'd learned to act quickly in matters of the opposite sex. He wasn't accustomed to taking so much time with a woman, even one he wasn't sure he should get involved with in the first place.

Living with Laramie was hell on his intentions. For a normal person, five days wasn't a long time. For Jake, five days spent in one place during rodeo season equaled an eternity. Particularly when they were spent with such an attractive, confounding, taxing woman like Laramie Jones.

No, not a woman *like* her.

It was Laramie that he wanted. Specifically Laramie. Only Laramie.

Beautiful, fierce, feisty Laramie Jones.

For five days, he'd gotten to know her. They'd chatted about little things, avoided the big, exchanged jokes and philosophies—preferably at the same time since he wasn't big on capital-letter Serious Discussions. They'd sketched in childhood histories and started to learn each other's personal habits, both good and bad.

He knew that she never ate breakfast even though every morning she swore she was going to start. He knew she wore a Jets jersey to bed when she felt cold and a Mets T-shirt when the temperature climbed. She treated her cowboy hat like a diamond tiara. Ate sprouts, wheat germ…and rich chocolate ice cream. Sang in the shower. Shaved her legs there, too. Said she never watched TV, but was a secret Letterman fanatic. Hated clutter and sloppiness. Called her mother every evening and fretted for fifteen minutes afterward. Worked as a travel agent, but seemed ready to quit, wasn't as sophisticated as she might hope, and had sworn devout loyalty to her friends and something called the Cowgirl Club.

She was tart, smart, independent. She hid her self-doubt and emotional scars beneath a quick-tongued, tough-girl veneer, just as he buried his with pessimism. She was as attracted to him as he was to her.

They were meant to be lovers.

He would break her heart.

And still…he couldn't stay away from her.

He found her in the living room, washing windows. The bowling trophies, 3-D artwork and ceramic dalmatians had gone to Helen; the rest of the trash had been carted away. Laramie had cleaned every surface, vacuumed and shampooed and revacuumed the vast expanse of shag carpeting, but nothing could make the room—or the house—look like the ranch she'd admitted to dreaming of owning.

"I think," she said with her back to him, "if I scrub hard enough, I can get the dried horse slobber off the picture window and its sill. All I can figure is that Goliath must have been pressing his nose to the glass and salivating over the fiberglass palomino."

Her voice was wound tight. A trickle of perspiration ran from her nape, sliding between her shoulder blades. Jake hesitated for a moment, battling his desire, and then slowly swiped a thumb over the trickle, his knuckles grazing her skin. The warmth and silky-smooth texture of it hit him low, where it hurts. Her quick inhalation and involuntary shudder of pleasure hit him higher. In his hard, cold heart, where it really counted.

Sonovabee. Turned out his heart was neither as hard nor as cold as he'd come to believe.

And that knowledge—that gift—gave him the strength to turn and walk away from her.

"I'M GOING TO SLEEP with him." Laramie had been saying it all evening to herself, just as only days ago she'd sworn there was no further need for kissing. Ha!

"You're going to sleep with him?" Molly Broome echoed from the lobby of the Triple Eight dude ranch. Laramie had caught up with her there at last, going over the upcoming month's reservations. "Wow. That's a fast turnaround."

"I know," Laramie said into the telephone. "It's not like me."

"You told Grace he's all wrong for you."

"Well, yeah. That hasn't changed."

Molly's caution and curiosity were palpable, even over the phone line. "Then...?"

"What happened?" Laramie said under her breath. "Good question." Putting her feelings into words was impossible. How could she explain that Jake had touched her once and then walked away, and that was when she knew there was nothing else to do but sleep with him? If they made love, she'd remember him forever; if they didn't make love, she'd remember him forever with regret. Once upon a time, Grace had said the same thing about Shane. Only now did Laramie truly understand.

She closed her eyes because somehow that made it easier to confess her most private thoughts. "Has a man ever touched you with such a simple, honest reverence that you could feel him inside you long before he was actually...inside you?"

Molly was silent, except for the soft sound of her breathing. Finally she swallowed audibly and said with such a fervor that Laramie's eyes moistened beneath their lids, "Oh, yes."

"Raleigh?"

"Of course Raleigh!"

"Of course." Laramie smiled sadly to herself. Molly was a woman who'd fallen in love once in her lifetime and couldn't imagine that it could be any other way. She didn't know how lucky she was that her fiancé, Raleigh Tate, agreed wholeheartedly.

"And it's like that with you and this Jake Killian character, huh?"

"I think so, yes." *I know so. I feel him.*

"But you're not..."

"No, Mol. It's extremely unlikely that the Cowgirl Club is going to go three for three in the cowboy department. Jake's just not eligible—by his own accord. I don't foresee a happy ending."

"And yet you intend to give him license to break your heart?"

Laramie's throat tightened. "What else can I do? The man has the sort of gruff charm that's lethal to me. You know I never go for the sappy, sentimental stuff." Not to mention that one look—one devastating touch—was enough to make her shiver in her boots and contemplate turning Buck's crap-o-rama into a love nest.

"Oh, Laramie...promise me you'll think this over. I imagine Grace told you to jump him—"

"More or less. You know Grace."

"Yup. With Grace, it's why look when you can leap. And with me, it's more why leap when there's a perfectly nice, safe view from right here. We're not exactly synchronized."

"Well, Molly, my dear, I can think of at least one instance when even you led with your heart. Does dashing pell-mell through the snow to Raleigh's cabin sound familiar?"

"Mm-hmm." Either Molly was purring or she was holding one of the young cats that had become the dude ranch's mascots. "But you said yourself that this rodeo cowboy of yours is refusing to be a hero. As I see it, that's a crucial sticking point. And jumping into bed with him won't resolve it."

Laramie twisted wrathfully on the hard kitchen chair. "I know, I know. But I can't help myself. I just have this feeling that we ought to be lovers." She gnawed her lip. "But is it the reasonable thing to do? Probably not."

"You don't need my approval."

"I guess I was hoping you'd be able to talk me out of it."

Molly laughed softly. "It sounds like your mind is made up, cowgirl. I only hope you know what you're doing."

"That's just it. I don't. I'm all out of whack. I swear, it's the Lazy J. Everything is upside down and inside out here, including me."

"No progress on the In Search of Buck Jones front?"

"Let's see. He was apparently a stubborn, lazy, antisocial pack rat who retired early on disability. I don't know why I keep hoping for more."

"Because we all expect our parents to be, oh, superhuman, I suppose. It's unrealistic, of course, but realizing that they're not flawless is part of growing up. Keep searching. You'll either find what you need or you'll find a way to deal with the disappointment of not getting it."

Laramie nodded. "You sound so wise, Molly. I was right to call you."

"Then maybe you'll consider following my other advice?"

Laramie gave an involuntary groan of frustration. "All right! I'll wait. A little while longer. We'll see what develops."

"Who knows what might happen?" Molly said, ever the romantic optimist. "Instead of your father, it could be that Jake is the cowboy you came west to find. He could even turn out to be the love of your life.''

"HERE WE ARE AGAIN, Goliath," Jake said from the ratty bench on the back porch. "Two of the sorriest cases I've ever seen." With a flick of his whiskery nose, Goliath flipped the bucket that had held his small ration of oats up into the air.

Jake leaned his head against the wall, waiting for the bucket to roll to a stop. In the kitchen, Laramie's hushed voice was barely audible—if he kept quiet. He hadn't intended to eavesdrop, but since there was no one to talk to except Goliath, he'd picked up on a passing phrase or two.

Sleep with him.

Change my mind.

Can't help myself.

Talk me out of it.

Talk me out of it.

Goliath walked over and head-butted the lattice trim for no apparent reason. "Tell me about it," Jake said, wanting a beer something wicked. He could have had one now that he'd quit taking the pain pills, but Laramie's disapproval had made him realize that lately he'd turned to alcohol far too frequently. And he had the Naylors on his tail to prove it.

All the same, it wasn't the craving for beer that was driving him up the wall. "Whatcha think?" he asked Goliath. "Should we go out on the town together, find us a couple of willing fillies for a change?"

No answer.

Jake put his heels up on the railing. If Laramie

came out, he was only watching the sun paint the clouds pink and gold, drape the hillside in purple. He was not talking to a pint-size horse. Not feeling sorry for himself. Definitely not listening to her come to her senses.

The hell of it was, with her keen tongue and her wry sense of humor and her searching soul, she'd managed to get under his skin.

Crept deep into his heart.

And he'd suddenly become too damn noble to do anything about it.

"A fine pickle," he told the little horse. "She wants me so much she's trying to make herself believe it's right. I want her so much I know that it's gotta be wrong."

Goliath put his front hooves up on the first step and tentatively stretched his head toward the porch floor. His nostrils whiffled air across the dusty planks.

"She needs a solid, stick-in-the-mud man." Laramie had explained some about her gypsy-caravan childhood and her determination to cling to one place ever since. There had to be a pretty strong motive for a woman who liked open spaces so much to stay put in New York as long as she had.

"But she's here now, Goliath. What am I waiting for?"

For it to be right.

Could he settle for honest? Would she?

The wrenching battle between his conscience and his libido screwed Jake's features into a knot. He'd never thought of himself as a weak man, but Lord help him, he felt weak when it came to Laramie. The thing to do was to pack up his gear, load up his horse, and hightail it out of town before he lost all reason and did something really stupid like kiss her and touch her and love her deep into the night.

Unless a guy had an easy ticket out, kissing and touching and loving led straight to trouble. In this case, he might even wind up making promises he couldn't keep.

"Man, oh man, Goliath, I'm all twisted up inside." Jake pulled his straw hat down over his face. Finding out that he had a heart was no picnic. Instead of being overjoyed, he was confused, frustrated and annoyed. "And that's makin' me ornery."

Goliath's hooves clopped on the porch floor.

Despite his mood, all Jake could muster was a lazy-ass "G'wan, git, shoo" that wasn't even strong enough to scare away the bluebottle fly that had landed on the tip of his boots.

6

"THINGS HAVE TO GET BETTER, because they can't get worse," Laramie complained from deep in Buck's bedroom closet. A drop of sweat slid down the side of her nose and plopped onto the silver-tipped toe of one of the size-huge black ostrich cowboy boots she'd just picked up. With every artifact she unearthed from the archaeological dig that passed as a closet, she became more mystified.

Thus far...

Buck was an enigma. A pack rat, he'd saved a lot of useless stuff: cigar boxes full of nails, screws and little bits of wire, all neatly separated (go figure); stacks of magazines (*Field and Stream* and *Western Horseman* were big); old horseshoes; a locked metal strongbox that seemed promising until she'd pried up the lid and found it filled with holey socks and empty tobacco tins.

None of this was of a telling personal nature. Except for a jumble of photocopied tax returns, a divorce decree from Iris Porter and the one baby photo of herself, she'd found no indications of a social life outside the flotsam and jetsam of Buck's existence on the Lazy J. Judging by the outdated decor, life here had stalled out in the mid-seventies and never really resumed.

Which happened to be around the time of her birth.

Significant?

"What gives?" Laramie muttered.

It wasn't that she expected to find a "Dear Daughter" letter that would make everything all right. She only wanted to gain a little knowledge about her parents' relationship. She needed some small sign that her father had cared about what had happened to her beyond a baby photo long out of date.

Shouldn't inheriting the Lazy J be enough? she wondered.

Particularly since it had led her to Jake?

Laramie jerked upright. The boots fell to the floor with a thud. She batted away the dangling chain of the lightbulb lit overhead. Was *Jake* Buck's legacy? Had he named them both in his will so that they'd meet and fall in—well, fall into whatever the heck you'd call their present circumstances?

Nah. Couldn't be.

Buck was neither that thoughtful nor that subtle.

"Hey, Laramie!"

"In here, Jake." She looked around her, winced at the mess, then started shoveling things back into the closet. Jake would think her a fool for trying to read tobacco tins like tarot cards.

He walked into the bedroom. "What are you doing?"

"Cleaning the closet."

He watched her toss a fringed Daniel Boone jacket over her shoulder. Metal hangers clanged. "Shouldn't you be taking things out, not putting them in?"

She brushed back her hair. "There's too much of it. I'm giving up."

"We can call Helen. She'll take it."

"Mmm, maybe." Laramie sought to distract him. "What were you doing outside?"

"Catching the sheep for you."

"Oh. Right. The sheep." She'd promised to shear the sheep and he was going to hold her to it. Thanks, cowboy. She scrubbed her hands on her jeans. "Shall we go?"

"Find anything interesting?" Jake asked as they left the house by the back door.

She shrugged, wondering why he cared. He'd made no bones about his lack of feeling for Buck. It didn't occur to her until a few beats later that he might have asked because he had feelings for *her*.

Too late. Jake strode ahead and opened Goliath's gate. He ushered her through, then slammed it shut just before the ministallion barged past them.

Laramie took a deep breath and looked around. The calendar was into June now, and a lazy breeze was dissipating the morning clouds, clearing the path for another warm, sunny day. They'd been working on clearing up the junk and fixing the fences; when she squinted, the back half of the Lazy J could almost pass for a small ranch or farm.

Jake was watching her. "Need your sunglasses?"

With a self-deprecating laugh, Laramie blinked her eyes wide open. "I was pretending to be a rancher."

"Think shepherdess."

Oh, dear. The sheep were tied to the fence, bleating piteously. No sweet little lambs were they. Their wool coats were dirty, scruffy, smelly. Very smelly. She longed for a washtub, nose plug and pair of thick gloves, but wouldn't dream of admitting it. She had to uphold the Cowgirl Club's reputation. And defend her father's ground.

"My clippers," she remembered. Reprieve.

Jake handed them to her.

"Electricity," she said.

He picked up one end of the extension cord he'd run from the house and plugged the clippers in.

"Forceps?" she tried.

Though the corners of his lips twitched upward, he shook his head. "This should do you."

She gritted her teeth, her smile insincere. "Thanks. You thought of everything." Experimentally, she switched on the clippers. Their buzz was menacing. She turned, her arm swinging wide, narrowly missing shaving a bald streak between the buttons of Jake's chambray work shirt. "Sor-ry!"

He held up his hands. "No problem. I'll step back."

When she looked at the sheep, crowding against each other in alarm, she knew she'd been too hasty in running him off. "You won't even help hold one down?"

"You're the cowgirl, darlin'."

"Not so's you'd notice," she muttered beneath her breath. Recalling how Jake had pinned Goliath, she untied one of the nervous sheep, lifted a leg high and tried to straddle the bleating ewe. Before she could close her knees, it bolted out from beneath her with a little hop, skip and jump, toppling her backward into the grass.

Laramie's head hit first, with a jolt, followed in quick succession by her jabbing elbows and her jouncing derriere. Jake said something she didn't catch because she was too busy saying "oof" and wondering where her city-style sophistication had gone. He offered her his hand; she waved him off and sat up on her own. The sky swung back overhead where it belonged.

"Was that what they call going ass over teakettle?" She put a hand to her wobbly head. "I've always wondered how it went."

"This is pathetic," he said, approaching from behind to encircle her upper arms with his hands and haul her up to her feet. His voice was rough in her ear as he steadied her, his hands sliding lower, spanning her waist. "You win. I'll help."

Her nape tickled. Despite the sunshine, the flesh on her bare arms was cold, then, suddenly, warm and tingling with awareness. Chills and fever.

Jake's body was pressed solidly against hers, hard as iron, honed to a lean perfection, potent with raw masculinity. Fever and chills.

This was not her. This pathetic bumbling creature who wanted only to sink into the grass with Jake on top of her and his tongue in her mouth was not her. It was...

"Laramie?" Jake said, his voice vibrating inside her ear like a honeybee. "I'll help you shear the sheep."

"Now you say," she croaked, looking down. His fingertips branded her midriff. She shouldn't have put on a sleeveless top that had shrunk enough to bare an inch of skin at her waist. Her nipples stood out like thimbles against the thin white cotton.

She crossed her arms over her chest and said stupidly, "I dropped the clippers." Great. Now she was clumsy, visibly excited *and* scatterbrained. Jake was lethal even when he was being charitable.

He released her. Retrieved the clippers. Grabbed one of the sheep by the scruff and neatly upended it.

"C'mon," he coaxed. "You've got to get down here with me, put your knee in her belly—like this. You won't hurt her. Watch the hooves. Make your first cut right along the shoulder..."

It wasn't a pretty procedure. Laramie made more stops and starts than a student driver. Even with Jake's help, the sheep were too squirmy for her to manage. They wriggled out from beneath her wavering clippers several times, resulting in haircuts that looked worse than a punk rocker's.

"Poodle cuts by Picasso," Laramie said, sitting on the grass watching the shorn sheep gambol across the small pasture. They sported crooked ridges of stiff short wool, pink bald patches, and many tufts the clippers had missed entirely. The clumps of wool they'd sacrificed for Laramie's cowgirl cause were pitifully sparse.

While a wool spinner would have discarded the remnants as useless, Laramie felt absurdly pleased by them. Maybe she'd knit a mitten. The sun was shining, Jake was grinning, she hadn't drawn anyone's blood. True, one lone mitten—there probably wasn't enough wool for a pair—wasn't enough to prove her point about the Lazy J. But there were other cowgirl feats for her to try.

Today, a mitten. Tomorrow, a cattle drive!

"Now I have a lump on *this* knee," Jake said, squatting on his heels and rubbing the spot where he'd been struck by a wayward hoof. He'd tackled one of the ewes after she'd run the clippers too close to an ear and set off a major panic.

"Matching lumps." Even her limited success had made Laramie goofy. She smiled fondly at Jake. "You won't find that on the rodeo circuit."

"No, all those lumps are uneven." He lifted off his straw hat, raked a hand through his dark wavy hair and resettled the hat at a cocky angle on the back of his head, giving his angular face a more open, optimistic cast. Daylight brightened the small gold flecks in his eyes. And revealed their gentleness.

She responded with a swelling heart, her feelings mushy enough for even Molly's approval.

"Your hand is better."

He waggled it back and forth. "The wrist even twists both ways."

Yet he was still here. Hope glittered inside her.

"Is there any word on the Naylor brothers? What were their names?"

"Reggie and Rusty. Reggie's the younger, a slick pretty-boy type, but god-awful mean. Rusty's a big redhead, the brains of the operation, which ain't sayin' much."

"I thought they might have tracked you down by now."

Jake's eyes crinkled. "I figure they're waiting for me to reappear. There's a big rodeo coming up in Fort Collins, Colorado. I don't plan to miss it."

She was concerned. "But, Jake..."

"I'll work it out. It's not your worry."

Of course not. He wouldn't want the burden of thinking that someone might care for him. She turned slightly and threaded her fingers through the sagging chicken wire fencing, bending it further out of shape. "When's the rodeo?"

He named a date.

She knew it. "That's the weekend you're signed up for the Rodeo Days cowboy competition."

"Outhouse races and hog roping? I'll give it a pass."

You're my partner.

"Sure," she said, swallowing. "I can see why you'd prefer confronting the Naylor brothers to hanging out here where there's only a couple of tame ewes and a dinky old stallion to beat you up." She sent Goliath a slit-eyed glare he didn't deserve.

"I'm not being cavalier. But I can't avoid them forever. This rodeo or the next. It's how I make my living."

"What about my month on the Lazy J?"

"You'll have your month. In fact, you can have as long as you like. I've been thinking that I'll sign my half of the house over to you." He swept his hands through the air. "All yours, darlin'."

She felt her jaw drop. It took a second or two to close it. To understand. "You want to leave that badly?" she asked, her voice stricken, her stomach gone hollow. Jake had never really wanted the Lazy J, she knew that. But now it was crystal clear that neither did he want her.

Not for good.

"I thought you'd be pleased." His brow furrowed. "The Lazy J's your legacy, that's what you claimed."

Nope, she wanted to say, with all her heart. *You're what I want. You're my keepsake cowboy.*

But that was playing against the rules. His rules. No tenderness. No loving. No commitment.

"That's right." She found the mettle to stand as though her heart wasn't breaking, even to gather the tufts of wool as though they still represented an important achievement. "The Lazy J's all I want. And you and Buck are so generous for giving it to me.

You and Buck.'' The liquid sensation in her eyes dried up. ''Two of a kind. Aren't I lucky that I didn't have to bother getting to know either one of you.''

She slammed the gate behind her and strode toward the house as if her heels were striking sparks. Even Goliath got out of her way.

SEVERAL DAYS LATER, Jake was still there. He didn't know why.

Laramie treated him with cool detachment. She wasn't rude. She wasn't friendly, either. Every morning they met in the kitchen and she drank a single cup of coffee while watching him fry eggs, responding to his occasional comments with stiff one-word replies. Yes, she'd slept fine. No, she didn't want eggs. No, she didn't need a hand feeding the animals. No, he couldn't help her clean closets. No, there was absolutely nothing he could do for her.

Other than leave, Jake thought. His departure would put an end to their mutual misery. It was what he decided to do every evening when he sat on the back porch and watched the sun set fire to the aspen and cottonwood trees that dotted the hillside.

And every morning, here he was, stuck in limbo.

Laramie was keeping busy. She worked on the house, cared for the animals single-handedly—at her own insistence—went shopping and sightseeing with Helen, took homemade lemon squares to the nosy neighbor lady across the street and came back with an empty plate and a puzzled frown. She had a long talk with the teenage boy who'd been hired to oversee the menagerie after Buck's death. She made phone calls to her girlfriends. To her mother, fruitlessly. Visited at the local cattleman's club, bowling alley and neighborhood honky-tonk bar, a waste of time, he'd have told her, except that she didn't want to hear anything he had to say about Buck or Buck's habits.

She was a stubborn woman. Reminded him more of Buck with each passing day.

Fortunately, Jake counted himself as a patient sort. He could withstand her temporary freeze-out because he'd felt his kiss light the fire inside her. He was willing to wait for her to accept him on his own terms, uncomplicated by expectations.

He was willing to wait, that was, until she went and accepted a date for lunch from Baby Bobby Torrance.

Now, *that* really got Jake's goat.

HE KNEW THE MOMENT she got home, and he made sure to look as if he hadn't been waiting. While she went in the front door, he stepped off the back porch and grabbed his coiled rope off the fence post, listening all the while for her sounds in the house.

Out of the corner of his eye, he saw the kitchen curtain pull back slowly, so he tossed a loop over Goliath's unsuspecting head. The little horse took exception to being roped, but Jake was able to reel him in like a flip-flopping bass. By the time he slipped the lasso off over the horse's head, the curtain had dropped again.

He heard her in the bedroom. In the bathroom, showering.

He amused himself by roping Goliath a few more times, then turned to the sheep, who were more of a challenge than usual. After such traumatic buzz cuts, they were chary about letting him near. His lasso snaked through the air, striking and recoiling with a flick of his wrist. Every now and then, one of the curtains would twitch, and he knew Laramie was watching.

It took her a good twenty minutes before she came outside, her hair pinned up, wearing blue jeans with a slim leather belt and that skimpy little sleeveless undershirt thing that he would have said left nothing to the imagination if not for the fact that his imagination seemed to be working overtime.

"There's a flood out front," she said, the tip of her elegant nose up in the air.

"I washed my rig."

"Getting ready to leave?"

On the hot seat again. He lifted a shoulder. "Maybe."

"You'll want to see Bobby before you do." Her face was icily serene. "Sign some papers."

Aha. The big date that had gnawed at his gut all day might have been no more than a business meeting. "Is that why you had lunch with Bobby—to set up the transfer of Buck's assets?" Was he relieved? Or disappointed?

She didn't respond satisfactorily. "Bobby took me to the Sweet Melissa Vegetarian Café. He likes health food."

Jake worked a large loop into his rope and started spinning it, several inches off the ground. It wasn't a show-offy thing with him, just something he'd learned to do as a kid. A way to keep his hands occupied and his mind off the strain of listening to his mother's screeching fights with the current stepfather.

"Neat trick," Laramie said, watching the spinning lariat. She slid her hands into her back pockets, her lips curving unconsciously as she relaxed.

"Step inside."

She laughed shortly. "I couldn't."

He cocked his chin. "You never played jump rope? Too clumsy, I suppose?"

Insulted, she rose to the bait. "Recent appearances to the contrary, I'm actually quite athletic."

"Then, c'mon." He stepped inside the spinning lariat himself, doing a figure-eight flourish with it overhead for good measure before bringing it low again, spinning even faster.

Laramie rocked on her heels, gauging the height and speed.

"Don't hesitate," he said, making the loop spiral up and down around his legs. "Trust your instinct."

She tossed back her head and hopped neatly inside the circle of the lariat. Her eyes glinted. "Not bad, huh, cowboy?"

While she was congratulating herself, he caught the knot behind her back, quickly shortened the loop and started it spinning again. Laramie looked down, realized what he'd done, and turned her accusatory eyes upon him. They were standing very close now, bound together by the smaller circumference of the lariat. "Let me take a wild guess," she said wryly, looking at him from the corners of her eyes. "This is a sneaky trick you cowboys pull on all the girls."

He grinned. "Who, me?"

She was a tall woman, probably five ten. Her face was nearly even with his. He could have counted each one of her lashes if he'd been of a mind to. He wasn't. Her mouth was too distracting.

"There's a problem, though." She blinked solemnly, giving him no more room to maneuver than he'd given her. "Your hands are occupied."

"Only one of them." He put his left hand on the small of her back and urged her hips a little bit closer to his. She let him do it, though her upper body swayed in the opposite direction, thrusting her high, round breasts into prominence, but keeping her mouth out of kissing range.

"Also…" she said, teasing him now. "You've forgotten something."

The pace of the lariat was slowing as their attraction thickened. He gripped the back of her braided belt, holding her in place as his mouth sought hers.

She put her hands on his shoulders, evading him. "You've forgotten that to escape all I must do is step—" she stepped high over the lariat "—right out of here." A flirtatious glance over her shoulder was all he got as she turned and walked away. "And there's nothing you can do about it, cowboy."

He allowed her five or six steps. She was reaching for the gate when he sent the lasso whistling through the air.

She let out a squeak as the loop settled neatly around her shoulders. It pulled taut, pinning her arms to her sides. "Hey!" Her voice was abnormally shrill. She squirmed, but he kept enough tension in the rope so she couldn't release herself. "Let me go."

He started walking toward her, gathering the rope in his left hand as he went. "Let this be a lesson to you, New York. Don't try to best a cowboy at his own game."

She spun toward him. "Another sneaky rope trick, huh? Well, guess what? I'm not into bondage."

"Neither am I." He loosened the lariat but ran his hand along the extra length of rope so that he could use it to pull her closer. A palpable heat flared between them. She could have gotten free if she'd really wanted to, but she didn't want to, and they both knew it.

He skimmed his knuckles across her breastbone. She inhaled, her eyes a deep liquid velvet as they searched his. There was a fine trembling about her mouth.

"You wore this shirt on purpose." He fingered the tiny flat bow centered on the neckline. "To tease me."

"I did laundry yesterday. It was on the top of the pile."

"Can I tell you how sexy you are without you biting my head off? Can I say that I want to kiss you?"

"You can do anything you—" Her voice cracked. "Anything you want."

"Is that so?" He rubbed his thumb over her nipple. "Can I do this?"

She gasped. "I didn't mean—" He didn't stop, so her eyes lost focus and she licked her lips and whispered, "Okay."

"Okay?"

Her arms reached around his shoulders. "Don't ask me any more questions, Jake. You might not get the answers you want."

He hesitated, reckoning she was saying that even though they were wrong together, she didn't want to think about it right now. Not a vote of confidence. But he was through with being patient. He wasn't going to think about it, either.

Her lips were warm. Her tongue moved against his. What was meant to be an introductory kiss fast became deep and insistent and solid with mutual need.

Kissing Laramie was both better and worse than he was prepared for. It was ecstasy; it was torture.

Because kissing Laramie was the one thing he could imagine wanting to do for the rest of his life.

She met him fully, her hands clasping his head, fingers in his hair. He palmed her breast, relishing the rounded weight of it and the sound of pleasure she made in her throat when he stroked her through the thin T-shirt. No bra. It was a difficult choice, but finally he left her mouth so he could tongue hot caresses over her tanned skin, stretching out the neckline of her shirt in his need to feel her flesh, her swollen nipple, her rapturous response against his tongue.

She cried out. He reached up with his hand, found her arched throat, then her open mouth. She took his hand in one of hers and pressed it to her lips, kissing, sucking, biting. The coiled rope was still wound around her and she pushed it aside, freeing an arm, raising her hands to his collar and wrenching at the snaps on his shirt so it split apart. She spread it wide, rubbing her cheek against his chest, pressing her lips to the base of his throat.

They found each other's mouths again and let their desire ignite. One kiss melted into another. They were both breathing hard, dizzy with heat and the rush of blood pounding in their veins, and they were both unwilling to stop.

"Not here," Laramie said. Jake's fantastic hands were inside her shirt and she found it difficult to think. Why not right there, right there where they stood?

"A bed might be more comfortable," he said, agreeing, nibbling at her lobe with his teeth and lips.

The man was touching her everywhere at once, too much to resist.

"Ye-e-es. No. Oh." She'd never been so indecisive. "I don't know…"

"I do." He was pressing his advantage, and she tried to remember Molly's words of warning. Something about overwhelming passion. Didn't sound like a warning.

"Wait, Jake. Wait a minute." Her shirt was around her neck, the rope falling past her hips. And her brain…her brain was still out to lunch.

"No," he said. "I've waited long enough."

His color was high, his eyes hot and alive, simmering like a cauldron. There was a boyish pout to his full lips. She couldn't help touching them with her own, a little gesture that built to a kiss that obliterated her momentary hesitation, even after she was forced to come up for air. "All right," she said, not thinking, not caring.

Only feeling.

All that could stop them now was a cataclysmic force of nature. Maybe not even that.

They were meant to be lovers.

And it didn't seem to matter that afterward only a miracle would keep them together.

7

RAINBOW MIRACLE ARRIVED as she always did—with color and clamor and the bevy of buddies who were her constant but changeable entourage.

Dimly, Laramie recognized the honking and shouting. She moaned beneath Jake's mouth, tightening her grip on his shoulders even though she knew she had to push him away.

He took her frustration for sounds of pleasure and continued kissing her. It was still so good that she would have gladly ignored the intrusion if that was even remotely possible. Since it wasn't, she finally broke free and said, "Listen, Jake. It's my mother."

A motor revved, then cut out. Car doors slammed. A babble of voices rose from the front yard.

Laramie dropped her forehead against his bare chest, swooning into its radiant heat, trying to gather her wits. Wits were a necessary requirement in her duty as Rainbow Miracle's levelheaded daughter.

Jake scrubbed a hand across his face in disbelief. "Your *mother?*"

Laramie was blinking rapidly, straightening her clothes, trying to assimilate. "I should have guessed. She hasn't been in touch for days."

"You're saying your mother drove out from New York?"

"Apparently. With her motley crew, by the sounds

of it.'' She clutched at his chest, realized she was pinching skin, and hurriedly began snapping shut his shirt. ''I ought to warn you. If you think Buck was a crackpot, my mother is—''

A high, thin voice interrupted her. ''Yoo-hoo-ooh!''

''My mother is—''

The back door swung open. ''Sweet pea!''

''Mom,'' Laramie said, unhanding Jake. She turned to greet the woman currently known as Rainbow Miracle, New Age maven. ''What a surprise.'' The tangled rope caught around Laramie's ankles. She kicked free. ''Stay on the porch, Mom. I'll come to you.''

''Pineapple,'' Rainbow said, opening her arms as she trotted lightly down the back steps. She was only a couple of inches shorter than Laramie, nearly as slim and limber, dressed in a loose gauze blouse and skirt so long it dragged in the dirt. She picked up the hem, revealing bare feet decorated with elaborate henna tattoos that matched the ones on her hands. Her face lit up as she sprinted toward her daughter.

''Rainbow—stop,'' Laramie cried. Jake saw why. Goliath's ears were pricked with interest. His pawed the ground like a baby bull.

Rainbow wasn't paying attention. ''Look,'' she called to the odd cast of characters who'd followed her out onto the porch. ''It's my pumpkin! My pickle! My peanut!''

The two women met in a hug. Laramie tried to keep the embrace brief and hustle her mother back up onto the porch, but Rainbow wouldn't go. With expansive gestures, she gibbered about the benefits of toxin-free air and how the siren song of the mountains had pulled her west.

Laramie figured that the real reason her mother had shown up sprang from a less mystical motive—simple human curiosity. "I'm glad you came," she said, casting a quick glance at Goliath. *Maybe now I'll get some answers.* "Please, let's go inside."

"This is the ranch?" Rainbow resisted Laramie's urging as she looked around the backyard menagerie. "You must be so disappointed, nutmeg. It really hasn't changed."

Laramie couldn't answer right then. Goliath was trotting toward them, head low, lips curled back from his menacing teeth.

Rainbow clapped her hands. "What a cute little pony."

"He's smiling," called one of the entourage from the porch.

"Rainbow—guess what?" Laramie said, out of sheer desperation. "There's a crystal ball inside. The hugest I've ever seen." She grabbed her mother's hand. Goliath was coming faster.

"Oh? Really?" Duly engaged, Rainbow stepped lively up the steps, completely missing both the miniature horse's last-second rush and the sudden strike of Jake's lasso. The rope tightened and Goliath was caught short, snapping at the women's heels in futility.

Laramie threw Jake a grateful smile as she prodded her mother and friends through the doorway. He was leaning against the rope at a forty-five-degree angle, his boot heels dug into the ground, preventing Goliath from charging up the steps and through the doggy door. His hair was a mess, his shirttail untucked, his lips reddened from their kisses.

A true cowboy hero, she thought.

"COCONUT, THAT'S NO crystal ball." Rainbow Miracle stared into the clear, crackled acrylic ball Laramie had hauled from the closet and set in the middle of the dining room table. "Why, I do believe it's a bowling ball."

"There are finger holes," pointed out the older woman who'd been introduced to Jake as Radha, Seeker of Enlightenment. Aka Dorie Rosenblatt from Queens, according to Laramie's whisper.

Radha put down her fork and poked a stubby finger into one of the holes. "Yep. It's a garden-variety bowling ball. No vibes at all." She took another big bite of carrot cake and beamed at Jake through the cream-cheese frosting as if they alone shared the joke. Radha was as plump and smiling as a Buddha, dressed in a bright woven poncho and practical overalls. Despite the name, he didn't think she was as far gone as the rest of the eccentric group.

"Imagine that," Laramie said, clearing the table. "I guess I was wrong."

Jake grabbed his plate and an empty pitcher. After settling in, Rainbow Miracle had taken over the kitchen and produced a meal that consisted of lots of wild rice, bean curd and tofu, but nary a bite of meat. Radha, wisely, had gone to a bakery for the cake.

Jake met Laramie at the sink. "This puts a crimp in our plans."

She took the plate without meeting his eyes. "Did we have plans?"

He touched her elbow. "We sure did." His fingertips danced up her bare arm. "And don't you forget it, New York."

Laramie tried to repress her shiver. Unsuccessfully. "Radha's sleeping in the van. Dominique and Herb brought a tent. I'm afraid I promised my mother and Yisrael the master bedroom. He's got a bad back."

"Yisrael's the weenie with the wispy beard?"

Laramie chuckled. "That's one way of putting it." She finished loading the plates and cutlery into the dishwasher. "He's been my mother's live-in boyfriend for three months now. Every time I mention his getting a job his bad back starts acting up."

Jake calculated. "That leaves me and you with one narrow twin bed between us. Or beneath us." He brushed aside a stray strand of hair and nibbled on her neck. "I'd say our plans are back on track."

Her head rolled, momentarily giving him better access before she pushed him away. "There's the pool table or the easy chair."

"You forget. I'm a broken-down rodeo cowboy— my bones can't take sleeping on a pool table."

"Now who's the weenie?" She laughed and darted out of the kitchen to evade his grasp.

He returned to the dining room at a saunter, feeling fine. Dominique and Herb, the mismatched pair of Wiccans who went together like salt and pepper—or, in their case, eye of newt and hair of frog—had gone outside to pitch the tent. They huddled inside it, tendrils of smoke rising from the unzipped flap. Laramie hadn't noticed, so Jake didn't bother pointing out that what they were smoking was illegal, especially on the front lawn.

Rainbow Miracle turned her attention to him when he took his seat in the dining room. "Your aura's throbbing, Jake."

Laramie's eyes got big. She sat down rather suddenly.

"Veritably pulsing," agreed Radha. She closed her

eyes and patted her splayed hands five inches from his face. "Hmm. Your colors connote passion. Do tell." A private smile puckered her rosebud lips.

The silent Yisrael nodded and stroked the feathery wisps growing on his chin.

Rainbow sipped green tea. "What are you planning on doing with my cabbage?"

Jake was quizzical. "You cook it," he said tentatively, "and I'll eat it." What the hell. He'd choked down the bean curd.

Odd strangled sounds rose from Laramie. He looked and saw that she was practically gnawing on her fist to keep from laughing.

"I meant my daughter," Rainbow gently explained. Beneath a frizz of dark, silver-tipped curls, her face was a serene—possibly bland—oval. She gave off an air of floating above it all. Jake couldn't tell if she was dim or merely oblivious. "What, pray tell, are you up to with my sweet child?"

"We're, uh, we're partners."

"Oh. My. Partners." Rainbow pressed her fingers to her temples.

"Temporary business partners," Laramie defined. "Sort of. In Buck's ranch. Sort of."

"I sense a presence." Rainbow hummed tunelessly as she rubbed her temples. "The spirits are restless."

Jake looked at Laramie. "Is this a seance?"

She shook her head. "Rainbow, please. The only restless spirit around this place is Goliath."

Rainbow blinked, holding her vacuous smile.

Laramie got a stubborn look on her face. "In fact, from what I've been able to uncover, once Buck had quit the bowling league he rarely even ventured out of the yard. I doubt that he's going to get adventurous as a ghost.''

''One shouldn't question the past,'' Rainbow murmured. She pulled her long-stemmed legs up beneath her, curling like a lotus in the baggy skirt and embroidered blouse. She tucked the hem around her bare feet. Her gaze slid away from the table, seeking distraction. ''Turnip, dear, I hate to ask, but what's that terrible smell?''

Besides dinner, Jake silently qualified, though Rainbow Miracle was correct. The room had been stripped down to bare plaster and subfloor yet retained a faint reminder of its previous incarnation as Goliath's powder room. It was a good thing that Rainbow Miracle and her Traveling Flea Circus weren't the sort to stand on ceremony.

''It's the odor of twenty-five years of denial, avoidance and loneliness,'' Laramie said flatly. Her face was a mask. ''Stinks, doesn't it, mother?''

Rainbow warbled. ''Oh-oh-oh, rutabaga. So harsh.'' She swooned toward Yisrael, but he was still doing his yogi-on-the-mountaintop imitation and wasn't alert enough to catch her. Rainbow had to brace herself on the table to keep from falling off her chair.

Radha patted Laramie's shoulder. ''The past is the present, dear child. Direct your questions inward. Only thine own heart can provide answers to a seeking soul.''

Something thudded against the windowpane. They all turned to look. Goliath was on the porch with his nose pressed to the dining room window, his ears pointed in two directions like a cockeyed TV antenna.

''There's a seeking soul for you.'' Laramie snorted.

"Say, Rainbow, maybe Buck's been reincarnated in Goliath."

"We do not honor the dead with ill humor," cautioned Radha.

"It doesn't jibe." Rainbow had taken the suggestion seriously. "Buck was not a small man."

"He was a tall, handsome cowboy," Laramie chanted in a singsong voice.

"That's right, radish. He was."

"Honestly?"

Rainbow drew herself up. "I do not speak untruths. They're bad for my karma."

Laramie's gaze narrowed. "They're not lies if they're fairy tales, right?"

"But, pea pod—you loved my stories."

"As a child. They fueled my cowboy dreams. But I'm all grown up now, and I want to know the truth."

Rainbow's voice wavered. "The storytelling tradition is an honorable—"

Laramie cut her off. "I need facts."

"Oh, papaya!" Rainbow's face crumpled. "You know how I feel about raised voices. My aura reacts badly." She pressed one hand to her forehead and extended the other toward her boyfriend. "Yisrael? Yissy? Take my hand. I must retire for the evening...."

Jake watched Laramie's face as the weenie led the fruit salad toward the bedroom. It was a fascinating portrait of all the emotions he didn't allow himself: frustration, pain, concern, longing. It all hit a little too close to home; he wanted to withdraw. Fought not to. The main difference between him and Laramie was that she had looked for her father, while he had purposely kept a healthy distance between himself and the rapid turnover of his own step-variations.

"She's never going to tell me the truth," Laramie said in a monotone. "Over the years, I've heard a hundred dreamy variations of her summer love affair with the tall, handsome cowboy, Buck Jones. None of them bear scrutiny. Particularly the notion that wearing a cowboy hat made him a cowboy."

Only Radha had retained full composure in the face of such anguish. "Dearest Laramie. Listen to your mother's heart, not her words." She shifted beneath the poncho. "Five people drove a van across seven states on Rainbow's insistence, and two of the people were Dominique and Herb. Let me tell ya. It was a sacrifice."

Laramie smiled and briefly clasped Radha's hand in thanks. "But why did my mother want to come in the first place? She still won't tell me anything."

Radha's silence was so long Jake thought she'd fallen asleep. He made the mistake of leaning forward to peer at her closed eyes. They flashed open and fixed on him. "Ask the cowboy," she intoned, then rose and floated from the room like a ship under sail. She could move pretty gracefully for a two-hundred-pound woman in overalls and hiking boots.

Laramie was frowning. "Ask the cowboy?"

Jake was equally mystified. Radha couldn't have meant him. He was clueless.

"Completely ridiculous." Laramie released a frustrated sigh as she stood. "Well, okay, then. Buck is Goliath, cowboys are oracles, and this particular piece of vegetable matter is going to bed."

TEN MINUTES LATER, when they met in Jake's bedroom, he took one look at her sitting at the head of the single bed, hugging her upraised legs, and said, "I'll sleep on the easy chair in the living room." Even though all she wore was the Mets T-shirt and a pair of white cotton panties.

Laramie's voice came low. "What about those plans you mentioned?"

He stoked her loosened hair. "Our auras are not aligned. It's obvious." *Mine's throbbing, yours ain't.*

She leaned into his caress. "Thank you."

"Hey. I'm not just a cowboy, I'm a gentleman."

"You are." Ignoring his throbbing aura, she twined her hands around his waist and looked up at him. "But fair is fair. I'll sleep on the chair."

"No, I insist. I've bunked in worse places."

"Okay." She released him. Turned aside and stroked the threadbare cowboy-and-cacti pillowcase instead. "I just wondered if…" She drew in a shaky breath, her face hidden behind the long hair draped over her hunched shoulders. "Oh, God, I'm such a wimp. Sorry, Jake. Just forget it."

She wanted to be held. Comforted. Consoled. It was a feminine signal that Jake had learned to either ignore or avoid with other women. Coming from Laramie, Miz Long Cool Drink of Water herself, it might possibly be significant.

Jeez, he thought, as wordlessly he drew her up onto her feet and into his arms…his platonic arms. This had better be earning him big points or the pain simply wasn't worth it.

Yes, it was.

She nestled her face into the crook of his shoulder and murmured something about this only taking a minute, but as they hugged the tension leaked out of her and their mutual comfort level increased, and several minutes later they still hadn't moved. Jake was, admittedly, in bad shape. Racked by desire, still trying to do the right thing.

Laramie was surprisingly soft in his arms. The floral shampoo and spicy scent of her infused his pores. He could feel her breasts, her heartbeat. Eventually he came to realize that the top of his head had blown off and was floating somewhere near the ceiling, sending messages to the rest of his body about how well he was taking this and how if he could hold on a few minutes longer without blowing it, everything would be all right. Laramie would be comforted, and it wasn't like he had to fall in love with her to accomplish it.

If he could withstand this for five minutes more.

Maybe ten…

THEY'D AWAKENED the next morning, as intimately entwined as lovers. Laramie savored the thought, smiling to herself while stretching as lavishly as possible when balancing on the edge of a mattress. She turned and burrowed against Jake. He smelled like warm leather. Delicious.

In retrospect, Jake might not have been as comfortable as she. As soon as he became cognizant, he said "Huh?" and abruptly rolled away, which was, in such a narrow bed, an unfortunate instinct. He hit the floor hard, face first, swearing a blue streak.

And the day managed to go downhill from there.

Breakfast was hectic, first the animals, then the people. Afterward, Rainbow and Yisrael set out their prayer rugs and tatami mats for a day-long session of meditation. Rainbow claimed her chakras were out of alignment. Yisrael said the same about his spine.

Laramie looked through the brochures she'd collected and sent the rest of the gang off to Wyoming Territorial Prison's Frontier Town, getting a kick out of the idea of Dominique and Herb sucking down sarsaparillas. By late afternoon, when Rainbow was coming out of her funk of avoidance and starting to talk about cooking dinner, Jake, who'd been silent as the Sphinx all day, suggested that the time was right for him and Laramie to have their first date. She was flattered until she realized that he simply wanted to get out of the house before the curdling of another bean.

Nevertheless, Laramie found herself getting excited at the prospect of a real date with a real cowboy. To calm down, she sought Radha's practical-minded counsel. As it turned out, there was enough of Dorie Rosenblatt, Queens matchmaker, left in the woman that they ended up chatting like best friends over dress, makeup and hair. Radha voted for va-va-voom. The upshot was that Laramie met Jake at the door wearing a dress that was short, tight and red enough to make him wish he hadn't been so quick to fall out of bed. The red cowboy boots were her own addition.

Dinner was very nice.

Their conversation was smooth—they avoided any mention of Buck Jones, Rainbow Miracle and the uncertain future of the Lazy J. Jake told rodeo stories. In his laid-back way, he made it sound exhilarating to flirt with serious injury on a weekly basis. Laramie volleyed with tales of a childhood lived in teepees, ashrams and a one-bedroom cold-water walk-up in Brooklyn. In her ironic way, she made it sound adventurous to sleep on a pallet or futon or pullout sofa, never knowing for sure where you'd be tomorrow.

Dessert—bananas flambé—brightened the remainder of the date. By the time they left the restaurant to stroll along the Laramie River, they were holding hands, glancing at each other out of the corners of their eyes and snickering like goofy kids whenever they caught themselves at it.

Once or twice, they stopped to kiss. Lazy, slow, indulgent kisses, not too serious, not too deep. Jake said she tasted like banana. She said as a man who'd been intimate with the floor that morning and still bore the taint of shag carpeting, he wasn't one to talk. They laughed and hugged and continued on their way.

They took their time returning to the Lazy J. Driving up in the pickup, they found the van gone and the house deserted. Rainbow had left a note; she and the entourage had embarked on an overnight camping trip in hopes of having a close encounter of the mystical kind at Devil's Tower.

"All the way to Devil's Tower," Laramie said, trying not to blush. Not so subtle, Mom. Rainbow had always gone overboard to prove her openmindedness concerning Laramie's dealings with the opposite sex. She didn't understand that a gawky teenager with no social skills to speak of might need guidance rather than a let-it-all-hang-out recitation of the benefits of free love. It wasn't until Laramie had gone into training with the Cowgirl Club that she'd gained a measure of confidence.

Jake draped an arm around her waist. "So, is the tower far enough away, you think?"

"For what?"

He traced the whorls of her ear with the tip of his

tongue. "Far enough away for them not to hear you scream when I make you—"

"Enough!" She stepped away. "I don't recall giving you a free pass."

"Better tell your lips—they've been making me promises all night."

She crumpled up the note. "Don't be so sure, Jake. I'll be sorry I kissed you."

"Have it your way, New York, but come and get me when you're ready," he said, utterly, irritatingly arrogant, flashing a cocky grin at her as he sauntered out of the kitchen in his black shirt, black jeans and polished black cowboy boots.

It was the shoe shine that got her. Knowing he'd sat down and polished his boots for their date made her feel all loose and warm and sappy inside. Previously, she'd had a reputation for being tough on guys, spurning them without remorse. Now, where Jake was concerned, she'd turned into syrup.

She opened the fridge. Took out a bottle of water. Delaying tactic, she thought, drinking. She knew very well that she would go after Jake. It just wouldn't do to be too eager about it.

She tapped the floor with the heel of her boots. Flicked her hair. Waggled her hips as she pulled on the hem of the crayon-red spandex dress.

Uncharacteristically fidgety, once again.

Darn that Jake for putting her in this position!

Male arrogance.

She smiled. Okay—if that's how he wanted to play it, she'd blast him away with a double dose of female pulchritude.

It should work...even though he'd seen her done

in by a miniature horse, an impotent rooster and a pair of squirming sheep.

"Ignore that part," she told herself, and went after Jake with her head held high and her heart beating like a tom-tom.

He was in the game room with only the neon beer signs lit, knocking balls around the pool table. She sucked in her stomach and sat directly in his sight line, crossing her legs with a slow, teasing deliberation.

He straightened. His eyes were very dark, his voice very rough. "If you're not going to play, New York, get your fanny off the table."

"Oh, but I do want to play." With a flick of her wrist, she sent the black eight ball spinning his way. "Care to make the game a bit more interesting?"

He chuckled lazily. "What did you have in mind?"

"A wager."

"Another one?" He bent over the cue stick. "You're already losing the first. Are you trying to renegotiate?"

She thought about it. "No. This wager will have nothing to do with the other."

He looked up from the table long enough to run his gaze along her legs, then unerringly sent a ball straight into a corner pocket, inches away from her firmly planted rear end. "You have my attention."

She leaned back on her arms, saucily seductive. "I propose a simple game of pool." She hadn't played in years and years. "Winner receives…"

"Yes?"

"Whatever they please." Her eyes looked directly into his—a challenge.

He smiled crookedly. "That covers a lot of ground.

I could ask for—'' his gaze lowered ''—oh, the moon, for instance.''

Her body torqued as she slid a hand over her hip, flashing her spandexed fanny at him. ''If that's what you want, you shall have it.'' Her brows arched. ''However, if *I* win...''

''You could ask for...''

''Whatever my heart desires.''

''The Lazy J,'' he said weightily.

She waved a finger. ''Don't forget. This wager does not concern the other.''

His knuckles were white where he gripped the pool cue. Its chalky tip skidded across the felt when he tried another shot. Laramie caught the wayward ball. Leaning low over the table, she rolled it slowly toward him, her hair draped like black spiderwebs over the green felt surface. Let him make the next move.

He stayed where he was, measuring the offer. ''Not much of a risk, I'd say, since I'm already handing over the Lazy J.''

She lolled indolently, arching her back. It was a centerfold pose—how much more obvious could she get? Why did he hesitate? It couldn't be that he believed this was only a ploy for her to get the ranch from him. The man had kissed her! He had to know, if only subconsciously, that *he* was her heart's desire.

Ah. *Maybe that was the holdup.*

''I thought you liked to play it fast and loose.'' She scooted off the pool table, strutted to the rack on the wall and chose a stick. ''The vagabond cowboy, so free of constraint he'll risk it all on a turn of the cards.''

''I'm sober now.'' He was preternaturally still. Except his eyes. They were darkly vivid, sliding back and forth to follow her every movement as she racked the balls. Without waiting for his go-ahead, she broke.

Passing up an easy shot on the other side of the table, she strolled toward stalwart Jake, turning aside at the last moment to line up her shot as coolly as if she couldn't feel his heat, their electricity. She bent over the table. He didn't move. Flirtatiously she bumped him with her hip, and when still he didn't move aside she pressed against him. Covetously he dropped his hand to her out-thrust derriere, giving it a lusty squeeze at just the right moment. The ball she'd been trying to pocket bounced off the bumper.

Her aim was off by a mile.

But she had ignition.

While Jake was no longer interested in playing pool, he certainly was into the game. Before Laramie could rise, he pressed tight against her, his body holding hers in place while he leaned down, reached around with his arms, and negligently took his own bad shot.

"You're not even trying to win," she said, letting her cue stick drop.

His lips touched her bare shoulder. "Yes I am."

Even though he wouldn't budge, she managed to twist around to face him. His palms were pressed flat to the table and she found herself sitting between them, her legs immodestly spread to accommodate his lean hips. His stance was aggressive, hers yielding, but it was she who put her hand up to his mouth.

He licked her fingertips. She rubbed the wetness over his lips, her own moisture levels rising precipitously. His were sexy lips. James Dean lips. Cruel and decadent. Promising only passion.

Her heart ached with wanting him.

Jake's breath was unsteady, his eyes feverish. And still he waited, silent and watchful, the neon signs washing bands of color across his face. A wondrous desire hummed inside her, seeking its outlet.

She saw the black eight ball out of the corner of her eye. Reached for it with trembling fingers. To push it into the side pocket, she had to lift her hips off the table. Her breath caught when she brushed against his arousal; he closed his eyes, sucking air through his teeth.

With a clatter, the ball dropped into the pocket. "I win," she said, and kissed him.

A lightning strike.

Sweet pressure, clever tongue, riveting pleasure. Jake gripped her hips, his fingers like metal clamps as he pulled her roughly toward him. Her dress had rolled up her thighs, and the intimacy was acute as she ground against the hard ridge of his erection. She needed...completion.

"Make love to me, Jake. Right here. Right now."

"Is that your greatest desire?" His voice resonated with a humility that was unnecessary but very poignant.

"Ye-e-es." *Keep it simple,* she thought. Knowing how much he meant to her would surely scare him off.

"A bet's a bet." He stroked his hands up her back, found the zipper, drew it open with a languid motion that was both frustrating and exciting. "Even when it's fixed."

She shrugged out of the bodice of the sleeveless dress. "Fixed?"

He gazed at her for so long she thought he'd lost track of the question. Only after his palms covered her breasts and began rubbing each of her pearled nipples with an exquisite, excruciating friction did he remember to answer. And by then, it was she who'd forgotten all but his name in the heady rush of sensation as her torso curled into his.

Jake.

"By definition," he said, lowering his head, "you're a wild card. No man could shoot straight with you waving your fancy tush in his face."

His tongue swiped a broad swath over her flesh. She clasped his head to her breast, arching into the wet suction of his mouth. "That, gamblin' man, was the plan." Bold talk when she was so distracted.

If she'd had a plan, it was lost to her by the time he finished savoring her breasts. He reclaimed her mouth, lapping it with his tongue. Blindly, she fumbled for the snaps on his shirt, unwilling to remain passive. She wanted to drive him wild.

She pushed the shirt off his wide tanned shoulders. Ran her hands over supple muscle, soothed the remnants of his bruises, extravagant in her appreciation. Her lips found the pulse of his throat. Her fingertips followed the tapering patch of surprisingly silken black hair to his belt buckle.

When she hesitated, he did not. His leather belt was unbuckled and his fly unzipped and her dress skinned to her waist before she could even recover an indrawn breath. "I hate panty hose," he said hoarsely, working them down her thighs. "They're hell to remove. Never wear them again."

She kicked off one boot, freeing a leg, and evidently that was enough for him. He spread her thighs with his hands at the back of her knees and she gasped and caught at his waist, tilting her hips, desperate now, too frantic for modesty. The need to be filled with him was burning her up inside.

She leaned back on one arm and wrapped her other hand around his shaft, felt the throbbing power of it as she guided him between her thighs. He drove into the center of her like a flaming arrow and she cried out, losing it, losing hold, dropping backward into the whirlpool of pleasure.

Pool balls scattered indiscriminately. The surface of the table was hard beneath her writhing body; she scarcely noticed. Her shoulders shifted, the tendons in her neck straining as she reached toward Jake. He put his hands on her breasts, leaning over her like a satyr, wayward locks of his long black hair falling forward around his face. "Right here," he said, touching her, stroking her, grinding his hips so that the sharp hot pleasure of it pierced her to the quick.

"Right now," he shouted, and together they reached a scintillating climax, all flagrant haste and fever and fury and flame, their half-dressed bodies fused in the rainbow glow of neon lights.

8

AFTERWARD, JAKE WAS NOT the lover she'd expected. Not by half.

A wonderful surprise.

"Are you always like this?" she asked, digging a spoon into the pint of toasted-almond, chocolate-chunk ice cream he'd brought her from the freezer. She wanted an almond, not a chunk.

"Like this?" Idly his forefinger caressed her leg just above the kneecap. They were sitting entwined on the single bed, facing each other, wearing only gray boxer briefs (him) and a pair of undies and a towel turban (her).

"You're being sweet," she said, showing her teeth as she delicately bit into the almond. "Cute."

"Sweet? Cute?" His eyes rolled. "Gimme a break."

"Cutie patootie." She ladled a spoonful of ice cream into his mouth. Though she was teasing, maybe it was true. He wasn't as hardhearted as all that.

"You found me out," he growled, trying to look ferocious. Not possible when surrounded by all those cavorting wallpaper cowboys.

"I won't tell anyone," she promised. She had her own reputation to protect.

After the pool table—*oy, the pool table!*—he'd stripped off her remaining clothes, gathered her up, carried her to the shower and washed her lovingly, with many gentle kisses and small caresses until, as kisses and caresses were wont to do, the intent of them grew into something bigger. So to speak.

"Life's strange, isn't it?" she said, looking around his teenage bedroom to distract herself from what they'd done in the bathtub beneath the pounding water. "I'll bet you never thought you'd end up here again, with a woman like me in your bed."

"I never thought I'd end up here at all."

She cocked her head. "Is it so bad?"

His palm coasted over her thigh. "It's getting better."

She saw his pupils shrink as his gaze narrowed to her bare breasts; her nipples tightened with a delicious tingling sensation.

"So there's some advantage to splitting an inheritance with a New Yorker after all?" She put the ice cream carton on the bed between their legs and unwound her towel. He frowned as her wet hair fell heavily to her waist.

"A bonus, maybe."

"Only *maybe?*"

With his hands on her hips he tugged her a little closer. "So long as you understand the limits."

She stiffened, then forced herself to relax. *No tenderness, no love, no commitment.* Did he even realize that he'd already achieved two out of three?

"You'll be leaving for a rodeo," she said, nonchalantly finger-combing her hair. She plaited it into two loose braids. "This weekend." Tossed them over her shoulders with a shimmy of her breasts. "Can't I convince you to stay? For the Rodeo Days competition," she qualified hastily. Don't ask for too much.

"*Can* you?" he challenged, a wicked smile playing games with his prodigal lips. And the hope that grew boundlessly inside her no matter how often she tamped it down.

The carton had made a wet circle on the cowboy sheets. She had him hold it while she scooped out a large dollop of the melting ice cream. Then she deliberately tipped the spoon aloft and let the chocolate ice cream slide slowly into her open mouth. His eyes ignited.

"Mmm," she purred when he leaned forward to lick a chocolate trickle from the corner of her mouth. His tongue skated across her lips, but she tucked in her chin, avoiding a full-fledged kiss. He looked disgruntled, so she scraped the edge of the spoon against his bottom lip until his mouth opened. She let him lick the spoon clean, thinking that the tangle of wet black hair on his forehead made him look boyishly sexy, regardless of the bristles already ghosting his chin. "Sweet and cute," she said, shaking her head. "Who'da thunk it?"

"I'll give you cute," he said, and pressed her supine upon the bed. He dropped the icy carton to the floor, parted her legs with a ruthless thigh. She caught her tongue between her teeth. He stretched wide the leg opening of her panties and put several fingers directly inside of her, without warning, just cold fingers, hot flesh, sudden shocking lust.

"Jake," she said, laughing, then repeated it— "*Jake*"—not laughing. Not breathing. Her eyes closed. Her hips began a slow, languorous movement. An exploration.

His fingers were no longer cold. They were perfect, gliding through swollen tissue to the heated heart of her desire. If only he was as agile and open with himself.

"This isn't fair." She squirmed out from beneath him. "Very nice, but not fair. I'm an equal opportunity gal." She pushed him down on the bed. "Get naked, bucko."

He did with alacrity, obviously amused by her determination.

She grabbed the black Stetson from the bedpost and put it on. "This," she said, her voice getting tight as she straddled him and felt the intimate prodding of his arousal, "is what we in the club call the *ride 'em, cowgirl* position...." Sinking lower—awed but incautious—she threw up one hand like a bronc rider. "Yee-haw!"

NEXT DAY. LOOKING OUT the picture window. They stood toe to toe, nearly nose to nose, staring into each other's eyes. She said, "You're not so tall."

It was their time that was short.

"Taller than you," he replied.

She rose on her bare toes. "Not in heels."

He smiled, unbothered.

"Size doesn't matter," she agreed. "I dated a football player once. A supreme jerk. His ego was way bigger than his muscles."

Hmm... "Why'd you go out with him in the first place?"

"Took me a few dates to figure him out."

"Since when are you so slow? You had me pegged from the first." He'd given up drink on her say. Hell, he'd given up more than that.

"Ah." Her eyes narrowed to slivers. "Only because you and I are...simpatico."

"Simpatico."

"We're alike."

"Yeah, we could be brother and sister."

"Oh, no, Jake." Softly. "No, definitely no…"

They kissed.

She pinched his chin, her face glowing with gentle affection. "I only meant…we understand each other."

He didn't think so.

"And I'm good at traveling," she said, apparently out of the blue.

He froze.

Suddenly she couldn't summon a smile, though she tried. "Just like you."

He knew what she meant. What she offered.

"And here I thought you were determined to put down roots." His tone was guarded.

"I can be flexible. I've had to be."

"And the Lazy J? Remember, it's yours if you want it."

"Oh. I see." Her face changed, losing its softness. He felt sorrow—the first pang of many to come—knowing that he could do that to her. "Yes, I do see," she murmured.

They were interrupted by the honking van before she could respond further, giving him reprieve from the realization that he wanted her to refuse the ranch house even though he'd offered it to avoid just such complications. He didn't like complications.

But he sure liked making love to Laramie.

It was safe to kiss her once more, quickly. Rainbow Miracle and the Traveling Flea Circus were back. He was almost glad to see them.

THE WHOLE GANG DECIDED to attend the Rodeo Days festival after they learned that both Jake and Laramie would be taking part in the—as Rainbow put it—cowperson competition. "Hey, dude, weren't you leaving?" Yisrael lazily asked Jake as they walked to their vehicles. Having taken to settin' on the back porch with Jake, Yisrael was privy to the nightly decision to depart. "Laramie convinced me to stay," Jake said, straight-faced, until he caught her eye as she climbed into the pickup. She met him inside with a mild punch to the rib cage and a deep, grateful kiss, which was interrupted by raucous catcalls from the group in the van. Jake let them back out of the driveway first, waited till they turned the corner, then returned to Laramie's kiss. Rainbow Miracle was far too obvious about giving the young couple their "privacy" for him to fully enjoy their past few days together.

He suggested they rendezvous back inside now that the house was free, but Laramie wouldn't go. She didn't want to be late, and if they went back inside they certainly would be. Her friends Molly and Grace were driving over from Treetop, and they were all to meet up with Helen Olney and her boyfriend, Karl. Jake started the truck, practicing tolerance. From what he recalled of Rodeo Days, he knew that tolerance must be his watchword for the day.

Rodeo Days was a small neighborhood festival rather than a major city-wide, tourist-rich event. Nonetheless, it was well attended. Several blocks had been cordoned off, with sections devoted to the flea market—Helen's bailiwick—craft fair, food tents and children's games. A parking lot covered in sawdust served as the site of a petting zoo, a cluster of simple carnival rides and the staging area for the tongue-in-cheek rodeo events. First up was the junior cowpoke and rodeo princess competition, so the group from the Lazy J had time to enjoy other activities before Laramie and Jake's turn.

Radha went in search of indigenous crafts. Rainbow hauled Yisrael off to a tarot-card booth. Dominique and Herb wanted to scour the flea market for psychedelic goodies to furnish the van.

Laramie and Jake walked along the crowded street, just looking. Within minutes, they were holding hands.

The day was bright and clear, pleasantly warm. The air was scented with cheap carnival food—sizzling hot dogs, deep-fried onion rings, hot-buttered popcorn and corn on the cob. Jake bought Laramie a rainbow-striped ice in a paper cone. By the time she finished, her tongue was stained blue and green and still he wanted to taste it, sweet and cold in his mouth. She must have known by the look in his eyes because she leaned closer, said, "Cold tongue, warm heart," and licked the hollow of his ear. He looped an arm around her waist and said, "Cold fingers, hot *sex*," so vibrantly she had to pull her cowboy hat over her face to hide her telling blush.

They watched a demonstration by the local volunteer firefighters. Laramie asked if he was one of those little boys who answered cowboy or fireman when asked what he wanted to be when he grew up.

He tried to remember, but he'd suppressed the years when his father and mother were still together. Some things were better forgotten. "I don't know," he finally said, aware that Laramie was watching his face with eyes too keen for comfort. "Anyway, these days, don't all little boys want to be rich doctors or lawyers?''

"We're both out of step. I think now they want to be Internet billionaires. Girls, too.''

"I missed the boat on that one.''

"You're a throwback," she said, glancing over a display of genetic farming and artificial insemination in the 4-H booth. "Luckily, I like throwbacks.''

"Remember that when you see me riding a milk cow in the cowboy contest." He winced at the thought. "Y'know, my ribs are startin' to ache. Maybe I should sit this one out...."

"It might be my only chance to see you in action.'' She put a hand up to his mouth when he started to protest. "Tussling with Goliath didn't count.'' She tugged him toward a quilt display.

"Oh, sure, now you say—'' He suddenly went silent.

Laramie, held in check by his hand, turned back. She frowned when she saw his face. "What is it?''

"Nothing.''

The automatic response didn't cut it with her. "Tell me," she said. "I'm not one of those scaredy girly-girls.''

"I know. It really was nothing." He said it not to pacify her, but to convince himself. "I thought I saw Rusty Naylor. My mistake. It was just a redheaded lumberjack type.''

She rocked on her heels, trying to see over the crowd. "You're sure?''

The prickles creeping along his nape said no. His mouth said yes. "The Naylors must have lost interest in me by now.''

"What did that cowboy friend of yours say?''

He'd told her that he was going to call Tack Corey, a fellow rodeo cowboy who was following the circuit and would have surely run into the Naylor brothers along the way. "I tracked him down in Fort Collins. He was pretty sure that the Naylors intended to compete there this weekend." Jake squeezed Laramie's hand. "There's nothing to worry about."

"Anyone could get to Lady Laramie at the Lazy J. And we left her there unguarded."

"Well..." Would the Naylors have plotted that far? He didn't think so. "There's Goliath. He's better than a guard dog."

Laramie's laugh wasn't convincing. "If only we hadn't been so quick to nail down the doggy door."

They moved on. Jake kept an eye out, and after another fifteen minutes of scouring the festive crowd he was pretty sure he'd been mistaken. The Naylors weren't known for their subtlety. If they'd tracked him down, he'd know it by now.

"Oh, look," Laramie suddenly said, and dread dropped through Jake like a stone.

She waved. "Molly! Grace! Over here!"

He breathed. It was only Laramie's girlfriends, the transplanted members of the Cowgirl Club. They greeted one another with enthusiasm—drawing attention Jake could have done without—then Laramie presented them for introductions. Molly Broome was a brunette in a wheat-colored dress; she had nice curves and a dimple when she smiled hello. They shook hands. That wasn't enough for Grace Farrow. She embraced him, clutching tight, her head bobbing with excitement. She was a bundle of energy, duded up in a white straw cowboy hat and boots, a sleeveless shirt, denim shorts and lots of cinnamon-coloured freckles in between.

They made apologies for their husbands. Grace's was a busy rancher. Molly's man was a husband-in-waiting—Laramie spent five minutes exclaiming over an engagement ring—off fighting crime with the Secret Service. That gave Jake pause. He wouldn't have minded having a lawman at hand. Just in case.

"It's getting that time," Laramie said, checking her watch. "We'd better head on over toward the cow-persons competition." Many in the throng were already moving in that direction; the three women joined the flow of traffic.

"Jake?" Laramie looked over her shoulder, her eyes anxious. Despite her good humor with her friends, she hadn't forgotten the possibility of the Naylors.

He smiled to reassure her and said, "Right behind you." Which was where he stayed. Tight up behind them, his protective instincts working overtime. Better safe than sucker-punched.

"Time to spill the beans, Lar. What the heck is this cowgirl competition, and is there still time for me to sign up?" Grace said. "Shane assures me I'm turning into an excellent ranch hand. Dulcie and I lost only three cattle and one hat on our last roundup."

Molly's dark head turned. "You're lucky. I'm so busy with guests at the dude ranch that I rarely get to ride."

"Ah, but I hear your fame has spread," Laramie said.

"Yup. It's crazy—every new group of guests wants to hear the story of how we foiled the counterfeiters, from the fire in the stuffed bear to the Christmas tree

showdown. Raleigh's quite the popular raconteur
when he visits. I've been telling him he'd make a
wonderful innkeeper.''

"He is the ideal cowboy," agreed Grace. "Straight
from central casting."

Laramie's eyes darted across Jake's face. "Any
progress convincing Raleigh to stay on at the Triple
Eight permanently?"

Molly chuckled. "I'm using my feminine wiles."

"And they're working?" Jake thought that Laramie sounded...envious. As if her own wiles were
lacking.

It would make it a lot easier on him if that were
true.

Still, he was glad it wasn't.

"Oh, who knows?" Molly said airily. "It's fun just
to try.''

Grace swung her hips. "Tell it, cowgirl!"

They approached the staging area, which was already ringed with voluble spectators. Bales of straw
set off several contest areas as well as a measured
length of the street. Nearby, temporary corrals held
squealing pigs and several milk cows and crates of
chickens. Other props didn't bear scrutiny, in Jake's
opinion. He didn't want to know what they'd be doing
with the row of child-size rocking horses put up on
wheels. He didn't even want to guess.

Laramie was telling her friends about the competition. Now that the moment was actually at hand, and
amid such a raucous carnival atmosphere, she looked
less sure of her involvement. "The entrants earn
points from a series of silly events. Helen says they
change them every year, things like outhouse racing
and buffalo-chip hurling and, oh—" Dubiously, she

studied the flustered chickens. "Something called chicken stuffing."

Grace clapped her hands. "I want to enter!"

"You need a partner." Laramie's eyes slid sideways. "I'll let you have Jake."

"Absolutely not." He put his hand on the back of her neck, beneath her long black braid. "No backing out. We're a team." His voice lowered to a whisper. *"You asked for this, New York."*

Rainbow Miracle and her buddies—decked out in flea market purchases—hailed them from the sidelines, offering to make room for Grace and Molly. Laramie's mother was draped with a fringed shawl, swaying in place on her sandal-clad feet, a bright blue balloon tied to one wrist. Yisrael's wispy beard and thin shoulders drooped beneath a gaudy Mexican sombrero that was clearly someone's castoff. Radha sat on a straw bale, content with a worn suede vest. Dominique and Herb didn't need embellishment— their pale skin and midnight-black hair and clothes drew plenty of alarmed glances as it was.

Helen arrived, with Karl in tow. They sported numbered placards and exaggerated cowboy-style garb. Burly Karl was buckled into fancy chaps and had a tin sheriff's star the size of a dinner plate pinned to his chest. Helen had done something creative with six bandannas and a bullwhip.

"Laramie, Jake. You haven't signed in yet." She pointed. "Head thataway for your costumes. They'll get you fixed up with some good stuff."

Karl and Jake exchanged suffering glances.

"Costumes?" Laramie repeated, her leery tone making it clear that the other cowboy boot had just dropped.

Jake decided there was no choice but to enjoy himself. He scanned the crowed once more for the Naylors, then escorted Laramie to the sign-in table. They were issued contestant numbers and directed to the costuming tent.

A small group of lady volunteers swarmed Jake like bees on a honeycomb. Within the minute his shirt and hat were gone. Someone spirit-glued an oversize handlebar moustache to his upper lip. They gave him a red ten-gallon hat, a black-and-white cowhide vest—no shirt—and a pair of jingling spurs. He absolutely refused the lariat stiffened to the size of a hula hoop that they tried to foist on him. The ladies settled on a pair of toy guns and dubbed him Six-Gun Killian.

He met Laramie outside. She was a saloon-hall girl, all feathers and shiny satin except for the Stetson and boots she'd insisted on keeping. "Someone got this wrong," she said, twitching her voluminous skirts. "How am I supposed to rope and ride like a cowgirl in such a prissy getup?"

"You'll win the fan vote." The male fan vote. For a woman who preferred jeans, she sure knew how to wear a dress. "Did they give you a name?"

She didn't get to answer because the emcee had begun announcing the contestants, one by one, who responded with flourishes that befit their characters. Bobby Torrance was decked out in banker's gear, complete with money bags. When Jake was introduced, he doffed his gigantic hat and shot off a round of caps into the air.

"And finally, we have Miss Laramie Manhattan, a saloon-hall floozie come all the way from New York Citay!" Laramie sashayed before the crowd. "Look out, fellas,'' the announcer cried when she lifted her skirts. "This one's a wildcat who'll steal both your kisses and your wallet." She pulled a tiny toy gun out of her garter and aimed it at the pop-eyed announcer, who quaked in his boots and threw his hands high overhead in surrender. Hammy overacting went over big with this crowd; the spectators cheered wildly.

The first event seemed simple enough to Laramie. The cowboys were crowded into an enclosure; the cowgirls were handed lariats in order to rope their partners.

Laramie had practiced with Jake. Trying for a fence post or a barrel, she was a passable aim. If Jake stayed very still, she might be able to—

Her vision went dark. O-kay. Someone had tied a bandanna over her eyes. "What gives?" she said, pushing one side of it up.

Helen squinted out from beneath her own bandanna blindfold. "We rope 'em by voice. If you catch the wrong cowboy, you're out of this round with zippo points." She was eyeing Karl and weighing her rope with a practiced hand. "Fastest lasso wins the most points."

Laramie was dismayed. "I can't do this."

"Just fling it. The guys are allowed to jockey for position."

Laramie's blindfold was tugged back into place. The emcee yelled, "Ready, set...*go!*"

She tried to listen for Jake and point herself in his direction, but apparently the cowboys weren't allowed to stand still. Even when she identified him through the hubbub, she couldn't seem to get a bead on him fast enough.

The onlookers yelled encouragement, shouting for a good lassoing, booing the many hilarious misses. Laramie flung her rope once and came up empty. Jake called to her, his voice low and soothing amid the noise. She swung her lariat in preparation.

A loud cheer distracted her. Someone had connected.

Then another. Helen whooped.

Laramie concentrated, going for accuracy rather than speed. Jake's voice seemed to be inside her head. She threw the lasso. There were shouts of encouragement from the spectators, but she couldn't tell if they were meant for her.

"Easy as she goes," called Jake.

She reeled in the rope hand over hand, feeling resistance on the other end. She sensed a body. Threw off her blindfold. Jake stood before her, smiling, the rope pulled taut around his right wrist. Although it had healed, she knew it was still tender.

"Sorry about that." She hugged him. "Are you okay?"

"Never say I don't sacrifice for the cause," he told her, and she realized that he'd probably managed to thrust his fist through her lariat rather than the other way around.

One of the judges waved a clipboard over their heads. "Number Sixteen—eight points!"

The Lazy J contingent whooped it up, with Grace and Molly shooting their fists and shouting, "You go, cowgirl!"

Laramie had never participated in such an ostentatious display. She was tacky. She was garish. She was, not to put too fine a point on it, a downright spectacle.

And she was ridiculously happy about it.

9

MANY MINUTES LATER, Laramie was sunburned, sloppy, exhausted...and still ridiculously happy. Her cheap satin dress had been torn during the hog-roping competition—the cowgirls had to tie a bow around the hog's neck. And she was spattered with barbecue sauce, rolled in sawdust and coated with feathers and egg goo—chicken stuffing had involved transporting live chickens and raw eggs from a stew pot to a frying pan to a table full of cowboys. The only redeeming event had been the roundup relay, because it had included splashing through a jumbo-size water trough. As a result, she was soaking wet, but a little less messy.

Laramie squeezed water from her limp skirts, smiling at Jake's equally drooping mustache. If ever she'd been a reserved cosmopolitan career woman, no one could tell. Not even herself.

"Ready for the last event?" he asked, picking bits of eggshell off of his dented ten-gallon hat before settling it in place. Despite his occasional protests—and her mishandling of the iron skillet—he'd been a good sport. He'd even relaxed about the possibility that the Naylor brothers had shown up, when she knew darn well he must be sweating bullets over their interest in his horse.

"I'd better be ready." Laramie rearranged her

skirts, tucking as much fabric as was decent into her waistband. "We're in third place in the point standings—we win the last event and we'll zoom up to first."

He tapped the flank of their trusty steed. "All you have to do is get on and stay on."

She made a face. "I should have practiced on Goliath."

The final competition was a horse race, of sorts. The twist being that their mounts were an assortment of carousel horses, jimmied-up sawhorses and child-size rocking horses that had all been affixed to wheels. The race itself was simple. The cowgirls rode, the cowboys pushed. First over the finish line at the other end of the street won the biggest points of the day.

There were only two complications. The cowboys had to race in full regalia—hats, chaps, lassos, boots and spurs. Jake assured her he'd outrun many a bull in just such garb.

Their other problem was steering. The wheels of their mounts spun in all directions, like wayward grocery carts. In anticipation of the melee—*gleeful* anticipation, in Laramie's opinion—the contest coordinators had supplied the cowgirls with elbow pads and crash helmets.

"Take your places," called the announcer.

Laramie pecked Jake's cheek, drawing a cheer. "Just in case I don't make it to the finish line in one piece," she explained, climbing aboard her little black rocking horse. When she put her feet on the stirrup spindles, her knees came up to her ears. Gripping the handles, she hunched forward like a jockey. "I'm ready."

"No tougher than riding Chauncey," Jake said

from behind her. His hands were positioned on the wooden horse's narrow hindquarters, ready to push.

She chuckled dryly. "Only faster, I hope."

"Just don't fall off."

Her eyes narrowed with determination when she glanced over at Helen, mounted on a fancy merry-go-round horse, sitting pretty in first place with a lot of muscle power behind her. Jake was quicker on his feet, Laramie decided. "Don't you crash me. I want to win."

"You realize this is a joke."

She nodded. "Doesn't matter. I want to win."

"For Buck?"

"Hell, no. For the honor of the Cowgirl Club." Laramie was only half kidding. Molly and Grace were waving from near the finish line. She looked for her mother, but Rainbow was lost in the crowd.

The emcee raised a starting gun. "Ready…"

Ready for anything. Laramie tightened her grip, but the sight of Rainbow's balloon bobbing above the throng was distracting.

"Set…"

She glanced to her left as several spectators picked up and moved off toward the finish line. There was her mother, behind the barrier of straw bales, talking to a dark-complected man in a cowboy hat. He turned, his eyes connecting with Laramie's across the short distance.

She said, "Jake?"

The emcee said *"Go!"*

And then all was pandemonium.

"THAT'S YOUR DAUGHTER, the one in the red dress?"

Rainbow said it was. She was proud of Laramie

today—for once her practical cabbage had lightened up, tuned into the good vibrations and let herself go with the flow. Perhaps it was returning to the land of her birth that had stirred her blood. Rainbow would have brought Laramie back to Wyoming and Buck's silly ranch years ago if she'd known for sure that he wouldn't put up a fuss about paternal rights and such. The archaic patriarchal court system was one big snooze as far as Rainbow Miracle was concerned.

"She's a beauty. And the guy with her is...?"

"Some cowboy." Rainbow frowned at the man who'd engaged her in conversation. He was polite enough, but there was something about him....

She wished Radha were here to read his aura. Try as she might, Rainbow could only pick up feelings, not colors.

The guy's smile was too quick. "You all live here in Laramie?"

"Oh, my, no. I'm a citizen of the world."

The stranger lifted his cowboy hat, bent and spat out a stream of tobacco juice. Nasty habit. Rainbow did not approve.

He was looking at Laramie again as she climbed onto a rocking horse. Rainbow smiled, reminded of how her sober child had returned giddy from camp the summer she was ten, chattering of nothing but horses and cowboys and her new friends Grace and Molly.

"Got a ranch?"

"Mmm. It's my daughter's inheritance." Within moments, Rainbow was lost in her memories. Buck Jones. Summer love. The little baby girl he insisted on calling Laramie...

When she looked, the stranger was gone.

"EEEEYAAAAHHHH!"

The rocking horse careened sideways. Laramie swayed with the momentum, taking the turn as if she were on a toboggan run. The contestants they'd just cut off swerved out of the way, banking on two wheels.

Laramie whooped again. Sheer exuberance. Her ruffled skirt flapped in the wind, baring her upraised knees. Jake's boots pounded the pavement; his spurs rang each time they struck the hard surface. His breathing was labored. It was too late to make him stop, and too fast for her to think about what she'd seen at the starting line.

A shrill cry rose above the buzz of the crowd. "Go, cowgirl!" Had to be Grace.

"Faster!" Laramie shouted, though the world was a blur. She clamped her arms around the wooden horse's neck as Jake caught sight of Bobby Torrance and renewed his speed. They swooped past the flagging team, missing crashing into the straw bales by an inch.

The finish line loomed. Spectators cheered.

The Naylors, she thought suddenly, dread draining the adrenaline from her veins. *Jake. His horse.*

Was she mistaken?

They had gained on Helen astride her carousel horse. She'd lost a bandanna or two and was caught between maintaining modesty or letting it all hang out for victory's sake. Karl's legs kept churning. His fringed chaps flapped like sails.

It was a dead heat.

Laramie set her teeth and reached out with both hands, straining for the tape. They were lighter, speedier. She'd lost her modesty in the pig corral.

One step ahead now. Two...

She lunged, breaking the tape. A raucous cry went up from the crowd. They'd won!

Jake tried to put on the brakes, but momentum had a mind of its own. As did balance. Laramie hung on to the petite rocking horse, her off-center weight tipping it toward the straw bales. Jake dug in his heels, spurs sending out sparks. The horse went over sideways, tumbling Laramie into the bales. She somersaulted over them in a ball of red satin and bare legs and gaudy cowboy boots, landing with a sharp "oomph" on the other side.

The spectators hushed. Jake threw himself atop the bales, calling her name.

Laramie lay on the pavement, smiling beatifically up at the sky, sucking air. Both knees were scraped raw, but her hands were folded behind her head as if she were lolling on the beach on a perfect summer day.

This gave Jake pause. "Did you hit your head?"

"We won, didn't we?"

He looked up. The throng was closing in on them. "Yup. Helen's fit to be tied." Panting, he eyed the remaining bandannas. "Good thing."

Laramie hadn't stirred. "Before we're crowned, I have to tell you. I think I saw one of the Naylors. Talking to my mother."

She *had* hit her head. "That makes no sense. The Naylors don't know you or your mother."

"All the same." She took his hand. Sat up. Straightened her spinning head and smiled valiantly at the circle of spectators.

Molly and Grace were galloping toward them.

"You're one heckuva cowboy," Laramie said.

He lifted her, his arm around her waist. "And you…" He wrenched off the handlebar mustache. All he could think of was that he'd fallen head over heels for her and it was worse than being tossed by Black Tornado. Since he couldn't say that, he settled on a gruff "And you, New York, are never doing this to me again."

"Hey." She stuck out her chin, regal even in wet satin and feathers and fragrant remnants of barbecue sauce. "From now on out, that's *cowgirl* to you."

"I COULDN'T GET MUCH out of my mother," Laramie said to Jake as the Lazy J group walked toward their vehicles. After they'd been crowned—with gigantic, floppy, foam cowboy hats, hot pink for her, electric blue for him—and the crowd had dispersed, she'd managed a word with Rainbow Miracle. "She said he was just a guy. They chatted briefly. She claims his aura was off—for all the good that does us. And he did ask about the Lazy J, in a roundabout way."

Jake slowed his pace. He didn't look happy. "You saw him…?"

She shrugged. "Just a glimpse. He was dark, sort of handsome. He stared at me."

"Reggie Naylor, for sure. He thinks of himself as a ladies' man."

"Aren't you guys coming?" Grace called from up ahead. "I am starving!"

They'd made plans for the entire group to meet at a nearby restaurant. Now Laramie sensed Jake's hesitation. She told the others to go on ahead and order appetizers; she and Jake needed to go home first to clean up.

''What are you doing?'' he said. ''I want you to go with them.''

''No. We have to check on Lady Laramie. The Lazy J's not exactly a discreet hiding place. If the Naylors have been nosing around, asking questions...'' She shrugged and climbed into the pickup truck. ''Besides, I'm still sticky. I couldn't go to a restaurant like this, anyway.'' Although she'd washed and changed back into her jeans and T-shirt after the competition, a hot shower was a necessity. ''You said yourself that the Naylors aren't really dangerous. No shoot-outs or showdowns to worry about.''

''But a confrontation could get ugly.''

''I can do ugly.'' She made a fierce face.

Jake shook his head, both amused and impressed by her fighting spirit. ''Darlin', you'll have the Naylor boys shaking in their boots.'' He backed up through the departing crowds, made an illegal U-turn and bumped over a curb to reach a cross-street shortcut.

Within minutes, they'd arrived at Buck's place. All seemed peaceful. The sun hung low in the sky, spreading a mellow golden light like thick honey through the air. Laramie breathed deeply, her head hung out the open window. The ranch house was not pretty, but neither was it astonishingly ugly. Their efforts had done wonders, elevating the Lazy J all the way up to nondescript.

''Looks like we're okay,'' Jake said, parking. ''No sign of the Naylors.''

''Let's go see your mare.''

They circled the house on foot. Laramie was halfway expecting the worst, but the horses were right where they should be, grazing in the pasture, idly flicking their tails at flies. Lady Laramie was a lovely golden color in the thick light, her black-tipped ears and dark liquid eyes alert as she swung her head up in acknowledgement of their arrival.

"Is she valuable?" Laramie asked, knowing that Jake cherished the mare in a way that had little to do with her monetary worth.

Cowboys and their horses. She sighed. What was a cowgirl to do?

Jake leaned against the fence. "She's a top-flight rodeo horse. So, yeah, that means she's valuable."

"You've had her for a long time."

"We're both seasoned."

"Oh, sure, you're a regular old broken-down rodeo cowboy." She nudged him. "I don't think so!"

He turned to her with a look in his eyes that stole her breath. Maybe she had no reason to envy his horse, she decided as he took her face between his palms and kissed her deeply. The man had feelings, they were just so bottled up he didn't know how to release them. Except in bed. If he could express himself as eloquently as he made love…

"Well, now, ain't this a pretty picture."

Laramie and Jake broke apart. Two men in jeans and cowboy hats stood watching them, one big and redheaded, the other the saturnine man who'd spoken to her mother before the rocking-horse race.

The Naylor brothers, she thought. Of course. She and Jake had probably led them straight to the Lazy J.

Reggie continued. "Pretty boy Jake Killian always did attract the best-looking cowgirl of the bunch. Ain't that so, Rusty?"

Rusty Naylor had a walking cast on his lower left leg. He took a lurching step toward them. "That's so.

Doesn't surprise me at all to find Jake run to ground with a foxy lady by his side.''

Laramie let out a snort of laughter. She couldn't help it. Foxy lady? Hilarious! "Pardon me," she blurted, unsuccessfully stifling a giggle. Jake looked at her strangely. "Foxy lady? That just struck me as—'' She waved her hands.

Rusty's broad, freckled face darkened. "Shut the hell up.''

Laramie sniffed. "My goodness. That's no way to talk to a foxy lady.''

Jake put his hand on her wrist. "You came for the horse,'' he said to the Naylors, his voice strong.

"Sheesh, Jake.'' Laramie wrested against his grip. "You don't have to offer—''

He interrupted. "*Laramie.* Why don't you go inside? The boys and I can settle our differences on our own.''

"Laramie?'' repeated Rusty Naylor, his eyes narrowing speculatively.

Reggie was staring at her as if she were a slice of birthday cake served up to him on a plate. "There's a coincidence, huh, Rusty?'' He rubbed his palms in slow circles. "We came here looking for a Laramie. We got one owed to us.'' A lewd chuckle. "Forget the horse. This one'll do me fine.''

Laramie blinked, sobering fast.

Fortunately for her, Rusty was not so inclined. "Keep it in your pants, Reg. The horse is worth more to us.''

"That's right,'' Jake said. He seemed very calm and cool, except for the unnatural brightness of his eyes. "Name your price.''

"Money won't do. We want the horse.''

Reggie leered. "Why not the girl?"

"Shut up," Rusty fumed. "I told you to shut up. So just shut the hell up!"

Jake had opened the gate. "Go inside," he muttered to Laramie. "Take Goliath to protect you."

Goliath? She backed through the gate. He'd be as likely to take a bite out of her as Reggie Naylor.

"Hold on." Rusty hustled to the gate as fast as his cast would allow. Reggie followed cockily, still eyeing Laramie in a way that made her skin crawl.

Goliath rushed the fence. Bless his nasty little heart.

Reggie recoiled, then caught himself and laughed with his mouth twisted into a sneer. "What is that thing?"

"Our guard pony. Laramie will take him inside." Jake sent her a look that brooked no nonsense. "Go on."

Obediently, she herded Goliath up onto the porch. He must have been confused by the switch in protocol, because he went with only a few halfhearted bucks of his hind end. Inside, she hastily threw a bag of Rainbow's organic carrots at him to keep him occupied and then crawled up onto the kitchen counter, keeping herself safely out of the ministallion's reach while she watched Jake's negotiations through the window.

The discussion was short. Before long, Jake was leading the Naylor brothers toward the buckskin mare.

Laramie hugged her knees, startled by his compliance. Then it struck her. Jake was doing this for her.

He was giving up his horse to keep *her* safe.

She couldn't let that happen.

She glanced around the kitchen. Goliath had shredded the plastic bag and was chomping on the carrots, green stems dangling from his mouth. She thought of calling 911, but what could she say? While the Naylor brothers might be cheaters, that didn't change the fact that Jake had lost his horse in a not-strictly-legit poker game.

There was Helen's cop boyfriend, Karl. He could probably help, but they were waiting at the restaurant with the rest of the gang. There simply wasn't time.

Outside, the men were talking heatedly. Rusty Naylor had his hand on Lady Laramie's halter.

Laramie's blood curdled. Jake was surrendering his horse.

She absolutely refused to let that happen!

"It's up to you and me, Goliath." She eased off the countertop. "Can I count on you to be as mean as ever?"

Beneath his overgrown forelock, Goliath peered at her from the corner of one white-rimmed eye. His tail switched. His nostrils fluttered. The carrots were gone.

Laramie edged over to the door. Jake was standing near the chicken coop, watching as the Naylors led his mare through Goliath's pen, right past the porch.

Silently she turned the knob. Now was the moment. Goliath was very territorial. The Naylors were in his territory. Hence…

She flung open the door.

True to form, Goliath shot outside, a furious piebald rocket, leading with his bared teeth. It must have been the sight of Lady Laramie being led away that did it. Making eager grunting noises, the tiny stallion lunged off the porch.

Rusty Naylor, at the lead, was Goliath's first target. The cowboy pivoted on his cast, saw the charging stallion and tried to hop out of the way.

Goliath hit him at the back of the knees. *Crunch.*

Rusty's hat flew off. His arms cartwheeled, hands grabbing at thin air. Goliath kept going, flipping the cowboy on his backside in the dirt. Lady Laramie shied, then trotted back to Chauncey, her lead rope dangling.

Goliath wheeled around to follow the mare, but Reggie Naylor must have thought the vicious little horse was coming for him. Hollering holy hell, he turned and ran, vaulting over the nearest fence.

Directly into the pigsty. *Plop.*

Jake was laughing.

Laramie didn't see the humor, especially since Rusty Naylor was scrambling to his feet. She grabbed Jake's rope off the porch post, made a fumbling knot and sent the lariat flying. In honor of her new title as Boss Cowgirl, the loop landed perfectly around Rusty's shoulders. With a jerk, she pulled it taut and fastened the other end to the railing. It wasn't a permanent fastening, but it would do for a few minutes. At least until Jake stopped laughing.

"Jake! Stop laughing!" She stomped toward him. "I can't handle the bad guys alone."

Reggie was crawling out of the pigpen. Somehow, he didn't look very threatening, what with his jeans a mucky mess and his boots squidging and oozing.

Still...

She gave Jake a shake. He said, "Okay, okay," and went to deal with the Naylors, chuckling all the way. In the pasture, Goliath was taking advantage of an unsupervised opportunity. He trotted after a nervous Lady Laramie, nipping at her hocks, whinnying like a lovesick calf. Even Chauncey and the sheep were agitated by the ruckus.

Laramie strode across the corral. If she had to, she would personally show the Naylors the gate. She absolutely, positively would not allow Jake's horse off the property.

Raucous honking announced the arrival of her cavalry. Dominique and Herb's trippy van pulled up into the driveway, followed by a police car.

Rainbow Miracle was the first to emerge. "Rutabaga!" she called, hurrying to Laramie with her shawl dragging and her arms open. "Don't worry, pumpkin. We're here!"

Laramie said a little prayer of thanks. Karl stepped from the police vehicle, looking stern, followed by Helen, looking thrilled. Molly, Grace, Radha, Dominique and Herb all converged. If nothing else, the Naylors were outnumbered.

Laramie accepted her mother's embrace. "How did you know we needed help?" she asked, although, being her mother's daughter, she knew the answer even before Rainbow spoke it.

ESP.

What else?

10

"I'LL TELL YOU WHAT we're gonna do," Laramie announced, trying to sound tough. She gave the Naylor brothers a look that said she'd sooner spit in their eye than compromise, but as there was a lawman on the premises she was forced to be nice.

Jake scowled, already unhappy about her pending offer.

She ignored him. "You've got a claim on Jake's horse. A stinkin', rotten, double-crossin' claim, but so be it." She zeroed in on Rusty. "Let's up the stakes, cowboy. Double or nothing. That's my only offer." Still ignoring Jake, she sent Yisrael inside for a deck of cards.

Rusty Naylor was suspicious. He scanned the Lazy J gang, trying to gauge their intent. It was big Karl, standing with his arms crossed, muscles bulging, who settled him. "I'm listening."

"Here's the deal. One draw. You put up your claim on Lady Laramie. I put up the deed to the Lazy J."

There were gasps. Helen, awed, said, "Holy cannoli."

Rainbow let out a trilling "Oh-oh-oh, pickle. Do be careful...."

Laramie threw her a significant glance. "Don't worry. I'm lucky at cards." Yisrael returned, moving faster than usual.

No one wanted to get too close to the fragrant Reggie, sulking and skulking in the background, so they closed in on Rusty, forcing a response. "Reckon I got nothing to lose," he said, disgruntled even though he was being offered more than he deserved.

Karl had already made it clear that the Naylors could be arrested for horse theft if they took Lady Laramie without Jake's say-so. It was Jake, obviously torn between his dubious obligation to the Naylors and his concern for Laramie, who had convinced her that the debt must be settled beyond Goliath's attack. For their peace of mind. Their future.

She shuffled the cards. Jake's face was pinched with worry. "Trust me," she said to him in a low voice. For a moment, her gaze held steady on his. *Love, trust, risk—it was a package.*

He gave her a silent go-ahead.

She slapped the deck on the hood of the Naylor's truck. "Make your cut, cowboy."

"Just a minute." Radha pushed forward, her palms outspread. "I must take a reading."

Rusty knocked her hands away. "Leave off, lady. I ain't gonna let no weirdo pull a fast one on me."

Molly clasped one of Radha's hands and pulled her away. The older woman said, "But the auras—" and Molly responded in her soothing voice.

"Laramie knows what she's doing."

Grace's head bobbed. "Oh, most definitely!" She gave Jake an encouraging squeeze. "Not to worry."

Overdoing it, Laramie thought. She blinked, trying to appear ingenuous. "Go on," she told Rusty. "Cut."

Resigned, he reached out and cut the cards. The

gang watched with bated breath as he drew. Jack of spades. Group exhale.

Calmly Laramie chose her card.

"Praise be, Allah," whispered Rainbow Miracle, and the others chimed in according to their current belief: Vishnu, Jehovah, Buddha, Almighty, Ra, Isis and Mother Earth.

Laramie didn't need divine intervention, and she didn't need to look. She held up the card for all to see.

Queen of hearts.

The gang exploded into celebration. Rusty grabbed the card from her hand and examined it for marks or other trickery. Reggie kicked the truck, spewing expletives. And Jake...

Jake simply smiled.

He'd trusted her.

A LONG WHILE LATER, after a double-celebration dinner and several bottles of champagne, Molly, Grace and Laramie convened in the master bedroom of the Lazy J. Rainbow and Yisrael were out front with the Wiccans, getting mellow, as they put it; Radha was snoring in the van; Jake was checking the horses...for the second time since they'd returned from dinner.

"Cowgirl Club's back in session." Grace sighed with satisfaction as she kicked off her boots and stretched out on the bed.

"It's been too long." Molly prowled the room, making evaluations with her innkeeper's eye. She'd already given Laramie suggestions for improving the ranch house's aesthetics. First on the docket was stripping the cowboy paper and painting the walls an earthy terra-cotta or warm honey-gold hue.

"But look how far we've come," Laramie said. "Eight, nine months ago, we were all stuck in Manhattan, bemoaning the dearth of cowboys...."

Grace giggled. "And now we've got three!"

"Mine was counterfeit," Molly pointed out.

Grace waved a dismissing hand. "Plus three ranches."

Laramie slumped at the foot of the bed; the trauma and high emotions of the day had started to kick in. She was drained. "If you want to call the Lazy J a ranch. I don't. Even with improvements."

"Mere details," said Grace. "The point is, the Cowgirl Club has triumphed."

"Then why do I feel so..." Laramie fell back on the bed. "So blah."

"Nitwit." Grace lazily tossed a pillow at Laramie, who drew it over her face. "You need to talk to Jake." Grace crawled forward and flopped on her stomach beside her friend. "Get things settled between you. Close the deal, cowgirl."

"Close what deal? Nothing's changed," Laramie said from beneath the pillow. "No, strike that. Circumstances *have* changed. Now that I've used my best card trick to nix the Naylor brothers' claim on Jake's horse, he's at liberty to leave for the next rodeo that strikes his fancy. He's told me all along that's what he intends." The scent of her mother's clove cigarettes had permeated the pillow. She flung it away, feeling wretched. *"Blah!"*

"Oh, Laramie." Molly's sympathetic face hung over the sturdy log bedstead. Laramie was relaxed enough to close her eyes—until Molly slapped her hip. "Get off your duff, cowgirl."

Laramie squinted an eye halfway open. "Huh?"

"You've never been obtuse," Grace said. "Figure it out."

"What Jake did for you today…" Molly's voice trailed off. She was looking at her engagement ring and getting all romantic-mushy-dreamy-faced again.

For once, Laramie understood. Boy, did she ever. If she allowed it, she could get pretty misty-eyed herself. "You mean…" She swallowed. "Because Jake was willing to give up his horse…"

"Well, *duh*," Grace said.

"Not just Jake," Molly pointed out. "It was a mutual sacrifice. He was ready to give up his horse for your sake. You were willing to give up the Lazy J for his. Love doesn't get any more obvious—and equal—than that."

Laramie felt herself drifting off to the sort of castles-in-the-sky dreamland she'd always regarded so cynically. "Love?" she said, filling with wonder at the thought of it.

"Of course, love."

"Definitely, love." Grace patted her arm. "Honey, it happens to the best of us."

"But what about the Lazy J? If I stick with Jake, I will have to give up the house. And while it might not be much, it's the only legacy I've got."

"Maybe your legacy is…" Molly paused, searching. "A new life. *This* life. Apparently your father let his slip through his fingers. But he's given you an opportunity to grab onto your own with both hands."

"Hold on real tight," murmured Grace.

Laramie sat up. "Never let go."

A soft chiming sound came from the hallway. A shadow shifted. "Rainbow," Laramie said softly. "Mom. Please join us."

"You'll be wanting the bedroom back," Molly said. She pulled Grace off the bed. "We've got to check into our hotel, anyway." She hugged Laramie; Grace kissed her cheek. They murmured encouragement, then said their goodbyes to Rainbow, stopping to hug her as well.

Laramie slid to the edge of the bed. "Don't go," Rainbow said. "I'm in no rush. Yissy's still outside, playing his guitar."

Laramie ran her hands through her hair. "It's been a long day."

"Oh, but I was so proud of you, pimento. Winning that cowgirl contest. Besting those scoundrels." Rainbow sat down beside her daughter, pulling her legs up onto the bed, belly dancer ankle bells jingling.

"I knew my misspent youth would come in handy one day."

"You must be at least a teensy bit glad that I'm not like other mothers. Molly and Grace never got to hang out with street hustlers and learn their card tricks like my little peach did."

"Yes, that's certainly true." Laramie found it wasn't so difficult to accept her mother for what she was. Even to appreciate her. "So, thanks, Mom. For bringing, um, shall we say, *color* into my life."

The shallow creases in Rainbow's plain face deepened for a moment, then smoothed out again as her placid countenance returned. Laramie could almost see the clouds begin to drift through her mother's eyes. "I did wonder..." Rainbow murmured, putting long, empty spaces between each word, "if...oh...I'd made a...mistake. Keeping you from your...father."

Laramie's pulse picked up. She held herself quite

still, knowing she must be careful now. "I would have liked to know him," she said softly.

"It wouldn't have worked."

Laramie didn't breathe.

Rainbow sighed. "Marriage," she said, looking at the Daddy's Li'l Cowgirl photograph on the bedside table. "I was only twenty. So young. I wasn't cut out for marriage."

"Buck did want to marry you, though?" *He wanted me to be his daughter.*

"And settle in one place. This house." Rainbow shuddered. "Too dreary for me, kumquat. So suburban."

Laramie had heard her mother's post-hippie take on marriage many times before. Just not in connection with Buck Jones. Though it stood to figure.

"Buck." Rainbow shook her head, smiling a little. "He was no traveler. But I did tell him that perhaps you and I would be back one day...."

Was that it? Was that all?

"You left," Laramie clarified. "He stayed." *Right here. Forever. Waiting...?*

What a waste.

Rainbow Miracle gazed into the distance, seeing neither the drab house nor the conventional life it had contained. "Buck Jones. Dear Buck. When I met him, papaya, he was a tall, handsome cowboy...."

JAKE DECIDED THAT SORTING out the stars studding the brilliant night sky would be an easier task than making sense of his feelings. Blast that Laramie Jones. She'd turned his life upside down, and done a better job of it than any piece of rough stock he'd ever put his legs around.

"Jake," she crooned, sounding like something out of a dream. Sweet heaven on earth. If he left her now, her face and her voice would haunt his dreams for the rest of his sorry life.

He looked up at the sky, asking for strength to do the right thing.

At one time, he thought the right thing was to leave her. Now...

"Jake." She padded through the grass. The delicate scent of clover rose in the air. "You should come inside."

He gave Lady Laramie one last pat and turned to look at the Laramie who'd surpassed his horse in significance. He'd come to understand Buck's fixation on the name.

She was beautiful. Her dark hair, uptilted eyes, elegant nose, wide, ripe mouth.

She was more than beautiful. Her quickness to challenge him was matched by a willingness to rise to a challenge herself. She had an indomitable spirit. A heart both fragile and brave.

Finally, *finally* he could admit that he—a man who thought he'd never learned how—had fallen in love.

The kicker was that it wasn't enough. Because even though the last thing he wanted to do was hurt her, he was so afraid that he didn't know how *not* to.

"Worried about the horse?"

"No," he said. "The Naylors won't be back."

She waited expectantly.

There was so much he wanted to say. Out of habit, he settled for the easiest. "Neat trick with the cards."

Her smile glowed, even in the dark. "Just call me the Queen of Hearts."

"Much as I appreciate it, darlin', don't think I've

forgotten that you pulled the same trick on me. Our first night here..." *Right before we kissed and changed our lives forever.*

"Uh, yeah." She peered at him. "Do you mind?"

"Not a bit."

Her exhale was audible. "Good. I wouldn't have done it if I hadn't known that underneath your curt exterior you really wanted to stay."

He said, "I did," surprising himself. He'd missed a shot at a couple of big jackpots in Greeley and Fort Collins, but what the heck. He'd won something far more valuable.

If only he could find the words. If only he dared speak them.

She shrugged. "The Lazy J has a certain slipshod appeal. Even Goliath has grown on me."

Jake's laugh rasped like a rusty hinge. "Yeah, old Goliath's always good for an opportune head butt."

They fell silent, moving toward each other in a cautious, roundabout way. Laramie took a step sideways, glanced at him, rocked on her heels for a moment before inching closer. He'd never seen her so tentative; it made him realize that she, too, was groping for the right words.

He braced himself. "You're saying you want to keep the house."

"Mmm, that's a possibility. I'm trying to be flexible, remember?" She reached out with her hand, then, when he didn't respond, let it drop by her side. He was a statue, a stone.

"There's no reason..." She was faltering. "We could..."

We're a pair, all right, thought Jake. Neither of them dared take the final leap of faith.

"Let's be brave," he said.

Laramie must have understood. Her eyes widened, dark pools, deep desire, rich emotion. "You're a cowboy," she whispered. "Courage is your way of life."

No. He'd been a coward.

There was outer strength and there was inner strength. Already loving Laramie was building him up inside, making him strong enough to risk the pain and pleasure and uncertainty of opening his heart, pledging his love.

He swallowed and said, "I love you," just as mellifluous strains of strumming guitar music drifted from the front yard.

The perfect timing of it made Laramie smile. She said, "I love you, too, cowboy," and with one step was in his arms as solidly as if they'd never been apart.

After a while, he stopped kissing her long enough to comment. "You don't seem surprised."

"I knew it. Molly and Grace knew it, too. When a cowboy offers to give up his horse for you, there's no room for doubt. It's gotta be love."

"Agreed." He hesitated for a heartbeat. "And on your side?"

"Me?" Her fingertips danced across his lips as if talking wasn't enough; she had to keep touching him as well. "Well, me. The thing is, I'm a cliché. I came here looking for explanations of Buck's life and instead I found out how to live my own. I'll never have all the answers, but one thing I know for sure is that I don't want to stay on the sidelines like my father did, waiting for a knock at the door."

"Which brings us back to the Lazy J."

She tilted her face, lashes lowered. "Why not use

it as a sort of home base? I mean, we can't stay on the road three hundred and sixty-five days a year—''

"We?"

"Oh, didn't I mention that part? See, the plan is for me to track down a good barrel-racing school. I'll acquire a speedier replacement for Chauncey, get some intensive training, and since you've already got the double trailer and the rodeo know-how…well…'' *Ask the cowboy.* She pinched his chin, needing his approval. "What do you think?"

"I like a woman with a plan." Jake squeezed her tight. "In fact, sonovabee if I don't downright *love* a woman with a plan."

Laramie's eyes stung with tears, but this time it was okay. They were tears of joy, of relief, of anticipation for the tens of thousands of miles and rodeos and adventurous days and glorious nights she'd have with Jake.

So she laughed through the tears and said, "That's *cowgirl* to you, bucko, and don't you forget it."

Epilogue

Five years later

EACH SPRING IN THE ROCKIES was better than the last, or so it seemed to the members of the Cowgirl Club. They'd adopted the mountains as their cathedral, the glades of aspen as their raiment and the children gamboling among the columbine flowers as their congregation.

Thus exalted, the Cowgirl Club lived on, even though between marriage, careers, homes, traveling and babies, they'd narrowed the number of their official meetings down to one fabulous barbecue blowout each year. The location varied, but always they chose springtime.

For the promise of renewal, Molly said.

Because their juices were running wild, insisted Grace.

Merely a matter of practicality, according to Laramie. After the long winter, the roads were finally clear.

This year they were picnicking at Goldstream Ranch, overlooking a green pasture dotted with glossy mares and frolicking foals. Shane and Grace McHenry's ranch had thrived in accordance with their burgeoning family. Three children in five years— Johnny, named after Wayne; Lucy, a peace offering to Lucilla, Grace's virago of a mother-in-law; and Danielle, the baby, born that very spring and already nicknamed Vanilla Bean by Shane. Grace's life, once constrained by doormen, concierges and maitre d's, was now filled with as much happiness, frivolity, confusion, disorder and laughter as one woman—even a spark plug like Grace—could stand.

Molly Tate had known both sorrow and joy. She and Raleigh still owned and ran the Triple Eight Dude Ranch. Her happy marriage and prospering business had given her a deep contentment that needed only children for completion. Two miscarriages and a long, difficult pregnancy and birth had left a shadow in Molly's wide brown eyes. The sight of her cherished two-year-old daughter—gentle, dark-haired, dimpled Gemma—always drew an especially loving smile. This spring, looking forward, Raleigh and Molly were bursting with plans to upgrade the dude ranch that was already Treetop's busiest social center.

Laramie Jones and her husband, Jake Killian, had recently retired from the rodeo circuit after a long, successful run that had included more travel, adventure, prize money, broken bones and greasy-spoon diners than either of them cared to recall. As Laramie was now six months pregnant with their first child, and Jake had determined not to miss even a day of fatherhood, they were looking for a small ranch of their own in the Treetop area. The infamous Lazy J, where for five years homeless broken-down rodeo cowboys had been welcomed with a hot meal and a soft bed, had recently been sold. Laramie had kept only her black Stetson and one leftover lawn ornament—a roly-poly elf who'd be given a place of honor in their new yard.

Life was good, the three women agreed.

And cowboys were better.

Shane, Raleigh and Jake stood near the barbecue in a haze of smoke, arguing over the best way to cook the ribs. They did this every year. Their wives egged them on, developing rival seasoning and sauce recipes and issuing stern challenges that invariably concluded with "May the best cowboy win."

Five years later, the men were getting wise.

"You notice how the chicks are lolling on their fannies while we labor over a hot grill?" Jake said.

"How'd that happen?" Shane wondered, even though Grace, what with chasing after Johnny and Lucy, didn't get to sit for more than a few minutes at a stretch.

"We need to stand together," Raleigh suggested, wiping his face with a bandanna.

"Yep." Shane nodded. "Get us a sweet deal going. Something like…"

Raleigh spread his hands. It was obvious. "What else?" he said. "The Cowboy Club."

When the men suddenly interrupted into shouts, raised fists and self-congratulatory hand slaps, Grace, Molly and Laramie looked at one another and rolled their eyes.

"We're in for it now," said Laramie, with a palm pressed to her rounded belly.

Grace flung her floppy limbs in four different directions. "We knew they'd figure it out. Eventually."

Molly's eyes widened. The apron-clad men were marching toward them, barbecue tools in hand, impressive in their husbandly outrage and defiant masculinity. There was nothing to do but throw up her hands and say, with an anticipation that still thrilled her, "Oh, holy cowboy!"

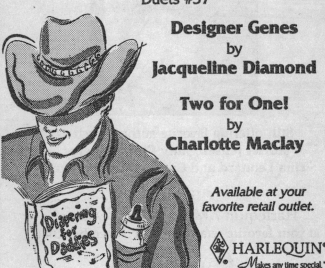

Coming in October 2000

brings you national bestselling author

ANNE STUART

with her dramatic new story...

A man untamed, locked in silence.
A woman finally ready to break free.

Available at your favorite retail outlet.

COMING NEXT MONTH

HARLEQUIN®

Duets™

#39

SHE'S GOT MAIL! by Colleen Collins

Ambitious editorial assistant Rosie Myers is *finally* getting her big break. When the writer of the "Real Men" column runs away with a stripper, Rosie is given the assignment. There's only one catch—she has to *write* like a guy. No problem until she starts getting letters from sexy lawyer Ben Taylor. He thinks he needs a man-to-man talk, but Rosie knows what he really needs is a woman....

FORGET ME? NOT by Darlene Gardner

Straitlaced, by-the-book Amanda Baldwin is at loose ends. Her fiancé has just dumped her without so much as a by-your-leave! What's Amanda to do? Easy...let the most charismatic, hunky beach guy show her the wild side of life. Zach Castelli is irrepressible, unpredictable and uncommitted! He just wants to help Amanda forget her fiancé, but after a few close encounters, will *he* want the title? And will Amanda approve the change?

#40

MISTLETOE & MAYHEM by Cara Summers

Librarian Jodie Freemont's New Year's resolution is to get a life! Plain, predictable Jodie is going to turn into a daring, free-spirited femme fatale. And she gets her chance when rugged bounty hunter Shane Sullivan comes to town. Shane's got a reputation for always getting his man. But he doesn't stand a chance when Jodie decides to catch hers—under the mistletoe!

SANTA'S SEXY SECRET by Lori Wilde

Working undercover as a jolly department-store Santa is no holiday for Detective Sam Stevenson! He's *supposed* to be checking out a large-scale theft ring, but meantime he can't help checking out his gorgeous assistant elf Edie Preston. The cute little pixie is a definite distraction. And now thanks to a little holiday mistletoe, Santa Sam is suddenly hearing wedding bells instead of jingle bells....